Honoré straightened up, raking her hair out of her eyes. "Majungasaurs and Komodo dragons aren't motivated by personal vendettas, Jack."

"Maybe not…but maybe whatever—or whomever—is nudging Stinky along has one."

Honoré blinked at him in confusion. "Are you proposing that this attack was planned?"

"And the kamikaze dive of the Quetzalcoatlus and maybe even the Sarcosuchus."

"I think you've been out here in the tropics so long, you've let your imagination run rancid. There was blood in the water, remember,and McQuay's wound had begun bleeding again, too. You said yourself that the Stinko—Majungasaur—hunted around the river banks."

"Yeah, but I never heard of one camouflaging itself before."

"That was probably due to foraging at the shoreline and it just picked up a covering of detritus by accident. I'm sure that wasn't a deliberate act."

"I wish I could be. What's that old saying: 'once is happenstance, twice is coincidence and three times is enemy action'?"

"That applies to mobsters in Chicago, not dinosaurs."

"It doesn't matter," Kavanaugh replied impatiently, "What does matter is we're going to have to take action if we plan to stay alive on this island long enough to get off it—unless you just enjoy running around screaming like an extra in a Japanese monster movie."

"No," she stated stolidly. "I do not."

"All right. Let's go do something about it."

As silently as they could, they retraced their steps, alert for any sounds, but they heard nothing but the inquisitive cheep of birds.

They entered a small glade and looked all around.

Worriedly, Honoré said, "Perhaps it decided to give up on us and go after Captain Crowe, Mouzi and Bai Suzhen."

Kavanaugh nodded as if he considered the possibility, and turned slowly. The Majungasaur crashed through the foliage, running at full speed with its head low, jaws wide in an unmistakable posture of attack.

Honoré cried out incredulously, "It was laying in wait for us—!"

"You're still a young man, Charles. You must think of the future, of the consequences to the sciences."

Copyright 2010 by Mark D. Ellis.
www.MarkEllisInk.com
www.Cryptozoica.com
Interior artwork & cover art copyright 2010 by Jeff Slemons
Art Director & Incidental Art
Melissa Martin-Ellis
Logo Design
Deirdre DeLay-Pierpoint

Published by Millennial Concepts • 48 Bedlow Avenue • Newport, RI 02840

DEDICATION:

*For Melissa. Nothing would be
possible without her.*

*In loving memory of our friend
Jim Mooney
1919-2008*

Other Books by Mark Ellis

- *Hellfire Trigger*
- *Devil's Guard*
- *The Everything Guide to Writing Graphic Novels* (w/Melissa Martin-Ellis)
- *Doc Savage: The Man of Bronze*
- *Death Hawk: The Soulworm Saga*
- *The Miskatonic Project: The Whisperer in Darkness*
- *The New Justice Machine*
- *Nosferatu: Plague of Terror*
- *The Green Hornet Chronicles*
- *Star Rangers: The Spur*

As James Axler:

- *Stoneface*
- *Demons of Eden*
- *Nightmare Passage*
- *Exile to Hell*
- *Destiny Run*
- *Savage Sun*
- *Omega Path*
- *Parallax Red*
- *Doomstar Relic*
- *Iceblood*
- *Hellbound Fury (The Lost Earth Saga, Book 1)*
- *Night Eternal (The Lost Earth Saga, Book 2)*
- *Outer Darkness (The Lost Earth Saga, Book 3)*
- *Armageddon Axis*
- *Encounter*
- *Shadow Scourge*
- *Hell Rising*
- *Doom Dynasty (The Imperator Wars, Book 1)*
- *Tigers of Heaven (The Imperator Wars, Book 2)*
- *Purgatory Road (The Imperator Wars, Book 3)*
- *Tomb of Time*
- *Devil in the Moon (The Dragon Kings, Book 1)*
- *Dragoneye (The Dragon Kings, Book 2)*
- *Far Empire*
- *Equinox Zero*
- *Talon and Fang (Heart of the World, Book 1)*
- *Sea of Plague (Heart of the World, Book 2)*
- *Mad God's Wrath*
- *Mask of The Sphinx*
- *Evil Abyss*
- *Children of The Serpent*
- *Cerberus Storm*
- *Aftermath*
- *Rim of The World*
- *Hydra's Ring*
- *Skull Throne*
- *Satan's Seed*
- *Dark Goddess*
- *Grailstone Gambit*
- *Ghostwalk*
- *Warlord of the Pit*

Books featuring art by Jeff Slemons:

- *Hollow Earth Expedition Sourcebook*
- *Hollow Earth Expedition: Secrets of the Surface World Sourcebook*
- *Luan Moon Hunter*
- *Armor Quest*
- *Spectrum 17: The Best in Contemporary Fantastic Art*

CRYPTOZOICA™

By

Mark Ellis

Illustrated by Jeff Slemons

"Tombstone" Jack Kavanaugh

Bai Suzhen

Augustus Crowe

Honoré Roxton

Aubrey Belleau

Mouzi

Hamish Oakshott

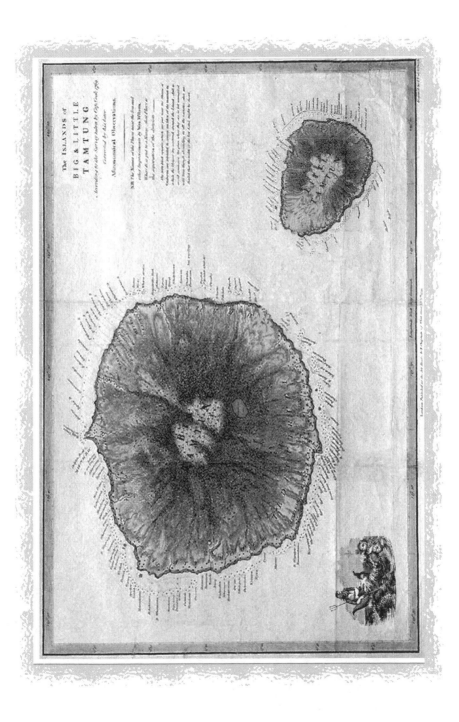

If (and oh! what a big if!) we could conceive in some warm
little pond, with all sorts of ammonia and phosophric salts,
light, heat, electricity, etc., present, that a protein compound
was chemically formed ready to undergo still more complex
changes at the present day such matter would be instantly
absorbed, would not have been the case before living
creatures were found.

—*Charles Darwin to Joseph Hooker.*

The megatherium, the icthiosaurus. They paced the earth
with seven-league steps and hid the sky with cloud-vast wings.
Where are they now? Fossils in museums, and so few and
far between at that, that a tooth or knuckle-bone is valued
beyond the lives of a thousand soldiers.

—*George Bernard Shaw*

Mythology is shorthand. It is condensed history and it lives
on in analogy.

—*Brinsely lePoer Trench*

Prologue

May 7th, 1836: *The Island of Big Tamtung, 518 kilometers southwest of the Makassar Strait*

The *Beagle's* longboat rode the wild breakers at the shoreline, rising and falling and rising again. Waves lapped over the sides, drenching Darwin, Martens, Belleau and the three sailors. Salt spray stung their eyes and stiffened their beards. The smell of brine and kelp filled their nostrils

Darwin vainly tried to shield the wounded man from the waves, but sea-water splashed over the gunwales. It spilled into the raw gashes slashed through Hoxie's torso, sluicing away the blood and dragging a cry of agony from his lips.

Bassett and Phyfe leaned their considerable weight against the oars, rowing desperately to break free of the combers before the stormy seas smashed the boat back onto the beach or piled her up on half-submerged rocks. With teeth bared and biceps bulging, they strained against the wooden sweeps.

Darwin hoped that once the boat cleared the breakers, the violent, up-and-down buffeting would cease. A white skein of lightning broke through the cloud cover, flashing over the waves. Thunder boomed, the air shivering from the concussion like the striking of a gong.

Clearing his vision with swipes of his hands, Darwin glanced over his shoulder at the rock-strewn beach. It was surrounded by thick clumps of palm trees and flowering brush. High above the treeline towered dark ramparts of volcanic stone. He saw no movement there but wind-whipped foliage.

Belleau leaned close and shouted triumphantly into Darwin's ear, "Charles, *mon coquin*, I think we have escaped from Hell!"

Dr. Jacque Belleau's English was so heavily accented, Darwin could understand only every other word. He just nodded in response. Hitching around, he squinted toward Conrad Martens. The middle-aged artist clutched his oil-cloth bound sketchbook tightly to his chest, both arms crossed over it protectively. Water streamed down his bald pate and flowed over his round-lensed spectacles. His lips moved as he recited the Lord's Prayer over and over.

Darwin couldn't help but feel sorry for the man. The round-the-world voyage of the HMS *Beagle* had already presented its fair share of dangers, but so far without loss of life or even a serious injury amongst the crew. Now, with the end of the five-year long trek less than six months away, Bosun Hoxie's blood mixed with the sea-water puddled around Martens's ankles.

Long ago, Darwin had accepted the perils of the voyage, but even his own broad imagination could not have anticipated the horror that came roaring out of the jungle on Big Tamtung Island.

The courageous Hoxie faced down the beast with a misfiring musket. Belleau, the botanist who served as the ship's surgeon, had already expressed his doubts that the injured Scotsman would live until they reached the *Beagle*. The survey barque lay at anchor barely an eighth of a mile from the spit of beach upon which they had landed the afternoon before.

Thunder exploded directly overhead, as stunning as the detonation of artillery shell. Lightning crowded the sky, the brilliant flash turning the dim gray dawn to blazing noon. Within seconds, a howling squall hit the longboat broadside, tossing the craft about as if it were a twig caught in rapids. A swell peaked like a hillock beneath the keel and the boat slid down it.

Belleau cried out, *"Merde! Non!"* and snatched madly at the capped metal canteen that slipped from his fingers. He managed to catch it and he exhaled a long, relieved sigh.

Darwin glanced sourly at the tall, broad-shouldered French-man. He could not understand why he had risked his life to fill the flask with slime from the pool he had discovered at the center of the island. Belleau had traipsed off alone to collect a sample and when Hoxie went off into the jungle in search of him, he had been attacked by a savage animal.

The ocean heaved and roiled, and more water flowed over the sides. Darwin cupped his hands above Hoxie's waxen face, trying to keep the sea from filling his mouth. Belleau tugged down the makeshift bandage wrapped around the man's mid-section to examine the wounds. Darwin averted his gaze from the blue-sheened intestines bulging through the three vertical gashes torn in the man's belly.

As they drew closer to the ship, Darwin saw how the *Beagle* rocked beneath the storm's pummeling. The sails of her two masts were tightly furled. He could barely make out the people on deck, a handful of sailors who crouched in the lee scuppers, draped in tarpaulin cloaks. He felt certain the sailors were pro-fanely wondering about the sanity of the crew of the longboat for braving such wild seas at such an hour. He couldn't blame them.

The boat dipped down in the green trough of a wave, then rose up on its foaming slope. Darwin gestured frantically to the sailors on deck. The boat fell again and when the seas lifted it once more, he saw the rope ladder unrolling from the deck rail above them.

Bassett and Phyffe cast fevered glances over their shoulders, gauged the distance to the survey ship and rowed even more single-mindedly, the oar blades biting deeply into the ocean. The two men breathed through their open mouths, blowing out droplets of water in fine sprays.

When the prow of the boat bumped against the hull of the *Beagle*, a sailor tossed a coil of rope down to Belleau, who expertly knotted it around a cleat. Working in tandem, he, Phyffe and Bassett handed the unconscious Hoxie up to the waiting crewmen, after first making sure the man's bandage fit snugly.

Darwin waited until his companions were aboard the barque before he clambered up the ladder.

Captain Fitzroy hauled him over the side and both men staggered when the ship rolled. A slurry of warm rain and foam splattered against their faces.

"What in God's name happened to Hoxie?" the burly, flaxen-haired officer bellowed. He shouted because he was angry and also to be heard over the keening of the wind through the rigging.

Darwin opened his mouth to answer, but Belleau interjected quickly, "He was attacked by a wild animal, possibly a leopard."

"Did I not advise against going ashore?" Fitzroy glared balefully at the waves slamming against the hull and the dark bulk of the two islands then transferred his gaze to the tall, blond-bearded Frenchman. "The Tamtungs have never been explored by white men. They're completely unknown."

Rather than respond to the captain's accusatory tone, Belleau said, "Let us get this poor fellow below so he can be treated."

Sailors carried Hoxie down the forward companionway to the far cabin and the cramped, makeshift surgery within. They laid the red-haired man down upon a table, his arms and legs dangling over the edges. Darwin and Martens joined Belleau.

To the seamen, Belleau snapped, "Leave us."

Their eyes flashed with resentment at the man's autocratic manner. More than one member of the *Beagle*'s crew had served aboard a Royal Navy vessel during the Napoleonic wars. They didn't make much of an effort to disguise their dislike of the French in general and Belleau in particular.

Martens made a move to follow the sailors out of the cabin, but Belleau laid a hand on his arm. "One moment. Leave your sketchbook with me, Conrad."

The slightly built man froze, blinking from behind his salt-smeared spectacles. Seawater dripped from his muttonchops. "What are you going to do with it, Jacque?"

"I will keep it safe, never fear. What is within it is for no eyes other than our own."

Martens considered the man's words for a thoughtful moment, and then slowly handed it over. He closed the door firmly
behind him. Darwin and Belleau stripped out of their wet coats
and lit the whale-oil lamps. Rain drummed heavily against the
glass of the cabin's porthole.

"I will do what I can to dress his wounds," Belleau declared,
placing his canteen on the table and slipping on his white clini-
cian's coat. "But I have faint hope that I can do anything for
the poor fellow, except to ease his suffering for a few minutes.
Fetch me the lint, Charles."

As the ship's surgeon, Belleau often decried the poor quality
of the medical supplies available to him. Darwin didn't blame
him. Everyone on the barque performed various duties and over
the last eighteen months, he had become the de facto medical
aide to the French doctor.

As Belleau snipped away Hoxie's scarlet-soaked bandages
with a pair of scissors, Darwin poured vinegar into a saucer
and placed a handful of lint within it. Sponging away the blood
from the man's torso, Belleau shook his head at the sight of the
three gaping wounds, all of them four to five inches long. The
flesh around them was swollen and inflamed. Both men caught a
whiff of a punctured bowel. Belleau uttered a wordless murmur
of dismay.

The Frenchman removed the lint from the saucer and carefully applied it like a paste around edges of the slashes. He said
sorrowfully, "He will not live out the day. He has lost too much
blood. For all intents and purposes, he has been disemboweled.
Such savagery—"

Darwin's hands began to tremble. "You saw?"

"From a distance, only a glimpse. I was at the pool when I
heard Hoxie scream. I turned just as the creature sprang away."

Darwin's throat constricted and he had to force out the
words. "Conrad and I saw it, too. It came to the outskirts of
the camp and shrieked at us. A devilish thing, a scaled monster
howling up from Hell. I believe it would have attacked all of us
if not for the birds."

Belleau glanced up from Hoxie, eyes narrowing. "Birds?"

"We heard birds singing…the creature seemed distracted by the song and then it fled." Darwin shook his head. "I cannot speak of it."

Belleau nodded. "That is good, Charles, that is undoubtedly for the best. We must never let the world know about this place. Our visit to the Tamtungs must not be recorded in the ship's logs or your journals."

Darwin frowned. "Why?"

"Isn't it obvious? It will undo all our work, all of the gallant battles we scientists have fought to replace religious superstition as the dominant force in human culture. The voyage of the *Beagle* is devoted to advancing biogeography, paleontology, embryology and morphology. Those sciences must become the world's new scriptures and there is no place in them for tales of monsters."

Bewildered, Darwin exclaimed, "You confound me, Jacque! How will telling the truth of the Tamtungs set back science? I would judge that allowing the world to know about all the life-forms upon it would have the exact opposite effect. The thing is done. The island has been discovered, it cannot be undiscovered."

Belleau straightened up from Hoxie. Softly, he intoned, "He has lapsed into a coma. I fear he will never awaken. I have done all I can."

Then he turned toward Darwin and cuffed him across the right side of his face, leaving an imprint of bloody fingers on the younger man's cheek. Darwin staggered against the bulkhead, gaping at him in astonishment.

"Jacque, are you mad?" he cried, struggling to keep his temper in check.

Belleau retorted grimly, "I am far more sane that you, Charles. The creature that attacked our poor comrade is completely unknown to science, more of a monster of myth than of nature…a basilisk, a sirrush, the dragon slain by Daniel—and where there is one, there are bound to be many more.

"Once that revelation reaches the rest of the world, then all of the scriptural literalists, whether they are Christian, Jew or Muslim, will use the island's existence to dismiss and denounce scientific thought for the next hundred years

"By documenting what we have seen, you will restore the power to churchmen to act as the final arbiters of what is true and what is not."

Darwin rubbed the stinging side of his face with a handkerchief, wiping away the blood. "Your argument is without merit. Perhaps the creature was an unclassified species of lizard, or perhaps a larger version of a Galapagos iguana or a giant specimen of the New Zealand tuatara. I think you're overwrought."

Belleau voiced a derisive laugh. "Am I?"

With sharp, violent movements, Belleau snatched up Martens's sketchbook and yanked away the oilcloth covering. Crowding Darwin up against the bulkhead, he flung open the cover, stabbing with a finger at the first charcoal rendering. It depicted deep parallel tracks sunk deep into mud.

The outside edges of the prints showed a pattern resembling splayed, three-clawed feet. "Have you ever seen an animal track like that before, Charles?"

He flipped to another sheet of paper, and to a hastily done portrait of a horse-shaped head, grinning jaws baring double-rows of dagger-like fangs. A pebbled pattern of scales coated its snout. A crest of feathers stood up from the center of its skull.

"Or an animal like that?" Belleau demanded. "Not even in Africa would you find such a beast! To the churchmen, it is not a new species of reptile, but a creature from the ancient bestiaries, a cockatrice, a dragon or a basilisk. They will cite the ancient legends to support their belief in superstition."

He turned the sheet aside, revealing another grey and black rendering beneath it, of a creature whose outline resembled that of a kangaroo. It stood on powerfully muscled hind legs with a thick tail tapering to a sharp point. Both of three-toed feet were equipped with a large, cruelly hooked talon, curving out from the third claw like a sickle.

"You and I are versed in the elements of naturalism," went on Belleau. "This is *not* an animal known to modern zoology. No, rather it is a product of an isolated environment where the ordinary laws of nature have been suspended…creatures survived that would have otherwise disappeared."

Slapping shut the sketchbook, Belleau declared emphatically, "Don't you see, Charles? The fundamentalist fools who promote the supernatural belief that God created the Earth and everything upon it a mere six thousand years ago will point to the Tamtungs as absolute proof of their contention, that life did not evolve from common ancestors, and that it remains exactly as God originally envisioned it. They already contend that the fossils of ancient animals, millions of years old, were recent creations.

"Remember the fossil tracks that were discovered in America twenty years ago? The so-called scholars claimed they were the tracks of Noah's raven! The Tamtungs will only supply more fodder to the literalists, who will no doubt describe the animal we saw as belonging to the same genus of dragon as described in the Book of Daniel! Scientific thought will be turned back to the level of the Dark Ages, when men like us were hounded from their homes and burned at the stake as heretics."

Darwin cast his eyes downward. He knew how ingrained most people's spiritual convictions could be. As an undergraduate at Cambridge he had studied for the clergy, before realizing his true vocation lay in science. More and more he found himself trying to reconcile his religious beliefs with his naturalist's point of view, if for no other reason than to maintain peace between himself and his devout family members.

Exhaling a weary breath, Darwin asked, "What would you have me do?"

In a calmer voice, Belleau answered, "You're still a young man, Charles. You must think of the future, of the consequences to the sciences. If you do that, then you will be rewarded. The society—the school—to which I belong and which has helped finance this voyage, is devoted to the advancement of a rationalist view of the world, to the exaltation of science over the strictures of religious thought. You will be accepted gladly as a fellow scholar and your future as a scientist will be secure…but only if you do as I bid."

For a long moment, Darwin didn't answer or lift his gaze. He murmured doggedly, "That environment must be studied."

Belleau laid a hand on his shoulder. "It will be, Charles, believe me. But the secret of the Tamtungs must be shared only among the scholars of the School of Night. We will finance a thorough study."

The deck shuddered underfoot as a heavy wave crashed broadside against the ship. The two men stumbled the length of the cabin. The lanterns swung to and fro. Darwin caught a fragmented glimpse of Belleau's canteen toppling over, the cap popping free of the short metal neck. A trickle of gray-green slime spilled onto the blood-damp table.

Crying out, Belleau shouldered Darwin aside and hurled himself forward to grab the flask. As he hastily recapped it, Darwin demanded, "Why are you so obsessed with the muck you found in that pool, Jacque?"

The Frenchman gave him a long, searching stare. "You mean you do not know? You really don't?"

"No, I really don't," Darwin replied impatiently.

Belleau started to speak and then smiled wryly. He glanced over his shoulder at the door, then back to Darwin.

"Tell me, Charles…in your studies did you ever come across references to Prima Materia?"

Darwin's flesh turned clammy. "Only in the most abstract sense. Something to do with alchemy, isn't it?"

Belleau's smile widened, his hands tightening around the container. "As you say…only in the most abstract sense. In the broadest terms, the concept of Prima Materia states that all particular substances are formed out of one and the same original substance. The most prevalent notion of the Prima Materia to be found in modern thought is the atomistic theory which we inherited from the ancient Greeks. In this conception, all material structures are composed of tiny building blocks of indestructible matter. The alchemists called it the 'One Only Thing'."

He nodded toward the narrow ribbon of slime glistening on the table. "You've heard the term primordial ooze or soup, I am sure. So, if we accept that—"

Belleau broke off, his body stiffening, his eyes widening. *"Sacredieu! Incroyable!"*

Darwin leaned forward. "What is it?"

With a forefinger, Belleau pointed toward Hoxie's body.

Following his finger with his eyes, Darwin saw nothing different from the last time he had looked. Then, a stirring, a shifting of shadows caught his attention. For a second, he attributed it to an illusion caused by the flickering lamplight. He felt a pressure in his lungs and a sudden loosening of his bladder..

The slime that had spilled from Belleau's flask mixed with Hoxies's blood, but the fluids had done more than mingle. The sludge flowed along the trail of blood, like drops of liquid trickling down dangling threads.

Shocked into speechless immobility, Charles Darwin and Jacque Belleau stared at the substance as it progressed up and over Hoxie's pallid flesh, crawling toward the open gashes in his midsection. Darwin heard a faint rasping sound. Distantly, he realized the short hairs on the nape of his neck had lifted, scraping against the collar of his shirt.

The thick fluid oozed into the largest wound, bubbling along the edges of the slashed flesh. Then Hoxie's body began to quiver, the fingers of his hands flexing and unflexing. His limbs twitched spasmodically. Foam flecked his lips. For an instant, Darwin feared they were watching the man's death-throes.

Hoxie's eyes and mouth flew open. He screamed. He jack-knifed up from the waist, staring around unfocusedly.

Belleau broke the chains of paralysis and threw himself atop Hoxie, bearing him back down onto the table. "Be calm, *vaillant ami.* You are back aboard ship in the company of your comrades. You are safe."

The man twisted his head around, looking toward Darwin. A little of the unreasoning terror left his eyes. "Sir—"he whispered hoarsely. "The dreams I had!"

Barely able to speak himself, Darwin placed his hand on top of Hoxie's. "Rest easy, there, old man. Rest easy. You have been sorely wounded, but let the doctor do his work and you'll be right on the mend."

Belleau gazed at Darwin with wet eyes. In a voice made husky by awe, he said softly, "Do you agree now, Charles? We cannot let this gift be exploited by the witch-burners or their modern counterparts."

Darwin ran shaking fingers through his hair, his senses reeling. He nodded. "I need air, Jacque. I am feeling rather faint."

Belleau's face registered relief. "Go on, then. I am fine here. I will attend to my patient and we will talk later."

Darwin stepped out into the companionway and turned into Harper, the orderly. He held a tray bearing a bowl of biscuits and a mug of tepid tea.

"Breakfast, sir," he said.

The sight of the tray made Darwin realize he was intensely hungry and thirsty. He gulped down the tea and swallowed a biscuit nearly whole. Thanking the man, he carried the mug up the stairs to the deck. Weariness and lack of sleep combined to make him feel as if he were walking through a dream. He hoped he would suddenly awaken in his bed at his home in Shropshire, with the smell of kippers and eggs in his nostrils instead of kelp.

The ferocity of the gale slackened, but rain still fell and the slate-green sea heaved, capped with white. He walked to starboard. Although the sun had risen, he could see only gray emptiness stretching to a deeper gray on the horizon.

Moving with care, he walked to portside aft. He stood at the *Beagle*'s rail, gazing at the dark bulks of the two islands rising from the sea. Curtains of rain blurred the view. The heavy barque creaked and groaned as she rode at anchor. The sounds were interwoven with the humming vibration of rigging as strong gusts sang through the ropes. The warm wind carried with it the musk of the tropics and Darwin felt a sudden revulsion, wishing for the icy touch of the North Atlantic breezes.

Captain Fitzroy came to his side, slapping his open palm with a brass telescope. As if he were picking up the thread of a prior conversation, he said, "The bosun is a good shipmate, a good friend. He has sailed with me for the last two years. It would break my heart to lose him."

Darwin said, "I don't believe you will, Captain. I think Mr. Hoxie shall pull through."

Fitzroy eyed him with suspicion and surprise. "And why do you think that, Mr. Darwin?"

Rather than lie to the man, Darwin chose to evade the question. "May I borrow your telescope for a moment?"

After a second's hesitation, the captain handed it to him. "Take a final look at your Tamtungs. I doubt we will ever come back this way again. I would hazard a guess that no other ships have come this way in centuries."

Darwin peered through the eyepiece, sweeping the lenses over the more distant and smaller island of Little Tamtung, over three kilometers away from Big Tamtung. It looked peaceful, unremarkable, with a crescent of white sand beach, palm trees and tropical ferns growing lushly on all sides. The somber verdant hue was relieved by brilliant yellow blossoms of flowering plants.

He returned his attention to Big Tamtung and the castellated cliffs of volcanic rock looming at least three hundred feet above the jungle. Through the telescope, he studied the high ramparts, briefly noting the fluttering of big wings. He tried to focus on them, but it flew from sight too quickly. He lowered the lens to the shore, watching waves crashing and breaking on the bare stone, foaming spray splashing in all directions.

"When the tide is with us, we'll weigh anchor," said Fitzroy bleakly. "There are some places on Earth where Mankind doesn't belong. I think that bloody island is one of them...an unending war for survival that keeps the life there dangerous and violent."

Quietly, Darwin intoned, "Yes, survival of the fittest…a process of natural selection."

Fitzroy grunted, putting his hands in his pockets. "It's a place where man would not be among the fittest. He would be naturally selected to serve as prey."

Darwin didn't reply, staring at the figure stalking out of the foliage on the far side of the beach. A shudder shook him and his mouth filled with sour saliva.

The creature was bipedal and although there was nothing around by which he could judge its height, he guessed it stood six feet tall. The saurian snout bore a pair of flared nostrils that dilated and twitched. The head, about the same size as that of a dray horse, turned to the left and the right upon an extended, scale-coated neck.

Huge cold eyes, like those of a serpent's magnified a hundred-fold, stared unblinkingly out to sea, as if they gazed directly at Darwin. A pair of legs almost as big around as some of the palm trees surronding the beach supported the lean body. Beads of water shone like tiny pearls on the ridge of feathers running down its spine. A muscular tail trailed out from behind, disappearing into the undergrowth. The claw-tipped forelegs were drawn up to its chest in a parody of prayer.

Out of foliage behind the creature stepped another figure, moving with a slow, shuffling sidestep. For a wild instant, he thought it was a man. When he realized it was only man-shaped, his tongue froze to the roof of his mouth.

Shadowed by the overhanging fronds of a palm tree, Darwin could barely make out a naked body, the gray, hairless flesh glistening with moisture.

Darwin's gaze was drawn to the large yellow-green eyes, the dim light of dawn making them luminous, molten pools. The eyes radiated a savage anger, outrage and a threat.

A cold thought, like the slithering of a reptile, crawled across the surface of his mind: *If you return, you will die. All of you will die.*

Biting back a cry of fear, Darwin lowered the telescope.

Panic weakened his joints, and awakened nausea in his belly. Desperately, he rubbed his eyes with a thumb and forefinger.

"What is wrong, Mr. Darwin?" asked Fitzroy.

Taking and holding a deep breath, Darwin raised the telescope to his eye again. He focused on the same area, but both the creature and the man-shape were gone, as if they had never existed, except in his imagination.

For a few seconds, he continued to scan the shore and the brushline, struggling to convince himself that what he had seen had been only a gnarled tree trunk, its bark glistening with rain and the uncertain light cast by the cloud-shrouded sun. His scientific reason told him that the monsters were no more than tricks of the light and eyestrain. His primitive gut instincts knew otherwise.

"Mr. Darwin?" Fitzroy's tone was peeved.

Darwin removed the telescope from his eye and handed it back to Fitzroy. "You're absolutely right, Captain."

Lines of confusion furrowed the man's brow. "Right about what?"

Darwin turned away, back toward the companionway. His legs trembled, and he grabbed a length of rigging to support himself. In a voice scarcely above a rustling whisper, he said, "You were right about the Tamtungs."

"How so?"

Slowly, Charles Darwin answered, "In the struggle for survival, the fittest win out at the expense of their rivals because they succeed in adapting themselves best to their environment. There are some places on Earth where Man cannot possibly adapt. I understand that now."

Chapter One

Present Day, May 9th: *The Island of Little Tamtung, 520 kilometers southwest of the Makassar Strait*

When Kavanaugh heard about the throat-cutting, he knew exactly where to find Mouzi.

There had been a brawl at the Phoenix of Beauty. A Papuan deckhand had gotten too rough with one of the girls and the pair of wicked little butterfly knives Mouzi always carried came out of her pockets. After Mouzi was done with him, the bouncer threw the man onto the embankment so Huang Luan could eat what was left.

As sunset fell out of the deep blue sky, Kavanaugh came across the dead Papuan. He lay twisted over on his back, black eyes wide and glazed, his slashed throat leaking a ribbon of blood across the muddy stones. Light winked dully from a heavy silver ring on the middle finger of the man's left hand.

Huang Luan was barely eight inches long, although its wingspan stretched over two feet. A long beak full of serrated teeth, talon-tipped wings and unblinking onyx eyes made the raptor look like a demon dressed up in the feathers and plumed tail of a green macaw. It crouched on the Papuan's chest, claws sunk deep into his rib cage, chewing tiny gobbets of flesh torn from the man's double chins.

Kavanaugh had often considered wringing the little hell-spawn's neck, but he figured Bai Suzhen would take a dim view of the decision and cut off his credit as well as his testicles. As it was, he had presented the archaeopteryx to her as a peace offering and she had grown very fond of it. He assumed she thought the feathered reptile was close enough to a phoenix to serve as her establishment's mascot, since Huang Luan meant Beautiful Phoenix in Mandarin.

Kavanaugh stepped around the Papuan, his hand reflexively touching the butt of the old Bren Ten holstered at his hip, just in case the archaeopteryx decided it wanted to sample meat on the hoof. The creature paid no attention to him, either because it remembered Kavanaugh as the human who had first caged it, or because it knew from a prior taste-test that he wasn't particularly palatable.

Carefully, he worked the toe of his boot under the dead man's back, looked around and pushed him off the embankment into the sullen waters of the cove. He slid down into them with scarcely a splash. To his disappointment, the archaeopteryx didn't sink with its meal, but squawked in outrage and flapped up to a nest atop a nipa palm tree.

Kavanaugh hoped that since it was getting on toward dark, the monster would settle down for the night, despite the oppressive humidity. Sweat filmed his face and his T-shirt stuck to his back. The air was heavy with moisture, tainted with the thick perfume of jungle and swamp.

The last downpour of the day had finally tapered off but the dripping of water from the interlaced tops of the trees continued with a maddening monotony. Normally, Kavanaugh didn't mind the daily tropical storms, but at this time of year on Little Tamtung, leeches fell from the saturated branches along with the rain drops and set their suckers into their victims, injecting an anticoagulant into the blood to keep the wounds open.

When the leeches were gorged, they dropped off, but the wounds they left behind were slow to heal and prone to infection. No one came ashore during or after a rain shower without being instructed to check themselves regularly.

Kavanaugh lifted his gaze from the ripples spreading around the sailor's body and glanced toward the rust-streaked ship anchored in the flat waters of the bay. He recognized it as *Mindanao's Folly*, a slow, lumbering merchant freighter that ran military supplies, food and medicines to tsunami-devastated Indonesia.

Looking beyond the harbor, he stared at the rain clouds swelling above the black volcanic peak of the island christened Cryptozoica. Although several miles away and shrouded by mist and the blue darkness of the night, he could still see it.

However, he didn't see the *Keying*, the junk of Bai Suzhen, so he assumed she and her crew of Ghee Hin still cruised the Sulawesi Sea northeast of Sarawak, looking for cargo more profitable than that carried by old freighters.

Bai Suzhen blamed Kavanaugh for being forced to return to her first career as a black marketer since her legitimate investments in Cryptozoica Enterprises had hit rock bottom. Over the last two years, whenever they met, she greeted him with the same bitter, yet almost laughably formal mantra: "I, the white serpent of good fortune, am still not prospering."

But nor had anyone else who poured their hopes, dreams and savings accounts into the venture. Neither Kavanaugh nor his stubborn partner, Augustus Crowe were exceptions, so he had stopped feeling guilty about Bai Suzhen long ago. Her White Snake triad still owned the majority interest in the Phoenix and held the mortgage on his chopper.

Even Howard Flitcroft had lost sixty million dollars but he hadn't resorted to smuggling or pandering, although like Bai Suzhen, he held former USAF Captain Jonathan Kavanaugh personally responsible. In fact, Flitcroft himself coined the name "Tombstone Jack" and it fell into common usage so quickly, Kavanaugh often suspected the industrialist of paying the Tamtung Islanders to address him as such.

Kavanaugh turned toward the Phoenix of Beauty just as the neon sign mounted above the veranda blazed with brilliant light. Against a yellow background, the green outline of a shapely nude woman with outspread wings in the place of arms, buzzed and flickered.

He walked up the pathway made of crushed seashells. Bright flowers with big orange blossoms grew in borders on either side of the path. He knew Bai Suzhen had personally planted the flowers, so he took care not to brush against them. As he reached the broad steps, a mottled Tokay lizard, its scaled hide iridescent in the neon glow, darted along the wooden rails encircling the veranda.

The Phoenix was the second largest building on Little Tamtung, which really wasn't that much of an achievement. Built in the old Thai style with a long, gracefully upturned roof and eaves, a colonnaded façade with intricately carved bas reliefs faced the bay. The orderly row of Bombay chairs arranged on the veranda was vacant, holding only the shadows cast by the close-growing oleanders.

Kavanaugh pushed open the door and stepped into the interior of the club. Although it was an oasis of relatively cool air, it was not particularly quiet. The juke box blared out the sugary Chinese lyrics of CoCo Lee and crimson-winged parrots cawed along from elaborate cages hanging overhead, making for a cacophony of gibberish.

The main room of the club was furnished with rattan tables and wicker chairs. The slowly churning wooden paddles of the fans in the plank ceiling stirred the air but did not refresh the dank and musty atmosphere.

Three plastic buckets half-filled with brown water betrayed a roof badly in need of repair. The green baize covering of the billiard table was as stained and threadbare as Kavanaugh's own shirt. The bar itself was of polished black bamboo, the corners inset with brass fittings.

Although barely two years old, the Phoenix of Beauty exuded an atmosphere of faded grandeur, emulating the colonial establishments of old Indonesia. It had been built to suggest those more opulent times, of decadent nightclubs in exotic climes, and the irony that the Phoenix of Beauty had become what it sought to superficially imitate was not lost on anyone, least of all the White Snake triad of Bai Suzhen.

Jarlai the barman, a small Malay wearing an immaculate white jacket, sat quietly upon a stool in a corner, watching Mouzi dab at the abrasion on the cheek of a sniffling girl. Kavanaugh knew the man didn't like his job, but he needed it and it was far better work than anything else available on Tamtung. His duties were relatively simple, so he could endure watching a little homicide.

Mouzi glanced toward Kavanaugh, not reacting to the appearance of the tall, scarred and dark-haired man wearing a drab T shirt with the legend Horizons Unltd Tours emblazoned in peeling letters across his chest.

Mouzi's own Horizons Untld T shirt showed blood spattered in an artless pattern and Kavanaugh assumed the dead Papuan had supplied the medium. She wore her jet-black hair in long ponytails sprouting from both sides of her head. Although he knew next to nothing about current tonsorial trends, he guessed the girl was still trying to appear current, regardless of her distance from the fashion centers of the world.

Mouzi's mocha complexion was flawless, except for the Maori spirals blue-tattooed below her eyes. Small and slender, with piquant features, her eyes were the color of obsidian and just as fathomless.

Kavanaugh didn't know the name of the girl whom Mouzi tended, but he knew she was a mixture of Achenese and East Indian, a refugee from a homeland devastated by the tsunami. A bruise spread over her broad left cheek, surrounding a raw scrape he guessed had been made by the Papuan's silver ring. She wore a torn sari of translucent blue silk. The imprints of fingers showed dark on her bare shoulders and around the slender column of her throat.

Kavanaugh glanced at Cranio, busy slopping water around on the floor with a mop, smearing a red stain, diluting it, not necessarily absorbing it. Gesturing to the noise-vomiting jukebox, he asked loudly, "Can you turn that thing down?"

Without otherwise moving, the Samoan used the mop to hammer at the top of the machine. CoCo Lee's song was interrupted by an electronic belch, and then it fell silent.

Kavanaugh nodded. "Thanks."

Cranio grunted in response, but said nothing, returning his attention to widening the scope of the red smear on the floor. Amber-skinned, he was at least six and a half feet tall and over half of that wide. His hair clung tightly against the scalp of his big head, like a coarse-curled black helmet.

Kavanaugh stepped up beside Mouzi. "What happened here?"

Mouzi's eyes flicked toward him. "What does it look like?" Her sharp voice held a broad New Zealand brogue.

"It looks like you killed a deckhand with your knives and if you don't have an iron-clad reason why, you and I will have to talk to his captain."

"Why?"

"So he can file a report and charges, if he sees the need."

Mouzi snorted. "As *if.* Sanu, tell him what happened."

In a halting, soft voice, the girl in the blue sarong said, "Dai Chinnah was very drunk, even before he came in. He wanted me to go with him to my room. I refused."

Kavanaugh arched a questioning eyebrow. "Why? Because he was drunk?"

"That and—" Sanu paused as she gingerly fingered her swollen lip. "He has been here before. He hurt me then. Bai Suzhen told him never to come back or he would die."

"He came back," stated Mouzi flatly. "And so he died. All there is to it."

"As *if.*" Kavanaugh looked over at Cranio. "Did you tell this man Chinnah to leave?"

Still mopping, Cranio inclined his head in a short nod.

"The bastard knew Bai wasn't here," Mouzi said. "That's the only reason he came back."

"What were you doing here?"

Mouzi gestured toward the back. "I was fixing the air conditioner."

"It broken," offered Jarlai.

Kavanaugh wiped at the film of sweat on his forehead.

"No shit."

"I heard the ruckus," Mouzi went on, "and came out and saw the bastard beating up on Sanu. He'd gone raw prawn."

Kavanaugh fixed his gaze on Cranio. "Why didn't you throw him out then?"

"He had a gun," explained Mouzi. "Show him, Cranio."

The bouncer dug into a voluminous pocket of his khaki pants. His right hand pulled out a .38 caliber revolver. It looked like a toy in his big dusky paw.

"He didn't see me," Mouzi continued, reaching into the back pockets of her denim shorts with both hands. "I came up behind him. And—"

She whipped her hands in front of her, blades of the butterfly knives dancing over her fingertips. Red stains dulled the sheen of the steel.

Kavanaugh looked at Jarlai. "Did you see any of this?"

The barman nodded. "All of it. Happen 'xactly like Mouzi say, Cap'n K."

Kavanaugh gusted out a sigh. "I don't know how the man's commander will take it, but at least we have witnesses and a weapon to support your story."

He paused, ran a hand along his unshaven jawline and wearily asked Mouzi, "Did you really have to kill him?"

She shrugged. With a flick of her wrists, returned the knives to her back pockets. "Guess we'll never know."

Kavanaugh turned toward the bar, putting his elbows atop it. "A gin and tonic. Light on the tonic, heavy on the ice."

As Jarlai mixed the drink, Kavanaugh's eyes passed over the half-dozen fly-specked photographs framed on the rear wall. One of the largest had been taken a couple of years before. It was of himself and Howard Flitcroft. Howard still had a full head of wheat-white hair and a toothy grin split his bland, boyish face. He held a cashier's check from Maxiterm Pharmaceuticals made out to Cryptozoica Enterprises for the sum of fifty million dollars.

The frame beside it held not a photograph but a front page

from the *Weekly World News*. The red-ink headline read: "When the Rich Feel Poor, Billionaire Vows Ancient Drug Will Restore Youth!"

Dominating the rear wall above the liquor shelves was a lurid yet bizarrely fascinating black-velvet portrait. Enclosed within an ornately scroll-worked frame, the image rendered in garish hues of gold, green, red and Pepto-Bismol pink depicted a Siamese dancer.

She wore the traditional conical headpiece of a temple dancer that rose to a high, ball-tipped spire. The hat, gilded and gem-bedecked, had an almost three-dimensional quality. Beneath it, the dancer's face was a fixed white mask of heavy green eye-shadow and lips painted in blazing scarlet. Black hair cascaded down almost to her hips. A dozen gold hoops encircled the slender column of her throat.

Although she wore white panungs—baggy Siamese bloomers—the dancer was nude from the waist up. Her arms, held at stiff angles barely concealed her bosom.

Emblazoned on her torso was the sinuously looping body of a python that stretched up from her waistband and twisted between her breasts, extending over her left shoulder and along her arm. The scales of the serpent were edged in gold.

No matter how many times Kavanaugh looked at the portrait, he always experienced a disquieting combination of sexual arousal and intestinal distress.

Jarlai placed the glass down on the bar before him just as Kavanaugh heard the door open. He turned around as Augustus Crowe strode in. The big man loomed well over six feet tall and like Mouzi and Kavanaugh, he wore a Horizons Unltd T shirt.

The spread of his shoulders on either side of his thickly corded neck was very broad. Because his body was all knotted sinew and muscle covered by deep brown flesh, he did not look his weight of 250 pounds. The stub of an unlit cigar jutted from between his teeth and a black Greek fisherman's cap was perched at a rakish angle on his head.

"What's this about another throat-cutting?" he demanded.

Still dabbing at Sanu's abrasion with a cotton ball, Mouzi said cheerfully, "For such an underpopulated shit-hole, word sure gets around fast in this place."

Crowe grunted and sat down on a stool beside Kavanaugh. "Especially if it's about hookers, fucking and murder."

"It wasn't murder," Mouzi protested. "Not in the first degree, anyhow. And it never got around to fucking."

"Cutting somebody's throat has that effect on horniness, I guess," Kavanaugh commented dryly.

Jarlai placed an open brown bottle of Guinness before Crowe.

"What did you do with the body?" Crowe asked, removing the cigar from his mouth and lifting the bottle to his lips.

Kavanaugh took a sip of his gin. "Are you asking me or Slingblade Sally here?"

Crowe swallowed a mouthful of the dark beer and answered, "You."

"I pushed him in the canal, just in case."

"Just in case what? Her story didn't add up?" Crowe reached across the bar and took a book of matches from a glass jar. The cover showed stylized illustrations of crisscrossed palm trees superimposed over the bright yellow Cryptozoica logo.

"That's basically it," Kavanaugh replied.

Crowe put the cigar back in his mouth and tore off a match. "Well, as interesting as it is, I'm not here to find out about you two conspiring to cover up yet another capital crime."

"No?"

"No. I just got a satphone call. Howie Flitcroft is on his way here. I was told we should expect him early tomorrow morning."

Kavanaugh felt his stomach slip sideways, but not in reaction to the liquor. "Howie hasn't been here since..." His words trailed off.

"Since those investors of his were eaten?" Mouzi supplied helpfully.

Kavanaugh scowled at her, and then shifted his gaze toward the two men who pushed open the door. They were both wiry

Moros, wearing a kind of uniform consisting of white turbans, dark slacks, shirts, and black sneakers. Each man had a small automatic pistol holstered at his belt. The letters EAC were hand-stitched in gold thread on their breast pockets. Kavanaugh didn't need the reminder that the East Asiatic Company owned *Mindanao's Folly*.

At first, the pair of men seemed startled by the diverse collection of people in the big barroom, then they tried to slip on stolid masks of officialdom.

"We've been sent by Captain Lars Hellstrom," said the tallest of the pair in passably good English. "We are looking for Seaman Dai Chinnah. Does anyone here know him?"

Chapter Two

"You're not jackos," Mouzi said, back-stepping away from Sanu. She moved with smooth grace, her high-cut white shorts snug on her hips. Casually, she put her hands behind her back and kept them there, hooking her thumbs into her pockets. Sanu slid off the stool and moved to the far corner of the bar.

The eyes of the two men flicked to and fro cautiously. The taller man said, "No, we are not policemen. We are EAC security officers, assigned to *Mindanao's Folly*. May I have your names?"

"You go first," suggested Kavanaugh.

The man's face registered irritation, but he said smoothly, "I am Lieutenant Azahan. This is officer Ruipender."

Crowe tried to strike a match but due to the humidity the sulfur only fizzled, sending up a pungent stench. "Neither of you have any authority here, you know."

Azahan stiffened. "There is no authority here at all, not even a provost marshal. That is why the Captain sent us, Mr. Crowe."

"If you knew our names, why'd you ask us for them?"

"*Mindanao's Folly* has put into port here before. The crew knows all about you here on Little Tamtung."

A contemptuous smile touched Azahan's lips. "Especially about you and Tombstone Jack Kavanaugh."

Kavanaugh raised the glass to his lips, feigning disinterest. "Is that a fact."

Ruipender spoke for the first time. "It is a fact that all of you here are liars and thieves. Tricksters. You defrauded many powerful, wealthy people and some of those people died. You stay here because you are afraid of their retribution if you go back to your own country. They will have you killed or imprisoned."

Angrily, Mouzi said, "You don't know what you're talking about."

"We know enough," snapped Azahan. "We know you fear coming under the hand of United Bamboo."

"Bai Suzhen, Madame White Snake herself, owns this place," Mouzi declared defiantly, pointing to the garish portrait of the Siamese dancer behind the bar. "She won't be happy when she finds out you came here to harass her friends."

"The United Bamboo Society controls a hell of a lot of ports in this part of the world," Crowe said casually, still trying to strike a match. "You piss her off, you piss them off. I'm pretty sure that's how it works."

Azahan's eyes narrowed for an instant, but he drew himself up haughtily. "We are looking for a member of Captain Hellstrom's crew, that is all. We were informed about a disturbance here that might have involved him."

He gestured to the dark pink stain on the floor, then to Sanu and finally to the speckles of blood on Mouzi's shirt. "Do you deny there was a disturbance?"

Mouzi didn't answer. With a weary sigh of exasperation, Kavanaugh pushed himself away from the bar. "We don't deny anything. Dai Chinnah was the cause of the disturbance."

Quickly, Ruipender drew his pistol but he didn't aim it at anyone in particular. "You will come with us to the ship."

Kavanaugh walked toward Azahan, seeming to ignore the gun in Ruipender's hand. "There's no need for that. We can give you a report right now. We have witnesses."

Then he lashed out with his right hand, his fingers closing around the gun in Ruipender's fist. He squeezed, grinding the smaller man's delicate metacarpals into the unyielding steel frame of the pistol.

Instinctively, Ruipender tried to jerk away but Kavanaugh

turned with him, locking the man's right wrist under his arm and heaving up on it with all of his upper body strength. The pain was so overwhelming, Ruipender couldn't even scream.

As the pistol dropped from his nerve-numbed fingers, Kavanaugh maintained pressure on the captured arm. He forced the man down to the floor.

At the same time, Crowe came up off the bar stool. He hurled his half-full Guinness bottle in an overhand throw toward Azahan, the heavy base striking the man directly in the throat, a quarter of an inch to the left of his larynx. The bottle didn't break, but Azahan reeled away, clutching at his neck. He clawed for his pistol.

It had barely cleared the holster when Cranio used his wet mop like a bludgeon, slapping the water-soaked strands across Azahan's face to send him staggering into Crowe's arms. He easily wrested the gun out of the smaller man's grip and swept his legs out from under him with a swift kick.

He sat down hard on the barroom floor.

Lips writhing over his teeth, Ruipender fumbled to draw a knife from his pocket with his left hand. Kavanaugh drove his foot into his diaphragm and the man's features squeezed together like an accordion. His legs drew up in the fetal position.

Releasing the man's arm, Kavanaugh removed the folded butterfly knife from Ruipender's pocket and tossed it to Mouzi. "Add this one to your collection."

Wisely, Mouzi had kept her own blades in her pockets during the brief struggle.

Kavanaugh briefly inspected the Guardian .32 ACP automatics and snorted. They were ridiculous little things with ivory grips and one-inch barrels. He figured the only reason Azahan and Ruipender carried them was because slingshots hadn't been available in the ship's armory.

Cranio lumbered over to the pair of men and hauled them to their feet by the collars of their shirts, twisting the fabric so it constricted their throats like choke leashes. Azahan uttered gagging sounds, but he appeared to be in less pain than the whimpering Ruipender, so Kavanaugh addressed him.

"Tell Captain Hellstrom that Dai Chinnah was here but we don't know where he is now. He roughed up Sanu and was asked to leave. You might want to check the canal. He could have had an accident. Little Tamtung is as dangerous a place as Big Tamtung, you know."

"Yeah," Crowe said. "Good thing we're here to walk you back to your boat, isn't it?"

Cranio marched the two men to the door and shoved them out on the veranda. He refrained from delivering departing kicks to their rear ends. Kavanaugh, Crowe and Mouzi walked out with them.

The sun had fallen completely beneath the horizon, giving the ocean a coppery sheen. Although purple bougainvillea and pink hibiscus flowers turned the road into a surreal kaleidoscope of color, no amount of perfumed flora could disguise the fact that Little Tamtung was scarcely more than a frontier outpost. The houses were all prefabricated structures set upon stilts, rising up out the kunai grass. Painted on the window of a Chinese trade store they passed was the notice: American Cash Only, No Cheques, No Plastic.

Kavanaugh, Crowe and Mouzi walked behind the EAC officers until they reached the quayside. Azahan and Ruipender marched to the end of a rickety dock and to a small motor launch tied to a piling.

Rubbing his bruised neck, Azahan turned to face them. "You have our guns."

Kavanaugh nodded. "That's right."

"We would like to have them back. Captain Hellstrom told us he would make us pay for new ones if we lost them."

"Technically," said Crowe, "you didn't lose them. Just tell him you know exactly where they are."

Azahan gathered a little courage and squared his shoulders. "Hellstrom will be very angry when we report what happened tonight. He will be even angrier when we tell him how you stole company property."

"Yeah," taunted Mouzi. "But he'll be a lot angrier at you."

"He will take it out on you people, the protection of Madame White Snake notwithstanding. He does not like Tombstone Jack."

"Not many do," drawled Kavanaugh. "So?"

Azahan held out a hand. "Our guns. Please."

Kavanaugh stared at the two men and shook his head in disbelief. He popped the magazines out of the pistols, put them in his pocket and tossed the empty Guardians to Azahan and Ruipender, who caught his left-handed. "There're your guns. Now get back to your ship."

Azahan didn't move. "If you could leave the ammunition on the dock so I could come back for it later—"

Kavanaugh drew his Bren Ten and shouted angrily, "Get the hell out of here!"

The two men swiftly scuttled across the dock and jumped aboard the boat. When the engine started and the mooring line was cast off, Kavanaugh turned toward Mouzi and Crowe. "Unfucking-believable."

"Think that'll be the last we'll hear from them?" Mouzi asked.

"Hell, no," Kavanaugh half-snarled, holstering his pistol. "They'll report to their captain who'll make a report to the Malaysian Maritime Enforcement Agency. The best we can hope for is that Chinnah didn't have any influential family or friends."

Mouzi nodded, and then smiled almost shyly. "Thanks for covering for me, Captain K."

"It's my job," he replied gruffly. "You're part of the Horizons Unlimited crew."

Crowe snorted. "She's the *only* Horizons Unlimited crew. That reminds me—I'll need you tomorrow when I tear apart the *Krakatoa*'s bilge pump. It'll be a good excuse not to take Flitcroft out fishing."

The *Krakatoa* was a thirty-six foot converted trimaran motorized sail boat, built by Denmark's Quorning Company. It had served as Crowe's home for the last couple of years. They could see the boat in her customized berth, lovely and clean-lined. The scrubbed deck was as white as her furled canvas, the teak railings polished to the color of old honey.

Mouzi put an index finger to her nose and snapped it away in a short salute. "Aye, aye, Captain."

Gaze fixed on the EAC launch cutting a foaming wake toward the distant bulk of *Mindanao's Folly*, Kavanaugh remarked absently, "Two captains but with a single crewman between them."

"Crew-woman," Mouzi corrected testily. "If you can't tell the difference by now, you've been here *way* too long."

Kavanaugh favored her with a slit-eyed glare. "You're about half right."

Crowe finally managed to strike a match into flame. As he applied it to the end of his cigar, he said, "Not much like the old days, is it?"

Kavanaugh nodded gloomily. "Nothing is. See you tomorrow. I'm sure Howie will expect a breakfast meeting."

"He can expect his ass off," Crowe growled, blowing twin streams of gray smoke through his nostrils. "He's not the boss of me."

"Not anymore," Kavanaugh replied, turning away. "He's just one of our landlords…and we owe 'em all big-time back rent."

Sunset made a pale rose haze against the dark humid sky, dimly lighting the footpath Kavanaugh followed to his stilt house. A bamboo handrail and six steps extended up to a small porch. Behind the house was a concrete landing pad with a tall stone wall protecting the area from the storm surges that occasionally boiled in from the bay.

Secured to the pad by a webwork of steel guy-wires and eyebolts was a six passenger ASTAR B2 helicopter. A peeling red and yellow decal on the portside door panel declared the big chopper was the property of Horizons Unlimited Tours, Little Tamtung Island, a Subsidiary of Cryptozoica Enterprises.

Kavanaugh walked up the short flight of stairs and opened

the screen door. He hadn't bothered to lock it. Like the exterior, the interior of the house wasn't very memorable. He did not turn on the overhead lights. There wasn't anything in the room he cared to see. There was a daybed, an old TV he almost never watched because the reception was so problematical, a bookcase, a couple of wicker chairs along with a few odds and ends that might have been junk or rare *objet d'art*.

The grinning, bleached-out skull of a Deinonychus he used as a paperweight could have been both. It rested atop a scattering of Horizons Unlimited promotional brochures, advertising package tours to the Cryptozoica Spa and Living Laboratory.

The house felt like a furnace, despite the cooling rain shower. Even after five years in the South Seas and two and a half on Little Tamtung, he still suffered from the heat. He stayed because the island had become his home as well as his prison, his own Elba.

Kavanaugh had never quite managed to think of the house as his home, even though he had paid too much for it. Raised in a big old Indiana farmhouse, his idea of a home was three stories high with an attic full of junk cast off and forgotten by four preceding generations.

He unclipped the Bren Ten's holster from his belt and put it on a shelf above the day bed. Taking off his sweat-soaked shirt was like stripping away another layer of skin.

He tossed it over the back of a kitchen chair, ignored the two cockroaches that shook their feelers at him indignantly and opened his small, college-dorm refrigerator. It wasn't much cooler than the rest of the house, but the bourbon bottle was still on the top shelf.

He poured an inch into a nearly clean glass and slid the *Blue Train* CD into the player. With the haunting notes of Coltrane's trumpet as an accompaniment, he carried the bourbon out to the porch.

Kavanaugh stood and sipped at the tepid liquor and absently traced the scar tissue along his right rib-cage, then fingered the weal curving down from his hairline that pulled the outside corner of his right eye slightly out of line.

The scars had matching saddle-stitch patterns. A couple of times women in the Phoenix of Beauty had remarked about the symmetrical way the scars lined up along his body. He knew they were hinting to hear the story of how he had incurred the injuries, but he never told them, for several good reasons.

His memories of the attack were hazy, like a nightmare dimly remembered from childhood. Primarily, he didn't talk about it because he knew no one would believe the culprits were a pack of vicious Deinonychus. Even pointing out the skull of the creature that had sunk its fangs into his right side wouldn't have convinced them.

Kavanaugh sat down on the porch railing. He heard the flapping rustle of wings overhead and reflexively jumped, biting back a curse. The trilling cry of a night bird did not comfort him. He half expected to hear the clacking screech of the archaeopteryx, flying out of the darkness to bite off his nose. It wouldn't be the first time Huang Luan had attacked and inflicted scars on him.

During the struggle to cage the feathered monster, it had latched onto his thumb and damn near gnawed off the top joint. Recollecting the incident, he stared at the black peak rising above Big Tamtung, wishing he had the courage to take Huang Luan back there, but the archaeopteryx had become accustomed to being pampered and dining on the occasional dead sailor.

Memories tumbled over each other in his mind, as they always did when he looked at the pinnacle of volcanic rock while his belly was full of bourbon.

After resigning from the Air Force eleven years before, he had gone into partnership with Augustus Crowe and formed an exclusive travel agency that specialized in guiding people with stratospheric credit ratings to very exotic, very off-the-beaten path locales around the world. The more money a certain type of person had, the more they yearned for rare and unusual experiences.

Very often, those experiences involved the outright breaking of international and sovereign laws. Kavanaugh knew the world's back alleys, the places most people wouldn't think of visiting, even if they knew they existed.

Crowe could sail any kind of vessel, from a tugboat to a three-masted schooner. He had made his living piloting motor sailers through the Panama Canal to the Caribbean and back again. Several times he'd brought craft over from the Shanghai and Singapore boatyards.

In the *Krakatoa*, Crowe escorted seekers by sea and in a second-hand Cessna, Kavanaugh conveyed them by air. Sometimes they combined the modes of transportation. The Upper Amazon, the Himalayas, the Congo and even the interior of New Guinea—no place was beyond the reach of Horizons Unlimited, as long as it was not out of the reach of a client's bank account.

One of Horizon's repeat clients was Howard Flitcroft, a man who had amassed several fortunes through real estate development. Even while on vacation, the man was always tuned in toward the opportunity for profit.

When the tsunami devastated coastlines along the Indian Ocean and South China Sea, Kavanaugh and Crowe turned their skills and vehicles to delivering aid on the behalf of several international relief agencies, coordinated by Howard Flitcroft and his companies.

During that period of chaos and suffering, Kavanaugh made the acquaintance of the beautiful Bai Suzhen, a former nightclub owner turned representative of the White Snake triad, one of the twenty-four affiliates of the United Bamboo Society.
As he had with Flitcroft, Kavanaugh found enough commonalities on which to build a friendship of sorts. Although Bai Suzhen could not have been more different from Flitcroft than if she had fallen from another planet, the two people shared a disquieting similarity in their ability to sniff out business opportunities.

Kavanaugh and Crowe fervently wished they possessed the same talent. After the tsunami, all they thought about was money and ideas of how to make more, but they were fast running out of both.

When a storm squall drove Kavanaugh's Cessna far from the shipping lanes, instead of thousands of empty miles of ocean waiting in the darkness, he found the rarest of business opportunities. Flying over a pair of islands all jungled green with occasional black outcroppings of volcanic stone, Kavanaugh and Crowe realized they had rediscovered what was left of the Tamtungs, originally charted nearly three centuries before, but never explored.

He wasn't overly surprised to find the islands. He knew that many clusters of tropical mud heaps existed between the Celebes and Sulu Seas. There were hundreds, maybe even thousands of them. No one really knew how many.

Kavanaugh piloted his plane over the deep-shadowed valleys of Big Tamtung, and although the scenery was beautiful, he wasn't inclined to linger—not with a cargo compartment full of perishable and exceptionally valuable antibiotics.

Then, as the treetops streaked by beneath the shadows cast by the Cessna's wings, he glimpsed another pair of wings. Huge and leathery, they were attached to a body that for an insane instant reminded Kavanaugh of a plucked turkey, but the creature didn't look like a turkey in any other particular.

The long beak that snapped at his passing plane was spiked full of sharp, needle teeth and he knew he looked at a pterosaur, flapping down an unmarked back alley of the global village. He also realized he looked at a fortune.

Upending the glass, Kavanaugh drained it of bourbon. Thunder rumbled faintly in the distance, but he didn't see lightning reflected on the surface of the sea. On some nights, he painfully felt the absence of the sounds of civilization—the rumble of trains, the blare of car horns, the distant drone of jet airliners.

The dead heat and silence touched him with the shuddery feeling that life itself had melted and poured into the gutters of Little Tamtung. Vague tendrils of mist coiled along the shoreline, writhing like souls trying to escape the dark purgatory of the sea.

He knew how they felt.

Chapter Three

Four kilometers off the coast of Sarawak, Borneo

Bai Suzhen stood on the pitching mahogany deck of the launch as it approached the *Bĺo Kù Chan*. The treasure ship of the United Bamboo Society reminded her of a gigantic jeweled water bug, bobbing on the dark surface of the Sulawesi Sea. Colored lights and paper lanterns flared incandescently from the rigging of the big craft.

Although a junk like her own vessel, the *Bĺo Kù Chan* was twice as broad in the beam and length as the *Keying*. The ship had very high poops and overhanging stems, looking somewhat top-heavy because of the exceptionally tall pole masts and huge sails with batten lines running entirely across the fore and afterdecks. The three masts held huge sheets of ribbed sailcloth folded up as neatly as paper fans.

The evening breeze sweeping over the flat surface of the ocean held a cool touch, but it was far from chill. The setting sun cast streaks of copper and gold over the hulls of the motorized sampans, launches and water taxis clustering around the four boarding ramps that extended down from the ship's starboard side.

The sight of so many water craft was a familiar one to Bai Suzhen. Although Chinese by birth, she had grown up around the open canals and *klongs* of Bangkok, which were always crowded with fishing boats, sampans and dugouts.

The pilot of her launch expertly ran the boat alongside a VIP ramp, so close that the hull scraped the aluminum edge.

Then he reversed the engines, backing water into a smother of foaming spray.

Bai Suzhen stepped from the deck to the foot of the ramp, waving away the proffered hand of an attendant. Her two bodyguards, Dang Xo and Pai Chu followed her. They wore European-cut black business suits and narrow black neckties over spotless white shirts. Double-edged, flat-bladed jian swords rested in lacquered scabbards strapped across their backs. They wore their weapons openly as was the custom of Ghee Hin soldiers.

Bai Suzhen went up the steps of the ramp swiftly, her stilt heels tapping out a snare drum rhythm on the metal risers. Slim of build with the soft, matte tan skin of the northern Chinese, her face was smooth and calm, with high cheekbones under contemplative almond eyes. A touch of lipstick outlined her wide mouth, damp now with a misting of salt spray. Her straight black hair was drawn up into a thick chignon on the crown of her head and made her appear taller than five foot five.

She wore a satin kimono jacket of scarlet and a black silk sheath skirt slit up to mid-thigh. The high military collar of the jacket did not detract from the elegant column of her throat.

Bai Suzhen could feel the eyes of the ramp attendant upon her. Although the glimpse of her leg visible between edges of the skirt's slit alone was tantalizing enough, she also knew the serpentine tattoo that writhed up from the ankle and slithered around her small kneecap riveted the man's attention. The delicately-detailed scales were edged in gold ink and the twisting body itself colored in tints of blue and green, with white highlights.

She knew the men she would meet with might be offended by her mode of dress, particularly by the golden imperial dragon of old Peking embroidered on her jacket, but she didn't care. Nor did she fear their disapproval.

Beneath her jacket she carried a CZ75 autopistol snugged in a nylon shoulder rig.

As she reached the deck above, the smells of incense, burnt

grease and human sweat became more pronounced. To her, the odor symbolized greed and therefore profit. The scent was perfectly fitting for a treasure ship like the *Bĺo Kù Chan*.

The vessel combined the best elements of a floating bank with that of the classic den of iniquity, while maintaining the fine Asian tradition of organized criminality. Over a century before, pirates plying their trade in the South China Seas and Indian Oceans rarely headed for land after successful raids.

Instead, they deposited their plunder in an offshore bank owned by one of the Tongs. Soon, the concept of a floating vault was blended with that of a seagoing pleasure palace pandering to all tastes, however mundane or perverted. The United Bamboo Society had further streamlined the template and turned the *Bĺo Kù Chan* into the primary vault and money-laundering center for all triads with interests in east Malaysia.

Bai Suzhen hated the ship, knowing that too often young girls and boys were lured onto it with the promise of employment, only to end up addicted to drugs and forced into prostitution.

A huge pavilion built like a pagoda arose from amidships. Double rows of colored light bulbs illuminated the wide entrance which blared forth with a cacophony of Cantopop music. Bai marched down the passageway, wincing at the volume and the incomprehensible, screeched-out lyrics. She still found it difficult to believe that the tawdry palace of pleasure was anchored only four kilometers from the port city of Sarawak. Although modernized, the *Bĺo Kù Chan* was still little improved from an opium den and gambling hell from the old Tong days.

Dong Xo and Pai Chu shouldered a path through a crowd of elegantly dressed Arabs and Japanese businessmen on holiday. A French woman with a sun-pinked face shouted angrily at the three people but closed her mouth when Bai Suzhen cast her a cold glare.

Flanked by her bodyguards, Bai climbed up a short flight of stairs to a balcony that ran around all four walls of the pavilion. She looked down into a casino decorated with Chinese lanterns and rotating mirror balls that reflected distorted birds-eye views of the blackjack, roulette, Pai-kow and Fan-tan tables. The beeps, burps and bells of electronic slot machines added to the clangor.

Barely audible over the noise rose the murmur of a dozen languages, as varied as the clothing styles worn by the men and women clientele—white dinner jackets, saris, Malay sarongs and *bajus*. She also glimpsed young men and women in Western-style garb and fashion—Chinese girls with breast implants, bleached blond hair, made up to resemble Paris Hilton and boys who affected the dress and swagger of American gangsta rap stars. She didn't understand the intercultural mimicry, nor did she care to. She classified everyone who patronized the *Bĺo Kù Chan* as mental dwarves, hopelessly stunted by avarice and desperation.

Bai Suzhen moved around the balcony. On the walls were cages filled with parrots, cockatoos and birds of paradise. She felt far more pity for the captive birds than the people who gambled away their savings at one of the rigged games in the ship's casino.

The balcony led to a carpeted hallway decorated with delicate Chinese porcelains behind glass cases. At the security checkpoints, the uniformed guards greeted her with deferential bows. The corridor ended at a door of teakwood. Seated on facing benches were the bodyguards of the other members of the conference. The soldiers of the Ghost Shadow and Blue Lotus triads were dressed identically to her own Ghee Hin, except they didn't carry swords.

Bai Suzhen didn't need to tell Dong Xo and Pai Chu to remain behind. Silently they took seats on the benches, hands resting on their knees. She pushed opened the heavy slab of wood and entered a formal indoor garden, lit by glowing lanterns. Sculpted shrubbery surrounding a central court. When she closed the door, the din from the casino became little more than a faint mutter.

In the center of the court rested a long, low table of black enamel. The surface was intricately carved and inlaid with ivory and jade figures depicting pagodas, tigers and elephants. Seated on cushions around the table she saw Zhou Zhi, mountain master of the Blue Lotus triad, and Jimmy Cao, vanguard boss of the Ghost Shadows.

"*Chi dao.*" The harsh, whispery voice sounded like it bounced around inside a cast iron throat and then passed a pair of rusty steel tonsils on its way out into the world.

Bai Suzhen ignored Zhou Zhi's observation that she had arrived late. She bowed toward the woman who sat at the head of the table. Lady Hu, the *wáng hòu* of the White Snake triad was very old and wrinkled, her bone-white hair tied back in a bun. She wore a layered silken robe of burgundy, embroidered with gold thread in dragon forms and tiny figures of Manchu nobility.

"I am actually two minutes early, grandmother," Bai Suzhen said in Mandarin.

Lady Hu nodded, gesturing with one trembling hand that she should seat herself at the opposite end of the table.

Zhou Zhi snorted. The middle-aged Asian's flabby pectorals and enormous belly strained at the buttons of a yellow silk shirt that barely contained his girth. His crew-cut dark hair was as stiff and grizzled as the bristles on an old hog's back. Barely visible within the creases and folds of the man's triple chins wealed the trace of a cicatrix scar, the memento of a long-ago throat-cutting.

"No woman is ever late," he said in a voice barely above a slurred whisper. Bai Suzhen knew that Zhou Zhi had suffered a minor stroke a few years before due to his obesity. He had never fully regained his faculty for speech, although his appetite remained unaffected.

"Late or early, let's get down to business," Jimmy Cao said impatiently, consulting his gold Rolex wristwatch. "I've got a date."

A young man in his mid-twenties, Cao wore a tailored black business suit and snakeskin cowboy boots with thick soles and high heels to make him feel five feet seven instead of five feet four. To Bai Suzhen, he looked ridiculous with his thick black hair slicked up and combed back in a high pompadour which added another inch to his height. Long wispy sideburns barely covered a scattering of acne on his cheeks.

"And I have an appointment with a masseuse," said Zhou Zhi.

"Oh, please," Bai Suzhen murmured wearily.

"No, really," he said defensively, slipping off the Italian loafer from his right foot. He probed the instep with careful fingers and grimaced. "I've got a condition."

"Let's do this thing," said Jimmy Cao impatiently. "Condition, my ass."

Lady Hu's seamed face turned toward the young man. "Business such as this cannot be rushed."

Jimmy Cao uttered a snicker of derision and placed the filtered tip of a cigarette between his lips.

"Please do not smoke," said Lady Hu.

Cao ignored her, setting fire to the cigarette with a gold-plated lighter engraved with the ideograph of the Ghost Shadows.

Reverting to English, Bai Suzhen asked coldly, "You like the bling, don't you?"

Cao didn't answer. He drew in a mouthful of smoke, then exhaled slowly, defiantly in her direction.

Zhou Zhi said bluntly, "Our investments in Cryptozoica Enterprises haven't made a penny's worth of a return. The two-year time limit has expired."

Bai Suzhen turned her attention to the heavy-set man. "I am well aware."

"Then maybe you're aware that we're calling the note due. One hundred and forty million dollars...with interest."

"My triad doesn't have that kind of available cash."

"There are some assets. We want them liquidated and all of the interests sold off. We've already found you a buyer. Or he found us."

"What's his offer?"

"It doesn't matter," said Jimmy Cao.

"You expect me to sell off everything without knowing how much he's willing to pay?" Bai Suzhen asked, arching her eyebrows.

"A small return is better than none," Lady Hu said quietly. "Our holdings in this part of the world are already imperiled by political unrest and the vicissitudes of the weather."

"United Bamboo ain't a philanthropic organization, babe," Jimmy Cao stated, lapsing into English again. "The motive is profit and profit is the motive. The white serpent of good fortune ought to know that."

Zhou Zhi slid a slab of a hand into his jacket and brought out a tri-folded brochure. "The Blue Lotus invested in Cryptozoica Enterprises because you presented what seemed to be a once-in-a-lifetime opportunity to own a large piece of a legitimate and self-perpetuating tourist and pharmaceutical venue. We were fools to expand our base in such a way."

He slapped the full-color Cryptozoica brochure down on the table in front of Bai Suzhen. She did not so much as glance at it. She knew it by heart—she had actually designed the logo and had final approval over the copy. She had even chosen the color scheme.

Although she understood Zhou Zhi's issues, she had little sympathy for them. Over the last five years, the White Snake triad had drawn the majority of its profits from legitimate businesses in Hong Kong, Shanghai, Singapore and Sydney. The Blue Lotus and Ghost Shadow triads still employed the old ruthless Tong tactics of murder-for-hire, extortion, houses of prostitution, gambling dens and drug trafficking.

"The nightclub makes no money," Lady Hu stated almost sorrowfully. "Nor does the brothel. The housing development produces no rent revenue. Obviously there are no tourists. You hold the mortgage on a very expensive aircraft that does not make flights. We have been patient, but now it's time to sell everything and get on with our normal business practices."

Jimmy Cao blew another stream of smoke and said in English, "Cryptozoica, my ass...like we're the goddamn Disney

Corporation or some stupid shit like that. We invest in casinos and whorehouses, not tourist destinations."

Although it wasn't easy, Bai Suzhen managed to maintain her composure. "People still live on Little Tamtung. They have no other means of making a living or anywhere else to go. Most of them are refugees from countries devastated by the tsunami. They came to Tamtung to make new lives, working for Cryptozoica Enterprises."

Zhou Zhi chuckled. "Like the American pilot who got you into this shit in the first place...what do they call him? Tombstone Jack? He sure as hell buried your reputation with United Bamboo."

For a moment, the world seemed to fall utterly still and silent. To Bai Suzhen, it was as if all the air had been pumped out of the room, leaving only a vacuum.

Voice steady, head held high, her face not betraying the rage that filled her, she said softly, "I will not tolerate disrespect from you, Zhou Zhi."

"I have my sources of information," Zhi retorted. "Maybe I don't know how reliable they are about you and the American, but I know he's more to you than a business associate."

"Your sources of information are not only unreliable," stated Bai, "they are liars. I met Kavanaugh when he flew relief missions after the tsunami. I met many Americans then...many Australians, many Englishmen engaged in the same work. They all came to the White Snake club to see me dance."

"But you set only one of them up in business," Lady Hu pointed out.

"Not just me—Howard Flitcroft, too. Kavanaugh showed respect to our triad's influence in the area by coming to me. He dealt with us honorably and so we entered into an arrangement. It was not personal."

"*Not* personal?" echoed Jimmy Cao incredulously. "The man brought you a crazy story about finding an island full of mud that cured diseases and you fucking bought into it! The fountain of youth, my dick."

"Shĩo luô suô!" Lady Hu hissed venomously. "Watch your language!"

Jimmy Cao brayed out a scornful laugh.

"He brought me a story," replied Bai Suzhen. "And he brought me proof. I saw the material, I read the scientific analysis from accredited universities, scientists and Maxiterm Pharmaceuticals."

"He also told you about dinosaurs on the goddamn place— did he show you proof of them?"

Without hesitation, Bai said, "Yes."

"Be that as it may," Zhou Zhi said snidely. "All of us must answer to United Bamboo when they ask questions, even Madame White Snake."

"I answered everyone's questions over two years ago," Bai Suzhen retorted, sweeping the three people with a challenging stare. "The notion of owning a piece of a luxury resort and spa on a private island awakened a kind of greed in you that surprised even me. You didn't care whether the spa delivered what it promised. When you were offered the chance to exploit it in return for start up capital, none of you hesitated. Particularly *you,* Zhou Zhi. You wanted to be the first to take the magical mud bath and put the stick back in your old carrot."

Zhou Zhi fidgeted, averting his gaze. Bai repressed a smile at even so small a victory.

"Our plans were not realized," she continued. "The death of the other investors, the legal and political fallout that resulted, the civil lawsuits, the manner in which Flitcroft kept the undertaking a secret…all of that contributed to, in corporate jargon, 'a lack of alignment.' "

Brusquely, Zhou Zhi said, "You're wrong."

Bai lifted a shoulder in a shrug. "No one is to blame."

"Kavanaugh is to blame," Cao said. "He escorted the investors into the place without proper security. They all died."

"He nearly did, too," Bai countered. "It's a waste of time to go over this again. If you want to sell off our remaining assets of Cryptozoica Enterprises, you don't need me as your go-between."

"Yes, we do," said Lady Hu. "You are the senior shareholder."

"Flitcroft is the senior shareholder," Bai Suzhen replied.

"He controls all of the intellectual property and ancillary rights," the old woman said. "The tangible assets are ours. You will sell them and divide up the proceeds to reduce the White Snake triad's debt."

Bai Suzhen did not even try to repress her outrage. "*Reduce* the debt? It was a risky venture. All of you knew that. Now you react like members of an investment club from Fresno when you didn't get the big payday you were hoping for?"

"We were not playing the stock market," Zhou Zhi growled. "This was a loan to build a business. The business did not materialize but the debt remains...with accrued interest."

Struggling to tamp down her rising fury, Bai demanded, "How much interest are you talking about?"

Jimmy Cao smirked around the cigarette in his mouth. "We haven't decided yet. But you could start paying it down right now, babe."

He touched his fly suggestively.

Zhou Zhi chuckled. "I like that idea. You're older than my usual masseuses, but you could probably be trained."

Grunting, he pulled off his sock, exposing a tiny foot. The arch was crisscrossed with a livid blue and red network of blood vessels broken by trying to support his ponderous weight. The nails on the nubbins of his toes were thick and brown. Bai was put in mind of a pig's hoof. The disgust surging within her did not show on her face.

Grinning, Zhou Zhi said, "I suffer from certain decrepitudes, from bad feet to other parts of my body that don't work as well as they used to. You could help me with that and I could help you with your money problems. It's only fair."

Bai Suzhen glanced from the leering face of Zhi to the grin creasing Jimmy Cao's lips. The cigarette dangled from the corner of his mouth. Lady Hu's expression was impassive, all emotions locked away behind a seamed and wrinkled mask.

With a sigh, Bai Suzhen ran a hand over her forehead and whispered, "All right, Jimmy."

Leaning toward him, she plucked the cigarette from between Cao's lips and shoved the red, glowing tip up the man's left nostril. He howled, clawing at his face, falling over backward.

Bai bounded to her feet with a dancer's grace, uncoiling from the floor, right hand slipping inside her jacket and withdrawing the CZ75 from the holster in the same smooth motion. She leveled it at Zhou Zhi's shock-slackened face, then adjusted her aim a trifle and squeezed off a single round.

The sound of the shot was lackluster, like a distant hand-clap. She doubted the report penetrated out into the foyer where the bodyguards waited. There was nothing lackluster about Zhou Zhi's reaction when the bullet trimmed off the top of his big toe, taking the horny nail with it in a spray of blood.

Squalling in fear and agony Zhi toppled over sideways, plucking at his foot. Bai Suzhen whirled back toward Jimmy Cao, who dislodged the cigarette from his nostril and groped beneath his suit jacket. She jammed the barrel of the CZ75 hard against the side of his neck.

"You'd better be grabbing for something to blow your nose with," she said flatly. "Babe."

Cao raised his hands and she reached in under his coat, found the butt of a Glock 9mm and pulled it out of the holster. She tossed it across the room, into the shrubbery.

"You have a buyer?" she demanded, digging the bore of her pistol against the underside of his jaw.

Swallowing hard, Cao said hoarsely, "An Englishman."

"His name?"

Cao's lips peeled back over his teeth. "I don't remember. Something French."

Bai Suzhen pressed harder with the automatic. "You said he was British."

"He lives in London, but he has a French name."

"Send him to me and I'll deal with him on my own terms. If you and Zhi want your cut, you'll stay out of my way."

Bending close, she switched to English and whispered into his ear, "Or I'll have your balls cut off, pickled and sent to me in a Ming vase. Do we understand each other, you little Taiwanese piece of shit?"

Jimmy Cao couldn't nod because of the painful position of the gun barrel, but he said hoarsely, "Yes."

"Yes, what?"

"Yes—Madame White Snake."

Bai Suzhen whipped the gun away from Cao's neck and he sagged over the table, coughing violently. Returning her pistol to the shoulder holster, she glanced contemptuously at the whimpering Zhou Zhi, still vainly groping for his bleeding foot.

Turning toward Lady Hu, she inclined her head and upper body in a deferential bow. "I regret you had to see this, grandmother."

The old woman's lips twitched. "Do not. I found the display very entertaining. I wondered when you would lose your tempers with these two pigs."

Bai Suzhen smiled fleetingly and asked, "Do you know the name of the buyer?"

"Aubrey Belleau," Lady Hu answered. "I shall report to him that our business meeting concluded satisfactorily and he may contact you on Little Tamtung. You are truly the white serpent of good fortune. May you prosper and enjoy a safe passage, granddaughter."

Chapter Four

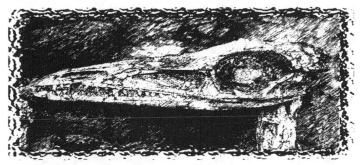

Chubut Province, Patagonia

Honoré Roxton pushed up the brim of her white Stetson and returned the hollow-eyed stare of the Troodon skull, half buried in the loose dust and dirt. She said, "This is just one of an amazing treasure trove of fossils that have been unearthed in Patagonia, giving paleontologists our first view of the whole range of life in the mysterious middle Jurassic period."

She spoke with the crisp and ear-pleasing enunciation of a well-educated Britisher. "The Upper Cretaceous and Tertiary deposits here have revealed a most interesting vertebrate fauna. This, together with the discovery of the perfect cranium of a chelonian of the genus Myolania, which may be said to be almost identical with Myolania oweni of the Pleistocene age in Queensland, forms an evident proof of the connection between the Australian and South American continents.

"The Patagonian Myolania belongs to the Upper Chalk, having been found associated with remains of Dinosauria, like this sample of the Troodon. Aaron, what can you tell us about this species?"

Aaron Edwards carefully brushed dust away from the fangs of the skull with a whisk broom, but the incessant breeze blew it right back, filling the crevices between them.

In a quavering, nervous voice, the young blonde man said, "Well, it's generally believed that predatory theropods like the Troodon had developed fully functional binocular vision and that controlled the coordination between running, hand movement and visual information about moving objects."

The twenty-one year old graduate student from Muncie, Indiana glanced up at Honoré and she nodded encouragingly for him to go on. He said, "If you examine this structure here—"

He blew grit away from a partially exposed vertebra, then sneezed explosively. Honoré managed to keep from laughing, although she wasn't able to repress a grin. Turning toward the cameraman, she said dryly, "I believe that calls for a cut."

Byerson, the director stepped forward, his bearded face locked in a frown. "That's my call, Doc."

"And that's my student," Honoré replied, nodding toward the young man. "I'd prefer his respiratory distress not be televised."

Aaron smiled up at her gratefully, then sneezed again.

"Go blow your nose," Honoré directed.

As the young man climbed out of the shallow, square-cut pit, Honoré brushed dirt particles from her long red-blond hair that spilled in a wind-tangled cascade from beneath her hat. Thin to the point of being gaunt with lean muscles curving down from her shoulders to her forearms, Dr. Honoré Roxton fought back a sneeze herself. Wearing a white shirt with the sleeves rolled up, old jeans and scuffed hiking boots, she knew she presented a decidedly unglamorous image of a female paleontologist.

She wore wire-rimmed glasses over her leaf-green eyes even though Byerson had begged her to wear contacts instead, claiming that the intense color of her eyes was her best feature. However, she knew her eyes would quickly become wet and red when particles of grit worked themselves beneath the lenses. Already she felt chafed and sticky from the sand that had crept through her shirt, into her bra and clung to her skin.

Byerson glanced at the sky lowering over the snow-capped Andes. "We might have time for one more setup before we call it a day."

"For example?" Honoré inquired.

"How about you holding up a leg bone or something and

talking about it?" the cameraman asked. Like Byerson, he was an American, but he seemed to be the product of a distinctly low-end educational level.

"And pretend I'm the host of a Home Shopping Network program?" Honoré demanded. "You *do* understand that fossils are imitations of the bones, not the real thing? Various minerals form a mold around the original material, but it's not always perfect. For example, pterosaur bones are very thin and rarely escape crushing during fossilization."

"Great," replied the man, peering through the view-finder of his shoulder-mounted camera. "Grab a bone out of the ground and say the same thing while I'm rolling."

Byerson rolled his eyes in good-natured exasperation. "Shut up, Bill. Doc, how about we get some scenes of you sketching the skull? I understand you're a superb scientific artist."

Honoré smiled self-consciously. "Nowadays, a detailed record of a dig is maintained by digital cameras."

"Yeah, but it's an old tried and true technique dating back to Victorian-era paleontologists, right? I think our viewers would get a kick out of seeing how you guys used to do it."

Honoré's smile vanished. "Just how old do you think I am, Mr. Byerson?"

A chill gust of wind threw a pinch of dust into Byerson's face and he grimaced. "To be honest, doc, filling an hour of air time with one scene after another of college students digging in the dirt doesn't make for good TV, not even on the Discovery Channel. But you've got a great speaking voice and you'd be majorly telegenic if you took off those damn glasses and put on some lipstick."

"Would you like me to flash some cleavage, as well?" Honoré asked coldly. "I could borrow a pair of low-riders from one of my interns and bend over more often than I have been."

Byerson shrugged. "It might not be a bad idea, but I think a 30-second spot of you drawing pictures of a dinosaur skull, with the appropriate voice-over, ought break up some of the academic monotony."

Honoré sighed. "All right, then. Amanda—!"

A brown-skinned girl standing at the rim of the excavation turned toward her. Her hair was a rat's nest of wind-blown dreadlocks and beaded braids. "Yes, Dr. Roxton?" Her voice held a strong Liverpudlian accent.

"Would you mind fetching my sketchbook and a few pencils from the op center?"

Amanda Redding formed an OK sign with her thumb and forefinger and jogged toward the main camp. For miles around was basically flatland, with not even sproutings of scrub to relieve the sameness of the terrain. A lifeless and sere lake basin spread out like a vast bowl of desolation.

Nothing was left of the lake, not even a few puddles. It looked as though an impossibly huge animal had stomped a hoof print into the center of the basin, sinking it well below the foothills of the mountain range.

Mineral deposits in the rugged Andes range glittered dully with the reflected radiance of the sun. The jagged serrations of the white peaks resembled the points of diamonds.

A dozen dust-filmed Land Rovers and a cluster of tents formed an uneven wall around the outer perimeter of the site. Rock hammers clicked, dental picks ticked and the little red marker flags fluttered in the constant breeze. Twenty people labored among four square-cut, sectionized pits, sifting through sedimentary gravel and carefully whittling away at stone with putty knives.

Honoré Roxton glanced at the cameraman and sighed. She didn't feel comfortable lecturing students in her paleontology classes at Oxford, so to look and sound at ease in front of a camera was a real stretch. But, she had learned that in order to acquire funding for her research projects as well as guarantee her tenure, she had to present herself as something of the Jane Goodall of paleozoology, the attractive, fairly youthful public face of a largely misunderstood scientific discipline.

If she had to give the impression that she was a cross between Lara Croft and Indiana Jones while she made the rounds of talk-shows or served as the anchor of Discovery Channel specials, she had resigned herself to it.

"Doctor Roxton!"

Honoré turned in the direction of Amanda's voice. She gestured to the big main operations tent that held most of their equipment. "London calling on the Wi-Fi!"

Honoré frowned, confused. She glanced at her wristwatch. Not only was it very late in England, she had no immediate family in London and most of the people she considered friends were with her at the site.

Quickly, she climbed out of the pit and crossed the open ground to the tent. As she reached Amanda, she asked, "Who is calling me out here?"

The young woman mimed patting a child's head at waist level and made a face as if she tasted something sour. "Himself the elf."

Honoré instantly knew to whom Amanda referred and a shudder shook her frame. "Oh my God," she murmured.

Despite its size, the tent felt crowded, filled as it was with packing crates, drafting tables, tool-boxes and three state-of-the-art computer consoles. By the time she sat down in the camp-chair before a monitor screen, taken off her hat, put on the headset and adjusted the video feed, she felt nominally prepared to speak to Dr. Aubrey Belleau.

As one of the preeminent curators of London's Natural History Museum as well as her self-appointed mentor, Belleau's credentials were worthy of respect, even if his personal behavior had earned little more than contempt.

The screen framed only Belleau's head and shoulders but that view was sufficient exposure for Honoré. She had seen the man naked in a hot tub several years before, the memory of his gnarled, misshapen body still gave her occasional nightmares.

Aubrey Belleau affected the kind of neatly trimmed beard once known as a Van Dyke. His dark blond hair swept back from an exceptionally high forehead. Under level brows, big eyes of the clearest, cleanest blue, like the high sky on a cloudless summer's day regarded her intently. He wore a fawn-colored blazer. A silk foulard swirled at the open collar of his black shirt. A gold stickpin gleamed within its folds, topped by a tiny insignia resembling the Masonic all-seeing eye. She had never inquired about it, but she assumed he held membership in a local lodge.

Although his size was not apparent on the monitor screen, Dr. Aubrey Belleau could have been classified as a dwarf, since his height did not exceed four feet, even with lifts in his shoes.

"Hello, Aubrey," Honoré said into the mouthpiece. "You're up early—or staying up very late."

The man showed the edges of his teeth in a perfunctory smile. He wore a headset identical to Honoré's. "It's worth losing a bit of sleep so I may see and speak with you, darlin' Honoré."

He emphasized the last syllable of her name, drawing it out like taffy so it sounded like "Honor-raaaay."

"You didn't make a satellite call at this hour just so you could get a peep at me, Aubrey."

His eyes widened in mock hurt. "Would it be so bad if I had?"

Honoré sighed. "The last I heard, you had just exchanged vows with Mrs. Aubrey Belleau…version three point oh."

"Your information is out of date, darlin'. My divorce from that soddin' cow became final last month."

Honoré smiled slightly at his use of vulgar slang. Despite his name, Belleau had been born in England fifty-six years before and she had never heard him so much as whisper a word of French, even to order wine.

"Aubrey, I'm very busy."

He uttered a short, barking laugh. "I know. I arranged the whole Discovery Channel special, of course."

"Of course," she said patronizingly. "You're a grand arranger."

"Ain't I just. Well, now I'm arranging something else."

"What might that be?"

"The museum and the board of department directors at the school of Anthropology all agree you're the best candidate—no, strike that. You're the *only* candidate to carry through with this."

Trying to soften the sharp edge of impatience in her voice, she said, "I'm waiting, Aubrey."

Belleau paused. She didn't know if he was doing so for dramatic effect or if it was due to a transmission lag in the wireless transmission. "Tell me…what do you know of Cryptozoica?"

Honoré did not respond immediately. Wonder and conjecture wheeled through her mind as she flipped through her mental rolodex. "Do you mean that fraudulent eco-tourism business a year or so back?"

"I do. And it was a bit over two years ago."

"I really don't know anything specific about it," she stated. "I do remember several universities were solicited to fund a scientific research station on an island somewhere in the South Seas. It all turned out to be some sort of elaborate con perpetrated by an American multi-millionaire, wasn't it? Howard somebody."

"Howard Philips Flitcroft," Belleau said.

"Right. A typical blustering Yank showman. Far too much money and too few brains as a balance."

"Perhaps. But Flitcroft didn't perpetrate a fraud. If anything, he was the victim."

"As I recall, there were hucksters pushing a fantasy about an island spa where the rich received longevity therapies…it was supposed to be populated by prehistoric survivors and in return for outrageous fees, the hucksters would schedule and arrange scientific tours."

"It all depends upon your definition of outrageous fees, I suppose," replied Belleau. "Thirty-five thousand pounds doesn't seem too outrageous in exchange for observing and perhaps interacting with actual dinosaurs."

"True enough," she said dismissively. "If there were truly dinosaurs on the island instead of moving models or some other mechanical replicas that can be found at any well-financed theme park or seaside holiday town. There are similar attractions in Brighton."

Belleau smiled. "I'd agree entirely, if the creatures in question were fabrications. However, in the instance of Cryptozoica, the dinosaurs were indeed real animals."

It required a few seconds for Honoré to fully comprehend the implications of Belleau's comment. She demanded, "Are you implying that Cryptozoica *wasn't* a fraud?"

"Hardly," he answered calmly. "I'm implying nothing of the sort. I am announcing to you without fear of repudiation that Cryptozoica is definitely *not* a fraud. It is the largest of a two-island chain recorded on the old seventeenth and eighteenth century charts as the Tamtungs. Dinosaurid survivors do exist upon it. How many, the actual genus and pedigree remains to be fully documented. Honoré, we want you to be instrumental in that documentation, to tell the world about it and legitimize the discovery."

Honoré stared unblinkingly at the image of the bearded man on the screen. Because of the fluttering pixels and grainy reception, it was impossible to tell if Belleau was joking or merely deranged.

"Aubrey—" She broke off and angrily began to remove the headset. "I don't know what the bloody hell you're trying to pull here, but I don't appreciate it."

"I'm completely serious, Dr. Roxton." Belleau's voice came as sharp as a whip-crack over the earpiece, causing her to wince. "I can prove what I say. You bloody well know I don't go in for practical jokes. Foolish wastes of time and concentration."

Honoré knew he spoke the truth, but she said, "Perhaps not, but you could be the victim of one or fallen prey to a hoax. That was the general consensus of opinion in the scientific community about the Cryptozoica business, right—an elaborate hoax that didn't quite come off? Who is reviving it now?"

"No one, because it's not a hoax." Belleau exhaled a slow, weary breath. "I'll be blunt with you...a handful of people have always known of Cryptozoica's existence but they also knew that it could conceivably be the single most influential discovery in modern human culture. I know it sounds fantastic, but there it is."

"It sounds more than fantastic." Very slowly, very deliberately enunciating each syllable, Honoré said, "It sounds *im*-possible. It's ridiculous for two scientists such as ourselves to even discuss such a thing."

Belleau nodded. "I once felt as you did. But I came to learn that living dinosaurs are not a zoological impossibility, particularly in areas that have been geologically stable for the past sixty million years. Larger ectothermic dinosaurs would have a more successful chance of thriving in stable, warm, equatorial regions than warm-blooded animals with faster metabolic rates. Ectothermic creatures also require only ten percent of the amount of the food taken in by fully endothermic animals."

"I can't argue that," Honoré admitted. "But determining dinosaur energetics and thermal biology without studying living models is pure pseudo-scientific speculation, the realm of cryptozoologists, not paleontologists. There's no evidence that humanity and dinosaurs coexisted, for even a short period of time. The Cretaceous-Tertiary extinction event occurred 65 million years ago, long before the appearance of the most primitive hominid."

"One with an open mind could argue that legends and ancient works of traditional art depict dinosaurs interacting with Man," replied Belleau. "The Ica stones found in Peru bear carvings of both humans and dinosaurs, not to mention fossilized footprints of hominid and dinosaurid that were found imbedded in rock strata from the same era. There is the carving of an apparent *Stegosaur stenops* found on a column in Angkor Wat.

"Less dramatically, there is the coelacanth, a fish believed to have died out even before the dinosaurs that is still swimming off the coast of Africa, not to mention a wasp thought extinct for twenty-five million years was discovered to have survived in California, of all places."

Honoré brushed away Belleau's remarks with an impatient gesture. "Yes, yes. It's also been suggested that a species of plesiosaur account for tales of sea and lake monsters, such as the Loch Ness Monster. Sheerest eye-wash."

"Entertain for a moment just the suggestion that you are wrong," Belleau said. "That a group of dinosaurids from the late Cretaceous Period managed to survive the K-T extinction event and continued to breed and reproduce in virtual isolation for millions of years. What do you think the impact of this revelation would be on the world at large, let alone the scientific community?"

"Before or after all scientists are tarred, feathered and our degrees burned at high noon in the village square?"

Lines of irritation appeared on Belleau's high forehead. "It's a serious question."

Honoré considered the man's words for a moment, then said quietly, "Possibly such a discovery could challenge everything, perhaps all of our beliefs about science and evolution and even our perception of the very process of creation. Such a finding would deal a crushing blow to the hypothesis of a unique evolutionary sequence. Darwinism might have to be re-evaluated… not to mention the boost it could give to creationists."

"Exactly! That is why we need completely trustworthy public principals to release the information, in a controlled, rational manner. A ridiculous holiday park endeavor would have completely discredited and destroyed the scientific and cultural value. Howard Flitcroft understands that now."

"That blowhard is still part of this?" she asked skeptically.

"Minimally. Believe me, the highest authorities in scientific institutions around the globe are deeply involved. In return for your own involvement, we are willing to grant you exclusive rights to any and all developmental research that arises. You'll have first right of refusal of anything in the zoological and paleontological fields connected to Cryptozoica. Your career, your fortune and future will be assured."

Honoré blinked, her thought processes alternately staggering and freezing in place. She shook her head. "I don't quite… Aubrey, you're serious? Really serious?"

He grinned. "As the proverbial broken leg, darlin'. I need to meet you at the Buenos Aires airport no later than tomorrow noon. Transportation has already been dispatched to fetch you."

"But I haven't agreed to anything!" she protested. "I don't have enough information on which to base a decision. I've got to think this through."

"You'll have plenty of time to think it through. But while you're doing so, please don't let me—and yourself—down. This project is proceeding apace, regardless of your participation. Without you, there's no way to ascertain its direction, but with you on board, everything will be validated. You'll be supplied with all the information you require. I hope to see you in the lovely flesh very soon, Dr. Roxton."

The image of Aubrey Belleau faded from the screen. Slowly, Honoré took off the headset. She felt as if she were under water, floundering in a sea of confusion and even madness.

Amanda suddenly threw the tent flap aside, her eyes wide with excitement. "Doctor!"

"What?"

Wordlessly, the young woman pointed to the helicopter that flew over the top of a ridgeline. Honoré rose and went to stand beside Amanda. The spinning rotors kicked up a cloud of dust as it landed on the far side of the perimeter. She saw an insignia imprinted on the fuselage, a blue circle with the letters HFP overlapping in the center of it.

Honoré muttered sourly, "Howard Philips Flitcroft. Minimal involvement."

Chapter Five

The pinnacled towers of the Natural History Museum rose from the foggy heart of London like the ghost of a medieval cathedral. It wasn't often that Aubrey Belleau had the opportunity to appreciate its ornate terra-cotta façade acrawl with the sculpted likenesses of apes, fish and human skulls in the blue-gray hours between midnight and dawn.

Sitting in the back seat of his Rolls-Royce Silver Spur limousine, Belleau eyed the arches and flying buttresses with appreciation. Heavy yellow fog wafting in from the Thames pressed against the windows. Still, the temperature was moderately warm for London at hard on three o'clock in the morning.

He didn't find the looming edifice of the museum at all intimidating. However, as he was the latest in a long line of Belleaus whose professional and personal life was inextricably linked to the fortunes of the institution, he found the sight of it inspiring.

Oakshott swerved the Rolls-Royce into the private parking lot at the rear of the Darwin Centre. The guard leaned out of his glass-walled booth, recognized the automobile and the ID sticker on the windshield and waved it through the checkpoint.

As Oakshott braked the big car to a stop, Belleau made sure the computer and video uplink were disconnected. Honoré hadn't asked him from where he was transmitting, nor would he have told her the truth if she had. Neither he nor any member of his family had ever violated the secrecy oath of the School of Night.

Oakshott parked the car and turned off the engine. Quickly, he got out, placing the step stool down before he opened the rear door. A gigantic man in gray chauffeur's livery, he stood nearly seven feet tall and tipped the scales at three hundred pounds. His long face was dead-white. In his uniform, complete with a peaked cap and jodhpurs, Oakshott looked like a store window manikin from the late nineteenth century.

Aubrey Belleau slid from the car seat and stepped onto, then off the stool, twirling his miniature silver-knobbed walking stick like a Victorian dandy. He walked with a rolling gait along a flagstone path. "I shan't be long, Oakshott. Wait in the car, take a nap if you've a mind to, that's a good fellow."

As he approached the service entrance, he heard the distant bong of Big Ben striking three. Reflexively, he glanced in the direction of the clock tower but because of the fog he could barely make out its outline.

At the door, he removed the gold stickpin from his scarf and gave it a brief visual inspection. It was tipped with a symbol resembling a caduceus, depicting a pair of serpents coiled around a staff topped by an eye within a pyramid.

Inserting the end of the pin into the keyhole below the doorknob, he probed for a second, then with a click of a solenoid, the door swung silently open. He stepped into a foyer containing janitorial and cleaning supplies and closed the door behind him, the solenoid catching automatically.

Angling his walking stick over a shoulder, Belleau strode into a broad gallery filled with iguanas and tortoises, frozen in attitudes of arrested movement. Masterpieces of the model-maker's art, the scaled bodies and staring eyes glittered like unfinished gems. Terns and albatrosses hovered overhead, suspended by almost invisible filaments.

He marched swiftly past the reinforced glass tank holding the preserved remains of Archie the squid, the eight meter long example of *Architeuthis dux* floating in a solution of saline and formaldehyde. He didn't so much as glance at the thousands of animal carcasses encased within glass. His footsteps echoed and re-echoed within the vast gallery.

Passing beneath an arch, he opened a narrow, nondescript door and entered a big chamber, shaped like the inside of a drum, with oak-paneled walls. High bookshelves rose nearly three meters above the floor. A wheeled library ladder leaned against the far wall.

Bronze busts mounted on marble pedestals occupied the spaces between the shelves, each one haloed by a small light fixture. Belleau's gaze passed over them one by one, an almost unconscious form of paying homage to Charles Darwin, Sir Walter Raleigh, John Dee, Gerardus Mercator, Christopher Marlowe, Sir Isaac Newton, Herbert Spencer, John Stuart Mill, Sir Richard Owen and Thomas Huxley.

A big round Japanese lantern hung from the center of the conical ceiling where the heavy beams converged, shedding a rich yellow light over a plank table made of bird's-eye maple.

The four men seated around the table were all direct descendants of the men who had founded the School of Night in 1592, and each one was a respected representative of a different scientific discipline, ranging from biochemistry to quantum physics.

"Good evening, class," Belleau said jovially, then as was the custom upon entering the chamber, he recited the school's motto, quoting from Shakespeare's *Love's Labour Lost:* "Black is the badge of hell/The hue of dungeons and the school of night."

The other men responded with grunted monosyllables. Andrew Wadley didn't even try to pat back his yawn. He demanded, "Why must we convene these meetings at three A.M.? It's becoming *damned* inconvenient."

"Tradition frequently is," replied Belleau stiffly. "Three A.M. is the midnight of the human soul, when the blood trickles at low tide and the heart beats at its slowest rhythm. We're more receptive to new ideas, more suggestible, more inclined to entertain different ways of contemplating and reevaluating our narrow view of reality."

"It's also the time when the elderly most often die in their sleep," interjected Jacob Haining dourly. He was the senior member of the group, eighty-three years old. Short, silver-haired and rail-thin, his brown suit was the same color as the oak paneling.

"According Dr. Dee's Codex," said Francis Dee smugly, "the original school met at three A.M. so as to avoid the prying eyes of palace spies."

Belleau took his chair, using the special crossbars to push himself up into its elevated seat. "As I recall, John Dee never received his doctorate."

Dee, an astronomer in his sixties with a moon face and eyes that blinked nervously from behind the round lenses of spectacles, said irritably, "My ancestor was a founding member of the school, nevertheless."

Belleau only smiled superciliously. He knew the man spoke the truth, but his habit of exaggerating John Dee's influence during the formation of the School of Night never failed to annoy him. As it was, Belleau resented how his own great-great-grandfather owed his pre-eminent position in the School to Dee's skills as an Elizabethan era cryptographer.

Conceived by Sir Walter Raleigh, the original cabal of scholars secretly studied science, philosophy, and religion, and all were suspected of being atheists.

Atheism in the court of Queen Elizabeth was a charge nearly the equivalent of treason, since the monarch was the head of the church and to denounce the church was to be against the monarch.

However, inasmuch as atheism was also a synonym for anarchy, that was a charge frequently brought against anyone who was the slightest bit religiously and politically troublesome. Guy Fawkes was a member of the earliest incarnation of the school, or more accurately a pawn.

The School of Night was not particularly unique. It was but one of many secret societies that sprang up in Europe in the tumultuous period between the reigns of Henry VIII and Elizabeth. Religious and alchemical cults arose among the nobility, convening in the shadows to evade ecclesiastical inquisitors.

By its very nature, the School of Night was heretical, working toward a rationalist view of society and human destiny free of biblical influence. It traced the roots of its progenitors to the so-called mystery schools of ancient Egypt, which allegedly passed on great secrets about creation and the earliest civilization, and through symbolism and allegory taught lost mathematical techniques, as well as advanced science and philosophy. Although wielding a degree of covert influence in the pursuit of scientific thought over the last century, the school had existed primarily to keep a single discovery hidden.

In its present incarnation, the School of Night wasn't a large organization, nor was there any reason for it to be. It had a four-hundred year old legacy preserved from generation to generation, although Belleau was concerned about passing on the torch to unworthy hands. Although the membership rules excluded females, he had suggested more than once that the School modify its stringent entrance requirements.

The sexism was one of the carryovers from the original founders, none of whom could have been accused of holding enlightened views about the equality of women, particularly Raleigh.

Belleau felt positive Honoré Roxton would make an exemplary member, but he knew none of his colleagues shared his enthusiasm. Therefore, he had no intention of giving them a choice in the matter.

"I'm getting a wee too old for these late hours myself," complained Gregor McArdle in his guttural Scots brogue. A big, rawboned man in his mid-50s, a red spade beard bristled at his chin.

"It's only one night a month," retorted Haining peevishly.

"Aye, but you're a bachelor. You try explaining to a wife why your lodge holds regular meetings at three o' clock in the bloody morning. The looks I get at the breakfast table—" McArdle shook his head in frustration.

Belleau rapped the knob of his walking stick on the table edge. "Then let us convene the meeting, get our business out of the way and you can go back to bed and to your wife."

"What precisely is our business again?" Haining demanded, his nasal, strident voice punching painfully against Belleau's eardrums.

"The Tamtungs...or to be specific, the main island so quaintly rechristened Cryptozoica by Howard Flitcroft's public relations firm."

"There is news?" asked Dee.

"Excellent news, in fact. My offer to buy the interests held by Bai Suzhen has been tacitly accepted."

Haining's wrinkled face screwed up as if he smelled or tasted something foul. "Words cannot express my disgust at our dealings with a criminal organization...an Oriental one at that. Sir Walter is no doubt revolving madly inside his crypt."

Belleau ignored the comment. "Through our intermediaries in the States, Flitcroft has been convinced to finance our film project in the hopes of recouping his investment losses. It took several months of persuasion, but he finally saw the wisdom in the proposition."

Belleau paused, chuckled, and added, "Of course, the stipulation is that we will have ultimate approval over the final edit."

McArdle shook his head. "I understand your worry about leaving the Tamtungs unsecured, but all these efforts, all this subterfuge and money we're pumping into the project...well, it's tantamount to trying to bribe the genie to return to the lamp, isn't it? The truth is bound to get out...even what happened to poor Dr. Perry all those years ago."

"I agree," said Wadley. "We were able to contain the problem over the last hundred years, but if we allow a film crew in there, especially into the interior—"

"—The whole point is that the truth of the place will indeed be known," broke in Belleau impatiently. "But we will control the degree of truth that is disseminated and to do that, we must have the complete cooperation of everyone involved. That's why I have taken the liberty of contacting Dr. Roxton."

Dee cocked his head in puzzlement. "Honoré Roxton? What does she have to with this?"

Belleau smiled at the man patronizingly. "Honoré is one of the best-known paleontologists in the world. She will be the voice and the figure of final authority regarding the 'truth' of Cryptozoica."

He crooked his index fingers to indicate quotation marks. "She will essentially be the star of the television program…or if all goes according to plan, the television series."

Haining spoke up in a sharp shout of outrage. "Then she will share in the secret. She will have to be told about the Prima Materia!"

Belleau nodded. "Exactly."

"She'll never believe you," argued Wadley. "She would have to be shown the sample and the lost journal of the *Beagle*. In which case, she might as well be accorded full membership of the school."

"Exactly," said Belleau again, this time with a smug smile.

The four men stared at him, shocked into speechlessness. Finally, Dee ventured, "My dear fellow, as much as we respect Dr. Roxton, she's still a woman. It's just *not* done."

Placing his hands flat on the tabletop, Belleau surveyed the men seated around him with a challenging stare. In a low voice, heavy with conviction, he said, "Even after all of these years, you still do not understand. As of 1836, we of the School of Night were no longer scholars or intellectuals engaged in the pursuit of studying and compiling esoterica.

"We became caretakers, guardians of the secret of creation, of the very source of all life on Earth. As such, we may very well become the saviors of all life when the inevitable next mass extinction becomes a reality, instead of sensationalistic fodder for talk television or cheap science periodicals.

"Our group must exert complete control over the resources of the island by any means that are expedient, even if those measures include entering into business arrangements with Asian criminal organizations, deceiving American millionaires, discrediting and silencing witnesses or even granting a woman membership in our sacrosanct order."

The last two words were spoken with undisguised sarcasm.

Haining bristled at Belleau's tone. "You spoke of our traditions earlier...be mindful of them now!"

"I can be mindful of the spirit of our traditions without adhering to the substance of them. We have kept many centuries worth of knowledge hidden from traditional science, have we not?"

With the silver ferrule of his walking stick, Belleau pointed to the bookshelves, moving it from left to right. "There we have forty-two sacred writings by Hermes Trismegistus, his so-called Emerald Tablets that encapsulate all the training of ancient Egyptian priests, rescued from the Temple of Neith by students of Plato...there are the alchemical tomes of Henry Cornelius Agrippa and the damned texts of Giordano Bruno, smuggled from his home on the very day he was burnt at the stake in Rome as a heretic.

"There are the notations of Paracelsus regarding the Philosopher's Stone, the Enochian alphabet as translated by John Dee and the formula of the *elixir vitae* concocted by the Comte de Saint-Germain, and much, much more."

He jabbed the tip of his cane at Haining like an accusing finger. "All of those men whose writings we have in our possession postulated the existence of Prima Materia, the primitive formless base of all organic matter. But due only to the foresight of my great-great-grandfather, the School of Night has had an actual sample of it in our possession for nearly two centuries."

"Yes, we're all aware of Jacque Belleau's contribution," said McArdle impatiently. "You've reminded us of it often enough over the last twenty-five years."

Francis Dee sniffed. "Belleau only acted upon my ancestor's code-breaking discoveries. It could have been any scholar of the School."

Belleau ignored the jibe. "I want the sample and the journal of the *Beagle*. If I'm to convince Honoré Roxton of the importance of our undertaking, I will need proof, visual aids at the very least."

Haining stared at him with incredulous eyes. "Do you mean to remove them from our hall?"

"Why not? We wouldn't even have a hall or the support of the museum if not for my influence."

"But if they should be lost or stolen—" Wadley broke off, unable to utter the awful implications.

Belleau grinned. "Oh, pooh. At this point, they serve no real purpose except as artifacts, trophies in our collection, two more items hidden from public eyes in our private repository."

Frowning, McArdle said, "We have a file containing photographs of the life-forms on Cryptozoica, taken at the blind in the early 1900s...the ones shown to Doyle. That should suffice to convince her."

"She will reject them as fakes, Photoshop forgeries. No, Honoré Roxton will require proof a bit more substantial."

The four men exchanged questioning glances. After a long, awkward silence, Haining turned toward Belleau. "I am opposed to this, but we need no further dissension. You may have what you request, but their safety is solely your responsibility. Do you accept that?"

Belleau shrugged. "Of course."

Haining nodded in McArdle's direction. "Gregor, you're the most able-bodied among us. If you would be so kind—" Not bothering to swallow his sigh of aggravation, McArdle rose and strode across the room to the library ladder. Belleau watched him wheel it over to the shelf to the right of Darwin's bust. He couldn't help but smile in triumph.

Noticing the smile, Dee said bitterly, "You're an ambitious man, Aubrey, but usually your ambitions coincide with the interests of the school. I'm not sure of your motives this time...particularly since you brokered the deal between Maxiterm Pharmaceuticals and that ridiculous ecotourism scheme of Flitcroft. Am I correct in assuming the company still holds you responsible for their losses?"

Belleau's face feigned hurt feelings. "You wound me, Francis. I don't inquire as to the source of your disposable income or how your gambling debts are always paid."

Wadley said quietly, "I'm glad you find such entertainment in this, Aubrey. I, for one, suspect we're making a tragic mistake."

"As do I," Haining said in his reedy voice. His eyes glinted with malicious amusement. "We've certainly made them before in regards to the Tamtungs. But assuming there is such a thing as a moral balance in the universe, the consequences of this mistake will be restricted to falling upon *your* head alone."

Belleau did not respond. He was barely able to keep himself from spitting at the old man. The School of Night was composed of sterile intellectuals, doddering old pedants. Despite all of their knowledge and staggeringly high IQs, none of them had accepted the fact that morality was relative, only a variable, not an absolute.

What constituted sin in one culture could very well be a virtue in another. Belleau knew with soul-deep certainty that objective morality existed only as his means to accomplish an end.

Grunting with effort, McArdle tugged a dark green metal case from the top shelf, two feet long by two wide. The lid was secured by a clasp and a small padlock. Hugging the case to his chest, the bearded man slowly climbed down the ladder, the flat rungs creaking beneath his weight. He carried it over to the table and with an almost reverent care, laid down the case before Belleau.

Fingers trembling, he lifted his stickpin and inserted the

eye-within-the-pyramid insignia into the base of the padlock. He twisted it to the right and for a long moment of frustration and fright, it did not turn. Then, with a faint click, the lock popped open.

Slowly, he raised the lid, aware of his colleagues craning their necks to see within, even though all of them were familiar with the contents. With both hands, Belleau lifted out a slim, leather-bound book, the dark front cover bearing no title or markings of any kind. He flipped aside the cover. Affixed to the underside by a metal clamp was a glass vial four inches long and no thicker than his middle finger. Soldered metal and wax served as a seal.

When Belleau plucked the tube from the clamp, both Haining and McArdle drew in sharp, apprehensive breaths. A kind of sobbing, crooning moan came from Wadley's lips. Revolving the vial between thumb and forefinger, he held it up to the light.

A grayish-green gel half-filled the glass tube. Belleau tilted it to the right, then to the left. The thick, semi-liquid substance oozed to and fro. Tiny bubble-laced streaks formed within it, little jeweled patterns that looked almost pretty.

In a husky whisper, Belleau said, "The bioplasm still in the same condition as when I first saw it upon my induction into the school ...there has been no change in its molecular density or color, almost as if it was dipped from the pool in the last hour instead of over a hundred and seventy years ago."

Wadley, Haining, McArdle and Dee stared at the gel with rapt eyes. Haining husked out, "There's no reason why it should change...it is primordial ooze, the *Prima Materia* from which all substances on Earth were formed. What is within that container is the *vita force*, the source of all life itself, unchanged and unchanging after six billion years."

Voice quavering with awe, Dee quoted a passage from the Emerald Tablets: " 'All things owe their existence to the Only One, so all things owe their origin to the One Only Thing.' "

The vial of Prima Materia within Belleau's fingers exuded not just a sense of antiquity but a vibration of pulsing force that surrounded him with a tingling, buoyant web. The vibration clung to him, caressing his nerve endings, slipping through his mind in delicate, rippling waves of excruciatingly pleasurable fire.

"The sperm of the Earth," murmured Belleau.

Just holding the Prima Materia made him feel like a god.

Chapter Six

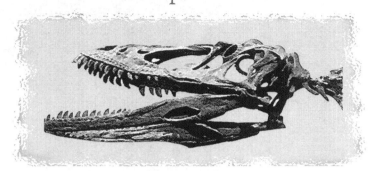

May 10th - The Island of Little Tamtung

Kavanaugh did not know how long he had been running or when the sun went down or when he stumbled and fell into the bed of wet ferns. All he knew was that he feared the night. The screeching of the archaeopteryx and the grunting of an animal somewhere in the vine-shrouded wilderness terrified him.

He knew he was being hunted. The beating of wings and the snarls of the raptor mingled with the crash of the surf beyond the tangled thicket. There was a madness in the noises that gave a little comfort to the insanity lurking in the shadows of his mind. He thought he heard voices mixed in with the other sounds, but they were garbled and he could make no sense of them.

The voices frightened him. They seemed louder than the screeching of the archaeopteryx and the growls of the Deinonychus. One voice shouted directly into his ear, the words filtering into his brain so vividly the individual letters flashed with color, red for blood, yellow for danger.

"Get up, Jack! Get up and run or you will die."

Kavanaugh was too afraid to get up, much less run. If the archaeopteryx saw him, it would call to the Deinoncychus and he would be disemboweled, his guts unwound, just like Jessup, Cranston and Shah Nikwan. A man-shaped figure moved slowly into his field of vision, limping as if crippled. A high-pitched whistle vibrated against his eardrums, like the trilling of birdsong and he heard a faint, dry rustling. Light gleamed dully from an intricate pattern of tiny, glittering scales.

The figure stood taller than he, taller even than Augustus, erect upon thick-thewed legs. From down-sloping shoulders dangled long arms, the five fingers tipped with spurs of discolored bone. The neck was very long, supporting a narrow, elongated skull with a nose that consisted of a pair of flaring slits.

Under knobbed brow ridges, the eyes gleamed golden with opalescent irises, bisected by vertical black slits. The loose flesh at the juncture of its underjaw and throat pulsed.

Kavanaugh stared, transfixed, into those eyes. He heard a faint, agonized groan and distantly realized it had been torn from his own lips. The fathomless eyes held his captive, peering deep into the roots of his soul.

Get up, Jack! the creature sang to him. *Get up and run, or you will die.*

Kavanaugh got up and ran toward the brief flares of light, reaching for them as if he were a child trying to catch fireflies. The flashes took on the appearances of faces that somehow resembled his mother, his father, his brother, and his ex-wife Laurel, all at the same time. He had a dim, faraway awareness that he had broken promises to those faces, but he couldn't remember what they were.

If you return, you will die.

He felt an insistent, prodding pressure against his right rib cage. It wasn't painful, but it wasn't pleasant. He tried to roll away from it, but he couldn't seem to move. Finally, he realized a hard object was pressing against him. Reaching down, his fingers closed on something that felt like the damp toe of a deck shoe.

"Rise and shine, Cap'n K. Howie Flitcroft and his flunkies wait for no one."

Kavanaugh struggled to open one eye. Crowe's scowling mahogany face filled his field of vision. He looked distorted, like a ferocious tribal mask viewed under a magnifying glass.

Coughing, clearing his throat, Kavanaugh massaged his

eyes with the heels of both hands. They felt as if they had been filled with hot sand. "Flitcroft is here?"

"About ten minutes ago, him and Pendlebury. I guess they expected you to be waiting in the office."

"What time is it?"

"A little after eight."

"A.M.?"

Crowe sighed, holding up the empty bourbon bottle. He pinged a fingernail against the glass. "Of course, dipshit. You weren't drunk for a whole goddamn night and day. I wouldn't be surprised if you pulled a bender like that in the future, but so far your problem drinking pattern consists of getting drunk, passing out and waking up the next morning with a hangover, wanting to know what time it is."

"What a coincidence," Kavanaugh croaked, "sort of like now." He realized he was lying on his daybed, still wearing his jeans and boots.

"You really ought to stick to Guinness…it's a food source. There's all kinds of vitamins and essential minerals in it. There's nothing remotely nutritious in bourbon."

Kavanaugh forced himself into a sitting position, his temples pounding. "Yeah, well, you know how I am about my figure."

Getting his arms under him, Kavanaugh heaved his body off the daybed, not even trying to stifle his groans. Pain ripped at the walls of his skull, like a clawed animal trying to escape a box. He stumbled into the tiny bathroom and ran a sink full of tepid water. He plunged his face repeatedly into it, blowing like a whale.

"Want some breakfast?" Crowe called. "Mouzi is frying up some fresh oysters."

Kavanaugh's stomach boiled like a percolator and face submerged, he mumbled, "You're hell on a hangover."

"Kill or cure, Jack."

Kavanaugh fought back his nausea. After his headache abated a bit, he straightened up and caught a glimpse of himself in the mirror. He flinched at the sight. His eyes were dark-rimmed and netted with red. His complexion was like mildewed drywall, his jawline bristling with three days worth of whiskers. However, he took a bit of satisfaction in knowing he looked exactly as he felt—like a man who had started drinking early the evening before and kept it up all night.

Squeezing a dollop of toothpaste onto his tongue, he swished it around his mouth, then swallowed it. Pawing through the pile of dirty laundry on the floor, he found a T-shirt that didn't smell as if it had been used as a burial shroud for a dead skunk and he pulled it on. After finger-combing his hair, he decided he was about as presentable as he was going to be under the present circumstances.

He returned to the living room, noting sourly that although Crowe wasn't dressed appreciably different than he had been the night before, he at least looked and smelled fresh.

Crowe eyed him critically. "That's what you're wearing to the meeting?"

Kavanaugh gestured to the man's fray-cuffed jeans, the tank-top bearing the seal of Temple University Girl's Volleyball Team and the fisherman's cap. "Is that what *you're* wearing?"

Crowe shrugged. His exposed arms and upper chest showed four puckered bullet scars, inflicted during his short career as a unit commander in the Navy SEALs. Like Kavanaugh, the man bore other scars beneath his shirt and on the backside of his psyche.

"Uniform of the day," Crowe drawled. "What's your excuse except that a forty-seven year old man still doesn't know how to operate a washing machine?"

"Neither do you," retorted Kavanaugh resentfully. "Mouzi does your laundry."

Crowe snorted. "If she did, do you think I'd be wearing this rig?"

Assuming the question to be rhetorical, Kavanaugh did not answer. Slipping on a pair of sunglasses, he moved toward the door. "Let's go. Maybe Pendlebury will have made some coffee."

The morning sky melted, pouring down heat. Crowe put on dark glasses as well. Wings flapped overhead and Kavanaugh glimpsed the green plumage of Huang Luan, the archaeopteryx.

"That goddamn thing is stalking me," he said.

Crowe squinted upward, shielding his eyes with his hands. "You're crazy."

Kavanaugh didn't argue with the observation. "I got to get some money…got to get back to the world. Make it or borrow it so I can get the fuck out of here."

"Borrow against what?"

Kavanaugh gestured behind him. "My house."

"Nobody would want that shit shack." Crowe shook his head in disgust. "You're pathetic on top of being crazy."

Kavanaugh inhaled deeply. The air was heavy with the smell of the sea. In the full light of day, both men were reminded again of how quickly Little Tamtung had deteriorated from a prospective A-list tourist resort destination to just another moldy settlement on an insignificant island in the South China Sea.

It wasn't much of a town, although a sincere effort and a lot of money had been expended to build one. On the harborside stretched a paradise of white sandy beach, leaning palm trees and a dark mangrove swamp. The village center itself was a sprawl of white prefab storefronts, souvenir shops and restaurants. Almost all of them were closed, the windows boarded up.

Water-filled holes pitted the narrow streets. Although most of the buildings were barely three years old, they seemed to have wilted at the edges, like the big decorative flower beds planted at all the intersections. In the tropics, decay was often swifter than growth. Overnight, mold bristled on a wet shoe, in a few hours, a body could rot, in a few weeks, a weak personality might fall apart.

Still, when Kavanaugh and Crowe had first seen the island, both of them felt that no new city could have had a more picturesque setting. A narrow river flowed through the town, streaming down from the tropical uplands. Four red-lacquered Thai-style foot bridges spanned it. The brightly colored bridges as well as the flower beds had been Bai Suzhen's idea, as were the stone Chinese lanterns along the walks.

The waterfront area was still in reasonable repair. It extended outward into the bay on a green, grassy promontory. Beyond a cluster of tin-roofed houses on stilts, they saw Flitcroft's big DHC-6 Otter twin engine amphibian tethered to the end of a long concrete jetty. Men clustered around the rear fuselage, unloading boxes from the cargo hold. The jetty had been built to serve as a debarkation and customs terminal. It led to a four-story white stucco building, set in the center of a lawn adorned with royal palm trees.

Although the words Cryptozoica Enterprises & Horizons Unlimited were whitewashed over on the façade above the double doors, the letters could still be made out when a shaft of morning sunshine fell directly onto them.

The few people Kavanaugh and Crowe encountered along the waterfront walkways were mainly fisher-folk and they wore mixed Asian and Western attire. Only one of them, a young man on a pedi-cab greeted them: "Mornin', Skipper, mornin', Tombstone."

Kavanaugh ignored him. Like every other would-be entrepreneur on Little Tamtung, Chou Lai blamed Kavanaugh for the failure of his business—in his case, Cryptozoica Pedi-Cabs and Sightseeing.

The freighter, *Mindanao's Folly*, was gone from the harbor, so either Dai Chinnah's body had been recovered or Captain Hellstrom decided he wasn't worth the effort of looking for and weighed anchor at dawn.

Humidity hung over the waterfront like a shroud, insufferably oppressive. Although the Tamtung islands resembled a pair of mythical Bali Hai paradises from afar, close up they stunk of dead fish, mud and the eternal heat of the tropics. The jungled bulk of Cryptozoica rising from the sea looked beautiful, too, but things with fangs and talons and appetites for blood crept among the colorful flowers.

The building that formerly housed the headquarters of Cryptozoica Enterprises and Horizons Unlimited Tours had been designed to perform double-duty as a four-star hotel, the entrance of which faced the sea. Augustus Crowe and Jack Kavanaugh entered through the office annex.

All of the furniture had long ago been removed from the big reception area, but glossy framed posters emblazoned with the bright yellow Cryptozoica logo still hung on the walls, each one displaying a different scenario and habitat of the proposed spa and clinic. The Jacuzzi, pool and steam baths were at the rear of the building.

They heard the murmur of voices from a corner office and they followed the sounds down a short hallway. Howard Flitcroft glanced up from a desk stacked high with papers, from release forms to brochures. Although the window was propped open and a ceiling fan spun, the air smelled musty and old. Flitcroft made an exaggerated show of consulting his platnium Rolex and arched his eyebrows.

"Right on time," Kavanaugh said blandly. "As usual."

"I was about to commend you on your punctuality," Flitcroft retorted dryly. "And also bring to your attention that you look and smell like a walking dog turd."

Kavanaugh shrugged. "Thanks. I wasn't sure. Good thing you've got personal groomers following you around, right? No telling when a *Forbes* magazine photographer might jump out at in you in a dark boardroom."

Bertram Pendlebury glared at him over a thick sheaf of papers in his arms. "Keep in mind who you're talking to, Jack! You owe him big."

Pendlebury was Flitcroft's right hand man, a position he secured when Flitcroft married Bertram's sister, Merriam. A thin man with short dark hair streaked through with badger stripes of gray, he wore a tropical print shirt three sizes too large for him.

"Suck up when you're ordered to suck, Smithers," Kavanaugh shot back.

Flitcroft snapped, "Enough of that...from everybody."

Both Kavanaugh and Pendlebury fell silent. Flitcroft wasn't a tall man, but he wasn't small either. Husky of build and in his early fifties, Howard Philips Flitcroft looked more like a high school PE teacher from an Iowa town than a millionaire several times over.

His thinning blond hair was blow-dried, sprayed, moussed, swept back and piled high to cover a sizable bald spot on the crown of his head. His blue eyes gleamed brightly with a challenge. He wore a short-sleeved yellow sport shirt, khaki pants and leather sandals. Sewn on the breast pocket of the shirt was Flitcroft's monogram—a blue circle with the overlapping letters of HFP.

"Why are you here, Howie?" Crowe asked.

Flitcroft's eyes narrowed momentarily. Augustus Crowe and Jack Kavanaugh were the only men he permitted to address him as "Howie" and he still didn't care for it.

"I'm straightening up, airing this place out."

"Not that it doesn't need it," said Kavanaugh, "but why?"

"I own this place, remember?"

"And you owned it two years ago when you flew out of here, claiming you'd never be back," replied Crowe. "What's changed?"

"What's changed is that I have a paying job for you, for both of you."

He stared at the two men expectantly. In unison, Crowe and Kavanaugh folded their arms over their chests. Their faces, still masked by sunglasses, remained impassive.

"Aren't you going to ask me about the job?" Flitcroft demanded impatiently.

"I have a boat," said Crowe.

"And I have a chopper," Kavanaugh stated. "If the job doesn't involve hiring us to sail or fly, there's no reason why we would be interested enough to ask you about it."

Flitcroft shook his head. "You guys are still so quick to cop the 'tudes."

"That's because we've done business with you before," said Kavanaugh. "Howie."

"It couldn't have been all that terrible…you're still here."

Kavanaugh uttered a scoffing laugh. "It's not like I had much choice, not with all the process servers out there looking for me."

"Have I charged either one of you a dime of rent in two years?"

"You haven't *collected* a dime," Crowe reminded him. "That's different from charging us. I always figured you'd get around to billing us one day."

"Charge, collect, whatever…if you two go back to work for me, we'll wipe the debit column clean and start all over."

"You still haven't said what the work is about," said Kavanaugh coldly.

Flitcroft smiled for the first time, showing his capped, bleached teeth. "By coincidence, the work is about you flying and sailing a film crew around."

"A film crew?" echoed Crowe.

Flitcroft's smile widened and he clapped his hands together. "Boys, I'm going into the reality TV business."

Behind the dark lenses of his glasses, Kavanaugh's eyes slitted suspiciously. "What kind of reality?"

"Real people, real things and real places." His smile widening into a grin, Flitcroft gestured expansively with both arms "A TV series about Cryptozoica."

Chapter Seven

"Whose stupid, suicidal idea was that?" Crowe demanded skeptically. "Not even the most desperate insurance company in Hollywood would issue a policy to cover a project that goddamn risky."

"*I'm* financing it," Flitcroft answered, tapping his chest. "I've got my own insurance company, remember? I'll cover the cost of everything."

Kavanaugh slowly took off his sunglasses, started to speak, then shook his head wearily.

"What?" Flitcroft stared at him. "Go ahead."

"I thought the whole strategy was to bury that fucking place and hope the world and most of the courts forgot about it."

"That was the strategy," Flitcroft agreed. "But I didn't get to where I am today by closing my mind to new opportunities."

"Such as?" asked Crowe.

"After I dissolved the Cryptozoica corporations, my attorneys settled the wrongful death suits and managed to get all but one of the negligent homicide charges dismissed."

"Which one?" Kavanaugh inquired, even though he knew the answer.

"The one the Jessup estate filed against you." Flitcroft lifted his hands palm upward in an attitude of helpless resignation. "Sorry, Jack. You knew I had to give them somebody and you *did* fly Cranston, Jessup and Shah Nikwan in-country, against the company rules."

A flush of shame and anger warmed the back of Kavanaugh's neck and unconsciously his body tensed, his fists clenching.

In a voice pitched low to disguise the tremor of building rage, he said, "I flew them there because they were my employers and they told me they'd fire me, Mouzi, and Augustus if I didn't do it."

"They wanted to shoot the animals," Pendlebury interjected shrilly. "The product!"

Kavanaugh didn't glance in his direction. He kept his eyes trained on Flitcroft's face. "They told me they were going to shoot the animals with cameras. It wasn't until they unloaded the chopper that I saw the rifles. I tried to talk them out of it, I told them we were in a restricted habitat. But no—it all boiled down to the fact that three of Cryptozoica's five main investors wanted their own private safari so they could bag some Hadrosaurs and mount their heads over the mantle, to have trophies no other sportsman in the world could ever have.

"You knew damn well that's what they had in mind all along—that's why you conveniently waited to attend to pressing business in Java on that very day…Howie."

Spots of red inflamed Flitcroft's cheeks. "Even if I did know what they had planned, you knew the security protocols. You and Gus drafted them, with the input of that homegrown Dragon Lady of yours. Yeah, okay, Jack—maybe I had an idea what those three spoiled assholes intended and maybe that's why I made myself scarce, so I wouldn't have to take responsibility for telling them no. But you accepted their money to fly them there…I found the thirty grand in the chopper, that's ten thousand apiece, right?"

Kavanaugh didn't respond, but his jaw muscles bunched into tight knots.

"So, the end result of you taking a bribe is that two weeks before the Cryptozoica Island Spa officially opens for business, the main money-men are slaughtered, you're gutted like a fish and the goddamn Ghost Shadow triad starts demanding its money back. Then it gets out that I'm doing business with the fucking Asian mafia and the SEC gets suspicious of me, and they drop a dime to the Financial Action Task Force. At about the same time I fly in a surgeon to sew up your intestines, the people we enticed to move here, put up the storefronts and open businesses see Cryptozoica Enterprises go belly-up before they make a single sale to a single tourist."

Flitcroft paused long enough to take a breath before he plunged on: "Oh, but wait—there's more. The families of the three chewed-up dinosaur hunters file wrongful death lawsuits and enough civil charges to keep me in international court twenty-four seven for the next ten years. But let's get back to you, Jack, because it's all about you and *your* suffering, right?

"You're responsible for raising tombstones over three men and a seven hundred-million dollar business deal, but you have your all medical bills paid and you get to hide out here, away from the reporters, the goddamn triads, the lawyers and the FATF. You got to keep the thirty grand in untaxable cash, a million buck helicopter and you live rent-free on a South Sea island and hang out at a whorehouse, drowning your sorrows in booze and hookers. Boo-hoo, Jack. You really got screwed with the shit-end of the stick, didn't you? Boo-hoo."

As Flitcroft spoke, Kavanaugh's expression first went remote, as if he weren't listening, then his face twisted into something dark and ugly. Tendons and veins swelled on his neck. He took a step toward Flitcroft's desk.

Alarmed, Pendlebury held out a restraining hand. "Jack, let's not do anything foolish! You're already skating on such thin ice—"

Kavanaugh's blow landed like a steam-driven piston. Mewling, Pendlebury folded over, clutching at his stomach. Sheets of paper fluttered to the floor. He stumbled, knees sagging and he would have fallen if Crowe hadn't caught him and eased him into a chair.

Quietly, he said, "Kicking the asses of Bertram and Howie won't do you any good, Jack."

Between clenched teeth, Kavanaugh said, "It's not supposed to do me any good. It's supposed to help them, and that's why I'm so tempted."

By degrees the furious glint in his eyes faded and he unknotted his fists, flexing his fingers. "Howie, if you're financing a TV show, then you must have a reason to believe that you'll triple your investment. You still go by the triple the minimum profit rule, right?"

Flitcroft nodded, relief that Kavanaugh wouldn't surrender to temptation evident in his face. "You're absolutely right. But I still need you guys."

"To act as your transportation department?" inquired Crowe, straightening up from the gasping Pendlebury.

"Yeah, but also to keep any triad goons off my neck long enough for me to get everything done."

"What's *everything* entail?" Kavanaugh asked.

Flitcroft's eyes glittered with sudden enthusiasm instead of anger or apprehension. "The film project—a TV miniseries in the US and the UK, and syndicated in the rest of the world. It's going to bring out the whole truth about Cryptozoica, but from a scientific, *National Geographic* kind of approach. I should've gone that way from the start, instead of going in the direction of a private resort so the rich could exploit the place."

Crowe rolled his eyes ceilingward. "Give us a break. Cryptozoica all of a sudden has a new profit smell and you're seeing a way to recoup your losses."

"Even if that's the case," Flitcroft countered, "so the hell *what?*"

"So," said Kavanaugh, "neither you n or Cryptozoica has any credibility. It's on your permanent record now and I don't think it can ever be scratched off. You promoted the place as being a retreat where the secrets of life extension used by the Bible boys could be found. Your price tag was so high that only the elite of the world could afford the treatments, but still the story got out to the general public. Then you pulled it back, claiming it was all a practical joke, a harmless hoax.

"The sad fact is, you're known as Howard Flitflake, a millionaire eccentric, a certified nut-job or just an ordinary scam artist. Take your pick, but whichever label you choose won't make any difference once the press gets hold of this story. They're not going to allow a do-over."

Flitcroft's lips tightened. "I'm going to keep a very low profile during the actual production. I'll be at the bottom of five levels of intermediaries."

"Whose profile will get the publicity?" Crowe asked. "Who'd you find who's gullible enough to let themselves be ridiculed on a global scale?"

Flitcroft's lips relaxed, curving into a smug smile. "None other than Honoré Roxton."

"Who?" demanded Crowe and Kavanaugh more or less simultaneously.

Still bent over in the chair, clutching at his middle, Pendlebury said haughtily, "Dr. Roxton is one of the world's foremost paleontologists and experts on dinosaur behavior. She's authored four books on the subject and she lectures all over the world. She's on the Discovery and the Science Channels a lot."

"Our TV reception is kind of hit or miss out here," Crowe said dryly.

"Take my word for it," Flitcroft said. "Honoré Roxton is extremely well-known and well-respected in scientific circles the world over. She's even been allowed to oversee digs in the heart of Muslim countries."

Kavanaugh smiled bleakly. "Which makes me wonder why she wants to get hooked up with you."

Defensively, Flitcroft retorted, "Over the last eight months, I've been corresponding with an English zoologist, a curator of the National History museum in London, no less. He persuaded me that Cryptozoica was far too important a scientific discovery to be relegated to the pages of tabloid newspapers or Internet legend."

Flitcroft spoke so precisely, both Crowe and Kavanaugh knew he was repeating by rote something he had heard numerous times.

"Does this Roxton woman know she's going to be your

shill?" Kavanaugh asked.

Pendlebury levered himself out of the chair and glared at Kavanaugh. "She won't be a shill. This is a sincere scientific endeavor that needs to be shared with the world."

Both Kavanaugh and Crowe laughed.

Flitcroft did not seem to be offended. "I've learned a lot in the last two years. One of the things is that you weren't the first white man to set foot on Cryptozoica, Jack."

"I don't recall claiming that I was. I knew the Tamtungs were on the old eighteenth century-charts, but like the Perhentians, they weren't explored until the twentieth century. Somebody had noticed the Tamtungs and taken notes."

Pendlebury drew himself up, massaging his midriff. "One of those somebodys was no less a personage than Charles Darwin. The *Beagle* made a stopover here in 1836."

Crowe favored the smaller man with a scowl. "Bullshit. There's no record of Darwin visiting the Tamtungs in any of the volumes or editions of *Voyage of The Beagle* or *The Origin of Species.*"

The three men glanced at him in silent surprise.

"I've read a few books, okay?" Crowe said self-consciously. "I studied to be a marine biologist after I got out of the Navy."

Flitcroft chuckled. "Well, Gus, you're right…there's no record of Darwin's visit here because he was persuaded not to publish his account."

"If he didn't write about it," demanded Kavanaugh, "how do you know he was here?"

"I didn't say Darwin didn't write about it, only that he didn't publish his account. According to what I was told, he made extensive notes of his explorations on Cryptozoica, complete with drawings by the *Beagle's* draftsman, Conrad Martens."

"Drawings of what?" Crowe asked.

"Of the flora and fauna," answered Pendlebury. "And that's one reason a small group of naturalists have kept Darwin's secret ever since."

"Kept it a secret *why?*" Crowe arched his eyebrows. "Because an island populated with survivors from the Cretaceous doesn't fit with Darwinian evolutionary theory?"

"Darwin and his colleagues were more afraid that the island would be exploited for material gain and not studied so as to advance the science of zoology and paleontology." Flitcroft again sounded as if he were reciting from memory.

"Oh." Kavanaugh nodded sagely. "That's so *completely* different from your own plans."

Flitcroft blew out a sigh. "I forgot how badly you get on my nerves, Jack. I was even feeling a little bit sorry for you. The historical truth behind Cryptozoica is a lot more complicated that you know. This is going to be a painstaking project to bring it forward.

"You can be a part of it and at the end of it go back to the States without being arrested...or you can just go on sitting on your ass here, getting drunk, pitying yourself and smelling bad."

"Nobody is going to believe your story," Kavanaugh said.

"You've got a story of your own about Cryptozoica that needs to be told," Flitcroft replied in a gentler tone. "Could be it's finally time to tell it."

Unconsciously, Kavanaugh's hand went to his face and traced the line of scar tissue curving away from the corner of his eye.

"Yeah," he said softly. "Could be."

Chapter Eight

May 11th

The C-21 Learjet knifed through the sky, following the corridor designated for commercial aircraft over the South China Sea. Looking out the window at the limitless expanse of the blue Pacific far below, Honoré Roxton reflected that only a few years ago the ocean would have been filled with rescue and relief craft, steaming toward tsunami devastated coastlines.

Now she saw only scraps of clouds and white-capped waves. A sense of the enormity of the world filled her, yet she still felt disoriented by the speed with which the far corners of the planet could be reached. Less than twelve hours before she had been washing Patagonian dust from her hair in a Buenos Aires hotel room.

The roomy cabin of the jet was decorated in beige trimmed with black. The front panel of the wet bar was engraved with the monogram of Howard Philips Flitcroft. Aubrey Belleau sat on one of the four stools, carefully mixing a Singapore Sling from the ridiculously well-stocked liquor cabinet.

"Are you sure I can't tempt you, Honoré?" he asked, pouring a dash of Benedictine into the glass. "You're supposed to keep hydrated on these long transcontinental flights, you know."

"Alcohol actually dehydrates," Honoré drawled. "You'll be far thirstier after you imbibe that poison."

"Really?" Belleau flashed her an impish smile. "Chemistry isn't my field, you know."

Honoré gestured to the rear of the cabin. "Perhaps your chauffeur will join you."

Oakshott, impassive in his grey uniform, sat strapped into a very wide upholstered chair, hands resting upon his knees. His great bulk made it seem like a child's booster seat at a barber shop.

"Oakshott is a teetotaler," replied Belleau, mixing in a teaspoon of grenadine. "Aren't you, old darlin'?"

Oakshott did not reply.

"I'm sure Howard Flitcroft was happy to give you the loan of his jet," Honoré said, "but do you think he'll appreciate you draining his liquor cabinet? Or will that lighten the load?"

"The load?"

"I noticed at the airport that the cargo hold is filled to bursting…mainly with camera equipment."

Belleau sipped at the drink and smacked his lips appreciatively. "It could use a thimbleful more pineapple juice."

"You're tart enough, Aubrey."

Belleau angled his eyebrows in an exaggerated leer. "Look who's talking."

Honoré sat up straighter in her seat. "What is that supposed to mean?"

Belleau laughed self-consciously and climbed down from the stool, ice tinkling in the fluted glass. "No need to go all stiff and proper on me. We have both been through the broken marriage mill, so we should commiserate. We're both professionals, colleagues and adults, are we not?"

"That last part remains to be seen," Honoré countered, her voice cold but her cheeks flushed with anger and humiliation.

Belleau tipped the glass toward her in sardonic salute. "Adult colleagues can engage in adult pursuits, can they not? Why can't you join me in a drink?"

Honoré refused to acknowledge the inquiry, suspecting that Belleau already knew the answer and enjoyed baiting her. She had first met the little man nearly seven years ago at a faculty party, shortly after separating from her husband Lucien.

He had first complimented her on her doctoral thesis, then on the plunging neckline of her dress. Although she found his intellect intriguing, Belleau's presence always made her distinctly uncomfortable. His high, refined forehead was that of the aesthete, the philosopher, but his eyes and the set of his jaw bespoke a ruthless nature. That, combined with his short stature, always reminded her of the so-called Napoleon complex.

As the man settled into the seat opposite her, Honoré said, "I agreed to all of this, leaving my dig and meeting you in Buenos Aires to fly to the Tamtungs, because your story interested me."

"Not to mention the inducement of five thousand pounds," Belleau retorted silkily. "Let's not forget that."

"The money made the proposition a little more attractive," she admitted, "but it wasn't the primary lure."

"Of course not. You and I are of a kind, Honoré, even if you are loath to recognize it. We're hands-on scientists, not academics. We respond best to the scent of a mystery, to the bugle call of adventure—"

"—Speak for yourself," Honoré broke in impatiently. "I want to know what I'm getting into *before* I get into it."

Belleau nodded. "Rightly so." He raised his voice. "Oakshott, be a good fellow and fetch my valise."

Unbuckling his seat belt, the big man stood up and opened the overhead luggage compartment. From it he pulled an old-fashioned black satchel and carried it down the aisle. Honoré winced at the deck vibrations caused by Oakshott's heavy footfalls. She fancied the entire jet quivered with each of the giant's steps.

Belleau took the satchel and rested it on his lap. "Thank you, old fellow. As you were."

As Oakshott returned to his seat, Belleau opened the case and removed a leatherbound book that at first glance reminded her of a standard volume of the *Encyclopedia Brittanica*. He passed it over to Honoré saying, "Take a look. I've arranged the contents in more or less chronological order."

Frowning, Honoré opened the book. Her frown deepened when she saw a sheet of ragged-edged paper, darkly yellowed with age and covered with copperplate, or English round hand, cursive handwriting. Thumbing through the sheaves, she saw ten sheets were sandwiched between sealed plastic sleeves. From a pocket of her blouse she took out a pair of square-rimmed eyeglasses and slipped them on.

The words, written in very faded ink, acquired a new clarity. *HMS Beagle, Personal Log, C.R. Darwin, 5ᵗʰᵉ May, 1836.*

Honoré's heartbeat sped up and an electric thrill streaked along her spine, but still her mind filled with a surge of suspicion.

Lifting her gaze, she stared challengingly at Belleau. "What is this supposed to be?"

Belleau sipped casually at his Singapore Sling. "Exactly what it looks like. As you know, Charles Darwin kept two journals, his public 'A' and his secret 'B'. You might consider this to be an excerpt from the 'B' or perhaps even his double-secret 'C' log."

Glancing at the page again, Honoré asked skeptically, "You've authenticated it?"

"Of course. I know its provenance. It was given to my great-great-grandfather for safekeeping by Darwin himself. Keep in mind this is a copy. I'll show you the full, untruncated version after you've had a chance to think all of this over."

Squinting, Honoré read the first few lines: *We are now in sight of the Tamtungs. The two islands are thickly forested with tropical jungle, but the larger also exhibits a more mountainous terrain, due no doubt to the extinct volcanic peak.*

Captain Fitzroy has never visited them and indeed claims that only Malay sailors have ever set foot upon them. They bestowed that name upon the islands because it means soiled or unclean. The Tamtungs are reputed to be the most inhospitable of environments.

However, from a distance, they appear far more inviting than the rugged, lizard-infested shores of the Galapagos. The vegetation is of the type usual to tropical isles. There is noni enata, ironwood, candlenut trees, hibiscus and pandanus. Dr. Belleau is most anxious to go ashore and collect botanical specimens.

Honoré looked up again, marking her place with a finger.

"*Doctor* Belleau?"

"Dr. Jacque Belleau," the little man replied. "My great-great-grandfather."

"I don't associate his name with the *Voyage of the Beagle*."

"There's no reason why you should. Like myself, great-great-grandpa was quite the accomplished arranger. He arranged to keep himself out of the history books."

"Unlike his more flamboyant descendant," Honoré observed dryly. "So he had sufficient influence to delete his presence from the journals and logs of the *Beagle*?"

Belleau nodded, smiling crookedly. "You may read on if you like, but the ink has completely faded away on some of the pages. I can fill in the blanks, if you prefer."

"I do."

Matter-of-factly, Belleau stated, "Charles Darwin, in the company of the ship's draftsman Conrad Martens, Bosun Samuel Hoxie, Jacque Belleau and two sailors made landfall upon the island of Big Tamtung on the afternoon of May 6th, 1836.

"Within hours, the party realized that the island might be the most extraordinary place on Earth, harboring as it did dinosaurian survivors from the late Cretaceous period."

Honoré rolled her eyes. "Oh, please."

"Please what?" Belleau asked, face expressing complete innocence.

"I told you before...the entire concept is ridiculous. Tales of such an island would have circulated for centuries, become part of folklore."

"Who is to say they didn't? Have you ever heard of the Isle of Demons?"

"No."

"Check it out on the Internet. The Isle of Demons is a legendary land that began appearing on maps in the beginning of the 1500s, and then disappeared in the mid-1700s. It was generally shown as two islands. It was believed that the islands were populated by demons and wild beasts. They would torment and attack anyone who was foolish enough to wander on to the island."

Honoré angled an eyebrow. "And the demons were dinosaurs?"

"Look in the back. The volume comes complete with illustrations."

Eyebrow still angled, Honoré did as he instructed, flipping the pages aside until she reached a black and white rendering of a bipedal, erect-standing dinosaur, with a large cruelly-hooked talon on its second toe. "A Deinonychus. Judging by the length of the neck, of the dromaeosaurid subgroup."

"Colloquially known as a velociraptor," commented Belleau. "If you look at the bottom right hand corner of the paper, you'll find the signature of Conrad Martens and the date, May 1836. Obviously, he sketched it from life since at that time no fossils of the Deinonychus had yet been discovered. For that matter, Richard Owen had yet to coin the term 'dinosaur'."

Honoré stared at the drawing numbly. She was barely aware of murmuring, "The Deinonychus wasn't discovered until 1964, in Montana."

Belleau took another sip of his drink. "Precisely. So the only explanation for Martens's accurate rendering in 1836 is that he actually saw a living, breathing specimen. In fact, it attacked and nearly killed Samuel Hoxie. Jacque Belleau was instrumental in saving his life."

Mesmerized, Honoré turned to the next picture, a profile view of the Deinonychus, with even the pattern of scales that coated the snout sharply detailed. A crest of feathers slanted back from the top of the skull. She studied it, turning the book this way and that. Softly, she said, "The cranial configuration is slightly different than the fossils that have been discovered. The occipital casing seems a bit larger. And are those feathers?"

"It's been sixty-five million years since they last roamed," Belleau remarked. "Naturally, there have been a few adaptive changes. Apparently, Ostrum's work on the Deinonychus and his theory that the smaller theropods developed feathers as insulation has been validated."

Honoré found herself starting to agree, then, as if a cold

bucket of water had been dashed into her face, she straightened up in her chair, glaring angrily at Belleau. "This is insane on so many levels, I don't know where to begin!"

Belleau swirled his drink, ice-cubes clinking. "Should we begin with Charles Darwin and why he kept the *Beagle's* visit to the Tamtungs secret?"

"Actually, we should start with why anybody would believe this rubbish."

Mildly, Belleau said, "I believe it. I have no reason not to. Many other people believe it too."

"Name two," Honoré shot back.

"I could name far more than that, but a head count of believers isn't relevant at this juncture. Are you familiar with *The Lost World*? The novel by Sir Arthur Conan Doyle?"

Despite herself, Honoré couldn't help but smile. "Of course. That book was probably the seminal influence on generations of children who became paleontologists."

"Would it surprise you to learn that Sir Arthur based the novel's Maple White Land, his 'lost world,' on scraps of information that came his way about Big Tamtung?"

"It would indeed surprise me," Honoré conceded. "I don't know if I'd accept it as truth."

"You might recall that Sir Arthur explained the survival of the prehistoric creatures and conservation of the flora due to the extreme isolation of the Amazonian plateau."

"It sounded semi-reasonable for a book written in 1910, but it's utterly unbelievable by the scientific standards of the 21st century."

"Not when judged by quantum evolutionary theory. Are you familiar with it?"

Honoré nodded uncertainly. "Somewhat. According to the foundation of the theory, some lineages in the fossil record evolved with extraordinary slowness, others more rapidly. Most phyletic lines of evolution occurred in a moderate and steady manner, while others showed fluctuating patterns of evolutionary descent."

"Just so. The most rapid of those patterns was dubbed 'quantum evolution.' Proponents believe that major evolutionary transitions arise when small populations—isolated and limited from normal genetic flow—would fixate upon unusual gene combinations. The unadaptive phase would then, by natural selection, drive a population from one stable adaptive peak to another and to a final stage."

"And you say that's what happened on Big Tamtung?"

"Partly." Belleau shrugged. "I realize this all seems a bit much to absorb in one sitting, but it's the truth. On Big Tamtung, the past has not stopped breathing. The evidence is there, darlin'."

Scowling, Honoré slapped the open book in her lap. "This is by no means evidence. At best, it's a fanciful footnote to actual history. At worst, it's a Cardiff Giant type hoax that never got off the ground."

Belleau shook his head. "Skepticism is a trait to be encouraged, but what you're exhibiting is closer to denial. You haven't looked at the entire photographic record."

Swiftly, angrily, Honoré flipped page after page, reviewing the photographs within the transparent sleeves. They progressed from blurry black-and-white plates of smudges that might have been animals or even shrubs, to color shots of distant quadrupedal and bipedal shapes.

Only one photo depicted a creature with any degree of clarity. A dark green mass with outspread feathery wings filled the frame. She prepared to dismiss it as an out-of-focus shot of a tropical bird, until she identified the three highly developed, claw-tipped fingers at the top wing-joint.

The word *archaeopteryx* jumped to the forefront of her mind, but she refused to utter it. Instead she asked, "When and how were these pictures taken?"

"A concealed duck blind was constructed in the 1840s and maintained until about thirty-five years ago," Belleau answered.

"Maintained by whom?" she demanded.

"All in good time, darlin'. All in good time."

Honoré thumbed through several other photographs, but they depicted human beings. She gazed at a candid shot of a tall, lean man wearing the dark blue dress uniform of the United States Air Force. Sunglasses masked his eyes and Captain's bars glinted on his collar.

"Who is this?" she asked.

Belleau craned his neck and snorted derisively. "A nobody. His name is Kavanaugh, a former officer in the US Air Force. As I understand it, he's known as Tombstone Jack."

The man's face was not conventionally handsome. In fact, it had a craggy, rawboned, American Indian stolidity, but she found something strangely appealing in it.

"He left the military and opened a rather disreputable travel agency in partnership with another nobody," Belleau continued contemptuously. "He's more or less responsible for the entire Cryptozoica debacle. I'll tell you about that later."

"Why not now?"

"Does he interest you for some reason?"

Honoré detected a hint of jealously underscoring Belleau's voice. Rather than respond to it, she turned the page to another photograph. Three men stood outside of a white-walled building in bright sunlight, all of them with cigars jutting at jaunty angles from grinning mouths. The blond man in the center had his arms draped around the shoulders of Kavanaugh and a big black man. The building in the background bore a sign reading Cryptozoica Enterprises & Horizons Unlimited.

"Who is this?" Honoré asked, turning the book toward Belleau.

"The man in the middle is Howard Philips Flitcroft himself…the other is Kavanaugh and his partner, Augustus Crowe. The other nobody I mentioned." He paused and added sourly, "All Yanks, of course."

Honoré smiled. "Of course. So am I to understand that these are the principals in the Cryptozoica affair?"

Belleau shifted uncomfortably in his seat. "Not quite all

of them. Frankly, I'm reluctant to share everything about the Tamtungs and Cryptozoica with you."

Honoré slitted her eyes. "Then I shall be equally reluctant to give you my full cooperation."

Belleau leaned forward, placing a hand lightly on her right knee, gazing earnestly into her face. "Honoré, I will be breaking an oath sworn to a brotherhood that male members of my family have been part of for nearly two hundred years."

Honoré crossed her legs, dislodging the man's hand. "The Freemasons?"

Belleau bared his teeth in a ferocious scowl, then it turned into a rueful grin. "My darlin' Dr. Roxton. You need to be indoctrinated so you can grasp the entire convoluted context."

Lifting the glass to his lips, Aubrey Belleau drained the last of the Singapore Sling, took a deep breath and stated, "We shall begin your indoctrination with a lesson in hidden history. What do you know of the School of Night?"

"Nothing."

Belleau's grin widened and he reached into the valise. "Tell me, Honoré…in your studies did you ever come across references to Prima Materia?"

Chapter Nine

The morning sky was as blue as a dream of summer, full of wispy white clouds and lazy shadows. Mouzi thought about all of her unfulfilled summer dreams and blinked back the stinging tears of self-pity.

Then the greasy socket wrench slipped on the nut and she skinned a knuckle against a flange of the bilge pump. Turning her face toward the sky, she shouted loudly and earnestly, "Fuck this!"

Crowe poked his head up through the hatchway and asked mildly, "Does that help or do you need another set of wrenches?"

Massaging her throbbing right hand, Mouzi said sullenly, "Another set of knuckles, more like."

Crowe heaved himself up onto the vaka, the main deck of the *Krakatoa*. His pants legs were wet from the cuff to the knee with foul-smelling bilge water. The noonday sun blazed down with a heat only a few degrees shy of merciless. The strip of cloth tied around his forehead was soaked through with sweat. Perspiration trickled down his face and clung to the ends of his mustache like tiny glass beads.

Mouzi wore a one-piece black thong leotard. It barely contained one sixty-fourth of her caramel-colored body.

She shifted position, allowing Crowe an unrestricted view of the bulldog's face snarling from her right buttock.

The small tattoo of the dog wearing a German coal-scuttle helmet symbolized her membership in the Mongrel Mob, the

Maori street-gang she had joined while running wild in New Zealand's Rotorura district.

The *Krakatoa* rocked slightly on the swells. The day had dawned mild, the seas fairly calm, the sun strong and so Crowe decided it was as good a time as any to work on the trimaran's bilge pump. If nothing else, it kept him and Mouzi from being drafted into house-painting detail by Flitcroft.

Shading her eyes with her hands, Mouzi gazed in the direction of the canal cutting past the Huang Luan. Seagulls swooped and dove at a dark shape bobbing on the water, trapped between a piling and the canal wall. She turned away disinterestedly, looking toward the hotel.

Several men hosed down the façade and sloshed soapy water over the windows. Old Tinh Bien, the island's self-proclaimed calligrapher, stood on a ladder and meticulously repainted the words Cryptozoica Enterprises & Horizons Unlimited over the door. She commented blandly, "Sprucin' up still."

Crowe grunted. "Howie wants everything spit on and polished up before the big-wigs get here."

"When's that supposed to be again?"

Crowe reached for the bilge pump housing. "Any minute now. He sent his own jet for 'em."

Mouzi smiled sourly. "In that case, maybe somebody should do something about the dead body over there."

Crowe straightened up, squinting in the direction of her waving hand. "Over where?"

"There...see them gulls?"

"How do you know it's a body?"

Mouzi shrugged and picked up the socket wrench. "You know how intuitive we South Sea islanders are."

Crowe blew out a disgusted sigh. "Don't I just."

Mouzi affected not to notice when Crowe strode across the deck and jumped onto the pier. He shouted toward Chou Lai who straddled his pedicab at the intersection of four footpaths. The two men exchanged words in what she took to be some form of pidgin Cantonese. Reluctantly, Chou Lai pedaled his vehicle toward the hotel.

Mouzi watched as Chou Lai yelled to the workmen. After a minute, three of them put down their hoses and brushes and trudged toward the canal. Crowe came back aboard and as he stalked past her, he growled, "Conscience of a shark."

Mouzi hawked up from deep in her throat and spit over the side. Crowe ignored her expectoration and Mouzi ignored him as he went into the wheelhouse. She knew the big man well enough to pick up on his anger. As a former lieutenant in the United States Navy SEALS, Crowe was no stranger to violence or death, but he preferred not to associate with either if other options were available.

Mouzi was steeped in the warrior tradition of her people and although she wasn't of pure Maori blood, she was most definitely proud of what did flow through her veins. Born in a sulphate-scented village on the banks of Lake Ngapouri, she had answered an ad for a tsunami relief service and through it eventually met Augustus Crowe and Jack Kavanaugh.

Within a month of the meeting, she found herself promoted to the position of chief grease-monkey for Horizons Unlimited. Even after Cryptozoica Enterprises had fallen apart, she stayed on Little Tamtung. She had no immediate family anywhere in the world and the island was as good a place to call home as any, certainly better than the ghettos of Rotorua's Fenton Street.

Besides, Kavanaugh needed looking after and Crowe needed a mechanic, even though she hadn't drawn a paycheck in nearly two years. But the men treated her respectfully most of the time and provided her with a house of her own and enough food to eat, so she didn't want for much. She and Crowe enjoyed a friends-with-benefits relationship and despite the difference in their ages, she supposed she loved the big man and didn't care to leave him. Besides, as a bail-jumper and fugitive, she had no great desire to rejoin what passed for civilized society in New Zealand.

After being arrested for strong-arm robbery in Wellington, Mouzi hid herself in the backwaters of the Third World. She made the acquaintance of twenty-first century pirates who were always on the prowl for the angle and the profit. Claiming to be representatives of tsunami relief organizations provided a good cover for the scavengers.

Mouzi fell for one of them, a dashing Russian who made a great lover but a terrifying enemy. Nikolai would lend her his last dime one night and then break her nose the next because she hadn't moved fast enough to fetch him a fresh bottle of vodka.

But from Nikolai and his *Mafiya* confederates, Mouzi learned how to be a shark swimming in those turbid waters—to bite fast and ruthlessly when the occasion called for it.

Cutting the throat of Dai Chinnah had not disturbed her emotional equilibrium overmuch. The Papuan seaman reminded her of the man who raped her shortly before her fourteenth birthday. Mouzi had cut his throat too, some weeks later when she came across him drunk and belligerent outside of a bar.

She had stabbed two of his friends in the same melee' but she never knew if she had killed them—nor did she give much of a damn.

"Looks like they found somebody," Crowe intoned. "Surprise, surprise."

Mouzi squinted across the harborside. The workmen hauled up a limp human shape from the canal water by a length of rope. She said quietly, "Poor bastard must've had an accident."

"That's what I figured," Crowe drawled. "He tripped and fell neck-first onto your knives."

Mouzi directed a glare at him. "I told you what happened."

"So you did."

"So why do you care?" she demanded angrily. "He was a rapist, a woman-beater—"

"—I don't give a shit about him," Crowe broke in. "But I care about police showing up here with outstanding warrants for Jack."

Mouzi shrugged dismissively. "Howie'll just pay 'em off like before."

Crowe shook his head. "He's got too many other things to throw his money at now."

"Like what?"

Crowe didn't answer. At the far edge of audibility, they heard a faint, droning whine. Tilting her head back, Mouzi saw a tiny speck in the sky, skimming across it like a tadpole through an azure pool. Between one heartbeat and another, the speck resolved itself into the bewinged shape of a jet. Sunlight winked from its white fuselage as it approached at a sharply descending angle.

"Like that, I imagine," Crowe said, taking a rag from his back pocket and wiping his hands.

"The big-wigs?"

"Who else? Want to go take a look at them?"

"Why not?" Mouzi put down her wrench, then rolled off the *Krakatoa*, falling into the water between the main hull and the portside outrigger hull. Her diminutive body barely made a splash.

"What the hell are you doing?" Crowe asked.

"Cooling off first." Mouzi spit a jet of water in his direction. "You mind?"

"Be careful of the sharks…don't be biting on any."

Grinning, the girl snapped her teeth at him. She knew as well as he did that just about every imaginable nasty creature swam in the Indo-Australian oceans, from venomous sea snakes, moray eels, to barracuda. Sharks constituted the least of the threats, but Mouzi had no fear of them. She made her way toward the beach with an inelegant but functional backstroke. There was nothing fancy about her swimming style, but it always got her to where she was going.

Crowe stepped off the boat onto the dock and walked quickly toward the airstrip adjacent to the hotel property. Like the harborside, it had been constructed several years before in anticipation of various holiday package flights.

Flitcroft's C21 Learjet was only one of three winged aircraft that had ever arrived and departed from the runway. The other two planes had belonged to the families of Jessup and Shah Nikan, when they came to retrieve the mangled remains of the financiers. Most of the island's supplies arrived by monthly freighter.

Crowe watched as the pilot of the jet trimmed the flaps and cut the throttle way back, subtly changing the pitch of the engine's rumbling whine. By the time he reached the edge of the tarmac, the jet touched down with a squeal of rubber tires and taxied to a lumbering stop. Heat-waves shimmered from the blacktop. Crowe looked for Kavanaugh but saw no sign of him. He figured the man was sulking someplace, maybe in the Huang Luan, but he was definitely aware of the arrival of the jet.

As Crowe strolled onto the runway, he stepped aside as Chou Lai rang the bell of his pedicab. The young man wheeled it past him, on a direct line with the jet, as anxious for paying customers as everyone else on Little Tamtung. Crowe felt a surge of annoyance when he spied Kavanaugh seated in the passenger box.

The jet rolled to a complete halt and the whine of the engines faded, leaving only humid silence. Crowe stalked up to Kavanaugh as he climbed out of the cab. "What are you doing here?"

"I could ask you the same thing," Kavanaugh countered, running his fingers through his hair, smoothing it down. "I was with Howie...he asked me to come and fetch his experts."

Crowe gave Kavanaugh a swift visual examination. Although his eyes were masked by sunglasses, his face was clean-shaved, his hair trimmed and his breath wasn't redolent of stale whiskey and potted meat. He wore his usual ensemble of tropical print shirt and faded jeans, but they smelled freshly laundered. He appeared to be as sober as a bishop.

Crowe observed dourly. "So you finally figured out how to work the washer and dryer."

Kavanaugh affected not to have heard the inquiry.

"I thought you didn't want any part of this deal," Crowe said.

"I never said that. You were the one who called Howie's idea stupid and suicidal."

"That's because I think it is," Crowe admitted. "But that doesn't mean I don't want to make money from it if there is any to be made."

"Good. Then we're both on the same page."

The portside hatch of the Learjet popped open, pushed up from the inside. Crowe and Kavanaugh moved forward, both men forcing smiles to their faces. Crowe's step faltered and Kavanaugh's smile vanished when a huge brute of man climbed out.

The giant paid the two men no attention at first, busying himself with pulling retractable aluminum steps out from beneath the hatchway, then he turned and regarded Crowe and Kavanaugh with bleak, blank eyes.

He wore a short-sleeved white shirt, khaki pants and sandals, but he looked uncomfortable in the ensemble. Kavanaugh guessed he was accustomed to wearing entirely different kind of clothes. His skin was pallid, as if it had never been exposed to direct sunlight.

Crowe extended his right hand. "Welcome to Little Tamtung. The name's Augustus Crowe. This is Jack Kavanaugh."

The man hesitated an instant before taking his hand, but the contact was more of a furtive palm brush than an actual shake.

The giant repeated the same swift, cursory move with Kavanaugh, but not before he glimpsed a three-character Asian ideogram red-tattooed on the man's thick right forearm. Kavanaugh had seen the symbol before in Okinawa—it denoted a high-ranking professional martial artist, a master of the *Shorin-ryu* style. The man's hand so briefly in his held a hard, leathery ridge of callus running along the edge of the palm.

"Oakshott," the man replied in a surprisingly high voice, touched by a British accent. He sounded like Mike Tyson impersonating an English valet.

Crowe tried hard to repress a smile, but he doubted he succeeded.

Oakshott said, "We are to meet a man named Howard

Philips Flitcroft. Where might he be found?"

Kavanaugh hooked a thumb toward the hotel. "In his office. The mountain will have to come to Mohammed in this instance."

Oakshott's eyes narrowed as if he suspected he were being mocked. "We have quite a bit of luggage and we will need reliable transportation—"

Chou Lai rang the bell on the handlebars of his pedicab.

Oakshott ignored him. "—For my employer and his guest."

"Guest?" repeated a well-modulated female voice. "I thought I played a more important role in this farce than that."

A tall woman wearing a pale green blouse, white jeans and western style boots leaped lithely down from the jet, ignoring the set of steps. A straight, thin-bridged nose with a pair of bright green eyes on either side of it led to a wide mouth touched with the hint of a challenging smile. Heavy red-gold hair tumbled down both sides of her face.

She wiped at her forehead, smiled and quoted, " 'Over the trackless past, somewhere, lie the lost days of our tropic youth'", then she thrust out her right hand toward the two men. Crowe clasped it first, noting the strength of the grip and the roughness of the palm. Turning to Kavanaugh, she pumped his hand formally.

"Honoré Roxton," she said. "I heard you introduce yourselves as Augustus Crowe and Jack Kavanaugh"

"We've heard of you, Dr. Roxton," Kavanaugh said releasing her hand.

"Really?" The woman arched an eyebrow. "Even in this very remote corner of the globe? I'm impressed."

"Don't be," Kavanaugh replied, deadpan. "We first heard about you yesterday when Howie said you were on your way here."

Honoré Roxton laughed and then gestured toward the edge of the field where Mouzi stood, dripping wet, watching with her hands on her hips. "Who might that nearly naked child be?"

"The chamber of commerce," Crowe retorted. "We call her Mouzi."

Kavanaugh beckoned to her with an arm wave. "Come on up and be introduced."

Mouzi didn't move or speak. She stared fixedly at Oakshott. The big man glanced her way, then looked in another direction, pointedly ignoring her. Mouzi heeled around and stalked back toward the waterfront so abruptly that Kavanaugh was a little taken aback. Mouzi had never been one for observing formalities, but she was rarely so outright rude to strangers.

Honoré inquired, "A bit shy, is she?"

"Not really," Crowe said. "Just sort of surly. She's the mechanic of Horizons Unlimited."

"And you are Horizons Unlimited?" The woman gazed at Kavanaugh boldly. He felt suddenly self-conscious, aware she eyed the scar on his face with a clinical interest.

"More or less," Kavanaugh replied.

"Which is it?' Honoré demanded. "Are you more or are you less?"

Crowe pointed to himself, then to Kavanaugh. "I'm more and he's less."

The woman laughed again and Kavanaugh couldn't help but grin. He liked the way Honoré Roxton's smile turned her stern features into something very appealing.

Honoré Roxton started to speak, then she fell silent, staring intently past Crowe and Kavanaugh. They involuntarily glanced over their shoulders at the black and green bulk of Big Tamtung rising from the sea. Masses of mist wreathed the face of the escarpment where it sloped down to meet the jungle. A waterfall glistened like a silver ribbon. The crescent moon of white sand reflected the sunlight so strongly that even at a distance of over three miles it stung the eye.

The woman cupped her hands around her eyes. "So that's the place...Big Tamtung?"

"Yeah," Crowe answered tersely. "That's the place, all right."

"Steamy, isn't it?"

"A lot of the time," agreed Kavanaugh. "Both Big and Little Tamtung are part of the same land mass, most of it submerged.

We think the steam comes out of thermal vent, from an underground shield volcano, maybe."

"That doesn't make it all that remarkable, you know. Islands formed by volcanic activity are not so uncommon in this part of the world. There are still active volcanoes on the Tonga Islands." Honoré sounded as if she were trying to reassure herself of the island's ordinariness. "That mesa or escarpment resembles Ball's Pyramid, off the Australian mainland. It's the remnant of a shield volcano."

When neither man responded, she lowered her hands and said dryly, "That was a conversational lead-in, gentlemen. You were to remark on how extraordinary Big Tamtung truly is. And, Mr. Kavanaugh, I understand you have your own extraordinary tale to tell about the place, is that right?"

Kavanaugh sidestepped the question by asking one of his own. "Aren't you supposed to have someone else with you?"

"She does, indeed," announced the bearded man who appeared in the hatchway. He gazed broodily at Crowe and Kavanaugh, then up at the sky, then at Oakshott. His blue eyes shone like the restless water of the bay. His gaze swept his surroundings, photographing every detail, committing them to memory.

Neither Crowe nor Kavanaugh had expected to see a dwarf climb out of the aircraft, but they kept their expressions neutral as he came down the steps, leaning on a walking stick. Dressed in a white shirt and white ducks with a straw panama hat placed at an angle on his head, he made a memorable impression. With his Van Dyke beard, Kavanaugh was reminded of old photographs he had seen of Buffalo Bill—that is, if Cody had ever worn tropical whites and was the height of a ten year old boy.

His legs were abnormally short. There was something grotesque about his fully developed torso and his diminished lower limbs. He carried a satphone bearing the AceS logo of the Asia Cellular Satellite company in a vinyl holster at his right hip.

The little man grimaced as he kick-stepped in a circle.

Leather sandals shod his tiny feet. "All of those hours in flight… my legs feel atrophied."

"If you go to Big Tamtung," Kavanaugh said flatly, "I can guarantee you a loosening up you won't forget."

The little man swung his head up and around, staring directly into his face. "Who are you again?"

Kavanaugh put out his hand. "Jack Kavanaugh."

"You may call me Dr. Belleau," the bearded man said, making no effort to take his hand. "You may address my guest as Dr. Roxton."

Honoré's shoulders stiffened. "I'll decide how I'll be addressed, Aubrey."

Belleau did not respond. He maintained his unblinking gaze on Kavanaugh. "You *are* employees of Mr. Flitcroft, are you not?"

Kavanaugh tamped down a sudden surge of anger. "Not exactly."

"No? Then exactly what are you? Why *exactly* are you out here? What *exact* purpose do you serve for this undertaking?"

"That has yet to be determined," Kavanaugh said quietly. "When it has been, you'll be one of the first to know…Aubrey."

Belleau continued to stare at him. "I shall hold you to that… Tombstone Jack, isn't it?"

"Sometimes." Kavanaugh kept his own gaze fixed on Belleau's eyes.

He realized that the little man possessed a mind like a computer constructed for a single purpose, a cold and analytical brain that sought opportunities first, last and always, whether they were personal or business. That computer had identified and categorized him as a rival, as a threat to the seizing of opportunities.

"Oakshott," Belleau intoned, not taking his eyes from Kavanaugh's face.

The big man stepped up beside him. "Sir?"

"Inform the pilots to disembark. Find some men to unload the plane. I'm sure we shall be here for quite some time."

Chapter Ten

By late afternoon it was too hot to work on the pump out on the deck and so hot Crowe could no longer think straight. Even down in the *Krakatoa's* bilge he sweated so much that it practically added another couple of quarts to the foul-smelling liquid swirling around his feet.

Working alone added to the strain and contributed to the volume of sweat flowing out of him. Mouzi hadn't returned to the boat after stalking away from the airfield and Crowe hadn't been inclined to look for her.

Jack was no help since he accompanied the little Belleau man and the Roxton woman to Flitcroft's office. Rather than stand around the jet and try to make conversation with Oakshott, who did not give the impression of being much of an idle talker, Crowe went back to the trimaran.

He noticed during the afternoon that Chou Lai put his prized *samlaw* to work, hauling boxes of equipment out of the jet's cargo hold and ferrying them over to the office and hotel. The motorized rickshaw with the rackety lawn-mower engine and striped canopy made at least six back-and-forth trips and Crowe wondered if Chou charged a flat fee or by the individual run.

Climbing out onto the deck a few minutes shy of sunset, Crowe sat down beneath the overhang of the cockpit's housing that had a little shade to it. Lifting the lid of a Styrofoam cooler, he found of a bottle of tepid Yinjang beer and twisted off the cap. He took a long swallow and shuddered at the bitter taste.

After a moment of groping behind him on the console, he

found the package of Golden Duck cheroots that had been shipped in from Rangoon the month before. He removed the next-to-last one and put it in the corner of his mouth, but he didn't light it. Looking for matches would require him to stand up, and he just didn't have the strength or the inclination at the moment.

Gazing toward the hotel, he watched Tinh Bien finish the detail work on the Z in Cryptozoica, adding a fancy drop-shadow. All Crowe originally wanted lettered on the building was the name of their travel bureau, Horizons Unlimited, but Jack fancied himself a wordsmith and considered just the two words decidedly unexotic.

After a couple of days of drinking and thinking it over, Jack had presented him with a square of cardboard on which the words Cryptozoica Enterprises were rendered in bright magenta and yellow, the colors exuberantly applied by felt-tipped pens, with stylized green palm trees worked into the block letters.

"What the hell is a Cryptozoica and what's so enterprising about it?" Crowe demanded.

Jack pointed to Big Tamtung then to himself and Crowe, announcing matter-of-factly, "That's Cryptozoica and we're the enterprisers."

"What's it mean?"

"Well, it's kind of a play on a couple of words….the place is cryptic and has cryptozoological animals running around, right? So if you sort of graft it onto Paleozoic and put an 'a' on the end, then you have Cryptozoica."

"It's a made-up word," Crowe said impatiently. "Why not something that nobody has to think about, like Monster Land or Dino Island?"

Jack gave him a pitying, patronizing look. "This isn't a god-damn gator-wrestling tourist trap on the way to Disney World, you know."

"It's not a goddamn tomb tour, either. Cryptozoica, my ass. We need to discuss this and come up with something everybody likes and agrees on."

Jack snatched back his square of cardboard and stomped off. A couple of days later, he saw Tinh Bien adding Cryptozoica Enterprises to the façade of the hotel, and Crowe just let it go.

Shifting position, Crowe watched the six people who had flown in with Flitcroft on his DHC-6 Otter walking down the footpath toward the Phoenix of Beauty, some of them lugging camera and recording equipment. Although his experience with a film production crew was limited, he hadn't been impressed with the men Flitcroft had introduced as the technical staff, particularly after he identified Pendlebury as the director. The concept seemed so ridiculous, neither Crowe nor Kavanaugh knew whether to believe the claim or not.

Still, Crowe reflected that there were more new people on Little Tamtung at the moment than had been in the last year and a half. For the first time, he began seriously considering Flitcroft's television series idea.

The man had never shown much interest in science before, mainly because it didn't pay as well as entertainment. But if anyone could figure out a way to profitably blend the two, it would be Howard Philips Flitcroft.

Crowe knew more than a little about marine biology, but he rarely had the opportunity to come up with ways to make his knowledge pay off, except through fishing excursions. He had studied oceanography at the US Naval Academy with an eye toward making that a career but events and fate pushed him in a different direction.

His Annapolis education had overlaid his Louisiana accent with an unidentifiable regional tone. Like Jack Kavanaugh, he spoke a number of Asian languages, even the Lao and Meo dialects of Thai. Unlike Jack, he envied the simplicity of the people who managed to eke out livings on Little Tamtung either by fishing or farming.

As Crowe took another sip of the Yinjang beer, he saw Mouzi sauntering along the pier toward him. She wore a Horizons Unltd T shirt over her leotard. Lithely, she jumped from the dock onto the portside ama hull.

When she stepped onto the deck of the *Krakatoa,* Crowe said gruffly, "You're fired."

"I quit," Mouzi countered, unperturbed by the man's hostile tone.

"In that case." Crowe took another bottle of beer from the cooler and tossed it in her general direction.

Effortlessly, Mouzi snatched it out of the air and unscrewed the cap. "Thanks."

"You seen Jack?" Crowe asked.

Mouzi took a long swallow of the Yinjang before replying, "Last I saw, he was over in Howie's office with the rest of them pommie bastards."

"Why'd you walk off like that? That was pretty damn rude, even for you."

Mouzi's lips pursed. In a soft, almost hesitant voice she said, "Seen that big-arse bloke before."

Crowe frowned. "Where?"

"In Bangkok, long about five years ago. 'Member me tellin' you about Nikolai?"

"Yeah."

"He used to take me to a private fight club…that Oakshott hoon worked for one of the local triad bosses. He'd get in the ring and kill them poor slopes he was matched up against, just twist their heads off like they was chooks."

Crowe eyed her skeptically. "Are you sure it was him?"

"Ain't like he's easy to mistake for somebody else." Mouzi touched her right forearm. "He had another name then, but I recognized his tat. Him all right."

Crowe tried to think about the implications, despite his heat-fogged mind. He mentally replayed the image of the tattoo. He shrugged. "Lots of people in this part of the world have connections with the triads. And they have tats. You included."

Mouzi's dark eyes flashed with annoyance. "What's a pommie professor doing with a professional killer as a valet? Don't that strike you as a mite unusual?"

Crowe nodded reluctantly. "A mite. But it's not like the unusual is unusual around here. Let's just stay out of his way."

Tilting her head back, Mouzi gulped down the rest of the bottle's contents, then uttered a deep, earnest belch.

"That won't be easy."

"Why won't it be?"

"I heard 'em talkin'…we're gonna have a reception over in the Phoenix tonight, so everybody can get acquainted."

Crowe frowned. "A meet and greet?"

The corners of Mouzi's lips quirked in a grim smile. "Everybody gettin' to know everybody. Won't that be nice? Attendance, as in *mandatory*."

Crowe pointed the neck of his beer bottle in her direction. "That means you, too."

Mouzi shook her head. "You just done fired me."

"Well, I just done unfired you. If I have to go, so do you."

Turning a grunt of exertion into a sigh of ennui, Crowe heaved himself off the deck. Assailed by momentary vertigo, he closed his eyes. When he opened them again, he saw Mouzi staring at him curiously.

"You okay?"

Crowe didn't answer at first. He gazed around the harborfront, appreciating the calm seas but also sensing a storm. The day died slowly, the peach and pink afterglow stretching upward in the soft sky above the island.

"Why wouldn't I be?" he muttered, stepping onto the dock.

The waters of the bay glimmered with the color of burnished aquamarine. He took a quick, almost apprehensive glance over his shoulder at Big Tamtung. The cliff-face was a rich bluish-purple in the fading light, the hue of a bruise. The setting sun looked like a ball of molten wax, burning into his eyes, filling his senses.

The air was still hot and steamy, so there was no reason for Crowe to feel so cold, but he did.

Chapter Eleven

Inside the Phoenix of Beauty, the music pounded at Kavanaugh with an almost painful intensity. The heavy, repetitive bass line made the smoke-laced air shiver. People crowded around the bar and milled about the verandah. The girls who worked and lived in the Phoenix flitted in and out of sight like a flock of birds plumed in tight sheath dresses of red, green and yellow silk.

Kavanaugh mopped sweat from his face. Despite the fall of night, the interior of the club was still sweltering. The air-conditioning had yet to be repaired and the body heat from the crowd in the barroom had built up the temperature to that of a sauna.

He winced as he passed the glowing jukebox. The moaning and high-pitched shrieking that substituted as lyrics in the Cantopop song punched his eardrums. Cranio stood beside the machine, hands on his hips, daring anyone to either complain about the volume or to change the selection.

Acrid cigarette smoke floated in a haze above everyone's heads, burning the eye and abrading the throat. Kavanaugh pushed his way between a man and a woman to the bar and gestured to Jarlai. The Malaysian affected not to notice him, but he quickly began mixing a gin and tonic.

A slender man wearing a flowered print shirt and baggy shorts that accentuated the pipestem thickness of his legs backed into him.

"Excuse me," Kavanaugh said loudly to his ear.

The man twisted his head around to look at him with wide, alcohol bleared eyes. It was Bertram Pendlebury, with his shirt unbuttoned to his navel. A gold medallion gleamed between his pale, flabby pectorals.

"Jack!" Pendlebury cried, slapping him on the shoulder. His breath smelled strongly of kava, licorice-flavored Polynesian liquor. "You crooked sumabitchbastard! Havin' fun?"

"I just got here so it's too soon to tell. How about you?"

Pendlebury's eyes widened, giving him the aspect of an eager frog. He gestured toward the women moving in and out of the crowd. "Why wouldn't I be, with all this dark meat in the deli aisle?"

He whistled sharply, "Hey, mocha-cream! Want to be in my picture?"

Kavanaugh glanced over and saw a mini-skirted Mouzi scowling at Pendlebury. Her full lips pursed as if she intended to spit at the man. Then she moved on.

"High-class pick-up material," Kavanaugh drawled as Jarlai slid the gin and tonic across the bar. "Fortunately for your testicles, she didn't go for it. Where's Howie?"

"You mean Mr. Flitcroft? He's out on the porch. Everyone has been waiting for you."

"Who's everyone?"

Pendlebury stepped unsteadily away from the bar, reaching for a slim Thai girl wearing a tight cheongsam of silver brocade. Grabbing her by the hand, he went into a frantic series of dance steps, his knobby arms and long legs flailing like the limbs of an insect caught in the electrified grille of a bug-zapper.

Kavanaugh sidled through the knot of people and walked through the open French doors to the verandah, avoiding the horde swarming around a buffet table. He couldn't help but smile. Although here and there he saw an unfamiliar face, the crowd was mainly composed of locals, drawn to the club by the siren song of free food and drink.

Tiki torches flamed in sconces on the wooden posts and cast a flickering illumination. On the far end of the verandah, furthermost away from the music and the smoke, he saw Crowe, Belleau, Flitcroft and Honoré Roxton sitting around a large table. The giant figure of Oakshott loomed near the railing, a brown beer bottle barely visible within his massive hand. A half-full martini glass rested on a coaster bearing the Cryptozoica logo near Belleau's elbow.

The heads of Honoré and Belleau were bent over a scattering of photographs and open file folders. The woman didn't so much as glance up when Kavanaugh pulled a chair away from the table, spun it around, and sat down, forearms resting on the back.

"Jack," Flitcroft said. He lifted his glass full of Agua de Azahar, a potent Philippine brandy, toward him in a laconic toast. "You're late. As usual."

Kavanaugh sipped at his gin and tonic. "The time got away from me."

Actually, after spending an hour in Flitcroft's office following the arrival of the British scientists, he had returned to his house to freshen up in anticipation of the party and of becoming better acquainted with Honoré Roxton.

Now, upon seeing the woman, he wondered why he had bothered. She wore faded denim slacks and a lightweight khaki shirt with the sleeves rolled up to the elbows. Her long sunset-hued hair was tied up in an untidy knot atop her head and wisps of it hung down around her face.

Honoré looked up, her large green eyes regarding him from behind the lenses of wire-rimmed glasses. "I've been reviewing your written accounts of how you found the Tamtungs and your initial explorations, Mr. Kavanaugh."

"Jack," he corrected her mildly.

She blinked in momentary confusion. "Pardon?"

"Call me Jack…that's my name."

Her comprehending "Oh" was dismissive. Picking up a sheet of paper from inside the folder, she said, "Over four years ago, you were flying medical supplies out of Kuala Lumpur when a storm drove you and Mr. Crowe off course."

"That's not quite accurate," Crowe interposed, chewing on the end of an unlit cheroot. "We flew off course to avoid the storm."

Lifting his martini glass to his lips, Belleau said diffidently, "Irrelevant."

"You found yourself within visual range of Big Tamtung," Honoré continued, "and so you made a flyover. Then you saw what you claimed was a pterosaur, buzzing your plane."

She did not ask a question—she made a flat statement. She stared at Kavanaugh from beneath an arched eyebrow, waiting for him to respond.

He took a leisurely swallow of his gin and tonic. "You're not calling me a liar or crazy, I notice."

Honoré smiled. "The fact that I'm even here and having this conversation proves that I have an open mind. Besides, I've been provided a grounding in the basics of Big Tamtung zoology."

"Provided by whom?"

Honoré glanced surreptitiously at Belleau whose bearded face remained dispassionately studious. But Kavanaugh caught the brief eye exchange and felt a surge of suspicion.

Flitcroft said, "I've let her go over every file that pertains to Cryptozoica, Jack."

"I thought you'd destroyed all those records," Kavanaugh replied.

Flitcroft uttered a short, patronizing laugh. "You should know me better than that. What seems worthless one year can be very valuable five years later."

Belleau stated matter-of-factly, "Particularly when you find someone who is qualified to evaluate their worth."

Crowe grunted, then struck a match and set fire to the tip of the cheroot, sending up a wreath of smoke.

Honoré asked irritably, "Must you smoke, Mr. Crowe?"

"In the tropics, smokers contract malaria far less often than non-smokers. That's a scientific fact. Maybe you ought to try it."

Impatiently, she fanned the air in front of her face. "That's because the nasty smoke drives mosquitoes away. There's your science for you—revulsion."

Kavanaugh reached toward the scattering of photographs and flipped through them like a deck of cards. He found the one he was looking for and passed it Honoré.

"There. Gus took this shot."

She held it up to the light. "A shot of what?"

"The pterodactyl or pterodon whatever it was. We saw it several times."

Honoré's eyes narrowed as she examined the image. A blurry outline somewhat reminiscent of a crane with outspread wings occupied the center of the frame.

"I enlarged it," Crowe said almost apologetically. "Lost some detail but you can still make out what it is...or isn't."

The photograph, taken from below, clearly showed a brown, leathery epidermis stretched tight over membranous bat-like wings. Four curving talons sprouted from the first joint juncture of the wings. The exceptionally long neck terminated in a narrow, sharply pointed beak.

Honoré Roxton stared at the image, as if she defied its reality. "Of the azhdarchid group, most probably a version of Quetzalcoatlus. They had enormous wingspans, over twenty meters."

"It was goddamned big," Kavanaugh agreed. "Nearly as broad as the Cessna we were flying."

"The question begs to be asked—and answered—" Honoré declared. "How a creature that size could avoid being seen for all these many, many thousands of years. Even the so-called flying Kongamato in Africa and New Guinea's Ropen is reported occasionally."

Flitcroft said, "The short answer is that no planes ever came close to the island and there was no reason for any ships to stop by. There's nothing out here to interest either merchant or fishing vessels. We're a couple of hundred of miles from the shipping lanes. The closest major port is Sarawak, in Borneo, well over a thousand miles away."

"What about satellite surveillance?"

"The analysts would have to know what they're looking for," Crowe said. "There are maybe five hundred islands out here that no one has ever set foot on. The Tamtungs are just two out of God knows how many. A lot of them weren't even placed on the charts until World War II. For example, the Spratly islands comprise more than 30,000 islands and reefs, and the majority of them have never been explored."

Belleau brought the martini glass to his lips. "Oceania has long been the dark continent of archeological, anthropological and zoological research. Keep in mind that barely ten percent of Malaysia's rain forests have been explored, much less surveyed. The percentage of the land surface of the Earth that is actually inhabited by humans is quite limited. In parts of the tropics there are areas of staggering immensity which no man as yet been able to penetrate. Just because a map is covered with names doesn't mean that the country is known, darlin'."

At the casually spoken endearment, Honoré's eyes flashed with annoyance. She riffled through the sheets of paper. "There was absolutely no scientific research performed except by layman."

She swept a challenging stare over Crowe, Kavanaugh and Flitcroft, then fixed it upon Crowe. "You theorized that the Tamtungs were part of the Laurasian coastline during the late Cretaceous?"

"Yeah, that's right," Crowe retorted defensively. "You don't need to be a degreed geologist to guess that the Tamtungs were connected to a larger land mass, either Gondwana or Laurasia. When the land began breaking away and submerging—probably due to seismic activity and changing sea levels— the animals gradually migrated to higher ground.

"Over a period of millennia, Big Tamtung became a closed ecosystem. That's what most likely saved an isolated group of dinosaurids from extinction. As it is, some of the surviving species have evolved into forms different from what the paleontologists have reconstructed."

"Like your so-called 'Quinterotops'?" Belleau inquired, reading from a sheet of paper. "That's what you named a type of ceratopsian you saw?"

Crowe held up a hand. "We counted five horns, so it seemed like the most logical name."

Sarcastically, Honoré said, "This whole thing sounds like the plot for a lot of B movies."

"Maybe," Kavanaugh replied with a studied indifference. "But when you don't claim to know everything about everything, then you're unwilling to be dogmatic about much of anything."

Belleau glared at him from across the table, but to Kavanaugh's surprise, Honoré laughed appreciatively. "I can't really argue with that. However, I hope you understand why I feel the way I do about following the proper investigative procedures and scientific methodology. The report of your discovery of the island should have been the most momentous of the last three centuries."

She paused for a handful of seconds. When she spoke again, her tone held an accusatory, bitter edge. "The Tamtungs should have been presented to the scientific community within days of you setting foot on them."

"Why?" Kavanaugh asked bluntly.

"So universities and private organizations like the Royal Geographic Society could have mounted the proper expeditions with the proper specialists in place. They would have dispatched zoologists and paleontologists and they could have—"

"—Could have, would have, should have," Kavanaugh broke in angrily. "And me and Gus would've been broomed off to a corner while the specialists and the universities and the private foundations made millions—maybe millions of billions—from our discovery."

Belleau snorted. "You didn't discover the Tamtungs, my boy. They've been on the nautical charts for centuries."

"So what?" countered Crowe. "We were the first to pay attention to them…at least in the last hundred years or so. We were the ones who took all the risks."

"And," Kavanaugh said, "we did what we could to catalogue the animals. We took pictures and filmed them when we could. We have a pretty good idea of what's there."

"Oh, yes." Honoré held up one of the photographs that depicted a bipedal smudge standing near an out-of-focus riverbank. Aloud she read the handwritten notation on the back: " ' We call this one the Stinkosaurus Rex, because it smells like shit.' "

She sighed. "Truly, a *very* scientific classification. Thank you very much."

Kavanaugh bit back a profane response. "For the first six months, there was only me and Gus…then Mouzi and finally Howie. We did the best we could do under the circumstances."

"What exactly were the circumstances?" Belleau demanded suspiciously, hand tightening around his glass.

"We set up a base camp here, right on this spot," Crowe answered. "We boated over to Big Tamtung a couple of times a week. Once we had enough photographic and taped evidence, we got in touch with Howie."

Flitcroft smiled blandly. "I'd used the services of Horizons Unlimited a few times so I knew Jack and Gus weren't liars, even if they weren't always reliable. I knew they weren't running a con on me."

"Only after you insisted on seeing the place yourself," Kavanaugh reminded him.

Flitcroft's smile widened. "Once I did and had the soil and water samples tested, I was convinced. I agreed to back the Cryptozoica idea."

"Biochemistry isn't my field," said Honoré, "but I'd be interested in reading the analysis and gauging the accuracy of the science."

Belleau cast her an impatient glance. "I already have done

that. The soil and water is rich in anti-viral chemical compounds. Conceivably, we could distill drugs that might kill HIV, slow the spread of cancer or halt the process altogether. There is nothing else like it on Earth."

"That's only speculation."

"So far," Flitcroft retorted. "But just speculation drew even more financing. We kept everything, even the smallest detail a secret."

"Hence the cover story about ecotourism and a health retreat," stated Belleau.

"Exactly. The plan was that after we had Cryptozoica up and running, we'd reveal the truth and allow the scientists to have access—a few at a time, under controlled conditions. If we had alerted the news agencies and the media from the outset, they would have been crawling all over the Tamtungs like locusts. I valued this piece of thunder too much to have it stolen by any scientist or reporter who wanted to make a rep for themselves."

"They wouldn't have just stolen our thunder," Kavanaugh said darkly, "but everything they possibly could carry away. Poachers, animal collectors, trophy hunters, agents for the drug companies, you name it—they would have gutted the place inside of six months."

"That seems a rather paranoid position," retorted Honoré.

"I'm a little surprised you didn't set up a black market for dinosaur eggs or the like," Belleau said with a snide grin. "Or at the very least a mail order business for raptor DNA and take out ads in the backs of magazines."

Flitcroft didn't appear to be offended. "The population of animals on the island isn't exactly what you'd call numerous."

A line of consternation crossed Honoré's brow. "Why didn't you offer up any live specimens for study?"

"First, we didn't want to take things away from the ecosystem," Kavanaugh answered tersely. "Secondarily, most of the live specimens are damn difficult to trap safely."

"So, you *did* try."

Kavanaugh nodded. "More than once…but I only managed to catch an archaeopteryx and even doing that was a major pain in the ass."

Belleau angled a skeptical eyebrow at him. "What did you do with it?"

"I brought it back here. It's sort of the unofficial mascot of this place."

Honoré leaned forward, eyes wide and bright. "Where is it? I want to see!"

Crowe laughed. "If you hang around Jack long enough, you'll see the damn thing. He thinks it's stalking him, waiting to swoop down and gnaw out his brains or something."

Honoré squinted first at Crowe, then at Kavanaugh, an uncertain smile playing over her face. When she realized that Kavanaugh's expression was somber, she inquired. "Really?"

Flitcroft waved away the topic. "Never mind. Starting up a trade in prehistoric animals was never what we wanted to do. Even if it was, trying to set up something like that would have drawn too much attention…most of it unwelcome."

"Why do you say that?" Honoré asked.

"The Tamtungs aren't in any specific territorial waters," Flitcroft said, "but we still had to get permission to operate here."

Belleau nodded. "From United Bamboo."

"Yeah," said Kavanaugh grimly. "The triads associated with United Bamboo think they own this part of the world, even the parts they never even knew existed. Some of the older triads have politicians and military officers in their pockets. Political and territorial borders don't mean a whole hell of a lot when a fortune in renewable revenue is at stake."

Honoré stared at him reproachfully. "From what I understand, you were the one who got the triads involved in the undertaking in the first place."

Kavanaugh smiled without humor. "They would've gotten involved eventually—they would have moved in and either demanded hundreds of millions in protection money or they would have burned us out by sabotaging the flights and tour boats. It made more sense to invite one in to act as the mediator of the others. I found a go-between who is fairly diplomatic. There was less chance of hurt feelings doing it through her, not to mention kicking up an international shit-storm."

"Her," Honoré echoed with icy irony. "Bai Suzhen, the so-called Madame White Snake who acted as your go-between with the triads. I'm interested in meeting her."

"If you're lucky," remarked Crowe, "you won't ever have to. She's a little quick on the trigger."

"She brought in more investors, is that correct?"

"The ones that didn't die unexpectedly, yes," Flitcroft said dryly.

Honoré gazed steadily at Kavanaugh. "And you came very close to dying unexpectedly yourself."

Kavanaugh managed to repress the automatic reflex to touch his scarred face. "Yeah, you might say that."

He folded his arms over his chest. "I've got a few questions for you now."

"Fire away...Jack."

He and Honoré locked eyes for a long moment. God, he thought, she really *is* lovely. In different clothes with her hair brushed, she would be—

Voices clamored in a fearful outcry from the barroom followed by a raucous squalling jerked him straight up in his chair, driving all frivolous thoughts from his mind. The music blaring from the jukebox stopped so abruptly, Kavanaugh knew the plug had been yanked from the socket. All the laughter and babble of conversation suddenly died, as if a giant bell jar had been dropped over the Phoenix of Beauty.

Kavanaugh shifted slightly, feeling the silent pressure build in the air, not unlike an approaching storm front. Even Honoré Roxton sensed it. She swung her head around, alarm glinting in her eyes.

Crowe pushed his chair back from the table and peered through the French doors. Feet scuffled and scuttered on the hardwood floors. "Something's going on in there."

The high-pitched squawk came again, followed by a flapping sound, as if a wet strip of carpet were being shaken out in the next room. Kavanaugh's belly turned a slow flip-flop of recognition.

Mouzi came rushing out onto the verandah, casting an apprehensive glance over her shoulder. She leaned over the table and whispered urgently into Crowe's ear.

Although the man's face remained impassive, he turned toward Honoré and said, "Well, Dr. Roxton, I guess your luck has run out—you get to meet Madame White Snake after all."

Chapter Twelve

When Huang Luan caught sight of Kavanaugh, the archaeopteryx fluttered its green wings and opened its tooth-lined beak, uttering a defiant screech that sounded like a nail being pried from a length of green wood.

Bai Suzhen caressed the breast feathers of the creature perched on her right shoulder and murmured a calming endearment. The face she turned toward the people standing between the open French doors held no particular emotion except a suggestion of her usual hauteur.

Her almond eyes slid over Kavanaugh and he felt as if he had been stroked by an electrically charged glove from head to toe. Elegant and immaculate as always, Bai Suzhen's glossy black hair was pulled smoothly back from her face and pinned up at the back of her head by an ivory comb.

Triangular jade earrings dangled on either side of her slender throat, encased in the high collar of a blue satin tunic. The tight fabric faithfully molded her high, firm breasts. The slit in her white linen skirt showed a round thigh encircled by a red and gold serpent.

She strode toward the verandah, her stilt heels tapping loudly on the floor. The crowd parted for her as if she were the figurehead of a ship. Dang Xo and Pai Chu, her two bodyguards, followed closely behind. Their eyes, masked by sunglasses, combined with the immobility of their features to emphasize the cold implacability of their expressions. As usual, their jian swords were sheathed in lacquered scabbards strapped across their backs

Bertram Pendlebury lurched into Bai Suzhen's path, holding out an autocratic hand. "Hey, excuse me, who do you think you are turning off the sounds?"

Bai Suzhen's eyes flickered with amused contempt but she continued striding toward him.

"Get out of her way, asshole," a man whispered from the crowd.

Pendlebury paid no attention. "If you wan' to see Mr. Flitcroft, you better make an appointment."

The woman halted less than inch from Pendlebury's outstretched hand. In a flat, dispassionate tone, she said, "I don't know who you are, but I suggest you step aside."

Pendlebury's lips twisted in a smirk. "An' I suggest that if you want to stay, you better behave yourself. We can always use more pussy at a party, especially of the Kung-Pao variety."

Pendlebury thrust his pelvis in her direction. "You want to be in my picture, Kung-Pao pussy?"

Bai Suzhen's expression did not alter, not even when Pendlebury reached out with his fingers to caress the swell of her left breast. The overhead lights flashed from steel, like a mirror reflecting sunlight for a fraction of a second.

Pendlebury rocked backward on his heels, clutching at his right hand with his left, blood squirting from the severed tips of two fingers. Lips writhing, his mouth opened and closed like that of a landed fish.

He gaped with disbelieving eyes, first at the ends of his fingers lying in little crimson puddles on the floor and then to the jian sword gripped in the hand of Dang Xo.

"A party," Bai Suzhen intoned softly. "I do not recall planning a party." She glanced around at the shocked faces on all sides of her. "But I *do* love a good party."

Pendlebury finally managed to drag enough air into his lungs to propel a shrill scream from his between his slack lips. Shrieking, he staggered wildly toward the verandah, running like a panicked deer, heedless of direction or obstacles in his path. He shouldered several people aside, bowling over tables and chairs.

Kavanaugh stepped aside as the wailing man stumbled onto the verandah where he pitched headfirst over the railing and down into the surrounding shrubbery. He thrashed madly and a little covey of geckos scampered away in all directions, chirping in alarm.

Bai Suzhen arched a carefully plucked eyebrow in Kavanaugh's direction as he was joined first by Crowe, then Honoré and finally by Belleau and Oakshott. "Are these the party guests, Jack?"

Flitcroft vaulted over the railing and helped the struggling, squealing Pendlebury to his feet. "Where's a first-aid kit?"

Crowe turned toward Mouzi who seemed content to lurk in the shadows. "Go get the one from the *Krakatoa*."

Kavanaugh said matter-of-factly, "Hello, Bai. I didn't expect you back tonight."

Despite himself, he felt like a teenager whose keg party had just been crashed by the unexpected arrival of a parent.

"Why should you have?" Bai Suzhen retorted. "I am not accustomed to apprising you of my schedule."

"Did you have a good trip?"

"No," she said coldly. "I, the white serpent of good fortune, am *still* not prospering."

Belleau spoke for the first time. "Perhaps I can change that, Madame."

Flitcroft stumbled back onto the verandah, holding the whimpering, bleeding Pendlebury in both arms. Face suffused with rage, he bellowed, "Are you crazy, Bai? What the fuck's wrong with you?"

Dang Xo made a motion to step toward him, but Bai restrained him with a hand. In a rather less formal tone, she demanded, "What are you doing here, Howard?"

"Business, what do you think?" Flitcroft sat Pendlebury down in a chair and Crowe wrapped the man's hand in a cloth napkin.

"I thought all of your business with the Tamtungs was over and done with quite some time ago. And if it wasn't, you should've told me you were coming."

"You weren't here," Flitcroft snapped.

"I am now." Her eyes swept over the faces of Kavanaugh, Honoré Belleau and Oakshott. "I'm guessing that the reason all of you are here in my establishment is due to Howard's business?"

Kavanaugh nodded. "Pretty much, yeah."

Honoré gestured to Pendlebury's fingertips on the floor. "You know, if somebody puts those on ice, it's possible they can be reattached."

Huang Luan spread its wings and sprang from Bai Suzhen's shoulders, swooped down, plucked the fingers from the floor with its claws and soared out between the French doors and into the night. The archeopteryx's long tail nearly feather-whipped Kavanaugh across the right eye. He flinched away, grimacing. Pendlebury wailed in anguish.

"I guess that's a never mind, then," said Honoré faintly.

"Who might you be?" Bai asked.

"Honoré Roxton," she answered. She started to extend her hand, glanced at the naked, blood-smeared sword and withdrew it. "Doctor Honoré Roxton."

Bai eyed her distrustfully. "You're a surgeon?"

"No, I'm a paleontologist."

"When did you arrive?"

"Today," Belleau said, stepping forward. "We both did."

"From England?"

"More or less, by way of Argentina."

Bai Suzhen's face remained a blank mask as she looked the small man up and down. "Are you a doctor, too?"

"That I am. Dr. Aubrey Belleau." He inclined his head in a respectful bow. "I believe you and I have business matters to discuss, Madame."

For the first time, Bai's face registered an emotion other than detached superiority. Her eyes widened in surprise. For a few seconds, she seemed to grope for a response, then she swiftly recovered her composure. "Yes," she replied stolidly. "I suppose we do, at that."

Oblivious to the astonished stare cast at him by Honoré, Belleau smiled broadly. "Shall we find a place a bit more private?"

Bai Suzhen waved toward the rear of the building, past the bar. "My quarters."

Addressing the crowd, she announced, "Everyone feel free to continue partying. That's what the Phoenix of Beauty is all about."

Honoré clapped a hand on Belleau's shoulder, her fingers digging in. "Aubrey, what the bloody hell is going on here? What business could you possibly have with her?"

Belleau carefully disengaged himself from her grip. "I'm full of surprises, aren't I, darlin'? I'll let you know all about it. While I'm otherwise disposed, I'm sure Tombstone Jacky will be pleased to tell you more of his amazin' adventures running opium and Oriental harlots and whatnot."

Kavanaugh felt the hot seep of anger on the back of his neck. In Thai, he said to Bai, "There's something underhanded going on here. You might need a witness just to keep matters on the up and up."

Bai nodded contemplatively and said, "*Bpen an dee.*"

Whether Belleau understood the brief exchange or guessed its meaning, he said curtly, "Madame, the business is between us."

"But it affects a number of people," she countered. "Friends of mine, more or less. You may bring a witness if you care to." She waved diffidently toward Honoré. "The doctor who is not a surgeon, for example."

Followed by Honoré,' Belleau, Oakshott, Kavanaugh, Dang Xo and Pai Chu, Bai Suzhen strode to the rear of the Phoenix of Beauty. She led the entourage into a large room filled with laquerware, Sukhothai carvings and colorful tapestries. On the other side of a very modern kitchenette, they glimpsed a canopied bed draped in pale yellow silk. A miniature gold Buddha sat in smiling meditation on a corner table, watching everyone come in. The far wall bore red, yellow and green tiles that formed a mosaic of the Naga, the seven-headed cobra of Asian myth. The room smelled of stale incense.

Bai Suzhen fanned the air in front of her face. "Why is it so hot in here? Is the air conditioning out again?"

"Afraid so," Kavanaugh said. "Mouzi tried to fix it. Want me to open a window?"

Bai smiled at him tauntingly. "And tempt my little Huang Luan to peck out your eyes?"

She flicked a wall switch and a large ceiling fan began to revolve, the wooden paddles stirring the humid air but not really cooling it down.

"May we get on with this?" Belleau inquired, wiping at the sweat filming his forehead.

Bai Suzhen glanced at him, then looked past him toward Oakshott who loomed in the doorway. "Instruct your man to wait outside."

"Tell your soldiers to leave, too," Belleau shot back.

Bai sat down in a high-backed Bombay chair and crossed her legs, the right over the left. Kavanaugh steadfastly refused to look at the serpentine tattoo writhing up from around her ankle. Although he appreciated her psychological ploy of presenting an attitude of a noblewoman granting an audience, he had been subjected to it once too often to find much novelty value in it.

"This is *my* place, Dr. Belleau," she said flatly. "You do not dictate to me here. Doing business in this part of the world is complicated and convoluted enough without you dragging poor manners into the mix."

Belleau glared at her. "Madame—"

The woman leaned forward slightly, hands on the arms of the chair. Under her tight blouse, her breasts lifted and fell as if she inhaled deeply, then held her breath.

Kavanaugh stifled the urge to tell the little Englishman he was risking a far more tragic amputation than a couple of fingers but Belleau gusted out a resigned sigh and turned toward Oakshott.

"Go back to the party, that's a good fellow. I'll join you in a few minutes. Ask Mr. Flitcroft if you can help with the unfortunate Mr. Pendlebury."

Reluctantly, Oakshott lumbered away, down the corridor. Satisfaction at the small victory glinted in Bai Suzhen's eyes. Quietly, she said, "Thank you, Dr. Belleau. I am told that you wish to purchase my interests in Cryptozoica Enterprises."

"You were told correctly."

"Told by whom?" demanded Honoré, impatiently swiping at a strand of hair hanging in her face.

"You look very uncomfortable, Dr. Roxton," said Bai Suzhen. "If you like, I can send for an iced drink of some kind. Perhaps a damp cloth?"

"Thank you, no. I want to know——"

"You are here at my sufferance," continued Bai. "As a witness to the proceedings, not a party to them. Is that understood?"

Eyes gleaming with barely suppressed fury, Honoré bit out, "Understood."

"Now, Dr. Belleau—why do you wish to purchase my interests here?"

The man's eyebrows rose. "What difference does it make? It should be sufficient that I'm willing to make the purchase. I was informed that you intended to sell them."

"You were probably told that I was willing to sell for whatever amount you offered me...isn't that right?"

Belleau shifted uncomfortably and cleared his throat. "Madame, my intermediaries made an offer to Mr. Zhi, Mr. Cao and Lady Hu. An agreement was brokered. I came here under the distinct impression that you were fully aware of the particulars."

"I am." Bai Suzhen cut her eyes toward Kavanaugh. "Howard didn't know anything about this deal?"

Kavanaugh shook his head. "If he did, he didn't say anything to me or Gus. As far as I know, he thinks he's bankrolling a film project. Are you saying he's been had or what?"

Belleau scowled up at him. "How dare you? The film project is completely legitimate. Dr. Roxton wouldn't be here otherwise."

"I'll go along with that," Honoré interjected. "As it is, if I don't get some clarity on what's going on, I won't be here for much longer."

Belleau said reassuringly, "My business transaction with Madame Suzhen is not linked to the film, darlin'. They're separate issues."

"Really?" Honoré's tone held the hard edge of challenge and suspicion. "So all of this is just one of those extraordinary confluence of coincidences I've heard so much about?"

Kavanaugh grinned. "Good point, doctor. Bai, is United Bamboo pressuring you into selling your assets?"

Bai Suzhen shrugged. "They are, but I've been expecting a move along those lines for quite some time. I owe them forty million dollars, after all."

Belleau spread his hands in a conciliatory gesture. "Well, there we have it. A selling price at last."

The corners of Bai's mouth twitched in a humorless smile. "And is that precisely the amount you were prepared to pay, doctor?"

He nodded. "It is."

"I imagine you have all the paperwork prepared as well. Another one of those extraordinary confluence of coincidences?"

Belleau's face reddened. "Does it matter about coincidence, Madame? You are very deep in debt. My bank draft can lift you out of it."

"What are you buying, exactly?" Honoré demanded.

Bai gestured negligently to the room, to the ceiling and toward the bar. "This place, primarily."

Honoré stared at Belleau incredulously. "You're buying a *brothel?* That's rather common even for you, isn't it?"

Kavanaugh stared steadily at Bai Suzhen. "He's buying more than that," he said grimly. "He'll be buying me."

The satphone at Belleau's hip suddenly emitted electronically synthesized chimes that sounded like the opening notes of Beethoven's *Ode to Joy.*

Chapter Thirteen

"**I** should've known better than to trust you, Aubrey." Honoré fumbled with the cigarette and a book of matches, inserting the unfiltered end between her lips, then angrily pulling it away. "You always have ulterior motives."

Belleau reached out for her, but she evaded his touch. "Honoré, you're jumping to conclusions and I honestly don't know why."

They stood on a gently arched foot bridge spanning the oily waters of a canal. Frilled geckos chirruped in the broad fronds of an areca palm tree. The musical cacophony from the Phoenix of Beauty had resumed its atonal blaring right after Honoré stormed out of Bai Suzhen's quarters. His short legs pumping, Belleau followed her, waving around his satphone and pleading for her to wait for him.

Honoré stopped trying to light the damp cigarette she had snatched from a table on her way out of the Phoenix. She flipped it into the canal and leaned against the carved wooden handrail. "I jumped to conclusions because you withheld the true purpose of your visit here…it's financially motivated, all of your blather about convergent evolution and a film about zoological miracles to the contrary."

Belleau shook his head. "Not at all. Granted, I arranged for the financing of the film, but I fail to see why that would preclude me from furthering a business arrangement that has been in the process for nearly a year."

"Why didn't you tell me about it, then?"

"First of all, it's not relevant to the reasons I enlisted you.

Secondarily..."

His lips clamped tight, then he exhaled a weary, exasperated sigh through his nostrils.

"What?" she pressed impatiently.

"I confess I had to go through rather unsavory channels to reach this point in the negotiations."

Honoré laughed scornfully. "You're not ashamed to consort with the criminal element, Aubrey. From rumors I've heard, your man Oakshott is wanted for a variety of crimes in a variety of countries. What's the real reason for your secretiveness? Why do you want to own half of Cryptozoica Enterprises?"

"I don't," he declared. "I want to own it all."

"Why?"

Belleau dabbed at the perspiration beading at his hairline. "If I own it all, I can protect the natural resources hidden there on Big Tamtung."

Honoré slitted her eyes in sudden suspicion. "The pool of Prima Materia you alluded to?"

"I did more than allude to it...I showed you a sample."

"Which you could have dipped out of a puddle in front of your Mayfair home," Honoré retorted. "I don't know how to break this to you, Aubrey...but there's no such thing as Prima Materia, the fountain of youth, the elixir vitae or the golden fleece. They're all myths and fairy tales."

Belleau chuckled, a sinister rattlesnake laugh that pimpled Honoré's arms with gooseflesh. "You may be as patronizing and as sarcastic as you wish to be, darlin'. I'm the one who knows the truth, who knows the true composition of the Prima Materia. On the island of Big Tamtung, somewhere in the middle of the quaintly named Cryptozoica is a substance that will revolutionize the fields of molecular biology and biochemistry...not to mention the pharmaceutical industry."

With thumb and forefinger, Honoré pinched the bridge of her nose. "Aubrey—"

"You're aware that researchers at the University of California's Exobiology Center successfully synthesized pantetheine, an ingredient considered essential for the development of life on the planet?"

"No," she said flatly. "I am not. Nor am I particularly interested at the moment."

"You should be. The researchers simulated environmental conditions as they are thought to have existed in prebiotic times… they're studying the abiotic synthesis of biomolecules to determine which ones could have been present on Earth before life arose and, thus, may have been important to the creation of the first living organisms."

Belleau paused, then in a voice pitched low as if he feared someone might be eavesdropping, said, "According to Darwin's secret journal, the conditions on Big Tamtung are much as they were millions upon millions of years ago…they found the last well of the primordial soup from which all life sprang. Percolating within it are the basic components of all modern genetic materials such as naked DNA plasmids and catalytic RNA. It is the basic substance from which non-living molecules turned into life forms and began to make copies of themselves."

Not bothering to disguise the edge of suspicion in her voice, Honoré said, "It sounds like you're talking about stem cells..

Belleau clapped his hands in triumph. "Exactly! But I'm talking about the source of *all* regenerative cells…for example, stem cells and progenitor cells act as the repair system for the body, replenishing the specialized cells that may be damaged due to a compromised immune system. Stem cells can be readily grown and transformed into specialised cells for the treatment of various nervous system disorders and even gene therapies."

Honoré nodded. "Except there is far too much opposition to their widespread use in medical therapies on moral and religious grounds, since the main source are human embryos, umbilical cords and bone marrow."

"Yes, yes." Belleau showed the edges of his teeth in a wolfish grin. "But what if there were a *natural* source for those cells? Not even the most fire-and-brimstone breathing fundamentalists would be able to find much to object to."

Honoré uttered a scoffing sound. "You mean harvesting stem cells that are floating around in a pool somewhere, free for the taking? Like the spring at Lourdes? That's very convenient, isn't it?"

"For the sake of argument, humor me and assume I'm talking factually. Wouldn't you prefer to have such a source for those substances with regenerative properties in the possession of scientists rather than gangsters, opportunistic showmen and alcoholic soldiers of fortune?"

"Assuming you're speaking the truth, of course I would. However, since you're *not* speaking the truth, whatever point you're trying to make is stupendously moot."

Belleau rolled his eyes skyward. "Ah, the ongoing torment of my life. Every woman in it casts doubts as to my sincerity."

"In this instance," shot back Honoré, "it's less your sincerity than your sanity."

Patiently, patronizingly, Belleau asked, "Do you think that the dinosaurid survival on Big Tamtung can be attributed only to a closed ecosystem, that the Prima Materia on the island does not have anything to do with it?"

"I'm not convinced of the one, so there's no reason why I should seriously entertain the likelihood of the other."

"You saw the archaeopteryx."

Doubt briefly clouded Honoré's eyes. Choosing her words carefully, she replied, "It was an unusual avian specimen, yes… but without examining it, as far as I know it could be a species of tree-climber, like the South America hoatzin."

"You're reaching, Doctor," Belleau said, frustration turning his voice raspy. "Even if all of this sounds like one of your movies from Hollywood, Big Tamtung could well belong to the same period as the prehistoric flora of the Carboniferous age found in Palm Valley, out from Alice Springs. The cycads and zamia palms go back millions of years. It's a land of living fossils."

"Now who's reaching, Doctor?" countered Honoré

Belleau's scowl deepened. "At first I found your skepticism

refreshing but it's turned to pig-headed denial. I can prove every word of what I say…and of what Charles Darwin himself said."

Folding her arms over her breasts, Honoré regarded him gravely. "You're very sure of yourself…Doctor."

"I am. Although the secret of the Tamtungs was first discovered and then safeguarded by my great-great-grandfather, I see no reason to keep it a secret when so many in the world can benefit from it. However, revealing the truth and controlling its release are two different issues."

"If you control the release of the truth, then you control the assets of the island?"

"Just so."

"Is buying the shares of Cryptozoica Enterprises from Bai Suzhen part of your overall investment portfolio? Do you plan to corner the market on stem cell research?"

"Would that be so bad if I did? You do know that I work as a consultant for Maxiterm Pharmaceuticals?"

"Are they behind this endeavor? Are they financing you?"

"No, of course not. However, they're extremely interested. You're aware of the mania for rain forest drugs by the giant pharmaceutical companies… over 100 pharmaceutical firms and several branches of the US government are engaged in research projects for drugs and cures for viruses, infections, cancer, and even AIDS.

"The research grants alone have become a multibillion-dollar industry, as scientists go hunting for the next miracle drug that can be synthesized from plants and herbs only found in rain forests. Quite possibly, the *ultimate* miracle drug can be processed from the pool of Prima Materia on Big Tamtung."

Honoré frowned. "You're doing this for the money."

"Not *just* for money," said Belleau sharply. "I embarked on this course of action after years of planning and consideration. It's a matter of conscience, of helping humanity learn of its lost origins so we may go forward on our next evolutionary step."

Aubrey Belleau's breath came faster. His eyes gleamed not just with anger but with a glint of fanaticism. "If the human race is to survive beyond this century, we must look to our collective past, to how life began on Earth. Charles Darwin and my great-great-grandfather understood this. Their ghosts made me the caretaker of the Prima Materia."

"I thought it was this School of Night lodge of yours that acted as the caretaker. Or are the ghosts still members in good standing?"

In a low, grim tone, Belleau said, "Don't make sport of me, Honoré. There is far more to this than you could possibly understand. Despite your inflated opinion of yourself, you really don't have all that much to justify your arrogance. Remember your broken marriage, the ugly divorce, with charges of alcoholism and adultery made by your ex-husband? If nothing else, extend my credentials a professional courtesy and don't mock me."

Honoré experienced a quiver of nausea and she made a move to step around Belleau. "All right, Aubrey. I'll take you at your credentials for the moment... but I will expect more proof other than a tube of sludge and some very bad photographs."

"You shall have them, darlin'." He caught her by the hand and drew her toward him. "And much more besides...there is far more to share with you."

She stole a glance at the crotch of his white ducks and saw the evidence of his arousal straining at the fabric, although the bulge wasn't much more pronounced than what an index finger could have poked.

Honoré's nausea increased. She tried to pull away, surprised by the little man's strength. "Let me go, Aubrey. It's late and I'm very tired. It's been a long, hot day."

Belleau clenched his teeth in a fierce glower, then he forced an abashed grin. He relaxed his grip on her hand. "You're absolutely right, darlin'. But be prepared to be convinced tomorrow. I intend to at least make a flyover of Big Tamtung. We'll have a proper cameraman along, too."

"In Captain Kavanaugh's helicopter?" she asked.

"In *my* helicopter," he corrected smoothly. "At least, it will be, once the papers are signed."

Honoré strode off the bridge. "I don't recall Bai Suzhen agreeing to your terms, Aubrey. Your mysterious phone call interrupted everything."

Belleau barked out a laugh. "Actually, that phone call put everything on track. So go on to bed…we'll speak more in the morning. Sleep tight and don't let the Deinonychosauria bite."

Honoré did not respond to the man's enigmatic remark. All she wanted to do at the moment was put as much distance between her and Belleau as she could. The concept of locking her hotel room door and taking a cold shower or bath seemed like the height of luxury. The night air was still oppressively humid and breathing was a labor. Only a few stars glittered through the cloud cover and a haze blurred the half-moon.

She strode swiftly toward the three-storied building with the Cryptozoica and Horizons Unlimited logos freshly painted on the façade. Curiosity warred with anger inside her. She damned herself for allowing Aubrey to talk her into leaving her cold and dusty dig in Patagonia. The situation on hot and humid Little Tamtung had taken on a surreal, almost hallucinatory quality which blunted her normal reasoning faculties.

As she strode up the main lane she smelled salted fish and garlic wafting from the stilt houses down along the waterfront.

Then she heard the scrape of footsteps behind her.

Chapter Fourteen

Honoré spun around, feeling the fire of fear scorch her nerves.

Kavanaugh and Crowe stood in the shadows of a boarded-up storefront to the right of the lane. Kavanaugh put a finger to his lips, then leaned forward to peer in the direction from which she'd just walked.

After hesitating a moment, Honoré stepped toward the two men. "What is going on here?" Unconsciously she lowered her voice. "Are you following me?"

"Not really," replied Crowe in a whisper. "Since we're ahead of you."

Honoré nodded. "Fair to say. Then why are you skulking around out here? Is this something you usually do, or only when you have visitors?"

"Little Tamtung is where we live," Kavanaugh retorted. "It's sure as hell not much, but it's the best we've got. If there's going to be a change, we want to know about it."

"We want to find out what your fun-sized biologist boyfriend is really up to," Crowe said. "Maybe you can give us an idea."

Honoré felt a rush of anger warm her cheeks. "My relationship with Dr. Belleau is not open for discussion."

"What if it was?" Kavanaugh asked, looking past her.

"Then I'd tell you it's strictly platonic."

"Good. You seemed surprised when he made Bai Suzhen the offer to become a major stockholder in Cryptozoica Enterprises."

"I was—am—but I don't think he's interested in engaging

in a cut-and-dried business proposition."

"Neither are we," grunted Crowe. "He's staying in the hotel with you, right?"

"Not with me…his room is down the hall from mine."

"And you're sure he's a stranger here? That he's never been here before?"

Honoré shrugged, annoyed by the questions but also intrigued. "That's what he led me to believe, although he certainly is aware of the history of the Tamtungs and the Cryptozoica debacle. However, I think he—"

"Sh." Kavanaugh back-stepped into the shadows, drawing Honoré with him. The touch of the man's hand on her arm did not feel like he was taking a liberty—instead, she found the pressure of his fingers somehow comforting.

The three people watched as Aubrey Belleau, followed by Oakshott marched at an oblique angle past their position down toward the harborside. The small man held the rectangular satphone to his ear, the digital icons glowing eerily in the darkness. They heard him speaking, but he was too far away for his words to be made out.

Kavanaugh whispered, "We'll be trailing along to see where he's going at this time of night. Just to make sure he's safe, of course. You should go on to bed, Dr. Roxton."

Honoré snorted derisively. "No, I don't think I should. I'm just as curious about my colleague as you two gentlemen."

Crowe and Kavanaugh exchanged a swift, questioning glance then Crowe said, "Be quiet, then."

"You were the one who made the noise that drew my attention to where you were cowering," Honoré said dryly.

A thin smile quirked the corners of Kavanaugh's mouth. "So we did."

The three people moved away from the storefront but were careful to stay within the wedges of shadow. Honoré felt a distant wonder that her overriding emotional reaction to being in the company of the two strange men in an equally strange environment was not apprehension, but was closer to trust.

The waterfront looked quite different at night than it had during the daytime. When she arrived on Little Tamtung, she had only caught a glimpse of its stilt-legged huts, plank walkways and piers crammed with sampans and brightly painted outrigger fishing boats. At night, the flickering glow of yellow lanterns cast an unearthly illumination over its byways. The moonlight danced in arabesque luminosity from the waves, delicate dabs of white light that shifted with the movement of the sea.

Only a couple of ships were anchored in the bay—one was a large, majestic-looking junk, its ribbed sails compressed like giant hand fans. A hundred or so yards away, a yellow and white sailing yacht rode on the low swells, near the mouth of the channel that led to the open sea. Even with her limited knowledge of seacraft, Honoré admired its trim, streamlined contours. Lights glowed from portholes.

"That's a pretty fancy boat," Kavanaugh murmured.

"Ship," corrected Crowe. "The LOA looks like it measures out to be about ninety feet. That makes it a ship."

"What's LOA?" Honoré asked.

"Length overall," answered Crowe. "That's where the distinction between a boat and a ship gets kind of fuzzy."

"You don't know who it belongs to?"

Kavanaugh shook his head. "No."

"What about that big junk?"

"That's the *Keying*, Bai Suzhen's boat."

"Ship," Crowe said.

Kavanaugh affected not to have heard the correction. "The sailing yacht must have arrived after Bai Suzhen did or she would have asked us about it."

"So you don't know who comes and goes here?"

"If we had a harbor master like we used to," Kavanaugh said, staring meaningfully at Crowe, "then we would."

"What happened to him?" Honoré asked.

"He quit when the checks stopped coming," Crowe growled.

Honoré, Crowe and Kavanaugh continued walking through the maze of the harborfront, crossing a plank runway that led to a short wooden pier. Over the bell-like tinkle of wind chimes, they heard the steady splash of water.

Coming to a halt between a pair of thick wooden pilings draped with fishnets, they watched as Belleau reached the end of the pier. A twelve-foot long passenger sampan creaked up to it, poled by a bent-backed man in a lampshade wicker hat. Crowe and Kavanaugh recognized the man as Den Lai, the older brother of Chou Lai. He and his brother had divided up their family-owned taxi service between land and sea. They knew the sampan had a small three-horse outboard motor clamped to the stern, yet Den hadn't started it. A green canvas shelter edged with yellow tassels was stretched over an aluminum framework.

The prow of the boat bumped against the pier and a thin man stood up, leaping lithely from the sampan to the dock. He shook hands with Belleau.

Kavanaugh squinted, silently cursing the overcast night. The newcomer wasn't significantly taller than the stunted Englishman but his body was much more proportionate. There was something about the tilt of his head and the way he moved that struck a faint chord of recognition within his memory.

"Who the hell is that?" Kavanaugh whispered impatiently. "He must have come from that yacht but he didn't want Den Lai to use the motor."

"Afraid of attracting attention?" Crowe inquired, but in such a way as if he already knew the answer.

"That would be my guess."

Honoré sighed in exasperation. "You know, I could just saunter on down there and ask Aubrey who he's talking to. I'm sure he'd introduce us."

Kavanaugh threw her fleeting, appreciative grin. "That would be one way of saving time. But before you do that, I'd like to find out one thing."

"Which is what?" Honoré wanted to know.

"Where his hired man, Oakshott, got himself off to."

"Not very far at all," said a mild tenor voice from the darkness. Kavanaugh began to whirl around when pain flared through his lower back. The impact of the straight-arm *oi zuki* punch drove him forward into a crossbar nailed lengthwise between the two pilings. It splintered beneath his weight and he fell sprawling to the sand.

Although startled by the sudden violence, Honoré did not cry out. She spun to face Oakshott, placing the flat of her hands on his chest, pushing him back. "Stop it! What's wrong with you?"

In his eagerness to reach Crowe, Oakshott shouldered Honoré aside but the motion threw him slightly off balance. His left arm shot out in a pistoning punch, a duplicate of the one that had knocked Kavanaugh down.

The blow did not land solidly, the knuckles only grazing Crowe's right side. Although red hot needles stabbed through his rib cage, Crowe caught Oakshott's wrist and yanked him forward by his own momentum. He kicked him in the back of his left knee.

Oakshott's leg buckled and he went down awkwardly, catching himself by his right hand. Gritting his teeth, Crowe locked the giant's wrist under his left arm and heaved up on it, hoping to dislocate it at the shoulder.

Simultaneously, a gasping Kavanaugh rolled to his knees. For a second, he and Oakshott were face to face. Then Kavanaugh punched him in the jaw with his right fist.

Oakshott grunted and tried to wrest his left arm free of Crowe's grip and he when he couldn't, he smashed his free hand into the side of Kavanaugh's head. The two men traded a flurry of blows, grunting with pain and exertion.

With each punch, Honoré cried out, "Stop it, you idiots! Stop it!"

Snarling, Crowe jacked up on Oakshott's captured arm and drove a knee between his shoulder blades.

Kavanaugh staggered to his feet, his head spinning with vertigo, his vision unfocused. Leaning against a piling, he massaged his lower back with one hand.

"Let him go, Gus," he said hoarsely.

Crowe released the man's arm and stepped back. Oakshott slowly pushed himself to his knees, then to his feet. Grimacing, he worked his shoulder up and down. He turned toward Crowe.

"You've had some training," he said inanely.

Breathing hard, Kavanaugh pushed himself away from the piling. "We both have. Want to go again, Francine?"

Oakshott took a menacing step toward Kavanaugh and Honoré stepped between them.

"Enough," she snapped curtly. "That's quite enough."

"With all due respect, mum," Oakshott muttered, "I don't work for you."

"That you do not," announced Belleau, jogging down the pier.

The sampan was still tied at the end of it. They watched the thin man climb back into the boat.

Honoré stabbed an accusatory finger at Oakshott. "This bipedal Doberman of yours attacked Captain Kavanaugh without provocation. Struck him from behind, in the back."

"His back was to me," declared Oakshott defensively.

Belleau swept Kavanaugh, Crowe and Honoré with a challenging stare. "I thought you were going to turn in, Honoré."

"I changed my mind," she said. "My bedtime is not the issue. The actions of your valet or bodyguard or whatever you call him are."

"Oakshot was only obeying my orders."

"To sandbag anybody he saw in the vicinity?" Kavanaugh demanded, rubbing the hinge of his jaw.

"Hardly. I instructed him to secure the area so I could conduct a business meeting in relative privacy. His standing orders are always to ensure my safety. He must have thought you presented a threat to it."

"Bullshit," grunted Crowe. "We were just standing here."

"Standing here to spy on me?"

When neither Crowe or Kavanaugh responded, Honoré interjected smoothly, "We were talking a walk."

Belleau's eyebrows rose. "The three of you?"

"The three of us," Honoré said matter-of-factly. "We saw the lights of that sailing yacht out there and came down for a closer look. That's all there is to it."

Belleau smiled without mirth. "Indeed."

Honoré matched his smile with a cold one of her own. "Indeed. I think your Mr. Oakshott owes Captains Kavanaugh and Crowe an apology."

Belleau did not reply. He stared unblinkingly at Honoré.

"That is," she continued in a silky soft tone, "if you want Captain Kavanaugh to fly us over Big Tamtung tomorrow."

Belleau's eyes narrowed while Kavanaugh's went wide. "I don't see that happening," he said with a studied indifference. "I've got kind of a back and jaw ache. But, if Dr. Belleau ends up holding the mortgage on my chopper, there's no reason he can't fly it there himself."

Belleau inhaled deeply. "Oakshott, apologize to the gentlemen, that's a good fellow."

The big man's face did not register any emotion. Inclining his head in a half-nod he intoned, "I apologize. I may have been over-zealous and I hope I did not cause injury."

With his tongue, Kavanaugh probed a small laceration on the tender lining of his cheek. "Nothing a couple of shots of hydrogen peroxide mixed with bourbon won't cure."

Belleau turned toward Kavanaugh. "Very well, then. May I call upon you in the morning to arrange a flight?"

"You know my rates?"

"I fear not."

"A hundred dollars an hour," answered Kavanaugh. When he saw the anger in the little man's eyes he added, "Of course, we can work out a flat fee. I'll still need a damage deposit, of course. My chopper cost over a million dollars."

"Of course," Belleau echoed in a sibilant whisper. "Now, if everyone will excuse me, I shall get on with my business."

Pivoting on a heel, he stalked back along the pier to the man waiting in the sampan. Eyeing Oakshott, Honoré said quietly, "Perhaps we should all do the same."

Oakshott rotated his left arm at the shoulder and winced. "That would be a wise idea, mum."

Crowe, Kavanaugh and Honoré walked away from the pier, adopting casual gaits, even though Kavanaugh's lower back throbbed fiercely. When they were beyond Oakshott's range of hearing, Honoré murmured, "My, that was unpleasant."

Crowe nodded. "Yeah, but we learned that Belleau doesn't want us to know what he's really up to....or who he's up to it with."

"Too late for that," Kavanaugh said. "It must have taken Oakshott's sucker punch, but I finally recognized the guy he was meeting. I only saw him once, in Sarawak, that's why I couldn't place him right off."

"Who is it?" Honoré asked.

"The name wouldn't mean anything to you," Kavanaugh answered. "But it will to Bai Suzhen."

Chapter Fifteen

May 12th

"Jimmy Cao?"

Kavanaugh nodded. "Yeah."

"You're certain?"

"Yeah...the boss of the Ghost Shadows himself."

"The vanguard boss. He's got a couple of years yet before he makes mountain master."

"Whatever. It was definitely him I saw meeting with Belleau."

Bai Suzhen voiced a sigh, seasoned with an under-the-breath Thai obscenity. She sat in a claw-footed iron bathtub in the center of a small enclosed garden at the rear of the Phoenix of Beauty. A small path curved to a corner where a mound of smooth stones and bonsai trees created the illusion of a distant mountain range.

A stream of water flowed down the face of the stones and formed a serpentine-twisting brook. On either side of it stood two small Naga statues, stylized representations of beautiful women whose lower bodies were coiled like those of snakes. Waxed-paper screens made a long decorative wall. The outlines of Dang Xo and Pai Chu were visible on the opposite side of the screens.

The tub in which Bai Suzhen reclined was filled mainly with ice cubes, collected from the bar's ice maker, and they did little to cover her nudity. Her sleek black hair gleamed like midnight velvet, caught up in an intricate knot at the nape of her slender neck. Although her slanted eyes were closed as if in meditation, Kavanaugh remembered how quickly passion could flame from them, as well as fury.

A small pert girl with mahogany skin wearing a pink silk cheongsam stood nearby with an ice bucket. Kavanaugh remembered that her name was Qui. She went to great lengths not to make eye contact with him.

Birds chirped in the overhanging oleanders. Although the sun was only at mid-point in the morning sky, a heavy, sultry heat had already settled over the island. The glass of iced mint tea Kavanaugh sipped had a stinging aftertaste, but at least it was cold. He pressed the chilled glass to his sweat-pebbled forehead. He wished he could join Bai in the tub, but he figured she would misinterpret his actions.

Bai Suzhen suddenly sat up with a clinking of ice, leaning forward, wrapping her arms around her knees, resting her chin on her forearms. "I shouldn't be surprised. Jimmy told me about Belleau two days ago aboard the *Bĺo Kù Chan*. Obviously, he was the Englishman's contact."

"That's what I figured," Kavanaugh said. "Cao called him last night to let him know he'd arrived."

Bai broodily eyed a yellow flower blossom. "The son of a bitch must have been only a couple of hours behind me all along."

"Yeah…but why?"

"Why what?"

"Why is he here?"

Bai lifted one bare shoulder in a shrug. "To make certain I obey the bidding of United Bamboo and sell my shares to Belleau…and to kill me if I don't…or maybe kill me even if I do."

"He wouldn't dare."

Bai Suzhen chuckled patronizingly. "Even after all this time, you still don't understand the nature of the triads. You still think the triads are criminal gangs, a bunch of professional crooks, like the Mafia in the states."

"And they're not?" Kavanaugh asked, eyebrows crooked at ironic angles.

"The triads are a political system, but one that's more powerful and has more influence than any local or national government."

"Except the heads of state are gunmen?"

"Using criminal methods to gain political ends is common everywhere, Jack, but sometimes criminal methods work best to establish law and order. If not for the triads, piracy would've taken over this part of the world after the tsunami."

Kavanaugh shifted position impatiently, knowing she spoke the truth. The South China Seas had always been a prime breeding grounds for pirates. In the wake of the tidal wave tragedies, they swooped in to loot and pillage, robbing both the victims and the aid organizations. He and Augustus had several run-ins with a group of Indonesian cutthroats led by Sarei ibn-Tom.

Bai gazed at him intently. "Why is your face bruised?"

"That man of Belleau's—Oakshott? We had a disagreement last night."

"You were very lucky, then. He is a trained killer." She touched her right forearm. "I saw his tattoo. He is a club fighter. A very skilled one."

"Mouzi says she saw him kill a couple of men in a club in Bangkok."

Bai nodded. "Belleau is a very strange Englishman to hire someone like that. He very much wants to own all of the shares of Cryptozoica Enterprises and that very much makes me reluctant to sell out to him."

"I didn't think you had a choice."

She smiled slightly. "The white snake of good fortune always has a choice."

"If the white snake's choice is to sell out, I really couldn't blame her."

"I've actually been fairly happy here, Jack...certainly far happier than I ever was as a nightclub performer, doing my sexed-up travesty of traditional dances for the tourist trade."

"You had your own place...you didn't have to dance if you didn't want to."

"The White Snake triad really owned it. I was only a name on paperwork and a face and body in the advertisements. But here..."

Bai leaned back, gazing up at the sky. "Our business did not turn out the way we planned but that didn't make it a complete failure. Of course, considering what happened to you, I don't imagine you feel the same way."

Kavanaugh said nothing, his fingers reflexively tracing the scar on his face. He glanced away from Bai's long, smooth body, just in case her mood changed in her characteristically tempestuous way. He looked toward Qui but she dropped her gaze to the ice bucket in her hands.

"What do you want me to do, Jack?" Bai Suzhen asked bluntly. "Do you want me to sign over the mortgage of the helicopter to you so Belleau won't hold it? Is that why you're really here?"

Kavanaugh gritted his teeth, then relaxed his clenched jaw muscles when the bruised side of his face began to throb.

"You know me better than that. I came here only to warn you about Jimmy Cao and Belleau being in collusion."

"Why do you care if they are?"

"Because—" He faltered for the proper reason to give, then said in a rush, "Because no matter what happened to Cryptozoica Enterprises and to us, to our personal relationship, I do care about you. More than that, I respect you."

Bai Suzhen laughed briefly, bitterly. "Is that why you never asked me to marry you?"

"I never asked because I knew you'd turn me down...especially after—"

He compressed his lips on whatever else he intended to say.

"Especially after your unfortunate accident?" Bai inquired with a mock innocence.

"Yeah."

"I know those raptors didn't bite off your cock, Jack. The

girls here have informed me of *that* much."

Automatically, Kavanaugh cast a glance at Qui who steadfastly kept her gaze fastened on the ice bucket.

"So," Bai continued, "what do you want me to do?"

Kavanaugh turned away, stalking toward the back door of
the Phoenix of Beauty. He placed the glass of tea down on a
wicker table. "I want you to do whatever you think is best for
you, Bai. Gus and me and Mouzi can manage."

"Very thoughtful. Why are you being so noble?"

Kavanaugh froze in place, then spun back around, glaring
angrily at the woman in the tub. He took a deep breath as if
fortifying himself, then stated matter-of-factly, "I let you down,
Bai. I never should've flown those three assholes to Big Tamtung, no matter what they threatened or offered.

"Greed got the better of me. So three men died, I was clawed
up, chewed on and spit out and you lost your life savings and
your triad's position with United Bamboo. It was all my fault.
How could I ask you to marry me after I'd done all of that?"

Bai Suzhen studied him silently through the veil of her long
eyelashes. Softly, she said, "You could have still asked. I would
have said no, but you could have still asked."

Effortlessly, she stood up. Water and ice cascaded down her
body, streaming over every curve. The bright sunlight struck
sparkles from the droplets. Standing in the tub, she was almost the
same height as Kavanaugh, a work of feminine sculpture crafted
in warm flesh tones. The glistening serpent tattoo writhed up her
right leg and over her torso, slithering between her firm breasts.

For a moment, Kavanaugh was mesmerized by her beauty, a
pulse throbbing at his temples and his groin. He instantly and in
total detail recalled the first time he had seen Bai Suzhen in the
White Snake Club, wearing the glittering costume of a Siamese
temple dancer.

He remembered how entranced he had been when the
dreamlike movements of the traditional Naga dance escalated
into a blur of flashing arms, thrusting pelvis and the way the
serpent tattoo between her breasts seemed to be endowed with

a separate life, undulating in rhythm to the wild music. Then, as now, Bai Suzhen's sensuality seemed all-encompassing.

He remembered another time, shortly after his guts had been sewn up and he came back to consciousness to see Bai leaning over him, her hair unbrushed and wearing no make-up. She looked exhausted but still beautiful and she smiled when his eyes opened. She had whispered, "You are a crazy man...you fight everybody, everything. Even death."

Bai Suzhen stepped out of the tub with a casual, relaxed grace. She drew on a sky-blue silk kimino with a heron embroidered on the left breast in red thread. Judging by the faint smile touching the corners of her mouth, Kavanaugh guessed the woman was very aware of her impact on him.

In a curt, businesslike tone, Bai said, "I haven't made up my mind what I'm going to do. Howard Flitcroft insists on talking to me before I reach a decision. He definitely does not want to find himself in partnership with Aubrey Belleau...which is no doubt what Belleau is counting on, to leverage owning my assets into a complete buyout of all outstanding shares."

"Belleau wants me to fly him and some people over Big Tamtung later today," Kavanaugh said. "I'll swing him by the Petting Zoo, then back here. That should give you a little breathing room."

"By that time, I'll have talked to Howard and made my choice." She stared at him expectantly. "Anything else?"

He shook his head. "Not at the moment. But with Jimmy Cao around, watch your back."

"That's why I have Ghee Hin soldiers to protect me."

Kavanaugh turned away. "Okay, then."

"Jack—"

He cast her an over-the-shoulder glance. "What?"

Bai Suzhen smiled at him with genuine affection. "For what it's worth, I have a feeling that I, the white serpent of good fortune, will soon prosper."

"Yeah, I have that same feeling...for what it's worth."

Chapter Sixteen

A few minutes shy of high noon, everyone making the flight to Big Tamtung assembled on the concrete helipad at the rear of Kavanaugh's house. He and Mouzi had spent two hours disconnecting the guy wires from the ASTAR B3-27 and running a complete diagnostic on the electrical and electronic systems. Almost as important were performing idiot checks on the fuel lines and oil well.

The ASTAR B3-27 was considered the Cadillac of tour helicopters and although Kavanaugh hadn't flown it any further than in a big circle around Little Tamtung in the last eighteen months, he kept the machine's monthly maintenance up to date.

Honoré Roxton and Aubrey Belleau showed up wearing what Kavanaugh assumed was explorer chic fashion—lightweight khaki and denim clothes as well as durable off-trail hiking boots. Although Belleau had exchanged his straw Panama hat for an Indiana Jones style felt Fedora, Honoré wore a battered white Stetson, an accessory that should have made her look a trifle ridiculous but for some reason did not. A Nikon digital camera hung from a strap around her neck.

Belleau carried an old-fashioned black satchel, clutching it possessively under his left arm rather than carrying it by the handle.

Oakshott wore much the same tropical ensemble as he had upon arriving, but if anything his face and limbs seemed even paler than they had when he climbed out of the jet the day before. The only spots of color on his body were the red-blue bruises on his face, the mementos of Kavanaugh's fist.

Crowe and Mouzi joined them. Crowe wore camou pants and a lightweight linen shirt bearing the Horizons Unltd logo. Mouzi was dressed in a pair of high-cut khaki shorts that showed off her gamine-slim legs to good advantage and high-topped, thick-soled combat boots.

The ASTAR's passenger compartment consisted of six burgundy-colored leather seats complete with safety harnesses. Kavanaugh removed the Plexiglass partition between the cockpit and the compartment to allow Chet McQuay to shoot through the forward nose ports without obstruction.

The blond-haired cameraman was stocky, under medium height and wore tan cargo pants with voluminous pockets. A silver stud in the shape of a Jesus fish glinted in the lobe of his left ear. Flitcroft had hired him based on a recommendation from the UCLA film school and McQuay balanced his mannerism of laid-back confident competence with thinly veiled contempt.

His general attitude was as if he only endured the assignment and the uncomfortable environment for as long as it suited him and he would quit without a second's notice if work more to his taste came along. He handled his bulky Sony ENG camcorder with far less care than Belleau carried his satchel.

If Aubrey Belleau objected to Mouzi and Crowe coming along on the flight, he said nothing, certainly not after Crowe took up the copilot's position in the cockpit. Although Mouzi had been introduced to everyone the night before, Kavanaugh explained that it was always a sound safety measure to bring a mechanic aloft if at all possible.

In truth, Kavanaugh didn't worry about mechanical problems so much as having witnesses on his side in case he ran into difficulties with the passengers, particularly Oakshott. His shirttail covered the Bren Ten pistol holstered at his hip.

Once everyone climbed aboard and seated themselves, Crowe made sure that they were securely strapped in. He showed them how to operate their Bose headsets so they could communicate with one another. He shut and latched the side hatch and took his copilot's chair.

Kavanaugh settled the earpiece of his own headset, put on aviator's sunglasses and announced over the comm system, "Hands and feet inside, kids," then turned the ASTAR's ignition key.

The powerful Turbomeca Arriel 2B engine caught immediately and the rotor vanes began to rotate, the steady swishing swiftly becoming a thumping purr. Placing the cyclic stick in the neutral position, Kavanaugh smoothly increased the throttle until he obtained the proper RPM then carefully pulled back on the stick until the helicopter's skids arose from the concrete pad.

Under the bright noonday sun, the helicopter lifted into the sky and inscribed a wide circle as Kavanaugh played with the torque, allowing the nose to swing to the right. Pressing the anti-torque pedal, he achieved a stable attitude even as the chopper continued to climb.

At three hundred feet, Kavanaugh made an adjustment in the collective controls and the ASTAR lanced out over the dark waters of the bay. He noted how Den Lai's sampan, propelled by the outboard motor, cut a foaming path toward Bai Suzhen's junk, the *Keying*.

Howard Flitcroft sat in the prow, barely under the canvas shelter. He waved up at them with a perfunctory, almost dismissive "off with you" gesture.

For a moment, Kavanaugh wondered why Bai had scheduled her meeting with Flitcroft aboard the *Keying*, but then figured she chose the junk to minimize outside distractions—not to mention that the air conditioner in her cabin worked whereas the one in Phoenix of Beauty did not.

Turning the helicopter to starboard, Kavanaugh flew over the sailing yacht, at anchor on the far side of the bay. He saw only a handful of men milling about on deck, but they didn't look like sailors to him. He figured they were Ghost Shadow soldiers, more comfortable spilling blood rather than swabbing it up.

A flotilla of fishing boats, most of them skiff-like sampans, were tied up along the shore near the yacht, but no one seemed to be manning them.

"Captain Kavanaugh," Belleau said with feigned weariness. "What are we doing and why?"

"I'm just getting the feel of the old girl," Kavanaugh said in a neutral tone. "Again."

He glanced over at Crowe and their eyes met in a silent, wry acknowledgement of the question and their low opinion of the man who had asked it.

Kavanaugh increased the chopper's airspeed and sent it across the whitecapped waters of the Celebes sea in the direction of the jumbled green, white and black mass of Big Tamtung. As the ASTAR crossed over the outer reef, the *laurabada* trade wind of the South China seas pushed down from above. Except for dark clouds far on the horizon, the sky was like a vast blue bowl inverted over their part of the Earth.

Dredging up fragments of the tour guide patter he had memorized years ago, Kavanaugh said into the mouthpiece of his headset, "Little and Big Tamtung are part of the same landmass, but the connecting strait is submerged under about a hundred feet of water. Little Tamtung is approximately five miles in diameter and seven miles long. Its highest point above sea level is about ninety feet. The interior is mangrove swamp and jungle. There is a river and a waterfall which is used to generate electricity for the village by a small microplant of the kind used in rural China."

The green-blue tapestry of the ocean below blurred by so quickly that waves and whitecaps became mere patterns of contrasting texture and color. Through the forward nose port, everyone watched as the black pillar of basaltic stone loomed ever larger in the forward windshield, rising high above the emerald sprawl of Big Tamtung.

"As you can probably guess," Kavanaugh continued, "Big Tamtung is considerably larger."

"Hence its name, I presume" commented Honoré, her amused voice filtering into his right ear.

Kavanaugh did not respond as the foliage cloaking the

escarpment of schist, shale and basalt turned dark green as the sun touched the eastern slopes. Planes of mist floated around its base, the haze lying close to the treetops.

"It's almost always foggy around the bottom of the cliff face," Crowe said. "We're not sure why."

"Probably a vent blowing out cool air from an underground spring or aquifer," Belleau said negligently. "In this climate, it takes a temperature differential only a few degrees cooler than the air to form a cloud."

Kavanaugh pulled back on the cyclic stick, slowing the ASTAR's airspeed as they approached the crescent of white sand beach, bracketed by stunted nipa palms and flowering tropical ferns of red and yellow. The foam of the surf spread wide at the shoreline. He circled slowly. "We planned on building cabanas complete with a wet bar down there."

"Very nice," Belleau drawled. "If we were here to play volleyball or to have one of your bloody barbecues, I'd be very impressed."

Although he felt an internal quiver of dread, Kavanaugh turned the chopper's nose inland, cruising over a seemingly limitless panorama of forested hills and wooded valleys. From the air, Big Tamtung Island looked like something out of a travelogue designed by either a liar or an expert at CGI. The billowed treetops were woven together like green fabric, with splashes of color made by the occasional orchid or bromeliad.

Bathed in the sunshine, suffused by the streamers of mist curling up from the treeline, the rain forest evoked a Garden of Eden sense of awe and peace. But he knew the jungle held murderous surprises and his belly turned a cold flip-flop. He struggled to tamp down his rising fear.

"Big Tamtung is shaped like a disk," Kavanaugh stated levelly. "With an area of 550 square miles, it's about the same size as the Hawaiian island of Kauai. The highest point is the escarpment there, rising three hundred feet and six feet. We think it's what is left of a volcanic cone."

Belleau muttered, "When will you Yanks join the rest of the

world and adopt the metric system?"

Kavanaugh affected not to have heard the question, assuming it was rhetorical as well as snide. However, he jerked the stick to port a few degrees and as the helicopter canted sharply to the left, he smiled when he heard the startled cry from Belleau.

"Gee, are you all right back there, Aubrey?" Kavanaugh asked, voice full of mock worry.

"Steady as she goes, Captain," Honoré said, laughter lurking at the back of her throat.

"Don't worry about it, Doctor," said Oakshott. "Everything is fine."

Kavanaugh kept the helicopter's air speed throttled down as he skimmed five hundred feet above jagged, razor-backed ridges that gradually rose up to blend with the escarpment. A flock of white feathered birds, disturbed by the chopper's passage, took flight, winging away in all directions. The cabin grew uncomfortably warm and Crowe notched up the air conditioner, with no change in the steady drone of power from the engines.

A broad river meandered through the valley below. It curved, twisted and turned, eventually meeting the sea in a little rock-sheltered cove on the far side of the island.

Peering out the window, Honoré said, "There appears to be a variety of topographies on Big Tamtung."

Crowe said, "It's mainly rain forest, but there are savannas and lowland swamps, too."

"In which case," Belleau said, "the different habitats should lessen the competition for food."

"Yeah," said Mouzi confidently. "That's what we figured."

Belleau snorted disdainfully.

McQuay spoke for the first time, in a laconic rasp. "Dude, I'm not seeing much worth taping. If you want me to get some usable footage, we need to fly lower or go somewhere these so-called prehistoric monsters can actually be seen."

"It's the heat of the day," Crowe said impatiently, hitching around in his seat to glare at the cameraman. "Most of the larger animals, the so-called prehistoric monsters included, are taking a siesta in the shade."

"I'll swing us over the grasslands," Kavanaugh said. "Maybe we'll see a few snufflegalumps grazing."

"Snufflegalumps?" echoed Honoré. "Oh, that's what you named a species of ornithopod?"

"That's what *I* named 'em," Mouzi announced proudly, tapping her chest with a thumb.

"They're a small version of Hadrosaur and Parasaurolophus," said Crowe. "We might see a couple of the larger sauropods, an Apatasaurus or two."

"Which is what? Worth photographing?" McQuay asked, checking the lens of his camcorder.

"It's what used to be called a brontosaurus," answered Mouzi promptly.

In response to the questioning glances turned toward her by Honoré and Belleau, she said defensively, "Hey, you can't live here as long as I have and not pick up a few things."

"I can imagine." Belleau chuckled. "Like a criminal record... or an STD."

Kavanaugh nosed the chopper in a climbing turn, awakening a sinking sensation in everyone's stomach. Below them, twisted ridges and deep gorges yielded to an expanse of open tableland, a vast green carpet folded in jumbled waves. The sunlight glinted from a narrow strip of metal that stretched across the savanna.

"What's that down there, dude?" McQuay asked, bracing his camera against his right shoulder and squinting through the eyepiece.

"A monorail track," Crowe answered. "It was built to ferry nature photographers and such across a couple of the habitats. Flitcroft got the idea from Busch Gardens, in Florida."

"Where do you board the train itself?" Honoré inquired.

Kavanaugh notched back the speed and arced the ASTAR in a sweeping semicircle. "A place we called the Petting Zoo."

"Pardon?" Honoré sounded incredulous and dubious.

Kavanaugh grinned at her tone. "We came up with three ways to tour Cryptozoica and three different prices. The most expensive is by air, the way we're doing it now. A thousand dollars for a full three hours, on top of the fifty thousand dollar three day entrance fee."

"Ridiculous," grunted Belleau. "Outrageous."

"Or," interjected Crowe as if he hadn't heard, "by tour boat, down the picturesque Thunder Lizard River. That was only a thousand dollars for six hours."

"And for the cheapies," said Mouzi cheerfully, "you got to ride twenty-five miles inland on the monorail. Five-hundred bucks per head, but there had to be at least five in the party. But to do any of them, you went to the Petting Zoo first."

"Which is what?" asked McQuay.

"It was built as a research center," Kavanaugh declared. "There's a jetty and the tour boat, a helipad and the monorail train station…not to mention a food concession and a little zoo where some of the smaller and less dangerous animals were to be confined."

"Confined why?" Honoré demanded. "So tourists could have their pictures taken with them?"

"No," said Kavanaugh. "So they could be studied by paleobiologists like yourself."

In tone thick with disgust, Honoré said, "This sounds so…*American*. Hot dogs and popcorn and dinosaurs. Bloody absurd."

"What I find absurd," said Belleau, "is that we have yet to see so much as a spoor or a footprint of these creatures. If they truly exist, where are they?"

"Don't worry about it, Doctor," said Oakshott. "Everything is fine."

Belleau ignored his valet's reassurance. "I'd like to take a closer look at the area around the escarpment, if you don't mind."

"There's not much to see," replied Kavanaugh. "Trees and rocks and fog."

"Nevertheless."

Kavanaugh resisted the urge to roll his eyes, and angled the ASTAR toward the north face of the rock formation. "Is there anything in particular you're looking for?"

Belleau did not answer for a long moment. When he did, his voice was tense. "Why do you ask me that?"

"Only because you seem so insistent on looking at the one place on the island where visibility is a problem. I was just wondering why."

"Quite the coincidence," challenged Belleau. "I was just wondering if this whole enterprise wasn't a hoax, after all."

"Like I said before," Crowe retorted testily, "It's the heat of the day. If you've ever spent time in the tropics, you'd know almost every jungle goes to sleep until late afternoon or early evening. The animal life conserves their strength for hunting at night."

"Don't lecture me about the tropics, young man," Belleau snapped. "I've been to more remote places on Earth than you could ever—"

A massive black shadow seemed to peel away from the shaded side of the escarpment. A booming clap of thunder was followed by a burst of turbulence that buffeted the ASTAR, causing it to pitch violently to starboard.

Ignoring the frightened cries crowding into his earpiece, Kavanaugh struggled with the stick, the vanes whining. The chopper surged upward at a steep angle.

"What the fuck was that?" McQuay yelled, no longer sounding laconic or bored.

Belleau's wordless shout of surprise compressed everyone's eardrums.

The huge black wedge swooped past the chopper and came into full view. Although he had seen it before, Kavanaugh felt his breath seize painfully in his lungs at the sight. The mottled mass dove and disappeared into the haze of vapor rising from the treeline, its passage tearing a great hole in the cloud.

Sounding as if she had just run a mile, Honoré husked out, "I could not have seen what I just did."

"It looked as big as the helicopter!" Belleau cried, his voice hitting a high note of fear.

"Don't worry about it, Doctor," said Oakshott. "Everything is fine."

"I didn't see much of anything but a big-ass shadow," Mc-Quay declared resentfully, jamming the camcorder against his shoulder. "Can you follow it?"

"It was probably one of the pterosaurs we told you about," Crowe said, striving to sound calm and even nonchalant. "Nothing to be concerned about."

"Nothing to be concerned about?" Honoré repeated in disbelief. "It was monstrous! If it's a form of Quetzalcoatlus, then it most definitely *is* something to be concerned about."

Kavanaugh said soothingly, "It's just curious about us. We'll be setting down at the Petting Zoo site in a minute anyway, and it'll lose interest once we're not airborne."

A stuttering screech penetrated even the earphones of their headsets. The winged creature glided alongside the ASTAR's portside, easily keeping pace. Its scale-ringed eyes coldly surveyed the chopper as if it were trying to figure out what kind of creature it was and if it were edible.

The jaws were enormous, longer than Oakshott's body and they led back to a round football of a head, covered in pimpled hide resembling discolored black leather. The membranous wings stretched out like those of a bat, folding and unfolding in flight, making a sound like huge sections of carpet flapping before a gale force wind. Four highly developed fingers, each one tipped with a curving yellow talon, protruded from the juncture of the first joint of the wings.

Clawed feet trailed out behind it and between them fluttered an appendage like the tail of a kite made of oiled rawhide. The creature's wingspan looked to be a minimum of fifty feet.

Peering through the view-finder of his camera, McQuay murmured, "Goddamn, godfuckingdamn."

"Isn't seeing that thing better than measuring footprints or putting poop under a microscope, Aubrey?" Kavanaugh asked, not allowing his own sense of awe and apprehension to affect his controlled tone.

Urgently, Honoré said, "Jack, that pterosaur is acting very aggressively--unusally so."

"Maybe we're flying over its nest," Kavanaugh replied. "It could be reacting like a mama bird protecting its eggs. Once we go past, it'll lose interest in us."

"It's not a bird," Honoré shot back. "Pterosaurs weren't the ancestors of birds, they were a form of theropod with wings, like a flying Deinonychus!"

At the mention of the raptor, a queasy, liquid sensation began to build in Kavanaugh's stomach. "It didn't bother us before."

"I think it's scopin' us out," Mouzi said tightly, eyes focused on the creature less than a dozen yards away from her seat. "Makin' up its mind about takin' a piece out of us."

"It just flew around us the first couple of times," Crowe said. "It didn't seem dangerous."

"That's because you were in a winged aircraft," Honoré replied, "and it probably thought the plane was one of its own kind—"

The Quetzalcoatlus swiveled its head toward them, arching its long neck and opening its jaws. It voiced a high-pitched cry that sounded like steam escaping from a leaky valve combined with a man gargling. Sunlight glinted on the needle-pointed fangs lining its dark red gumline.

"Quetzalcoatlus aren't supposed to have teeth!" blurted Belleau, sounding almost accusatory as if the creature had tricked him.

"All things being equal," said Kavanaugh, adjusting the ASTAR's attitude, "this one does."

The Quetzalcoatlus banked, climbing higher, and then it heeled over for another pass at the helicopter.

"It must've made up its damn mind," Mouzi observed.

"This is fucking great!" McQuay declared, unbuckling his seat harness and edging close to the window, camcorder pressed against his eye. "I can't believe the fucking great footage I'm getting! Oscar quality stuff!"

"Get back in your seat and buckle up, McQuay," Kavanaugh ordered.

"Not a chance," the cameraman retorted.

"Suit yourself."

Kavanaugh pushed the stick forward and the chopper went into a steep dive, toward the mist-shrouded treeline in the shadow of the escarpment. A dangerous maneuver, but with an unknown animal almost as large as the ASTAR swooping after them, it was the only chance worth taking.

He glanced up once and glimpsed the Quetzalcoatlus wheeling overhead, a scant five meters above the main rotor, wings stretched out to their utmost. The speed of its passage made the chopper jerk in the slipstream. Kavanaugh dropped more altitude while coaxing more speed from the engines.

"What are we going to do, Jack?" Crowe asked, worry evident in his voice for the first time.

"If we try to head on back to Little Tamtung, there's no guarantee that thing won't overtake and splash us into the ocean. I'm going to try to lose it in the fog, down around by the trees."

"Good plan," Honoré said approvingly, although her voice trembled. "A creature with that size wingspan can't maneuver well in close areas."

"Neither can we," Kavanaugh said flatly. "I'm still going to land at the Petting Zoo site, providing Rodan will let us get there."

They heard the banshee scream of the Quetzalcoatlus as it arrowed by, barely a yard from the nose of the ASTAR, before plunging into the mist. The downdraft hit them and the helicopter dipped. The haze left in its wake whipped over the forward windows, swept across the nose and limited Kavanaugh's visibility.

The chopper skimmed over three tall trees, shearing off the tops as if the landing skids were scythes. The helicopter shuddered brutally amid explosions of leaves. Kavanaugh struggled with the control stick, pressing the antitorque pedals judiciously. He followed the glistening windings of the Thunder Lizard River below, barely visible through the layer of mist and overhanging trees.

The Quetzalcoatlus burst out of the vapor right beside them, the tip of its left wing barely an arm's-length from the copilot's side window. Scraps of fog trailed from its feet and tail like froth. Turning its head toward the helicopter, the creature snapped its jaws open and shut in a threatening motion that resembled that of a hungry crocodile.

"That is one tenacious son of a bitch," Crowe commented.

"Isn't it just," said Belleau. "I can't help but wonder why."

"Where is this Petting Zoo place?" Oakshott asked, anxiety making his mild voice sound almost squeaky.

"Not far as the pterosaur flies," Kavanaugh answered. "It's been a while since I've been here. Landmarks tend to change."

"The jungle takes over everything," said Crowe, looking down at the vine-entangled treetops blurring by below. "But I think we're pretty close. Stay on this heading."

Mouzi said, "We got guns—why can't we open the windows and just shoot the fucker?"

Scandalized, Honoré demanded, "You brought *guns* aboard?"

"Hell, yes," said Mouzi.

"This was supposed to be a sight-seeing jaunt, just a fly-over—"

"—And you can see how quickly things change from the supposed to be's" broke in Crowe. "We're going to have to set down and even if we don't use the guns, it's better to have them and not need them than to need them and—"

"Oh, spare me," Honoré said irritably.

"Just do something, Kavanaugh," Belleau demanded.

Kavanaugh turned the chopper a few degrees to starboard, away from the pacing Quetzalcoatlus. Beneath the dark masses of foliage sliding by below, a flat expanse of ground came in sight, surrounded by a ring of trees. He glimpsed structures overgrown with vines.

"There it is," Kavanaugh announced. "I suggest everybody stay seated until we've come to a full stop and the seat belt signs are turned off. I'm talking to you, McQuay."

"Don't worry about me," declared McQuay defiantly.

Kavanaugh's hand pushed the cyclic stick full forward and the ASTAR dove down among the treetops. The chopping vanes flayed branches of leaves and peeled bark from the trees. Flat wide palm fronds slapped against the windows. Gently he pulled back on the stick, worked the foot pedals, brought up the nose and adjusted for the chopper's tendency to drift before achieving a stable hover mode.

"I think we're safe now," he said. "It'll be tricky, but if I can work us through and around the trees until we get to the landing pad—"

The Quetzalcoatlus plummeted out of the misty sky overhead, plunging downward and smashing against the rear rotor assembly. The spinning blades sheared through leathery flesh and hollow bone. Blood sprayed across the windows in an artless crimson pattern. The creature shrieked once, a painfully shrill cry and twisted away, its claws scrabbling and squealing on the hull like fingernails dragged over a blackboard.

The ASTAR sideslipped, hurling everyone to the left, their shoulder harnesses cutting into their flesh. McQuay clutched at a seat back with one hand and balanced his camcorder in the other. Kavanaugh hauled back on the stick as the chopper went into a wild spin. The onboard collision alarm blared discordantly. Voices blended in a frightened babble inside his earphones. Through the windows, it appeared as if the jungle wheeled crazily around them, a centrifuge whirl of greens, yellows and reds.

Kavanaugh worked the cyclic stick and foot pedals frantically. Their uncontrolled pirouette slowed, then stopped. For an instant, the helicopter hung suspended, swinging back and forth pendulum fashion, the vanes fanning the air. Then it spiraled down, crashing through tree limbs, jolted by one battering-ram impact after another.

With a screech of rupturing metal, the tail boom assembly broke away. The main rotor blades chopped through tree trunks, slicing into the wood with semi-musical chimes. They bent

backward at forty-five degree angles.

Kavanaugh's head snapped forward, slamming against the window. His body strained against the harness and then slammed back against the seat. The ASTAR continued to fall, leaves and vines covering the windows, adhering to the Quetzalcoatlus blood.

All the air exploded from his lungs as he was engulfed by a wave of shock, followed by red-hued pain.

And black silence.

Chapter Seventeen

Shielding his eyes, Howard Flitcroft watched the ASTAR helicopter inscribe a languorous circle over the bay. He glimpsed Jack through the portside window, looking down at him. He waved more by habit than a sincere greeting. His strongest emotional reaction was annoyance, since he felt like he was being pestered.

Flitcroft certainly didn't envy Jack ferrying around the supercilious Englishman and his party, particularly since Belleau presented a grave threat to the man's autonomy and lifestyle— what there was of it.

Flitcroft didn't look forward to his meeting with Bai Suzhen, either. The noonday sun shone down upon the waters of the bay with such dazzling intensity, he put on a pair of wraparound sunglasses. The heat was cloyingly oppressive. Sweat gathered on his face and his Hawaiian print shirt clung to his damp back.

Shifting position on the splintery plank that served as the sampan's bench, he grimaced as a needle of wood pricked his right buttock. He glanced back at Den Chu, sitting astern, hand on the outboard's prop control. The round brim of the man's lampshade hat cast his features into a semicircular shadow pattern. A long, cloth-wrapped bundle lay on the deck, his sandaled feet resting on it possessively.

Looking forward past the mouth of bay, Flitcroft saw towering cumulus clouds massing on the horizon. They were very far away, but still the clouds portended the imminent arrival of the monsoon season. Whatever form Cryptozoica Enterprises morphed into, he wanted it over and done with long before the first raindrops fell and turned Little Tamtung into a perennial steam bath.

Howard Flitcroft thought of himself as hard and canny, a man who knew his own mind, and after years of strategic planning had finally come into his own. Brought up in a world of savage economics where illusions of fair deals and honoring handshakes were the punchlines of happy hour jokes, Flitcroft had opened his first Atlantic City casino and hotel while still in his twenties.

He built the Sunrise Hotel and Sunset Casino with mob money because there was no way around it, but those finances had been bolstered when he married Merriam Pendlebury, heiress of the Pendlebury baked-goods dynasty. He had never loved her, he had never really loved anyone, but a five-hundred million dollar fortune served as an acceptable substitute.

Flitcroft's overriding ambition was not to be loved himself but to be respected and remembered as a great man, an adventurer, a risk-taker, a visionary. He had never met any man like that outside of cheap paperback novels he read while growing up in Yonkers, so he aspired to be one himself. He involved himself in a number of flamboyant stunts like epic hot-air balloon flights across the Pacific as well as transmitting a live TV special from the site of an erupting volcano.

Then he met Jack Kavanaugh and Augustus Crowe, men who were naturally what he strove to be. Through Horizons Unlimited, they had introduced him to a world he hadn't known existed except in the imagination, full of vivid color, extreme personalities and very often, big risks.

Cryptozoica Enterprises was Howard Flitcroft's biggest risk, his most foolhardy commercial venture, but he could still easily recall that first giddy thrill upon seeing the herd of Hadrosaurs and Parasaurolophus in the living, breathing flesh. No other experience in his life compared to that, not even when he opened a chain of highly profitable internet cafes around the globe. Everything else felt trite in comparison.

Although the collapse of Cryptozoica Enterprises had been

a financial disaster, emotionally his reaction was akin to that of losing a beloved child on whom he had lavished wealth, love and hope. Flitcroft blamed Kavanaugh for the catastrophe, but he also knew he could have put a stop to it with only a word.

Franklin Jessup, Maurice Cranston and Shah Nikwan represented nearly half of the world's wealth and even the five-hundred million dollars Flitcroft had married was little more than upkeep fees on their various properties around the globe. They were cold, grim men who had long ago lost interest in anything the world had to offer—except for the unique and the bizarre. They were collectors of rare items and many of those items were animals, whether they were King of Saxony birds of paradise or Asiatic lions. They became obsessed with the idea of being the only men in history with dinosaur heads mounted in their dens.

Even two-plus years after the fact, Flitcroft was not sure what had driven Jack to knuckle under to their demands, unless he was following a self-destructive urge to snatch defeat out of the jaws of victory. Flitcroft's own alcoholic father had been such a man, driven by personal demons, but he hadn't expected it of Jack Kavanaugh.

Jack was basically fearless but not foolhardy. He had brought in United Bamboo money through Bai Suzhen and managed to keep the entire undertaking under the media radar. Even the massive construction projects on the Tamtung islands had gone largely unnoticed.

Of course, Bai Suzhen had hired only people connected to the White Snake triad, either familial or through old, complicated business arrangements that dated back to the opium wars of the nineteenth century.

Flitcroft never questioned the setup too closely, partly because he wanted a layer of plausible deniability between his company and the triads, but primarily because his interests lay in the final result, not in the million niggling details of how the result was ultimately achieved.

However, he had no problem admitting to himself that Bai

Suzhen, Madame White Snake, scared him—badly.

There was something autocratic, aristocratic and even cruel about her bearing. Bai Suzhen was brilliant and beautiful yet she seemed untouchable, a woman of great power, remote from the caresses and even the understanding of men.

Although she was desirable, Flitcroft never dared to make a play for her. Upon their first meeting, Bai had made it quite clear that their relationship was one of business and it would remain so for the length of their partnership. Standoffish women usually aroused Flitcroft, since he suspected they were playing games. But he knew on a visceral level that Bai Suzhen did not play games, either in her business or personal affairs.

But Flitcroft had noticed the imperious glitter in her eyes softened a trifle whenever she was in the company of Jack Kavanaugh. He didn't think Bai Suzhen actually loved the pilot—he suspected she was as much a stranger to the emotion as he— but the man obviously meant a great deal to her.

The sudden trilling of his cell phone made him jump and caused the sampan to rock to and fro. The ring tone repetitively played the opening bars of Queen's "We Are the Champions." Digging around in a pants pocket, he pulled out his phone and thumbed up the cover, noting the name and number displayed in the caller ID window.

"What is it, Bert?" he demanded.

Without preamble, Bertram bleated, "That goddamn Tombstone Jack took my cameraman on a flyover without my permission!"

"McQuay is my cameraman. I gave the permission."

"I'm the goddamn director!" Bertram's strident shout stabbed into Flitcroft's right ear. He flinched away and glanced over his shoulder toward the building that housed his office and the hotel.

"You're also the director with two of his fingers cut off," Flitcroft retorted. "And the director who slept until noon."

"You gave me the Percocet!"

"Which you mixed with booze. You're better off where you are."

"And where are you?"

Flitcroft eyed the long wooden vessel riding high above the waterline, crafted so its configurations suggested sharp angles, arches and buttresses. The planking and timbers had been heavily varnished and lacquered to the rich bronze color of burnished brass.

Three masts held huge sheets of sailcloth folded as neatly as paper fans. Scarlet Chinese characters marked the junk's stern, but he could not decipher them. However, he assumed that the *Keying* could be identified as a ship belonging to the White Snake triad by the chops painted on the hull.

"I have an appointment with Bai Suzhen," replied Flitcroft. "We need to get this buyout business straight."

Pendlebury's voice hit a high quavering note of fury. "Tell that fuckin' slant-eyed whore she's going to jail!"

Despite his annoyance and agitation, Flitcroft laughed. "Yeah, I'll tell her that. She'll have your balls cut off and shoved into your mouth to shut you up. Let it go, Bert—you brought it on yourself. You got drunk and groped her. You don't want Merriam to know what really happened."

Only silence issued from the phone for a long tick of time. Then Pendlebury asked in a small, contrite voice, "What'll I tell her how it happened?"

"Make up something dramatic and heroic, like saving me from a barracuda. I'll go along with whatever you tell her."

Pendlebury blew out a relieved sigh. "You will?"

"Sure. You're my director, right?" Flitcroft didn't add, *And my wife's half-wit brother.*

"Thanks, Howard. When will you be back?"

"An hour or two. Do me a favor while I'm gone and monitor the GPS weather reports in the radio room. That way I can make travel plans."

"Will do. 'Bye."

Flitcroft folded his phone and returned it to his pocket just as the bulk of the *Keying* filled his field of vision. Den Lai eased up on the throttle of the outboard and pointed the sampan's bow toward the junk's hull. It bumped gently against the side, where a rope ladder hung from the deck railing.

"Do you want to wait for me?" Flitcroft asked Den.

The man nodded his head, his woven straw hat making him look like a mushroom caught in a breeze. "I wait."

Flitcroft checked his Rolex and said, "An hour from now."

Den Lai nodded. "Yes, sir."

Flitcroft clambered up the rungs of the rope ladder, hearing the sampan's outboard motor cease droning. He paid no attention to it after he reached on the *Keying's* deck

Although he saw sailors lounging about among the rigging, he also saw several sear-faced brown-skinned men wearing casual uniforms of black T shirts and khaki shorts. They wore Sam Browne belts with pistols holstered at their hips. Their round faces smiled as impassively as a Buddha's.

A slender man he recognized as one of Bai Suzhen's bodyguards stepped out of an open hatch beneath the elevated superstructure of the fo'c'sle. He gestured with one hand for Flitcroft to approach. A pair of stone Fu guardian dogs snarled on either side of the hatch.

Without hesitation, Flitcroft entered a dimly lit companionway, carefully climbing down a short ladder into a spacious cabin. The first thing he noticed was the blessed coolness of the room. The interior was air-conditioned and the temperature difference was akin to walking from a Turkish bath into a glacial cave.

The wooden bulkheads were hung about with brocades of the finest silk, many of them depicting scenes from myths. They were acrawl with golden tigers, crimson dragons and blue archers. Large-breasted, serpent bodied women were a recurring motif. A mahogany screen with circular yin and yang symbols on the two panels enclosed a round Chinese bed.

Bai Suzhen sat behind a desk in a chair made of tangled root-wood. The surface of the desk was intricately inlaid with ivory and jade. Illuminated by tea candles floating in large, water-filled glass bowls on either side of her, the woman's skin appeared almost golden. Her fine-pored complexion was unlined.

She wore a sleeveless blouse of white silk, studded with mother-of-pearl buttons and black knit slacks. She wore no jewelry except for a delicate silver ring on her left hand. It was made in the form of a scaled serpent, coiled in two loops. The snake body terminated in the head of a woman with cut ruby eyes. The scent released from the candles smelled delicate and exotic, like whiffs of distant honeysuckle.

Bai Suzhen's black hair was carefully brushed back and streamed over her shoulders. It caught the glow from the candles and the sunshine shafting in through a porthole and shone with glossy highlights. Her eyes held no expression, but they were hooded, like those of a drowsing falcon.

"Hello, Howard," she said softly, gesturing to a cane-backed chair.

Taking off his sunglasses, he nodded and seated himself opposite her. As always, Flitcroft felt extremely uncomfortable in Bai Suzhen's presence and that discomfiture put him on the defensive. Although he knew she was a minimum of ten years his junior, he always sensed she was much older and wiser and that she would *always* be wiser, no matter how many years he lived.

"Would you like a drink?" she asked, extending a glass tumbler toward him.

"No, thank you. I'm still a little hung over from last night."

Her eyebrows lifted like dark wings over amused almond eyes. "It's just a fruit juice blend, Howard. I assure you it's not spiked or poisoned."

Flitcroft took the glass and sipped at it, finding the taste a little acidic but still sweet. He smiled appreciatively. "It's nice, thank you."

"How is your brother-in-law faring today?"

"Still mad, but he knows it was his fault. I apologize for his behavior. He's not used to booze and women."

"So I gathered," Bai replied dryly.

Flitcroft waited for her to issue an apology or a word of regret for the actions of her bodyguard. When neither was forthcoming, he glanced around at the furnishings and said, "You've got some interesting decorating ideas here. What's with all the snake-ladies, though?"

"They're the Naga. According to both Hindu and Buddhist lore, the Naga were a race reputed to be half-human and half-reptile."

"Ugh," he said, exaggerating a shudder.

Bai Suzhen gave him a crooked smile. "Although it might seem like a singularly unpleasant combination, the Nagas were supposed to be extremely attractive race. The Naga maidens were so wise and beautiful that mortal males counted themselves blessed if they were taken for lovers or husbands."

Flitcroft eyed one of the tapestries dubiously. "Really."

"Most Nagas were benevolent toward humankind, but there were a few who were antagonistic. One, by the name of Naga-Sanniya, hated humans so much, later generations turned him into the prince of a pantheon of demons."

"What was his problem?" Flitcroft asked, interested in spite of himself.

"Heartbreak, mainly," Bai answered. "He was a lover scorned. According to one version of the myth, a Hindu Brahman named Kaundinya, armed with a magical bow, appeared one day off the shore of Cambodia. A female Naga, a dragon-princess, paddled out to meet him. Kaundinya shot an arrow into her boat. This action frightened the princess into marrying him. Before the marriage, Kaundinya gave her clothes to wear and her father the dragon-king built them a capital city, and named the country 'Kambuja'—Cambodia. The country thrived and so the princess became known as the white serpent of good fortune. However, the good fortune did not last, because her former lover, Naga-Sanniya, took vengeance on her husband and their children."

The woman paused and added, "In the Chinese version of the legend, the name of the princess was Bai Suzhen—Madame White Snake."

Flitcroft grunted and took another sip of juice. "Maybe

we should get down to business and talk about Oriental myths later."

"We haven't often spoken privately, just the two of us," Bai said. "Not since we signed the partnership papers. That was several years ago."

"And now we're discussing our partnership again…in regards to ending it."

"Yes," she drawled sardonically. "That's what is called irony, is it not?"

Flitcroft blurted, "I had no idea Belleau intended to buy your shares in Cryptozoica Enterprises, I hope you believe me."

Bai laughed, a sound he had never heard. It did not warm the blood. "You're a sharp operator, Howard, and your ethics are very elastic, but you're not a liar…at least not a very convincing one. Besides, if you wanted my shares, you could've offered to purchase them at any time over the last two years. I believe you. Tell me—how did this man Belleau insinuate himself into your life?"

Flitcroft shrugged. "He contacted me through an intermediary. His bona fides as a scientist were impeccable, so there wasn't much to make me think I was being conned. He proposed that through his connections to universities and museums all over the world, he could arrange funding for a film project that would legitimize Cryptozoica."

Bai said nothing. She stared at him.

Flitcroft gestured in frustration and resignation. "Hey, I believed him, okay? The little bastard wasn't an entrepreneur like Branson or a media mogul like Murdoch."

"Unlike our own ambitions," Bai said. After a thoughtful pause, she intoned, "It's apparent that forcing you into partnership with him was Belleau's plan all along. He must have figured that he could back you into a corner and buy your shares, probably at a loss."

Flitcroft felt the heat of shame and humiliation burn his cheeks. "He outfoxed me, I admit it. But it came out of left field, it really did. I liked his idea of turning Cryptozoica into a living laboratory and offering scientists and universities time-share franchises. It seemed like the perfect way to recoup my losses and fix my reputation."

"I understand. So, I might as well tell you that Belleau is colluding with the Ghost Shadows triad."

Flitcroft's stomach muscles clenched. "If you sell and I don't—"

"—You'll be a subsidiary of United Bamboo." The corner of Bai's mouth quirked in a grim smile. "I shouldn't have to tell you that millions of Asian businessmen curse that same arrangement every single day of their lives. With your casino and hotel holdings in the States, the triads would look at you like the proverbial golden goose."

Flitcroft swallowed against the increasing tightness of his throat. "They'll pluck my brains out."

"You might say that," Bai Suzhen commented dryly.

"I suppose I could back out of the whole deal and let the world keep thinking that Cryptozoica was a hoax pumped up to publicize a chain of health spas."

"That's one option, but then you might never learn what Belleau and the Ghost Shadows really want with Big Tamtung."

Flitcroft cocked his head in puzzlement. "What do you mean?"

"If Belleau owns all the shares of Cryptozoica," Bai declared, "even if he's bankrolled by the Ghost Shadows, it's obvious he would also own any prior proprietary claims that might pertain to it. For example, if Belleau knows of the medical and health benefits of the island, then he would own majority rights to it. I doubt even the Ghost Shadows know exactly why he's doing what he's doing. They just smell money, so they don't ask too many questions."

Comprehension glinted in Flitcroft's eyes, then anger. "What do you suggest I do?"

"What I'm going to do—delay as long as possible. Stall. There are issues here of great power and most likely great prof-it…either one is much larger than simply reviving Cryptozoica

Enterprises as an ecotourist destination or a health retreat."

Flitcroft stood up, his face a resolute mask. "Thanks, Bai. I'll put the arm on Belleau. Maybe you could get some answers from the Ghost Shadows."

She arose from behind her desk. "I could try, but their vanguard boss isn't fond of me...after our last meeting, I'm sure he'd be happier if I were dead. He's on the island. His name is Jimmy Cao."

Flitcroft opened his mouth to ask a question but immediately closed it when running footsteps thumped noisily on the deck above their heads. Both he and Bai Suzhen glanced up. Faintly, they heard men shouting and calling back and forth.

"What the hell is going on out there?" Flitcroft demanded.

Bai shook her head, her expression irritated, not perplexed. Then they heard the several flat cracks and the staccato hammering of automatic gunfire, followed almost immediately by the opening bars of "We Are the Champions" from Flitcroft's pocket.

Chapter Eighteen

Saddam Hussein and Howard Flitcroft had converted Radwaniyah Palace into a casino. Howard wanted Kavanaugh to play the roulette table and he agreed before he remembered that he was scheduled to fly a bombing run in his F-14 Tomcat.

So Kavanaugh ran through the palace, looking for the airfield. Instead he turned a corner and found himself sitting at a ringside table in the White Serpent nightclub, watching Bai Suzhen perform the Naga mating dance.

Surrounded by the pale green halo cast by spotlight, Bai's lithe arms weaved back and forth like cobras awakening from a nap. With her bare feet planted flatly and firmly beneath her, her hips rolled in tempo with the drumbeats. The gems encrusting her gilded headpiece glittered and gleamed with every sinuous undulation. Tiny finger cymbals chimed in counterpoint to the drumming.

Her arms and legs flashed in intricate movements within the aura of hazy light. Her body curved, bending forward and backward as if her spine were made of rubber, her long fall of ebony hair touching the floor. Her dance was a whirl of primal passions, the movements ancient and maddening.

Kavanaugh watched as she writhed in rhythm with the music, feeling his admiration and lust grow for the woman who danced with such elemental, abandoned artistry. He felt trickles of sweat flowing down his face from his hairline.

As if aware of his reaction, Bai Suzhen whirled on the balls of her bare feet, and glared directly at him, her eyes blazing crimson with contempt. A challenge glinted there as well, then she turned her back, defiantly frisking her buttocks at him with an ophidian flourish.

Rising from the table, Kavanaugh crossed to the stage and reached for the woman, his fingers brushing her bare shoulder. At his touch, Bai Suzhen recoiled and spun on him, eyes flaring bright with rage and accusation.

Beneath the conical headpiece of the temple dancer, her face was blunt of feature, with a wide lipless mouth. Her narrow skull held huge, almond-shaped eyes with black slits centered in golden irises. The greenish light gleamed dully from a pattern of tiny scales pebbling her flesh.

Bai pointed at him with one claw-tipped finger and in a voice like that of an enraged songbird, shrieked, "If you return, you will die, Jack!"

For a moment that seemed eternal, Kavanaugh could not move. Then the acrid odor of gasoline entered his nostrils and set nausea to boiling in his stomach.

"Jack!"

The shout rang in his ears and it took him a few seconds to recognize the voice of Honoré Roxton. The interior walls of his skull throbbed, as if hammers pounded away at the bone. A vibration, like that of a musical note refusing to fade, hummed against his eardrums.

"Jack!"

"I'm all right, I'm all right," he said, dismayed by how raspy his voice sounded. He reached up to wipe away the sweat from his forehead and his fingers glistened with blood.

Turning his head, he saw Honoré's stricken face behind a spiderweb pattern of cracks in the side window. Her tousled sunset-colored mane fell loosely around her shoulders. "I'm all right," he said a third time, even though he didn't feel particularly right.

There was numbness on the right side of his face and a fierce ache in his left leg. He fumbled with the catch on the harness, realizing that his body leaned painfully to the right at a twenty-five degree angle. He looked at Crowe and saw that the man had already freed himself of his seat. He turned toward the passenger compartment.

"You okay, Gus?" Kavanaugh asked, pulling off his headset.

"Just grand." Threads of blood inched from the man's nostrils. His voice sounded nasal and snuffling. "You?"

"Great." Kavanaugh opened the harness release and nearly fell atop Crowe.

Together, they stumbled into the passenger compartment. The entire ASTAR listed to one side, so walking upright was difficult. The compartment was a jumbled mess, with Oakshott, Belleau and Mouzi all struggling to get free of the straps. The hatch door gaped open.

"Everybody needs to get out fast!" Honoré Roxton's thin voice came from outside. She staggered out of the tangled greenery. "This bloody thing could explode any second! It's leaking petrol like the hind end of a goose!"

"As long as nobody lights a match," Crowe grunted, helping a cursing Mouzi get free of her harness, "we'll be all right. Choppers aren't that volatile, no matter what you see in the movies."

Oakshott reached over, and with his two massive hands, gripped the canvas straps, and tore them away from Belleau's torso. The little man half-crawled, half-slid out of the hatch and onto the ground, clutching his satchel in one hand and his walking stick in the other. He would have fallen on his face, if not for Honoré's restraining hand.

"Where's McQuay?" asked Kavanaugh, blinking back blood that dripped into his left eye from a shallow cut right above it. He opened the release catch on Oakshott's safety harness and the giant swiftly shrugged out of it.

"He's out here," Honoré said tremulously. "He's not in a good way, I'm afraid. That's why I got him out first."

After everyone had clambered out of the wreckage, they stood in knee high grass and breathed hard. The undergrowth stretched away on all sides.

Crowe planted his hands on his hips and muttered, "Well, at

least we're the first human beings to have been knocked out of the sky by a pterodactyl. That ought to count for something."

Kavanaugh surveyed the ASTAR, feeling a leaden weight gather in his guts. He felt very tired and very afraid. The helicopter lay between a pair of tall resak trees. The bent chopper blades had ripped away the bark and shredded the trunks so they looked like ears of shucked corn. The tail assembly lay several yards away, so bent and twisted that it barely qualified as a piece of machinery. Faintly, he heard the steady plop-plop of fuel dripping from the punctured tank.

He turned toward Honoré. "Are you all right?"

She rubbed her right hip. "A little bruised, but nothing is broken. How about everyone else?"

The rest of the party stated their physical conditions in monosyllables. No one complained of being in pain.

"Where'd you put McQuay?" asked Kavanaugh.

Honoré gestured toward a bed of ferns, where the man lay on his back, stirring feebly. He moaned between split and bloody lips. "He was unconscious when I got him out."

Kavanaugh eyed her lean frame and then the cameraman's burly physique. "All by yourself? You must do some serious working out."

She smiled wanly, settling her battered Stetson firmly on her head. "I'm stronger than I look."

"I'll keep that in mind." Kavanaugh kneeled beside the man, wincing at the flare of pain in his left leg.

McQuay's eyelids fluttered and he whispered hoarsely, "My head hurts."

"I don't doubt it," Kavanaugh said, carefully examining the laceration on the right side of his scalp. Although it bled profusely, painting the side of the man's face scarlet, the wound did not look critical.

He did not see the gleam of cranial bone, so he didn't think a skull fracture was likely. Still, he knew head traumas were tricky and not easy to diagnose or treat.

"I shouldn't have unbuckled," said McQuay, "but I wanted

to get the shot."

"Did you?"

He grinned, exposing red-filmed teeth. "Yeah. Hope my camera made it out."

"It did," Honoré said. "I don't know if it still works, but you can check it over later."

Crowe handed Kavanaugh a flat aluminum case marked with a red cross on the lid. "This came through, too...I have Mouzi testing the radio. I'll scout around and get an idea of where we are in relation to the Petting Zoo."

Kavanaugh propped McQuay up in a sitting position so Honoré could cleanse the scalp wound with a cotton swab soaked in liquid antiseptic. Watching her deft, expert movements, Kavanaugh said, "You're very good at this, doctor."

"I ought to be," she replied. "I've been out in the middle of nowhere and had to set broken bones with bootlaces and sticks. I even sucked rattlesnake venom out of one of my students."

"From what part?" Kavanaugh asked.

"Texas," she answered, deadpan, applying a gauze patch to McQuay's laceration.

Kavanaugh held the patch in place while Honoré wrapped the cameraman's head with a length of bandage. She examined her work with an appraising eye and said, "Best I can do, under the circumstances."

From a plastic pill bottle, Kavanaugh shook out two yellow pentazocine tablets into McQuay's hand. "Take these. It'll help with the pain."

Belleau, who had stood by silently watching the display of field medicine, asked, "What's the plan?"

"If we can reach anybody by radio, then we'll have one." Kavanaugh stood up, silently enduring the spasm of pain in his leg.

Honoré stood up with him, eyed his face and then dabbed at his forehead with an antiseptic soaked cotton swab. He flinched away from the sting. "Ow."

"Don't be a baby," she murmured. "Even nicks can become septic very quickly in a place like this."

Kavanaugh only raised a sardonic eyebrow and the woman responded in kind. Neither person said anything, but Honoré did a very poor job of repressing a smile. She applied a small butterfly bandage to the laceration.

"Pardon me," Belleau announced peremptorily. "Even if we can radio for help, can we be rescued this far inland? There's not an airstrip here, is there? And not another helicopter within a couple of thousand kilometers?"

"Not that I'm aware of," Kavanaugh replied, "no."

"You have nothing like a satellite emergency position indicating beacon?"

"Afraid not. The idea was to keep this place a secret, remember?"

"Then what are we going to do?"

"Walk, to begin with," Crowe declared.

He came striding through the brush, gesturing to the wall of undergrowth behind him. "The Petting Zoo is about a half a mile thataway. Once we get there, the worst-case scenario is that we sail downriver to the sea, around the headland and back to Big Tamtung."

"Sail in what?" Oakshott demanded.

"A Crossover Nautique 226," Crowe replied. "A cabin cruiser, an inboard tour boat. She's a sweet ride."

Mouzi called from the interior of the ASTAR: "Hey, I raised somebody!"

Crowe hurried over to the chopper and crawled into the cockpit. The light on the General Dynamic VHF radio console glowed green, but it flickered.

"Reception is in and out," Mouzi said, handing Crowe the headset. "But I reached Pendlebury."

"Better than nobody…sort of." Crowe heard the voice of Pendlebury filtered through the headphones, shot through with pops and hisses of static.

"—read me? Copy that, over. Read me? Ten-four? Breaker, breaker."

"Stop stringing trucker jargon together, Bert," Crowe interrupted. "Where's Howard?"

"On Bai Suzhen's boat."

"Call him and tell we have a situation out here The chopper crashed on Big Tamtung, pretty close to the Petting Zoo site. McQuay is injured. We need to be picked up."

"How can we do that?" asked Pendlebury. "The chopper is the only way into the Petting Zoo."

"We'll walk to the beach if we have to, but first we'll find out if McQuay is ambulatory."

Pendlebury's voice dissolved in a hash of crackles. Mouzi hammered on the radio console with the heel of a hand but the green power light faded completely. Grimly, she said, "I bet the battery casing is busted."

Crowe took off the headset. "We let them know our situation. Let's get moving."

Before leaving the chopper, Mouzi pried open a deck plate and removed several packages—a six-pack of bottled water, a box of power bars, a cellophane bag of beef jerky and a vinyl case containing two guns.

Crowe chose the M15 General Officer's autopistol, checking the action and making sure it held a full magazine. He tucked it into the waistband of his pants. Mouzi angled the Kel-Tec SU-16 semiautomatic carbine over her shoulder. Made primarily of high-strength polymer plastic, the carbine was perfect for a girl of her diminutive size and weight.

When they rejoined the group, Kavanaugh and Honoré were trying to help McQuay to his feet. "I think I can walk," the cameraman said. "As long as I don't have to run from Godzilla or anything."

Kavanaugh glanced sharply at Oakshott. "A little help from the gentleman's gentleman?"

The big man looked questioningly at Belleau who nodded his grudging assent. Oakshott stepped over, took McQuay by the right arm and the collar of his shirt and heaved him effortlessly to his feet. McQuay swayed as if he might fall, but Honoré steadied him. She held his camcorder in her right hand.

Crowe turned toward Belleau. "Have you got your satphone with you?"

Belleau patted his satchel. "It's in here. I tried it already. No bars."

"When did you try?" Honoré asked.

"While you and Tombstone Jacky were treating Mr. Mc-Quay."

"What else do you have in there?" Kavanaugh demanded.

"Nothing of any use to you," Belleau retorted primly. "Personal effects."

Mouzi's brown eyes slitted suspiciously. "Why would you bring personal effects on what was supposed to be a three-hour tour?"

"Maybe he's taking a cue from Thurston Howell," Kavanaugh said, an icy edge to his tone.

"I don't have to answer to anyone here," stated Belleau haughtily. "I could ask you why you brought weapons and food on what was supposed to be a brief junket."

"That's easy," said Crowe, snapping off a three-finger salute from his sweat-pebbled brow. "Navy SEALS and the Boy Scouts share the same motto—be prepared."

"Food, weapons and water are standard equipment in this part of the world," Kavanaugh replied. "You don't go anywhere without at least two of them."

Honoré gazed steadily at Belleau as if she dared the little man to speak further. He affected not to notice.

Instead, Aubrey Belleau turned toward the brushline, hefting his walking stick. "I stand corrected. Shall we get going?"

Chapter Nineteen

The hot yellow disk of the sun slowly darkened at the edges as heavy clouds scudded across the sky. By degrees, the sun was swallowed by huge black thunderheads. Cloud mountains massed in the west and a crooked finger of lightning arced across them.

Almost automatically, Kavanaugh counted the seconds. When the thick humid air shivered to a clap of thunder, he estimated the storm front was less than ten miles away and moving very fast.

After the thunder, he heard the chittering of curious monkeys and the clacking screech of birds. He also heard the buzz of flies winging over and settling on the bloody bandage around McQuay's head. The high humidity would prevent the blood from drying for some hours and the odor was sure to draw scavengers larger than flies. He hoped the rain arrived before that.

All around them, huge hardwood trees loomed, towering a hundred feet above the forest floor. Flowering lianas hung from every branch and bough. Bright red orchids bloomed between the gnarled buttress roots of the giant trees. Broad leaves and vines blocked the sunlight, creating a greenish labyrinth through which multi-colored butterflies darted back and forth.

Honoré stared upward at the intertwining boughs. "This looks like a very old growth forest. I wonder what kind of trees those are."

"Dipterocarps," Crowe answered promptly. "They share a common ancestor with the Sarcolaenacea, a tree family indigenous to Madagascar. So, that suggests the ancestor of the

Dipterocarps originated on Laurasia...and since these are very old trees, it seems pretty obvious that the Tamtungs were originally part of the Laurasian supercontinent."

Honoré threw him a fleeting smile of appreciation. "All of you here continue to surprise and impress me. I was led to believe that you were a bunch of ne'er-do-wells who concocted one con after another."

"Interesting," grunted Crowe. "I wonder who gave you that impression."

Kavanaugh came to a sudden halt, throwing out an arm. "Hold up."

Everyone stumbled to unsteady stops. Honoré, Crowe, and Belleau followed the man's gaze. A crumpled, bleeding mass of leathery wings lay in their path. Flies swarmed around the disemboweled corpse of the Quetzalcoatlus, crawling along loops of its intestines. The creature's humped, limp body resembled a collapsed circus tent made of greasy black leather.

"Almighty God," Honoré breathed, moving forward to nudge the tip of a wing with one boot. "It looks like the reconstructions of the animals I've seen, but there are a few significant differences."

"Like what?" asked Belleau.

Stepping carefully, as if she feared the monster was only asleep, Honoré touched the talon-tipped fingers curving from the apex of a wing joint. Each one was the length of her entire hand. "The digits are longer than the fossils would lead us to think they are. They seem built for grasping and holding. I'd guess when the Quetzal is on the ground, it walks on all fours, much like a bat."

Tilting her head back and lifting the brim of her hat, she squinted toward the dark bulk of the escarpment several miles distant, the summit barely visible above the treeline. "The Quetzal must roost on the ledges and outcroppings. Trying to launch itself from the ground would be exceedingly difficult, if not outright impossible."

"And they're not supposed to have teeth, either," Belleau

said resentfully.

Honoré frowned as she stared at the half-folded and broken wings. "I still say the level of aggression it showed us was not normal."

Mouzi said, "It thought we were something new to eat."

"The something new factor should have made it fly away from us as fast as it could, not made it hungry or put it on the offensive. Very odd behavior."

Kavanaugh edged around the creature's half-open jaws, glaring down at its glassy, staring eyes. "All I know is that the sonofabitch killed my chopper before my chopper killed it."

Belleau snorted. "Don't be childish. You can't blame an animal for acting like an animal."

"I don't." Kavanaugh swung his gaze toward the little Englishman. "I blame you. We stirred it up because you insisted on flying too close to the escarpment."

"If that makes you feel better," Belleau said, not unkindly, "then I will accept your blame. However, we really weren't all *that* close to the escarpment and we all managed to survive… unlike the last time you ferried people here. Of course, at that time your very expensive helicopter made it out intact, so you should look at this as a form of karmic balancing."

Balling his fists, Kavanaugh leaned toward Aubrey Belleau, as if he were on the verge of leaping atop the dwarfish man. Oakshott tensed. But Kavanaugh turned around and started walking again, giving the fly-encrusted body of the Quetzalcoatlus a wide berth. He favored his left leg. Needles of pain stabbed through it with every step.

Honoré caught up with him. "Are you sure you're all right?"

"Never better, thanks for asking. I just want to get to the site so we can figure out how to get home."

"It's only a few miles to Little Tamtung, right? Conceivably, we could even swim."

"Conceivably—if the riptides didn't carry us out to open sea and we didn't draw the attention of barracuda, sharks, sea snakes, sea wasps, moray eels, Portuguese Man o' Wars, and even more sharks."

Honoré mimed a shudder. "I don't like eels."

She looked at the jungle closing around them. Sunlight, filtered through the sky-filling, broad-leaved canopy, tinted everything with an emerald hue. "Are there snakes on this island?"

"Do you not like them either?"

"Not very much, no."

"You and Indiana Jones. Yeah, there are king cobras, spitting cobras and kraits, and a couple of different kinds of constrictor, like the short-tailed python. But they're not likely to bother us. They have other enemies to worry about."

A line of worry appeared on Honoré's forehead. "Like what?"

Absently, Kavanaugh, touched the scar on his face. "Like the Deinonychus."

Eyes widening, Honoré glanced around, and over her shoulder at the people walking single file behind. McQuay marched between Oakshott and Crowe, impatiently brushing flies away from his bandage.

"I read your deposition," she said quietly. "The one that was never submitted. When the Deinonychus pack attacked you and your party, you were far from here. Out in the grasslands, right?"

"Right. But that doesn't mean they can't smell blood on the wind. They move like lightning."

"You claimed they tended to follow the Hadrosaur herd."

"Yeah, but there's a competing predator."

Honoré's lips twitched in a smile. "The larger theropod you called a Stinkosaurus Rex."

Kavanaugh matched her smile, but it looked stitched on. "It's obviously of the Tyrannosaur family, but I think it's more of a scavenger than a predator. It eats everything, including the shit of other animals. That's why its breath smelled so bad."

"How many times did you see it? How many were there?"

"We only got one really good straight-on look at one of them. We spotted it around sundown, at the peat swamp, near the grazing grounds of the Apatosaurus. That's about ten or so miles away. We found its prints near the riverbank fairly often."

"What other animals are indigenous to Big Tamtung?"

"Monkeys, tapirs, and we've seen leopards from time to time."

Honoré nodded. "The *Neofelis nebulosa*, the Clouded Leopard. Mr. Flitcroft blamed the deaths of his investors on them, right?"

"That was the official story, but it didn't really matter what killed them. They were just as dead."

She paused and in voice barely above a whisper, she said, "There's something else here, too, isn't there? Some other form of life you've encountered?"

Kavanaugh cast her a sharp glance, then turned toward the faint sound of rushing water. "Let's pick up the pace."

After clawing through a thicket of vines, they reached the riverbank, breathing hard because of the heat and the exertion. Mosquitoes whined around them. The Thunder Lizard River flowed broad and torpid under overhanging tree boughs. The buttress roots of the giant hardwoods stretched out like gnarled tentacles to the river's edge. Because of their immense size, the trees were unable to send their roots down very far into the ground and extended them outward instead.

Several miles inland, the watery concourse lifted until the river seemed to issue from a crack between two towering cliffs expanding outward from the base of the escarpment.

The sky rolled with the echoes of a distant thunderclap. Crowe gestured. "Over this way, girls."

The seven people walked into the perimeter of the Petting Zoo, following overgrown limestone pavers inscribed with the Cryptozoica logo. A main thoroughfare ran between four brick and concrete block buildings, all of them only a single story high. The lane curved to the right and led to the helipad, a big square of concrete nearly covered with white flowering creepers. The logo of Cryptozoica Enterprises inscribed on the surface could be glimpsed through the greenery.

On the opposite side of a tin-roofed lean-to, a wide pier stretched out over the sluggishly flowing river. A canvas shrouded boat hung between a pair of metal hoists. Crowe gusted out a sigh of relief. "The Nautique is still here."

"Who would've stolen the bloody thing?" Mouzi asked dourly. "It's probably a home for snakes and face-huggin' spiders."

McQuay found a bench and sat down, examining his camcorder, absently fanning away flies from his bandage. Honoré surveyed the façade of the largest building. It bore an embossed red and yellow plastic representation of a grinning Tyrannosaur-like creature holding a hamburger between its paws. The picture window, even green-stained and streaked, still showed the legend: Try Our Brontoburgers With Jurassic Jump Juice!

Honoré read it aloud with undisguised contempt and turned away, shaking her head. "Did they hire anybody who even knew the difference between the Jurassic and the Cretaceous?"

Belleau chuckled. "I doubt the people they hired to put this farce together barely knew the difference between their arses and the proverbial holes in the ground."

A long bungalow with a faux thatched roof and vinyl bamboo siding occupied the largest tract of land. A veranda ran the length of the building. A metal sign hung askew above the door. The red letters in raised relief read Horizons Unltd Lounge.

"What did you charge for drinks in there?" Honoré asked Kavanaugh.

He shrugged. "We never got around to making up a price list. But they would have been reasonable, taking into account out transportation costs."

"I'm sure," she said coldly. "Just like I'm sure they wouldn't be watered."

The Petting Zoo site felt less like a prefabricated visitor's center and more like an abandoned frontier settlement, similar to the couple of ghost towns Honoré had come across while hiking in the American Southwest.

She walked down the avenue toward a vine-enwrapped concrete pylon. A spiral staircase corkscrewed around it up to a platform twenty-five feet above the ground. The monorail track extended straight outward, plunging into a mass of foliage. A couple of small outbuildings stood at the edge of the clearing.

"Where's the train?" Honoré asked.

Kavanaugh made a vague gesture. "Somewhere out in the savanna—we think. We sent it on a remote test-run and something went wrong with the electronics and it stopped dead. We never got around to finding it."

Belleau laughed derisively. "Dear God, this is *so* much worse than I imagined. Why on Earth wouldn't Bai Suzhen and Howard Flitcroft be desperate to sell their interests in this place—to anybody who has a checkbook?"

Kavanaugh suppressed the urge to mention Jimmy Cao and the Ghost Shadow triad. That bit of knowledge was a hole-card and he didn't want to play it in a transitory game of one-upmanship. He maintained a neutral expression.

Honoré strode over to a metal handrail spanning a concrete apron. The platform overlooked a square pit covered by interlaced steel bars. The sheer walls plunged downward about fifteen feet to the flagstone floor below. Where loose leaves and dirt didn't cover it, the floor showed dark stains. The dimensions were twenty feet by twenty feet. Two heavy metal doors faced each other at opposite sides of the pit.

"What did you plan on exhibiting down there?" Honoré asked.

"Something fairly harmless and fairly cute," answered Kavanaugh. "A baby snufflegalumpus, maybe. We never intended to keep them caged for long."

"Hey!" came Crowe's call. "I might need a hand over here."

They turned toward the pier just as Crowe, Mouzi and Oakshott dragged away the canvas shroud from the boat. The yellow and white craft was a twenty-foot long luxury runabout equipped with a 475 horsepower Crusader inboard engine. On the forward-planing hull the name *Alley Oop* was painted in bright cobalt blue. The big, concave-curved windshield swept back to the aluminum framework of a black vinyl sun-shelter.

As Kavanaugh approached, Crowe slapped the right-hand hoist and winch armature. "There's no power," he said irritably. "We'll have to lower it manually."

"Hope you chased out the tenants first," Mouzi commented.

The metal cable and pulley system was stiff with rust, so it took the combined strength of Oakshott and Kavanaugh to break loose the catch latches so the slack could be run through the drum. Crowe, Mouzi and Honoré guided the boat down, settling it gently in the water.

The interior of the craft looked surprisingly clean, with only a few spots of greenish mildew on the seat cushions. To Mouzi's relief she saw no evidence that snakes or insects had taken up residence.

She and Crowe clambered aboard and ran fast checks on the craft's systems and supplies. While they worked, a gusty wind rattled the leaves of the underbrush and the fronds of the trees. The sky rolled with a pair of overlapping thunderclaps.

"We're going to have a storm in our teeth in a minute," Kavanaugh called over to McQuay. "You might think about getting out of the rain."

The bandaged man pushed himself up from the bench and walked slowly to stand beneath the roof of the lean-to. He focused his attention on the playback window of his camera.

Crowe unscrewed the cap of the fuel tank and checked the dip-stick. With a note of surprise in his voice, he said, "There's half a tank. I thought it would've evaporated after all this time in this place."

"If you started with a full tank in an airtight container," Belleau said patronizingly, "then the rate of evaporation is about average."

Crowe checked the oil sump and found it full, although slightly dirty. "Mouzi, check the electrical system."

Mouzi climbed into the Nautique's cockpit and flicked the power switch of the shortwave receiver to the on position. Green lights glowed and the radio juiced up with an electronic whine. "Huh," she said dispassionately. "It works. Go figure."

"I went with only state-of-the-art equipment," Crowe said impatiently. "Don't act so surprised. Turn it off until we test the ignition. We'll need all the power to start the engine."

She did as he said. Crowe pushed the primer button on the exterior engine housing. "Give it a kick," he called to her.

Mouzi turned the key. The engine made a bubbly, burping noise, then died. Crowe pumped the primer again just as wind-driven sheets of refreshingly cold rain fell, first in scattered showers, then in a torrential downpour. The surface of the river dimpled under the barrage of raindrops. The wind tore at the treeline.

Water streaming from the brim of her hat, Honoré suggested loudly, "Captain Crowe, perhaps we should get under cover until you ascertain if the engine works."

She, Oakshott and Belleau joined McQuay in the shelter of the lean-to. Kavanaugh remained on the pierside, offering suggestions that neither Mouzi nor Crowe affected to hear.

Mouzi pressed the gas pedal and grasped the throttle. "I'll try 'er again."

There was a sputtering cough and a gout of blue-black smoke puffed from the exhaust. Then the engine roared and the entire length of the boat vibrated violently. Ripples spread out over the river. Kavanaugh saw the dark water roil and bubble ominously, as if something large moved off the bottom, attracted by the prop-wash and the noise.

Mouzi maintained a steady pressure on the throttle. Both Crowe and Kavanaugh expected the engine to stall and die but although it stuttered, it continued to run.

Kavanaugh stepped off the edge of the dock and into the boat. In Crowe's ear he shouted, "Do you want to see if you can get her moving?"

"First things first. Mouzi, try to raise to Pendlebury."

She turned on the transceiver, thumbing the channel scanner until she reached the correct frequency. She put the microphone to her lips. "Pendlebury, come in. Are you there? Do you read me?"

Pendlebury's high, shrill voice crackled out of the speaker, but because of the engine noise and thunderclap, they couldn't understand what he said.

Twisting the volume knob to full, Mouzi said, "Pendlebury, say again. Over."

"I said something has happened to Howard! When I called him to tell him what had happened to the chopper, he told me the boat was under attack by shadows!"

Scowling, Crowe moved forward and snatched the microphone from Mouzi's hand. "What the hell are you babbling about, Bert?"

"Howard just called me—he told me to tell you if I could reach you that you guys need to get the hell out of wherever you are…Belleau is in on it, too. They've got Bai Suzhen and once she signs her interests over to Belleau, she'll be killed. They're coming for you, too. Do you read me, Gus? *They're coming for all of you.*"

Chapter Twenty

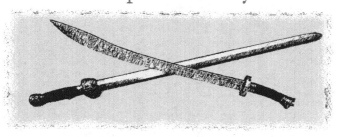

Footsteps slammed down the ladder from the pilot house, punctuated by frantic shouting in Thai and Cantonese. Interwoven throughout the thumps and thuds came the stutter of automatic weapons. A man's voice rose high in a scream of pain.

Bai Suzhen yanked open a desk drawer and pulled out a black handgun. Swiftly, she checked the action, working the slide, jacking a round into the chamber.

"What the hell is going on?" demanded Flitcroft, eyes darting from the pistol in her hand to the ceiling. "We Are the Champions" continued to trill from his pocket.

"Jimmy Cao and the Ghost Shadows," she bit out, whirling toward the door. "Answer your damn phone!"

Bai ran down the companionway and up the short ladder, shouldering open the hatch. Wood splinters flew in a spray above her head with the whine of ricochets. She ducked back into the hatch, holding her CZ75 in a two-fisted grip. Her security staff ran to and fro across the deck, but she didn't see either Dang Xo or Pai Chu. She had expected one or the both of them to make sure she was safe at the first vague hint of trouble.

Bai Suzhen counted to five under her breath, then lunged from the hatch and up the flight of steps to the pilot house so she could see more of the foredeck. Glass shattered and flew from the pilot house windows. More subguns opened up from below, bullets slamming against the hull. Wood splinters snicked through the air.

Ricochets went keening away as she reached the superstructure. Shielding her face from flying fragments of wood and glass, Bai Suzhen elbow-crawled around the corner of the cupola that served as a pilot house to a point where she could see most of the *Keying*.

Her crew and security men raced over the decks, all of them armed. Three of her men were down, dark blood pooling around their bodies. Bai saw six sampans circling the junk like sharks, water purling around their prows. The drone of overtaxed outboard motors was very loud. From the little cabins amidships stabbed muzzle-flashes, like clusters of mad fireflies.

Autofire rattled and bullets sent water fountaining up all around the junk. A hailstorm of slugs thudded into the hull, just above the waterline. Bai recognized the distinctive percussion of spidery-looking Chinese-made Type 64 subguns. She only caught glimpses of the men—they wore head-bands divided by equal rectangles of black and white, the colors of the Ghost Shadow triad. Half of them wielded curved, single-bladed dao swords, more meat cleaver than weapon.

She grasped the mechanics of the assault in an instant—the Ghost Shadows had hidden in plain sight among the daily flotilla of fishing sampans and then surrounded the *Keying* while Jimmy Cao's sailing yacht effectively bottled up the only exit from the bay. Steel-jacketed bullets sang through the rigging and sails. Holes appeared in the sailcloth, giving them the likenesses of giant lace doilies. One of her security guards doubled up and fell overboard, tumbling headfirst into the water.

Bai gritted her teeth in fury and rose to a knee, sighting down the length of her pistol. A man stood at the bow of Den Lau's sampan with a long-barreled Dragonuv SVD sniper rifle at his shoulder, peering through the scope. He wore Lau's characteristic lampshade hat and she realized how the Ghost Shadows had managed to get so close to the *Keying*.

Centering the sights of her pistol on the sniper, she squeezed the trigger. The single shot cracked, like the snapping of a whip. The man's hat floated away, propelled by a mist of blood. Legs twisting in clumsy pirouette, he and the rifle fell into the bay.

The rattling of the Type 64s drowned out the shouts and engine roars. She ducked down as bullets scooped out gouges in the side of the pilothouse, stinging her bare arms with splinters. Quickly, she backed up into the cupola and found Dang Xo sagged over the wheel, wheezing, blowing droplets of blood from his slack lips. A wet stain spread across his shirtfront. With a surge of horror, she realized the pink froth on his lips meant her bodyguard had taken a bullet through the lungs.

"My lady—" he managed to gasp out, his straight, double-edged jian sword hanging from his right hand.. "Tried to stop them, to warn you, but—"

Rising to her knees, Bai Suzhen pulled the man away from the wheel and sat him down, propping him against the wall. Judging by the size of the entrance and exit wounds in his chest, she knew Dang Xo had been one of the first casualties of the Dragonuv sniper rifle. "Don't talk," she told him quietly.

He nodded, lips writhing as he bottled up the pain. As formally as he could, he handed her his sword, pommel-first. He leaned his head back, closed his eyes as if he were lost in thought and died. Bai ducked her head in a respectful acknowledgement, then peered around the edge of the door.

The sampans had pulled close to the junk's portside and the Ghost Shadows hurled grapnels aboard, the metal hooks biting and holding into the deck-rails. A dozen of them swarmed up the knotted nylon ropes while their comrades in the boats maintained a covering fire.

The Ghost Shadow soldiers were stocky, saffron-skinned men. Their faces were broad and flat, their crewcut hair black and coarse. She guessed they were Nanai, from Manchuria. They were armed with subguns, pistols and curved dao swords. Nothing was orderly and organized about the boarding. They charged across the deck in a howling horde.

Cupping her right hand with her left, Bai Suzhen fired steadily into the first group of attackers. Some of them folded over, some fell down into the bay and a couple of others jumped back onto the decks of the sampans, clutching at wounds. She burned through the rest of the CZ75's clip, spent cartridge cases tinkling down around her in a glinting rain.

Bai squeezed off one more round, then the slide of the pistol blew back into the locked and empty position. She flung herself backward, behind the shield of the corner of the pilot house. Bullets crashed into it, tearing away long fragments.

The defense put up by the *Keying's* crew was disorganized and sporadic. They retreated toward the quarter deck while more Ghost Shadows hauled themselves over the rail until Bai estimated nearly a score were assembled on the deck.

Bai Suzhen glimpsed Pai Chu wielding his jian blade with expert ease, slicing halfway through the neck of a Ghost Shadow soldier. Blood spouted from the severed carotid artery, a scarlet fountain that splashed across the deck and slicked the boards.

Bai cast Dang Xo a final glance, put down her pistol, gripped his sword and then vaulted out of the cupola and off the superstructure. She landed directly behind two Ghost Shadow soldiers, bending her knees to absorb the shock of impact. She spun the mirrored blade over her head, cutting bright wheels in the air.

Bai's grandmother, Lady Hu, had begun matriculating her to take over the White Snake triad on her twelfth birthday. She had enrolled Bai in the finest martial arts schools in Asia, learning all forms of *wushu* with a strong emphasis on *Taijijian*, combat with the sword.

The two men stared at her in silence, their eyes wide, expressions registering a blend of confusion and fear. The man on her left uncertainly lifted his dao sword, as if he intended to shake it at her like an admonishing finger. Bai Suzhen bounded forward. The blade in her right fist sliced through his neck and blood splashed across the shocked face of the man standing next to him.

As he reeled away, trying to raise his subgun and clear his vision at the same time, Bai Suzhen performed a half spin on the ball of one foot and drove the sword into the man's midsection. As he doubled over she snatched the dao sword from his slack fingers.

A Ghost Shadow soldier shouted in wordless fury and

whirled toward her, stroking a short snare-drum rattle from his weapon. Bullets thumped very rapidly just above Bai Suzhen's head and then she was among the invaders. She thrust the jian at the man who had fired at her but he danced aside, managing to block the sword with the frame of his subgun.

She slashed the heavy edge of the dao across a man's wrist and with a faint wet sound, the blade sliced off the soldier's right hand. He screamed, clutching his blood-spurting stump, eyes bugging out. Whirling around him, back to his back, Bai Suzhen executed a half-turn, the dao and the jian cutting arcs in the air.

The crossed blades sank into a soldier's neck, catching it between a long scissors of steel. The razor keen metal grated against vertebrae, then she whipped the two swords free, leaving the man to clap his hands to both sides of his throat, trying to staunch the river of blood.

With the speed of a striking serpent, Bai Suzhen constantly shifted position so none of the men could achieve a proper aim with their subguns. If they fired, they would kill their own. She pivoted, slashing backhanded with the jian. The razored tip sliced through a man's belly.

When he staggered away, she received a jarring blow between her shoulder blades. She lurched forward, throwing her arms wide to avoid impaling herself on her own swords and managed to execute a somersault like an acrobat, bouncing back to her feet.

She regained her balance and faced Jimmy Cao. He aimed a big-bored Casull .454 revolver directly at her heart.

The barrel gleamed with a blue-satin finish. An unlit cigarette dangled from between the man's lips. He was dressed very casually in a multi-colored tropical print shirt and white jeans as if he planned to attend a beach party right after the massacre. Braided gold chains glinted at the base of his neck. His upswept black hair glistened with a combination of pomade and sweat.

Although he affected a calm semismirk, Bai noticed how the barrel of the pistol trembled and the sweat beaded in the sparse hairs on his upper lip. "Nice boat," he said in English. "A little too traditional for me."

"And it's all messed up with your men's blood, too," Bai retorted, not lowering her swords.

Jimmy Cao's smirk faltered. "We won, didn't we?"

Bai Suzhen didn't do a head count. Instead, she stated flatly, "There is no way in hell the council would have sanctioned this insanity, Jimmy."

His lips skinned back over his teeth in a malevolent grin. "You're right. But you made a very stupid mistake when you left Zhou Zhi alive."

"So you and he are working together? The Ghost Shadows and the Blue Lotus? I should have known when I saw those Nanai...that's Zhou Zhi's clan of pigs."

Cao gestured with the barrel of his pistol. "Drop the stickers, bitch."

"Why should I?"

Jimmy Cao turned his head and spoke rapidly over his shoulder. Two men wearing Ghost Shadow headbands dragged Pai Chu forward. His head lolled loosely on his neck and his face was masked by a layer of blood sliding from his hairline. They forced him to his knees.

Cao pointed the pistol at Chu "You should do it because not all of your men are dead. But I'll fucking make them all that way if you decide you're a complication instead of an asset."

Bai drew in a long breath through her nostrils and tossed the swords down on the deck, the blades chiming. Instantly, a man grabbed her wrists, twisting her arms up behind her in painful hammerlocks.

Between clenched teeth, she said, "None of the triads would authorize this kind of action against one of their own. What are you really up to, Jimmy?"

He swaggered close to her, idly passing the barrel of the revolver back and forth before her eyes. "I might tell you if you asked the right questions, white serpent-whore of good fortune."

"Which is what?" she snapped. "What size dick extender you use?"

Without warning, Cao kicked her, a whipping crescent kick with his left leg that caught her on the right side of her head. She would have fallen if not for the man gripping her arms. She sagged, knees turning to rubber, her vision blackening at the edges. Her ears rang and she tasted the salt of her own blood.

Then, slowly she straightened up, fighting her way out of unconsciousness. She blinked away the amoeba-shaped floaters swimming across her eyes, tossed her hair back and stared steadily at Jimmy Cao. His face had gone red, twisted with savage anger.

"You're a stupid, arrogant lesbian bitch and you have no place in United Bamboo." He spoke in Thai so she would be sure to understand him. "The council will reward me for getting rid of you."

"You still haven't told me what you want."

"What do you think?" He returned to English. "Your signature on a sales agreement to Aubrey Belleau. I knew you wouldn't do it willingly. I bet that fucking Tombstone Jack talked you out of it. I know you met with him this morning. So, I'm forcing the issue...you're going to sell your shares of Cryptozoica Enterprises to that limey midget and you're going to do it *today*."

Howard Flitcroft's voice announced, "That limey midget isn't here and he's not likely to be any time soon."

Heads and gun barrels swiveled toward Flitcroft as he walked casually from the direction of the quarterdeck. He held his hands up at shoulder level. A Ghost Shadow soldier grabbed him by the arms, twirled him around and roughly patted him down. The man pulled Flitcroft's cell phone from his pocket and tossed it to Cao who barely gave it a glance.

"I figured we'd have to hunt you down, Flitcroft," Cao said. "You saved me some time and trouble. What do you mean, Belleau isn't here?"

Matter-of-factly, making a show of straightening his clothes,

Flitcroft declared, "He's trapped on Big Tamtung."

"You're lying."

Flitcroft shook his head. "I have no reason to." He nodded toward the cell phone in Cao's hand. "A few minutes ago, I got a call from my assistant, Bertram Pendlebury. He received a short-wave distress call from Mouzi, that little Maori mechanic."

"So?" demanded Cao impatiently.

"She reported that Kavanaugh's helicopter had crashed and they needed a pick up."

Bai Suzhen stiffened, inhaling a nervous breath. "Was anyone hurt?"

Flitcroft shook his head. "Not seriously."

"You're so full of shit," Jimmy Cao sneered.

"Call Pendlebury and ask him."

"He'd lie, too. Everybody here is full of shit."

Flitcroft shrugged. "You saw the chopper flying away from here, didn't you?"

Cao nodded reflectively. "Yeah."

"You haven't seen it come back, have you?"

"Get to the point, Flitcroft."

"I'm sure you know Belleau and that valet of his were aboard the chopper. Now they're marooned on Big Tamtung with no way to get back here…and with about a dozen different kinds of animals that would swallow a pint-sized paleontologist in one bite."

Bai Suzhen laughed, despite the drill-bit of pain boring into her facial muscles. "In that case, it really doesn't matter if you have my signature or not, if the other principal is in some monster's belly. Financiers and Cryptozoica Enterprises always seem to cancel one another out."

Jimmy Cao's face became swollen with another surge of rage. His eyes slitted. His breath hissed out between his teeth and he set himself to kick her again.

Flitcroft interposed hastily, "There's another option."

Cao paused but he did not take his eyes off Bai. "I'm listening."

"You can buy my shares. I'm the majority stockholder."

Cao cut his gaze toward him. Contemptuously, he said, "I don't want your shares, Richie Rich. We'll get them anyway, by and by."

Bai Suzhen angled an eyebrow at the smaller man. "What does Belleau offer you, Jimmy? He knows there's something valuable on Big Tamtung besides some prehistoric wildlife… that's the only reason you started the major push for me to repay United Bamboo by selling my shares to him."

Cao snickered and tapped his temple with the bore of the pistol. "You finally figured it out? Took you long enough."

"What does Belleau know?" Flitcroft demanded, forgetting for an instant the guns directed at him.

"I might be inclined to give you a hint," Cao replied, "if you can give me a hint of how I can get Belleau safely off Big Tamtung. It would also be a good way for you to keep alive."

"So you'd just go and pick him up yourself?"

Cao nodded. "More or less."

"What about the people who are with him?"

"I'd rescue them, too, of course."

"Of course," Bai intoned.

"What happened here was business. I'd have no reason to leave anyone stranded over there on that shithole. Where would they most likely be?"

"Don't tell him anything," said Bai Suzhen, her tone edged with sharp warning.

"I know what I'm doing," Flitcroft countered. "This is just a negotiation. Belleau and the others are probably at the Petting Zoo site by now. It's about sixteen miles inland from the westside shore."

"Petting Zoo?" echoed Cao skeptically. "How do I get to it?"

"Without a chopper, there's only one way," answered Flitcroft, a smug smile tugging at the corners of his mouth. "By boat, up the Thunder Lizard River. You can reach the river on the east side of the island and you follow it right to the site, about twenty miles."

Jimmy Cao matched the man's smile. "That seems easy

enough, thanks."

Flitcroft's smile widened. "It's not really. You'll need a guide, someone who's been there."

"Hey, guess what," Cao said in a silky soft croon. "I have one."

He tossed the cell phone back to Flitcroft and from a holster at the small of his back, he produced an AceS satphone, a mate to the one Flitcroft had seen in Belleau's possession. "I'll have the midget just talk me through it."

Flitcroft swallowed hard, clutching his phone. "You're making a mistake, kid. You can't trust Belleau."

"What a coincidence," Cao said smoothly. "You can't trust me, either."

Cao raised the revolver and squeezed the trigger. The pistol banged like door slamming shut. Howard Flitcroft grunted, slapping a hand against his chest. He stood silently for a second, then carefully looked at the palm of his hand. It glistened with wet crimson. Without uttering a word, he toppled heavily to the deck.

Adjusting his aim slightly, Jimmy Cao fired another shot, the heavy caliber round slamming through the center of Pai Chu's forehead. A haze of blood surrounded the rear of his skull and he fell backwards, half on top of Flitcroft.

Cao focused his gaze on Bai Suzhen. "Both of them were complications. Are you going to be an asset or a complication?"

"What do you mean?" she demanded, pitching her voice low to disguise a tremor of fury.

"My boat can't navigate shallow waters. She has a fixed fin keel and she'd run aground in less than six feet of water. What about this obsolete hulk of yours? It's flat-bottomed, right? Can it make it up the river Flitcroft talked about?"

Bai Suzhen presented the image of pondering the question for a moment. She nodded. "I believe so…if you hadn't killed all of my crew."

"We didn't kill all of them, babe, just the ones who tried to kill us. Have you been up this river?"

"Yes," she lied.

"Good," Cao said. "That makes you an asset and not a complication. See how easy it is?"

In rapid-fire Taiwanese, Jimmy Cao shouted orders to his men, gesturing with his pistol for emphasis. They spread out over the *Keying* to assume various stations. The man standing behind Bai Suzhen released her.

Rubbing her wrists to restore circulation, she asked, "What about the dead?"

Cao shrugged as if the matter was of little importance. "Once we get underway, they go over the side...like all my complications."

* * *

Thunder boomed overhead and raindrops pattered against Flitcroft's face. He lay doubled up around the bullet wound, his eyes clouded with tears of pain. He breathed through his open mouth, tasting blood and bile. He ruefully eyed the raw, pulsing hole in the center of his chest. It bled profusely, and he thought he saw bits of lung tissue mixed in with the flow. Still, he didn't hurt as much as he thought he would after being shot through the clavicle, but then he had no other exemplar by which to measure.

He lay as he thought corpses would lie, boneless and frozen in a posture of pain. The body of Pai Chu draped awkwardly over his hips helped the illusion. He listened to men shouting back and forth and then the rattling clangor of the anchor being winched up.

Moving slowly, Flitcroft brought his cell phone up to his ear, flipped open the cover with a blood-coated thumb and punched the direct redial key.

Pendlebury's voice responded quickly. "What the hell is going on over there, Howard? Fireworks? Some sort of Chinese holiday?"

In a strained, guttural whisper, Flitcroft said, "I already told you about Jimmy Cao and the Ghost Shadows, Bert. Now you need to tell Jack and Gus. Cao is on his way to Cryptozoica in Bai Suzhen's boat. She's his prisoner. He'll kill her once she signs over her shares to Belleau."

"What?" Pendlebury demanded, incredulously.

"I don't care how you do it...just reach Jack and Gus—tell them not to trust Belleau. He's working with the Ghost Shadows. They'll kill everybody."

"Are you all right?" asked Pendlebury worriedly. "You sound sick or something."

"Or something," Flitcroft managed to husk out. "Just do what I said. And tell Merriam..." His voice trailed off when he realized he could not think of any message he wanted conveyed to his wife.

"Tell Merriam what?" pressed Pendlebury. "Howard, tell her what?"

With grim satisfaction, he decided that having no parting message whatsoever was a fitting epitaph for a man who had lived his kind of life.

"Goodbye, Bert," he said softly and folded the cover over the phone.

Chapter Twenty-One

The wind died down to no more than an intermittent breeze. The rain slacked off to a steady drizzle, then only a spritzing. Lightning still arced across the sky, but the heart of the storm moved away. The humidity rising in its wake was suffocatingly oppressive. Streamers of mist curled up from the surface of the Thunder Lizard River. The sun peeked out from behind the thick fleece of cloud cover, casting a sullen scarlet glow against the distant thunderheads.

Crowe eased off on the throttle of the *Alley Oop*, the engine roar becoming a muted, idling rumble, the props churning the water to foam.

"I think I've worked out the bugs," he said loudly. "We can cast off once everybody is aboard."

Kavanaugh climbed out onto the dock to disengage the hoist cables from the eyebolts affixed to the prow and stern of the Nautique 226. He gestured to Honoré. She left the shelter of the lean-to. "Celebrity lady scientists first and casualties second."

Honoré gave him a nervous smile and stepped down into the boat, sitting in one of the eight swivel chairs. McQuay followed, handing down his camcorder to Mouzi first. Belleau and Oakshott moved to the edge of the dock.

The big man began to step down into the boat, stretching out a leg. Kavanaugh planted a foot square on seat of Oakshott's pants and gave him a shove. With a wild waving of arms and a surprisingly deep-throated bellow, Oakshott plunged headfirst into the river between the hull of the boat and the dock.

Face contorting with shock and anger, Belleau whirled on Kavanaugh—and stared directly into the bore of the Bren Ten automatic. Confused and frightened, Honoré began to rise from her chair, but Mouzi kept her seated with a firm hand on her shoulder.

"Don't move," Mouzi ordered.

The pistol that appeared in Crowe's hand was another inducement to do as the girl said. Sputtering and coughing, Oakshott grasped the rail running the length of the boat and heaved his head and shoulders out of the water.

"Stay right there, tiny," commanded Crowe, leveling the M15 autopistol at his head.

Lips working as if he didn't know whether to yell, speak or laugh, Belleau's gaze jumped from Crowe to Kavanaugh to Honoré and then back to the gun in Kavanaugh's hand.

"What the bloody hell are you *doing?*" he finally managed to shrill. "Are you mad?"

"I'm royally pissed, if that's what you mean by mad," Kavanaugh said grimly. "We all are."

"What is happening?" Honoré demanded, bewildered. "Why are you doing this?"

"Ask the past president of the Lollipop Guild here," Kavanaugh said. "He's in on it."

"In on what?," Belleau asked, his eyes narrowed.

"Your pal Jimmy Cao just took Bai Suzhen prisoner," Crowe declared. "He and his Ghost Shadows are on their way to rescue you and probably kill us. For all we know, he killed Howard Flitcroft."

Honoré's face drained of color. Her *"What?"* was a ragged, aspirated half-gasp. "How can you know this?"

"Flitcroft told Bertram Pendlebury and Bertram told us," Mouzi said. "When we radioed him a few minutes ago."

Honoré started to rise again and when Mouzi held her down, she slapped the girl's hand away. "I didn't have anything to do with this."

"Me, either," McQuay said querulously. "I work for Mr. Flitcroft."

Oakshott grunted, fingers flexing on the rail. He peered

uneasily down at the surface of the river. "There's something swimming down here, mates…something large."

"Then it's probably best not to draw attention to yourself," Crowe said curtly.

Kavanaugh reached for Belleau's satchel but the little man hugged it close to his chest, turning away. "Don't touch me, Kavanaugh!"

"I want to see what you have in there, Aubrey."

"Nothing that concerns you."

"Except a satphone with a direct-dial option to Jimmy Cao. That concerns me very much."

"I'm warning you…don't trifle with me."

"I can guarantee you I won't be doing that." Kavanaugh put his hand on the handle. "Give it over, bad-ass."

Belleau's face molded itself into a mask of mad rage. He bared his teeth and bounded forward, head-butting Kavanaugh in the groin. Pain flared through his testicles and bile leaped up his throat.

Staggering back, Kavanaugh forced himself to remain erect, fighting the impulse to double over. He struck Belleau on the back of his head with the frame of the Bren Ten. Metal cracked loudly against bone and the little man fell to his knees, clasping his skull with both hands. He dropped the satchel and his walking stick rolled toward the edge of the dock and dropped into the water.

Honoré said angrily, "You don't have to abuse him!"

"Tell *him* that," Kavanaugh wheezed.

Repressing both groans and the urge to massage his crotch, Kavanaugh picked up the case and tossed it underhanded to Mouzi. "See what's in there."

She popped open the clasp, fished around inside and pulled out a satphone. She examined it quickly, then handed it to Crowe. "It's not powered up."

"Good. Cao can't get a fix on our position."

After feeling around inside again, she brought out a dark green metal box two feet long by two wide. The lid was secured by a small padlock. She shook it, listening to the contents bump against the interior walls of the container.

Kavanaugh prodded Belleau with the toe of a boot. "Get up. I didn't hit you that hard."

Belleau pushed himself to his feet and stood swaying for a moment, gingerly kneading the back of his head. He looked at his fingertips. They showed no blood. He glared at Kavanaugh with a pure, unadulterated hatred.

"You are a dead man, Kavanaugh," he said in monotone. "That's not a threat, either. It is a simple statement of fact."

Kavanaugh ignored him. Addressing Mouzi, he said, "Open that box."

"It's locked, Jack."

Kavanaugh stared down at Belleau. "What it's in it?"

Belleau only glowered.

Honoré said, "It's a journal, or a photocopy of one."

"Whose journal?" Crowe asked.

"He claims it's a secret journal of Charles Darwin, the lost log of the *Beagle*."

Crowe's eyebrows rose. "Do tell."

"There's also a vial of sludge in there."

Lines of puzzlement appeared on Mouzi's forehead. "Sludge?"

"He called it Prima Materia."

In a tone full of horror and betrayal, Belleau shouted, "*Honoré!*"

She spun to face him. "Honoré what?," she snapped. "You haven't played straight with me since you contacted me in Patagonia. I don't know what you really have planned but I won't be a party to it."

"I'm just here to shoot a movie," McQuay said faintly. "I work for Mr. Flitcroft. I don't want to get hurt any worse than I am now."

"Good," said Mouzi. "Behave yourself and you won't."

Kavanaugh gestured with his pistol. "Climb aboard, Aubrey."

Lips compressed, face stark and white, the little man did as he was told, sitting down in a chair astern.

"What about me?" Oakshott asked plaintively. "I tell you, there's something down here. It brushed my legs a couple of times."

Crowe tossed Mouzi a coil of yellow nylon rope. "Tie Pixie and Dixie up with some of those killer Maori knots you like so much."

Mouzi flashed him a devilish grin. "My pleasure."

Under the guns of Kavanaugh and Crowe, Oakshott laboriously pulled himself aboard the boat. It listed to port, but once the huge man stood dripping on the deck, he obediently put his hands behind his back. Mouzi swiftly began binding his wrists.

Honoré asked, "What are you gentlemen planning?"

"We're going downriver to lay in wait for the *Keying*," Kavanaugh said, jumping from the dock into the *Alley Oop*. He winced when a needle of pain stabbed through his groin.

"And then what?"

"That's all we've had time to come up with," said Crowe apologetically, turning his attention to the instrument panel.

"There will be more," Kavanaugh stated reassuringly. "Lots more."

"Of that," Honoré Roxton said dryly, "I have no doubt."

* * *

Sunlight shone down upon the hull of the Nautique in an intricately dappled pattern, filtered through the leafy boughs intertwined over the river.

Kavanaugh stood astern, studying the terrain on either bank as well as keeping his eye on Oakshott and Belleau.

Thick foliage grew right down to the water's edge. The prow of the cruiser cleaved through the rippling water smoothly, the big engine making a sound not unlike a protracted purr. The moisture-saturated air was tainted with the muddy, tropical fecundity of the jungle that brooded on either side of the

Thunder Lizard River. Mist floated above the surface in flat planes.

Mouzi sat with the metal box in her lap, trying to pick the lock with the tip of one of her butterfly knives. Belleau, his hands bound behind him watched her, his lips curved in a smirk.

"You won't be able to do it that way, young Miss Mongrel," he said.

Without looking up at him, she said blandly, "If I can't, then I'll shoot the lock off."

His smirk faded and Honoré said wearily, "Aubrey, if you have a key, why don't you just give it to her?"

"Why should I make anything easy for her?" he snapped. "Or for you?"

Honoré swiveled her chair away from him. "You're such a child."

Kavanaugh would have laughed, except he was too worried about Bai Suzhen. He felt the physical weight not only of the heat and humidity, but also of the vast rain forest itself.

Crowe maintained the *Alley Oop's* position in the middle of the river, trying to avoid passing beneath overhanging tree branches. Venomous snakes, face-hugging spiders, leeches and even nasty-tempered, diseased monkeys had been known to drop down on unwary boaters.

Within a couple of minutes of leaving the pier, the river flowed in such twists and turns that the banks behind them seemed to merge together to form an impenetrable thicket of greenery, shutting off any sight of the Petting Zoo site.

With Crowe at the wheel, and Honoré and McQuay seated amidships, the *Alley Oop* cruised past overgrown islets and narrow-mouthed tributaries. Kavanaugh's spirits lifted somewhat when the boat pushed through a profusion of huge butterflies wheeling over the water. Their orange and yellow wings fluttered with an almost strobing effect as they darted and skittered through the alternating bands of shadow and shafts of greenish sunlight.

After navigating another bend, the river broadened to a span of fifty yards. Kavanaugh kept watching both banks, thinking he glimpsed swift, darting movement in the underbrush. The faint whistling chirps he heard were voiced only by song birds, he told himself fiercely. Despite the heat, the back of his neck flushed cold.

"What is the depth here?" Honoré asked suddenly.

Crowe tapped a gauge showing green glowing digits. "Hard to get a true sounding because of all the debris on the bottom—fallen trees and boulders and the like. But I'd say the average depth on this stretch of the river is about twelve to eighteen feet...at least in the middle."

"Is that a sufficient depth for a junk the size of the *Keying*?" she inquired. "Without running aground, that is?"

Crowe shrugged. "The *Keying* is flat-bottomed, but it'll depend on how much weight she's carrying and how low her draft is."

"I can't understand why Jimmy Cao didn't come in his own boat."

"Ship. Cao's style of yacht has a fixed keel fin that could catch on anything under the surface and tear out her keel. She also has a higher mast profile than the *Keying*."

Metal clinked loudly against metal. Mouzi uttered a wordless snarl of frustration and held up her knife. "Broke the point."

"I told you so," Belleau said mildly. He glanced toward Kavanaugh. "Might I inveigh upon you for a drink of something wet?"

Kavanaugh smiled thinly. "You're asking favors of a dead man?"

"Thirst knows no classification, sir."

Reaching down into a small cardboard box at his feet,

Kavanaugh plucked out a bottle of water and unscrewed the cap. He stepped over to Belleau and tipped the plastic rim, putting it to his lips. "Say when."

As the man swallowed, sunlight glinted painfully from the golden stickpin piercing the collar of Belleau's shirt. Kavanaugh squinted away, then narrowed his eyes, giving it a closer look. It resembled a caduceus, a pair of serpents coiled around a staff topped by an eye within a pyramid.

Belleau leaned back. "Enough, thank you."

Kavanaugh screwed the cap back on and then snatched the stickpin from Belleau's collar.

"*Oy!*" the man cried. "What are you doing? That's my property!"

Revolving it between finger and thumb before his eyes, Kavanaugh replied, "I am aware, Aubrey. I'll give it back. What's this symbol?"

"Just a symbol," Belleau answered sullenly. "It has no significance. It's an heirloom. Please return it."

"*Please?*" Kavanaugh stared Belleau with exaggerated incredulity. "It must be damned valuable."

Honoré turned toward them. "Jack, I think that's the insignia of Aubrey's lodge."

"Like the Shriners or Elks?" Kavanaugh inquired dubiously.

"Nothing that mundane. He told me a bit about it. He called it the School of Night."

Crowe snorted and cast a glance over his shoulder, not taking his hands from the wheel. "Pretty over-the-top name for a men's lodge."

Kavanaugh handed the pin to Mouzi. "See if that little doohickey is really a key."

Mouzi examined it. "Looks about the same size."

She inserted the symbol into the base of the padlock and gave it a twist. With a little click, the lock popped open.

"Hey, presto," Kavanaugh said softly.

Belleau closed his eyes, as if by shutting out the sight, then he would not have to acknowledge to himself that the girl had managed to get the box open. Mouzi lifted the lid and took out leather-bound book, the dark front cover bearing no title or markings of any kind. She put it in Kavanaugh's outstretched hand.

Honoré moved up beside him, looking over his shoulder. He flipped open the cover. A glass tube was affixed to the inside by a metal clamp. Soldered metal and wax served as a seal. Kavanaugh took it out of the clamp and held it up to the light, tilting it to and fro. The substance inside the vial slid slowly back and forth.

Mouzi gazed at it with narrowed eyes. "Looks like phlegm or somethin'."

Honoré thumbed through the plastic-sleeved pages. "This appears to be part of the journal Aubrey showed me on the plane. There's a lot more here than he led me to believe."

"I'm sitting right here," stated Belleau diffidently. "You might ask me."

"Fine," Honoré said. "What's the difference between the journal I looked at on our way here and this one?"

Staring straight ahead, Belleau said, "What you have in your hands is the complete journal. Those are the original pages of the lost journal of Charles Darwin, protected within sheets of heat-sealed Mylar, as well as the suppressed log of the HMS *Beagle* as it pertains to the ship's visit here in May of 1836. It also contains the original drawings by Conrad Martens, the *Beagle*'s draftsman. There are also notations written by the *Beagle*'s physician, Dr. Jacque Belleau."

Kavanaugh cast him an inquisitive glance. "A relative?"

"My great-great-grandfather."

Mouzi stood up to peer around Kavanaugh's shoulder as he turned the pages. The yellowed parchment filled with florid, cursive penmanship looked exceptionally difficult to read. Honoré removed her wire-rimmed glasses from a shirt pocket and slipped them on.

Several of the pages held detailed drawings of Big Tamtung as seen from the sea, rendered in charcoal and ink. The quality of the work was very impressive.

"Doesn't look like the place has changed all that much since 1836," Kavanaugh commented.

"There's no reason why it should," replied Honoré. "No real estate developers have ever come calling, unless you count yourself and Captain Crowe."

Kavanaugh lifted a page by a corner, turned it over—and froze. All the moisture in his mouth dried up, leaving a foul tang on his tongue.

Inscribed on the page in ink was the head and shoulders portrait of a creature whose face consisted mainly of two huge eyes set in a round, hairless head. The skull resembled an inverted teardrop in shape, terminating in a long pointed chin and prominent underjaw. The huge eyes looked as big in proportion to its face as those of a tarsier's.

The nose consisted of a pair of flaring slits, and the pronounced maxillary bones gave the impression of a blunt muzzle. The wide, lipless mouth seemed stretched in a faint smile of superiority. A complex pattern of scalework pebbled the creature's long, tendon-wrapped neck.

"That's unique," murmured Honoré. "I'd almost say that it's an image of a Troodontid except that the cranium is too large and the snout isn't as pronounced as the fossil reconstructions."

Belleau snorted out a contemptuous laugh. "It's not a Troodon."

Honoré glared at him over the rims of her spectacles. "No?" she challenged. "Then what species is it?"

Shifting in his seat, Belleau stared levelly at Honoré. "Legends from all cultures have called it a Naga, a Sheti, the Anunnaki and even the Sarpa. But we've been calling it an anthroposaur."

"A what?" Honoré demanded.

"You heard me."

"Oh, I heard you—I just couldn't believe my ears. An anthroposaur? That's what you call it?"

Quietly, Kavanaugh stated, "Her, not it."

A sudden splashing from astern and a hoarse cry from McQuay made them sit bolt upright in their chairs, then they leaped to their feet.

Chapter Twenty-Two

McQuay cringed away from the rear of the boat, falling to the deck as he fumbled with his camera. "Something is in the fucking water! Something huge!"

Kavanaugh and Honoré stood at the gunwales, gazing at the water swirling with sudden movement, wavelets forming and cresting. A head resembling that of a crocodile broke the surface less than six feet away.

Its jaws were gigantic, nearly eight feet long, with thick masses of scale-coated muscle swelling at the sides of its triangular head. Its armor-plated hide was of a repellent gray-brown hue. Only dimly seen amid the churning waves created by its gargantuan body, the creature looked to measure out to at least fifty feet from its snout to the tip of its lashing tail.

The cold yellow eyes beneath knobbed ridges stared at them in silent surmise. It uttered a deep exhalation like a whale blowing, spray flying from dilated nostrils. The head and body sank beneath the surface, leaving only spreading ripples and a few bubbles to commemorate its appearance.

Clutching his camera, McQuay gasped, "I gotta change my pants! I gotta change my pants!"

Honoré declared matter-of-factly, "It looked like a *Sarcosuchus imperator*, a crocodilian...none of the fossil finds have been larger than ten meters in length."

Although she spoke with no discernible emotion in her voice, Kavanaugh noted her pronounced pallor and the way her hands trembled. "Maybe you'd better sit back down."

Apprehensively, Belleau asked, "Have you ever seen that thing before, Kavanaugh?"

"If I did, I probably thought it just a regular old crocodile. What about you, Gus?"

Still at the cruiser's wheel, Crowe shook his head. "Same here."

Mouzi's forehead creased with lines of worry. "Can it capsize us?"

Kavanaugh forced a condescending chuckle. "Of course not." He cast a glance at Crowe. "Of course not...right?"

"I wouldn't think so, but then I didn't think a goddamn pterodactyl could crash a helicopter, either."

"You like to fill a friend's day with sunshine, don't you?" Kavanaugh asked sarcastically.

The *Alley Oop* entered a stretch of turbulent rapids and she picked up speed as the prow clove through foaming white water. Crowe piloted the boat through the central cascade of the current, avoiding the largest rocks. Spray drenched them, but since the river water was only slightly cooler than the air temperature, the relief was minimal.

The Thunder Lizard River widened and the current quickened as it rushed over half submerged rocks. Brown and white foam splashed over the boat's prow. Kavanaugh returned the journal to the metal box, much to Belleau's obvious relief. Brightly plumaged birds, disturbed in their perches among the great fronded trees overhanging the river, squawked angrily.

Honoré peered upward as they took wing and exclaimed, "Hey, those are archaeopteryx!"

"Yep," Kavanaugh said shortly. "You didn't think Huang Luan was the only one, did you?"

When the current slowed, Crowe notched back on the throttle. "If we're going to meet the *Keying* halfway, we need to find a good spot to wait for her."

"You really intend to stage an ambush?" Belleau asked skeptically.

"Less of an ambush and more of a hostage exchange," replied Kavanaugh. "Whichever way it plays out, you'll have a front row center seat."

Belleau shook his head as if thoroughly disgusted. "You

arrogant Yanks with your fixations on shootouts and bush-whacks."

Crowe turned away from the cruiser's wheel. "If it disturbs you so much, we can dump your sorry mini-ass overboard right here. Then you can examine that prehistoric croc from the inside."

Belleau's lips tightened but he said nothing more.

Kavanaugh joined Crowe forward and they studied both banks of the river. "We can assume if Jimmy Cao hijacked the *Keying*," Kavanaugh commented, "that he has considerable firepower."

Crowe nodded. "The Ghost Shadows probably took con-siderable casualties, too."

"And," Mouzi put in cheerfully, coming to stand between them, "they don't know that we know they're on their way. So we have the edge with the element of surprise."

Crowe's lips quirked in a smile beneath his mustache. "That's always the best kind of edge to have."

"We still ought to have something resembling a plan," said Kavanaugh.

"I'm working on it," replied Crowe. "I'm a little out of practice."

On the right-hand bank, a copse of pagke trees rose on high roots like towers elevated by stilts. The last time Crowe had piloted past them, the river had been at flood stage and the roots were submerged. He examined the trees carefully, then pointed. "That one looks good."

He spun the wheel and held the cruiser's stern straight for an opening between a pair of roots arched like a cathedral doorway. He reversed the props, backing water into bubbling foam. Expertly, he eased the boat between the roots, the hull scraping the wood.

He keyed off the engine and as the boat bobbed in the shal-low water, Mouzi and Honoré cut broad leaves from overhang-ing branches, using them to camouflage the brightly-colored hull. Other than the sounds of cutting and snapping, the jungle was quiet. The late afternoon mist veiled the river and the marsh reeds on the far shore.

At a sudden startled cry from McQuay, Kavanaugh turned to see gray, leathery lumps of jelly pulsating on the right side of his bandaged head. Another leech had set its sucker into the base of his blood-crusted neck.

Belleau and Oakshott leaned away from the cameraman. "The ruttin' things dropped down from the tree!" blurted the big Englishman.

"They're attracted to the blood," Kavanaugh said calmly, picking up Mouzi's butterfly knife.

"Get 'em off, *get 'em off!*", shrilled McQuay, clawing at his head.

"Settle down," Kavanaugh said, using the edge of the knife to carefully scrape the leeches away and fling them overboard.

"How the hell do they smell blood?" demanded McQuay. "The fucking things don't even have noses!"

Kavanaugh didn't tell him that denizens of jungles the world over shared a supernatural awareness of the presence of blood. Leeches were no exception. Nor were crocodiles, prehistoric or otherwise.

Honoré examined McQuay's bandage and said, "You started yourself bleeding again. The dressing should be changed."

McQuay said, "I'm all right for the time being."

"Are you hungry?" she asked.

When he shook his head, she turned toward Belleau and Oakshott. "What about you two? Do you want something to eat?"

Belleau said stiffly, "No thank you."

Oakshott said, "I wouldn't mind some of that jerked beef."

"I'll feed him," Mouzi volunteered, taking her butterfly knife from Kavanaugh. "But if you get fresh with me, Jumbo, I'll fix it so you can't eat anything ever again."

Oakshott said, "There is no reason to be afraid of me."

"Yes, there is," Mouzi shot back. "I've seen you fight, in Bangkok. You play dirty."

Kavanaugh dropped into a seat, adjusting the Bren Ten in his waistband. "Now we wait."

Honoré sat down opposite him and reached for the metal case containing the journal. She opened the lid and removed the book, flipping to the page containing the drawing of the creature Belleau called an anthroposaur. "Why did you say this entity was a female?"

Kavanaugh opened his mouth to answer and then shrugged. "I don't know. Whatever I tell you won't sound very scientific."

"That's for sure," said Crowe, leaning against the console. "We always figured you were just out of your head from blood loss and shock."

"Or just out of your head, period," Mouzi put in with an insouciant grin.

Honoré thumbed through the pages. She paused at one, eyes flitting back and forth across the lines of handwriting. "According to this entry, Charles Darwin himself saw something very much like the bipedal anthroposaur creature, standing on the beach in the company of a theropod."

Belleau said, "Darwin claimed that a crewman was attacked by a Deinonychus and would have been killed except a bird's song seemed to distract it, drive it away."

Kavanaugh swiveled his chair to stare at the little man. "Bird song?"

Belleau smiled at him mockingly. "Does that sound familiar?"

Instead of answering the question, Kavanaugh glanced toward Mouzi who tentatively held out a chunk of beef jerky to Oakshott's lips. "Careful, honey. Don't let him bite you."

Belleau snickered. "If he did, I would imagine poor Oakshott would have to undergo a regimen of antibiotic shots."

Whirling on him, Mouzi put the tip of her knife against the hinge of his jaw. "What's that supposed to mean, Gollum?"

Oakshott started to push himself to his feet but Crowe said loudly, "Settle down, girls."

"Apologize to the young lady," Kavanaugh suggested.

Belleau didn't speak or even move. Only when Mouzi withdrew the knife from his throat did he say quietly, "I'm sorry, Miss. My remark was not only uncalled for but inappropriate and disrespectful. I hope you will forgive me. I used to be a decent fellow."

Mouzi nodded curtly and returned her attention to Oakshott. She shoved a piece of dried meat the size of a matchbook cover into his mouth. "Let your saliva soften it before you swallow it," she instructed, "or you'll choke. I'll be damned if I'll perform the Heimlich maneuver on you."

Honoré flipped back to the illustration of the anthroposaur. "You were saying, Jack?"

Kavanaugh dry-scrubbed his hair, sighed and said, "Cranston, Jessup and Shah Nikwan wanted dinosaur trophies, but they didn't want to risk their lives to get them. So they chose snufflegalumpus—the Hadrosaurs, which if any dinosaur can be compared to cattle, those are in it. So one afternoon, I took them up in the chopper and we landed about eighteen miles thataway."

He jerked a thumb over his right shoulder. "Near the tributary of this river, not much more than a stream."

"You said in your deposition that you didn't know they had guns aboard."

Flatly, he said, "I knew they did, even though I didn't see them until we landed and they all pulled out their custom .600 Nitro Express rifles. Elephant guns. I always carried a Winchester 30.30 whenever I went in-country. My old man's rifle."

Kavanaugh paused, his eyes growing vacant as if a veil passed before them. "It was about half an hour before sunset. The herd came out to drink at the stream. While I led the men over, I kept feeling like we were being watched, sized up, but not like by an animal. I don't know how to explain it but—I sensed intelligence."

Honoré's eyes widened. "A human intelligence?"

"Human level. I don't know about human."

"Are you sure you didn't imagine it?"

Kavanaugh smiled bleakly. "I'm not a very imaginative man, so I don't usually imagine much of anything. I used to be a fighter pilot in the Air Force and you don't get to be one of those if your mind has a tendency to play tricks."

She nodded in understanding. "Go on."

"By the time we got to where the snufflegalumpus—the Hadrosaurs—had gathered, it was just about sunset. I had the feeling that if we just turned around and left without firing a shot, everything would be fine. When I told Jessup, Cranston and Shah Nikwan that the deal was off, that we were going back, they looked at me like I was a lunatic. They threatened to ruin me, to ruin Gus and Mouzi if I interfered with them. So, because they'd paid me thirty grand, I went along with them, following the curve of the stream.

"Jessup was the youngest of the three idiots—about fifty— and the most impatient. He drew a bead on a Hadrosaur with a calf and fired. The animal went down. Then he killed the calf. The other animals got spooked and went running crazy, bawling and stampeding all over hell and gone. Nikwan and Cranston just opened up on them like they were in a carnival midway shooting gallery."

Kavanaugh paused, took a breath, held it then said, "Not to put too fine a spin on it, but they just shot the shit out the herd—adults, males, females, calves, wounding them, crippling them, maiming them. It was a slaughter. Those big bullets tore holes the size of my fist right through them…the way they screamed—"

Kavanaugh broke off, squeezing his eyes shut, lifting his hands as if to cover his ears. Belleau, with a surprising degree of civility said, "Not exactly sportsmen, I take it."

Opening his eyes, Kavanaugh shook his head. "Not unless you count the old-time buffalo hunters shooting from the backs of moving trains as sportsmen. Anyway, I can't begin to describe what happened next because even after all this time, it's still not clear. It was like being attacked by jumping shadows made of daggers or spears. They came out of the sunset, out of the underbrush, out of everywhere, all claws and fangs and shrieks."

"They?" inquired Honoré. "The Deinonychus pack?"

He nodded. "I'd only seen them from a distance before. Now they were all over the place, leaping, running, tearing. They moved faster than anything I'd ever seen, as vicious and as ruthless as monsters out of a horror movie. I managed to get off a couple of shots with my Winchester, then I was knocked down and ripped open. I had a knife and I fought back as best as I could. I killed one of them."

"What about the three men?" Belleau asked.

Kavanaugh didn't answer for a long moment, dredging up fragmented memories of Shah Nikwan, Jessup and Cranston firing their weapons in a frenzy. Nikwan ran pell-mell toward the distant helicopter, fleeing like a panic-stricken deer.

A Deinonychus caught up with the running man in one spring-steel legged leap. Its jaws closed over Shah Nikwan's head and the creature clutched the man in its arms as if it were embracing him. The Deinonychus chewed through his vertebrae, then let the man's head fall from its blood-flecked mouth. Nikwan's head tumbled across the muddy ground like an awkward ball. Hugging the decapitated corpse to its chest, the creature gathered itself and bounded from sight into the high reeds bordering the stream.

Kavanaugh wiped at the clammy film of cold sweat which had gathered at his hairline. He retained an exceptionally vivid recollection of the man's head rolling toward him, dead eyes wide with disbelief.

"Jack?" Honoré inquired.

Stolidly, he said, "All three of them died….ripped to pieces. Arms and legs torn off, disemboweled, even decapitated."

Reflexively, he fingered the scar on the side of his face. "I wasn't much better off. I could barely move, lying in a pool of my own blood, going into shock. Then I heard a bird singing… but it wasn't just a song. It was a voice. Or it was a song I understood, I don't know which. I never believed in telepathy or anything like that. But in my mind's eye, I saw her."

"Her?" echoed Honoré.

"Her. She had skin like a snake's hide and it shimmered with every step she took." Kavanaugh broke off, swallowed hard and said in a rush, "I don't know if I actually saw her or not, or if she transmitted an image of herself. But I knew she had sent the Deinonychus pack to drive us away. I was spared because she sensed I objected to the slaughter of the Hadrosaurs. I also knew she was not just a female, but the last of her kind, and females of her breed had been worshipped as goddesses by humans, thousands of years ago. She told me to get up and run...to never to come back...and that if I *did* come back, I would die."

Honoré arched skeptical eyebrows but did not speak.

"I don't know how I got there," Kavanaugh continued, "but the next thing I knew, I was climbing into the chopper. I had enough presence of mind to bring one of the raptor's bodies with me, as evidence. Even though I was in shock, I managed to fly back to Little Tamtung. The rest you know."

Crowe said quietly, "When I opened the chopper hatch, I couldn't tell where the blood ended and Jack began. I still can't understand how he lived or stayed conscious long enough to take off, fly and land."

Belleau drawled, "Well, now you've come back to Big Tamtung, Kavanaugh. What do you figure she'll do to you?"

Kavanaugh met the little man's eyes. "I couldn't say...but I know this much—if Bai Suzhen is hurt, I'll arrange it so that whatever happens to me will happen to you."

Oakshott glared at him, chewing slowly, with Mouzi still standing over him, knife at the ready.

Apparently oblivious to the upsurge in hostile energy, Honoré flipped through the pages of the journal, then stopped. She squinted. "These pages are written in French."

"Yes, by my great-great-grandfather," Belleau said.

Honoré turned to the next page and asked, "Did you ever see anything like this, Jack?"

He leaned close to her, their shoulders touching. An illustration of four square, squat stone columns dominated the page. Even though the image was rendered in charcoal and ink, Kavanaugh could tell that inestimable centuries of weather had pitted and scarred their surfaces so that the glyphs inscribed in them were barely visible. In the background he could discern a suggestion of ruined buildings. In the center of the cluster of structures was a pool or pond.

"According to what Jacque Belleau wrote," Honoré stated, "He came across ruins and a dark green pool. Apparently, he was following a map."

"A map?" repeated Crowe in surprise. "Where did he get a map of Big Tamtung's interior in the 19th century?"

Honoré cast Belleau a challenging glance. "You know, don't you, Aubrey?"

"Of course I do," Belleau said pridefully. "I memorized my great-great-grandfather's notes on his visit to this place."

The little man cleared his throat and quoted, " 'I would like to say that the columns and the buildings were built of sun-dried brick, but I am not sure of their composition. I judged they were many thousands of years old. However, there was none of the grace of say, classical Greek architecture. They seemed closer to Egyptian, perhaps even Sumerian or even a blend of all those styles.'"

"Is that what it really says?" Kavanaugh asked Honoré.

Tracing the lines with a forefinger, her lips moving as she read along with Belleau's recitation, she nodded. "Substantially, although the elder Belleau preferred to express himself in a vernacular form of French that has long since gone out of style."

"What was so special about the pool?" Crowe asked.

Belleau quoted, " 'Charles so often cited warm little ponds as being the source of all life on our world—if only he had been able to plunge his hands into the pool of primeval matter and let the very sperm of the earth run through his fingers. Ah, it was an experience like no other. Just holding the Prima Materia in my hands made me feel like a god!

"The cryptogram decoded by Brother Dee and Edward Kelley has led me to the greatest discovery in Mankind's history. It has come to pass that the School will safeguard the means of humanity's next evolutionary step, if only Charles agrees to remain silent.' "

"What the hell is all that gibberish about, Aubrey?" Kavanaugh demanded.

"I'd like to know about that myself," said Honoré. "What cryptogram was your great-great-grandfather referring to? Who is Brother Dee?"

Belleau hitched around in his seat, inclining his head toward the illustration on the journal page. "Do you see those inscriptions on the pillars?"

Honoré eyed them critically. "Yes."

⅂Ↄ ⅃ Ɓ ⍩ ⅂ ⅄ Ↄ

"What do you make of them?"

"They're not hieroglyphics or cuneiform. They almost look Greek."

Belleau chuckled. "They are letters in what is known as the Enochian alphabet. Most scholars and historians believe it was a coded language created by Dr. John Dee and his seer Edward Kelley during Elizabethan times."

"I read something about that," Crowe said. "Dee was a secret agent for Queen Elizabeth, right?"

Belleau smiled appreciatively. "You surprise me, sir. Yes, John Dee acted as something of a spy for the queen and was well-known for concealing secret messages in fiendishly complicated cryptograms. However, he did not create the language known as Enochian. Withal, he did spend most of his adult life trying to decode and translate it."

Honoré stared at the glyphs on the journal page, turning it this way and that. "What language is it, then?"

"Dee often referred to the alphabet as 'Adamical', because he theorized it was spoken by Adam and the early Biblical patriarchs. In reality, it is a language that predates humanity's first written records. It's a *pre*-Adamical alphabet."

"Talk sense, Aubrey," snapped Honoré.

"I am attempting to do that very thing, darlin'." Belleau's smile broadened. "The alphabet is called Enochian because the patriarch Enoch was reportedly the last man to have ever spoken it. You do know who Enoch was?"

"A Biblical prophet, I think."

Belleau nodded. "Enoch is mentioned in Genesis as the son of Cain and the father of Methuselah, and he is believed to be one of the antediluvian patriarchs who, along with Noah, personally 'walked with God'. Books written by anonymous scribes were credited to Enoch and were given great credence by early Jewish scholars. They influenced the writers of the Old Testament. Parts of the books of Enoch were found among the scraps of parchment in the caves of Qumran in 1947, having been placed there nearly 2,000 years before by the Jewish sect known as the Essenes."

"The Dead Sea Scrolls?" inquired Crowe.

"Yes…and although most of the books credited to Enoch were written in Aramaic, there were many scrolls rendered in the so-called Enochian alphabet. It was not code, but the actual language of a race of non-human creatures that once shared our planet with us—what some scientists have classified as the anthroposaur."

Before Honoré, Kavanaugh or Crowe could even begin to formulate a response, Mouzi's head whipped toward the river, her eyes narrowing, body tensing, as if she were a hunting cat that had caught a scent.

"Hear something," she whispered. "The *Keying* is coming."

Chapter Twenty-Three

"About half a mile downriver," Mouzi said. "Little less, maybe. Not travelin' fast, about five knots, max."

No one questioned the quality of Mouzi's hearing. Crowe swiftly examined the satphone, then pressed the power button with a thumb. With an electronic chirp, the surface of the phone lit up with various icons.

He stood over Belleau and said, "I'm going to hit the redial. I'm betting you'll be connected right to Jimmy Cao."

"And if I am?" Belleau's tone held a hard, defiant edge.

"Then you'll talk to him and tell him about your situation. But do *not* tell him where you are."

Belleau shrugged as best he could. "Fine."

"Don't think you can pull something over on us by talking to him in any other language but English." Crowe smiled menacingly. "I may not look it, but I'm multi-lingual."

"I would have taken you for a Baptist," Belleau muttered. "Of course, you realize that Mr. Cao wants both Bai Suzhen and myself. Separately, we are useless to him."

Kavanaugh made a show of popping the magazine out of the butt of the Bren Ten and sliding it back in. "We realize that, Aubrey. It's up to you to convince Cao that trading Bai Suzhen for you is an equitable exchange."

"But it isn't," Honoré protested. "Jack, while I certainly can't blame you for being angry with Aubrey, if this triad fellow went to such violent lengths to bring Bai Suzhen under his direct influence, he won't agree to give her up."

"We'll see." Crowe touched the redial icon and listened as the call was conveyed to a satellite and then to another telephone unit, less than half a mile away.

A man's voice, rich with suspicion but also pitched high with anger filled Crowe's ear. "Belleau, is that you?"

Crowe put the phone to Belleau's ear, but leaned close so he could listen in. "Hello, James. This is Aubrey Belleau."

"Where the hell are you? I've been trying to call you for over three goddamn hours!"

"I am on Big Tamtung. My helicopter flight ended with a bit of a mishap, stranding me here. Where might you be?"

"On my way to pick you up. I was told you were at the Petting Zoo place, is that right?"

Belleau evaded answering the question. "You are on a boat?"

"Yeah, the *Keying*, that junk of Bai Suzhen's. We're already coming down the river. According to her, we're about five miles from the Petting Zoo. Are we?"

"Is Bai Suzhen with you?"

"Yeah, she's right here. I'm keeping my eye on her." The suspicion in Jimmy Cao's voice acquired a sharper edge. "What about the people with you on the flight? Kavanaugh and Crowe and that scientist bitch you've got the hots for?"

"We're all just waiting to be rescued."

"Uh huh." Cao's tone turned abruptly non-committal. "They're standing all around you, aren't they?"

"Yes. They have proven to be the proverbial flies in the buttermilk."

"What?"

"They have it in their heads that once Bai Suzhen signs over her interests in Cryptozoica Enterprises to me, you'll kill her and probably them, as well. Therefore, since Madame White Snake can't sign the paperwork without me, they're not inclined to allow me to join you."

Cao didn't reply a long moment. Then he asked, "That man Kavanaugh—Tombstone Jack—is he there?"

"He is."

"Let me talk to him."

Crowe hesitated, then handed the phone over to Kavanaugh. He whispered, "Jimmy wants to speak with you."

Kavanaugh took the satphone. "This is Kavanaugh."

"You stupid bastard," Cao snarled, his voice made so guttural with rage that it was almost unintelligible. "Do you have *any* idea of who you're fucking with here? You got a death-wish, putting yourself in the middle of this?"

"What happened to Howard Flitcroft, Jimmy?"

"I killed him. Shot his ass dead and threw him over the side. He sleeps with the fishes, just like you and your friends will if you keep fucking with me."

Kavanaugh's hand squeezed the phone so tightly the molded plastic and metal creaked within his grip. "You're not offering much in the way of inducements to cooperate with you."

"Fuck cooperation! This isn't a bargaining table—"

"—I beg to differ," Kavanaugh broke in coldly. "You need both Bai Suzhen and Aubrey Belleau to complete the deal. I have one, you have the other. You really need to start bargaining."

Cao said nothing for such a protracted length of time, Kavanaugh wondered if he had dropped the call. Then, in a dispassionate voice, he said, "I'm not just going to turn Bai Suzhen over to you."

"And I'm not just going to turn Belleau over to *you*. So we've got a Shanghai stand-off here."

"I'm Taiwanese, asshole."

"Good for you. The best bet all around is for you to back water, reverse course and go back to Little Tamtung. We'll follow you in a few minutes."

"Follow me?" Genuine surprise shook Cao's voice. "How?"

"There's a boat here at the Petting Zoo. We have it running and we were just waiting to hear from you."

"So once I get back to Big Tamtung, then what?"

"We meet at the Phoenix of Beauty and have a formal paper-signing ceremony, all neat and legal with armed witnesses to make sure nobody gets out of line."

"And after that?"

"Everybody goes their separate ways, me included. You and Belleau can spend the next couple of years trying to outswindle and backstab one another."

"Why would we do that?"

Kavanaugh chuckled patronizingly. "Oh, come *on*, Jimmy—you know that if Belleau has told you this island is worth a hundred fortunes, you damn well can bet that it's really worth a couple of *thousand* fortunes."

"What do you know about it?" Cao demanded.

"We'll discuss that later. Do we have an agreement?"

Jimmy Cao's weary sigh whispered into his ear. "All right. I'll give the orders to turn us around."

"One more thing—I want to talk to Bai."

"No," Cao snapped.

"You talked to Belleau," Kavanaugh pointed out reasonably. "It's only fair. Quid pro quo."

Cao didn't reply. Kavanaugh heard a rustle, a muffled voice, then Bai Suzhen said, "Jack?"

"Are you all right?"

"More or less," she said calmly. "They haven't hurt me—much. What is going on?"

"Jimmy will fill you in. I just wanted to tell you that I've always admired you as a dancer."

"Thank you," Bai Suzhen said, sounding only a little puzzled.

"The way you're able to think fast on your feet, jump and back flip at a moment's notice is very impressive. That's true art, you know."

"Thank you," she replied again.

Cao's voice came back on the line. "What a bunch of bullshit. Okay, you talked to the dirty lesbian bitch, now let's get on with this."

"See you back on the island, Jimmy." Kavanaugh clicked off the connection, ending the call, but kept the satphone's power on.

Honoré asked, "Can't he use a GPS trace to pinpoint our position?"

"He thinks he can," Kavanaugh said. "But a GPS lock isn't as precise as the manufacturers want you to believe. We're too close to him. All Cao knows is we're on the island, but not exactly where. I'm hoping he assumes we're still at the Petting Zoo."

"What was all that blather about admiring Bai Suzhen's skills as a dancer?" Belleau demanded.

"Never mind." He turned to Crowe. "We'd better get ready for the party."

Without a word, Mouzi took the Kel-Tec SU-16 carbine and cradling it in her arms, crept out along the gunwales to the prow of the boat and stretched out on her stomach. She cycled a round into the breech.

Honoré watched the activity with a tight, strained expression. "Do you really intend to shoot at these triad fellows?"

"They certainly intend to shoot at us," Kavanaugh replied, flicking off the safety of his pistol. "They'll kill us if they can, make no mistake about that. The Ghost Shadow triad has a rep for hiring homicidal maniacs. If we had a peaceful alternative, we'd take it. But since we don't—"

Facing Honoré, McQuay, Belleau and Oakshott, Kavanaugh announced, "Things will become more than a little wild in a few minutes. We can't afford to have people onboard that we can't count on. I'm putting Aubrey and Oakshott ashore. Dr. Roxton, McQuay—I'll give you the option to share the risks."

The cameraman glanced at the overgrowth beyond the line of pagke trees and swallowed hard. "I think I'll share your risks."

"Me, too," said Honoré .

Belleau's face twisted in a mask of revulsion. "You can't be serious! Just leave us here to our fates? You can't do that!"

"Sure we can," Crowe said casually. "But don't worry—we'll untie you first."

Belleau cast a beseeching glance at Honoré. "You can't let them do this—"

"—She has nothing to say about it," broke in Crowe harshly.

Honoré said, "Aubrey, I don't pretend to understand what

you really had planned here on Big Tamtung, but I know one thing—you've played me false from the beginning."

"And on that note," Kavanaugh said breezily, hauling Belleau and Oakshott to their feet by the collars of their shirts.

With Mouzi's butterfly knife, Crowe cut through the ropes binding their wrists and then pushed Oakshott toward the railing. "Over the side."

The big man gingerly threw one leg over the edge of the boat, then slowly slid overboard. The river barely reached his waist. He said, "It's fine, doctor."

Belleau stepped to the side and gestured to the journal. "Please look after that."

Honoré nodded. "I will."

Aubrey Belleau awkwardly climbed over the side, into Oakshott's waiting arms. "The water is quite warm," the big Englishman said soothingly.

"And therefore the perfect breeding ground for parasites and bacteria," Belleau said bitterly.

Carrying Belleau like a child, Oakshott waded to the riverbank, grasping a root as a handhold to pull himself onto a hummock of grass and reeds.

Putting the journal back into the metal case and securing the clasp, Honoré said, "I'm sure it must have occurred to you that they may be no safer there than here."

"It's not their safety I care much about," rasped Crowe, turning the cruiser's ignition key

The engine purred to life, the props slowly churning the water. Kavanaugh stared at the GPS tracking screen on the satphone. "No change in their position," he said "Which doesn't necessarily mean anything."

"We'll hold position here until we have a visual," Crowe said, removing a compact set of binoculars from a drawer beneath the console.

Squinting downriver through the eyepieces, Crowe noted how the mist thickened, floating above the water, wreathing the surface with vapor. The fog felt like the touch of a clammy hand on his skin. A distant sound floated to him, vague and watery.

Out of the vapor a shadow appeared. Crowe stiffened, squinting as the shadow shape resolved into a looming, elongated outline. At the edges of his hearing he heard a distant, rhythmic throb which he recognized as the growls of twin diesel engines.

"There's the *Keying*," Crowe said, pushing the throttle forward.

The *Alley Oop* slowly eased from beneath the pagke tree and into the river. Despite the scraps of fog, Crowe's eyes still probed ahead. The cruiser hugged the bank for fifty yards, reeds whispering along the hull. The thudding of the *Keying's* pistons grew loud, far louder than the drone of the Nautique's engine.

Lying among the leaves and twigs on the cruiser's prow, Mouzi sighted down the length of the carbine at a dark silent figure standing on the deck of the junk. She figured he was a lookout, but not doing a very good job of it. He wore a black-and-white headband. She lined him up between the front and rear sights of her rifle, waiting for the man to spot the boat sliding almost soundlessly through the mist.

Suddenly, he leaned forward, stared and whirled around, mouth opening to voice a warning. Mouzi squeezed the trigger. She leaned into the recoil, letting the hollow of her shoulder absorb it. The shot sounded lackluster, like the breaking of a twig. There was nothing lackluster about the man's reaction to the impact of the bullet punching him between the shoulder-blades. Throwing up both arms, he screamed loudly and fell forward, out of sight.

Crowe slammed the throttle to full and the cruiser's engine bellowed. The boat lunged toward the *Keying*, its prow rising like the snout of a killer whale diving toward helpless prey.

Chapter Twenty-four

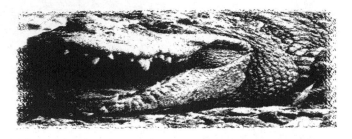

Gunfire crashed from the mist. A bullet tore splinters from the railing to Bai Suzhen's right. Jimmy Cao screamed orders in Cantonese and Mandarin. The *Keying*'s crewmen dropped flat to the deck while the Ghost Shadows came racing from all directions. The man in the pilot house wrestled with the wheel, turning the junk to starboard. He was not as experienced a pilot as Bai's man and had difficulty steering the boat.

Bai stood with Jimmy Cao on the foredeck. Despite the bore of the Casull revolver the man pressed against her ribs, she kept her face completely expressionless, except for an anticipatory glitter in her dark eyes. She instantly grasped Kavanaugh and Crowe's strategy—with their boat almost hull to hull with the *Keying*, the Ghost Shadows would have no choice but to expose themselves in order to effectively exchange shots with their attackers.

A bullet fired from a Ghost Shadow thumped the air between her and Cao. The man instinctively ducked, relaxing his grip on her arm. She exploded into motion.

She yanked free of his fingers, her right hand stabbing out and securing a handful of greasy black hair. Jimmy Cao's mouth opened but before he could scream or curse, she kicked upward, her left foot chunking solidly between his legs. Convulsively, he plucked at his crotch. She released his hair and he fell to his knees. At the same time, she grabbed his wrist, twisted and pulled the big Casull revolver from his grasp.

A man reached for her from behind, but she spun on her toes, the edge of her left hand chopping at his throat. The Ghost Shadow staggered away, trying to bring up the jian sword he had stolen from Pai Chu. She squeezed the trigger of the pistol and shot him in the chest, the heavy round bowling him off his feet. As the sword fell from his fingers, Bai snatched it from the air and whirled on the four men converging around her. She swung out with the jian, her arm curving up, then crossways across a man's torso. Blood sprayed as the Ghost Shadow lurched backward, careening into two his comrades.

Bai Suzhen moved with the deadly speed and grace of a cobra. She swept the blade at the three other men, spattering them with crimson droplets. They backed away. Anger possessed her, but not to the point where she became careless. The Ghost Shadows sidled around her, circling, their attention torn between the gunfire erupting from the cabin cruiser and the pistol in her hand.

The *Keying* surged at an angle across the river, the bow turning to starboard. Vines and low-hanging branches snagged in the masts, saplings snapped against the junk's bulwarks. There came a grinding, sucking sound as the vessel's flat bottom dragged in the mud of the shallows. The junk ran aground on her starboard side. The deck shuddered underfoot and men staggered, stumbled and fell.

Bai managed to stay on her feet. With a running leap, she gained the top of the portside railing. She paused for an instant, standing tall and straight, her taunting smile much like the enigmatic smile of the Naga princesses on display in her quarters.

Struggling to his feet, one hand cupping his testicles, Jimmy Cao screamed, "Kill the bitch!"

A subgun rattled as a Ghost Shadow panicked and fired a burst at nothing at all. Bai jumped from the *Keying* and landed on the leaf-shrouded prow of the *Alley Oop* a little less than six feet directly below her. She bent her knees to absorb the impact and threw herself forward, but the heavy revolver in her hand skewed her balance and she slid to the right.

Mouzi steadied her with a hand to her wrist.

"Thank you," breathed Bai.

The girl flashed a smile and went back to squeezing off shots with the carbine. A Ghost Shadow who ran along the railing slapped at his left leg, staggered and pitched headfirst into the water only a few yards away.

The man's arms flailed as he reached out for the hull of the *Keying*. A great sheet of foam-crowned water flew upward behind him. He abruptly vanished, snatched beneath the surface.

A heartbeat later, he reappeared, rising from the river, red water pouring from his open mouth. A pair of giant, fang-filled jaws clutched him at the hips. The Sarcosuchus lifted the screaming, writhing man high above the surface. His legs kicked in a futile spasm as the muscles at the hinges of the creature's jaws flexed. The huge fangs sheared through the man's flesh, crunching against, then pulverizing his pelvic bones. The upper half of his body splashed down into the river. The lower half slid down the monster's gullet, swallowed in two snapping gulps.

Mouzi cried out in wordless fear at the sight of the huge Sarcosuchus and adjusted the aim of her carbine, centering the sights on what she could see of its head, but she hesitated to fire. Once blood spread through the water, predators who hunted along the riverbanks would be drawn to their position.

The men crowding at the *Keying*'s rail howled with terror and directed their gunfire at the enormous crocodilian. It submerged quickly amid a flurry of bullet-driven water spouts.

Crowe yelled, "Mouzi, Bai! Hang on!"

Spinning the wheel to the left and gunning the engine, the *Alley Oop* surged away from the junk, the Sarcosuchus and the screaming men who fired their weapons in a mad frenzy.

The two women crouched down on the prow.

When the cruiser swung around a slight bend, out of direct range of the subguns, Crowe eased off on the RPMs, allowing Mouzi and Bai Suzhen the opportunity to climb back into the cockpit. The gunfire from the direction of the *Keying* tapered off and ceased altogether, although they could still hear men yelling.

Pistol in hand, Kavanaugh said casually, "I guess you understood my message."

Bai smiled slightly. "I'm somewhat surprised Jimmy Cao didn't understand it, too. Subtlety is not one of your strong suits."

Honoré's analytical gaze flicked from the woman to the man and then focused on the bruise darkening the side of Bai Suzhen's face. She asked, "Are you all right? Do you need medical attention?"

"An aspirin wouldn't be out of line." She looked around the boat and asked, "Where is your colleague, Dr. Belleau?"

"We put him ashore," Kavanaugh said. "If Jimmy Cao wants him so much, let him find him."

Bai shook her head. "We can't let him fall into the hands of the Ghost Shadows. Belleau is our only ace, our only source of information on the real agenda behind all this madness."

Mouzi handed the woman two aspirins and a bottle of water. "What agenda?"

Bai Suzhen swallowed the aspirins, washing them down with a swallow of water. "That's the point. I don't know. United Bamboo has apparently turned its back on my triad. My men and Howard Flitcroft have been murdered and I want to know what it's about."

"Mr. Flitcroft is really dead?" Honoré asked.

Bai nodded tersely. "His body was weighted down and thrown overboard, as were those of all of my crew who were murdered."

"Howie managed to get a warning out to Pendlebury," Crowe said. "Who got it to us. If he hadn't, we'd all have probably been killed by now. I can't say that I ever thought Howie was anything other than a jerk—"

"—But he was our jerk," Kavanaugh interjected grimly. "We won't let his killer get away, I can promise you that."

From his chair astern, McQuay said, "So after all this, everybody just ended up trading one for the other, didn't they?"

"More or less," Kavanaugh said. "Did you get of any that

shootout on tape?"

He shook his head, smiling abashedly. "'Fraid not. I was too busy ducking. Besides, I came here to shoot prehistoric monsters, not gang wars."

Bai asked, "Where did you leave Belleau and Oakshott?"

Crowe gestured upriver to the copse of pagke trees rising from the shoreline on their left. "Over that way. They couldn't have gotten far."

The *Alley Oop* cruised past a small island rising near the mouth of a narrow channel on the right-hand riverbank. It was thick with mud, marsh reeds and dead tree branches.

As the boat purred past it, a vile odor tickled Kavanaugh's nostrils. Absently, he fingered his nose, then realized the effluvium had a familiar scent.

Crowe reacted to the stench and glanced toward Kavanaugh. "You smell that?"

The small island of reeds and plant matter rustled violently and then arose, heaving itself out of the shallow water. A deafening bellow exploded from directly behind them, a mist of water spraying in all directions. Semi-liquid mud streamed down, splattering against the vinyl roof covering.

Beneath a layer of muck and gnarled twigs, grinning jaws bared double-rows of yellow fangs. The massive head reared fifteen feet above the deck of the *Alley Oop* .Two huge legs, as big around as pagke tree roots, supported its massive, barrel-shaped trunk. Tri-fingered forelegs tipped with six-inch long, scimitar-curved talons were held close to its chest. Its wet hide bore a golf ball-like pattern of pebbled, dark yellow scales.

Huge, soulless eyes, like those of a serpent's a hundred times magnified stared down from beneath arched, knobbed protuberances. A narrow ridge of bone rose from the center of the snout and extended to a point just above the pair the dilating nostrils. Thick swellings at the sides of its head told of the great muscles that worked its maw.

Although rooted in place by shock, Honoré Roxton breathed, "Majungasaurus."

The creature extended its massive head on the end of a long neck, opened its jaws wide and voiced a grunting roar. An odor like that of decomposing meat mixed with an open septic tank washed over their faces.

"*Stinkosaurus!*" shouted Crowe, reaching for the throttle.

Chapter Twenty-Five

The sound of the *Alley Oop's* engine rose in pitch and the craft churned forward. The Stinkosaurus leaned over so its upper body was parallel to the river, its forelegs lashing out.

Crowe spun the wheel, veering to port, but the creature's three-fingered forepaws slapped against the stern of the Nautique, the long talons penetrating the fiberglass, vinyl and steel hull with loud squeals and pops. The saurian gripped the boat tightly, as it slowly straightened up, water sluicing down its armored hide. In the suffused sunlight, the creature's scales glistened like a coating of molten metal.

The boat tipped upward, the bow rising like a whale leaping from the depths. A great geyser of water spumed from the engine as the vessel's stern was pushed beneath the surface. Everyone staggered, grabbing chair-backs and handrails. McQuay screamed as he clutched at a chair with one hand but kept the other on his camera. Everyone else added their own panicky shouts to his screams.

Bai Suzhen lifted the Casull, but the deck underfoot pitched violently and she fell to one knee. She was forced to drop the pistol to keep from sliding astern. The revolver skittered down, but Honoré scooped it up with her right hand.

The predator's head dipped forward and its massive jaws closed on McQuay's torso. Screaming in agony and terror, McQuay was torn away from the chair and lifted upward. His shrieks ended abruptly when the creature shook his body violently from side to side, like a puppy would shake a chew toy. Trapped between the tooth-lined vise of the creature's jaws, the man's arms and legs flopped as if they were filled with paraffin.

Bracing her feet against a chair-back, Honoré held the pistol in a two-fisted grip and squeezed off a pair of booming shots. Even at virtually point-blank range, the heavy caliber rounds did little damage to the monster's upper thorax. She could not draw a bead on the Stinkosaur's eyes, its really vulnerable points, because of the way it wagged its head to and fro.

But the bullets stung it, and drew little patches of blood on the scales. With a liquid snarl, the creature drew back, releasing its grip on the *Alley Oop*. The keel splatted against the surface and the boat shot forward wildly, like a cork spewed from a champagne bottle. Crowe fumbled with the wheel, trying to turn it. The bank, thick with marsh reeds, rushed up with appalling swiftness

The boat plowed through a mud-flat, rocking to a halt when the prow skated upward at thirty-degree angle, wedging itself between a gnarled pagke root and a thicket. The engine stalled, acrid black smoke curling up from the enclosed inboard module.

Kavanaugh struggled to his feet, helping Mouzi up. Bai, Crowe and Honoré slowly stood, shaken and very nearly paralyzed by shock. Silently they stared at the Stinkosaurus standing in the center of the river, examining the bloody corpse of Chet McQuay hanging limply in its paws. The man was only recognizable as a human because of his dangling arms and legs. His upper body resembled a crimson-seeping mass of freshly slaughtered beef, gutted and flensed.

The creature's head bobbed up and down, rolling its tongue within its maw. Kavanaugh was reminded of the way his childhood dog, Ajax acted after he had been given a peanut butter sandwich.

Then, with a sound like a man sneezing but many times

amplified, the animal spit out a small object. It sailed across the river and splashed down in the shallow water very near the boat. Before it sank out of sight, they recognized McQuay's treasured Sony ENG camcorder.

In a voice pitched low to disguise the tremor of fear running through it, Crowe said, "We'd better get the hell out of here before Stinky remembers us."

"I thought the vision of those Tyrannosaurs was keyed to motion," Kavanaugh whispered.

Honoré shook her head. "That's only a theory and a specious one at that. Besides, it's not a Tyrannosaur…it's a Majungasaur, of the family Abelisuridae and sub-family of Carnotaurinae. Late Cretaceous fossil remains have been found on the Indian subcontinent and Madagascar. While the animal is occupied, we should quickly and quietly collect everything useful and make ourselves scarce."

The five people carefully recovered their weapons, the first-aid kit, the metal case containing Darwin's journal, several bottles of water and the box of power bars. Crowe removed an emergency survival kit, a tightly latched waterproof vinyl box. While they worked swiftly and methodically, the Majungasaur seemed content to stand in haunch-deep water and nibble at McQuay's body.

The crunching of fangs into bone and the moist sound of flesh being chewed seemed unnaturally loud to Kavanaugh, but he hoped the noise would cover the scuff and scutter of their activity. He felt bile rise in a burning column in his throat when the giant saurian ripped out a chunk of cloth, flesh and viscera from McQuay's midsection and tugged at the intestines as if they were strands of pasta.

Honoré Roxton's face paled by several shades and her lips turned the color of old ashes, but she maintained a composed and controlled expression. But to Kavanaugh's surprise, Mouzi looked as if she were on the verge of fainting or throwing up or both.

One by one, they climbed out of the upward-canted *Alley*

Oop onto the marshy riverbank. Crowe said softly, "We still have Belleau's satphone, so we can call for help."

"The trick is to stay alive until help arrives," murmured Bai Suzhen, holding her appropriated jian sword in her right hand.

As Mouzi clambered out of the boat, carrying both the carbine and the first-aid kit, she put her foot down on a slippery stretch of reeds. She stumbling, sliding down the bank toward the river. As she tried to regain her balance, her finger closed around the trigger of the carbine.

Although the shot went ricocheting up into the trees and wasn't overly loud, the Majungasaur jerked erect with a startled snort. Its head swiveled on its neck like a gun turret. Everyone froze in mid-motion.

The carnotaur stared at them unblinkingly for so long that Kavanaugh began to wonder if Honoré's dismissal of the vision-keyed-to-movement theory wasn't too hasty. Then, the loose flesh at the animal's throat vibrated, and from its blood-flecked lips issued a hissing, rumbling snarl. The Majungasaur thrust its head forward, opened its jaws wide and voiced a ferocious roar that combined the worst aspects of a trumpet, steam valve and the howl of a dying dog. Its tail swept back and forth, whipping the water to froth.

"Ah, *shit*," rasped Crowe.

The Majungasaur dropped McQuay's mutilated corpse into the water and charged the riverbank with long, hopping steps. Water splashed in sheets before it.

"Run!" shouted Honoré, wheeling around. "Try to keep among the trees!"

The five people plunged into the rain forest, ducking under a canopy of overlapping ferns. The carnivorous dinosaur clawed its way up the bank, making a panting noise like a laboring engine.

The Majungasaur pounded across the ground toward them, lowering its head and opening its jaws wide, crashing through the undergrowth, showers of leaves flying in its wake. The ground shook to the saurian's thundering tread, the clawed feet tearing up great clods of earth, its counterbalancing tail held straight out behind it.

Kavanaugh glimpsed Honoré stumble and nearly fall, catching herself on a tree. She dropped the case holding the Darwin journal. The carnotaur turned its head toward her. Kavanaugh whirled around, diving low, knocking Honoré off her feet into the brush. Both of them rolled and tumbled, head over heels. Unable to slow its charge, the gigantic reptile crashed into the trunk of a tree with a splintering impact, stumbled and wallowed clumsily in a copse of vegetation.

Honoré and Kavanaugh staggered to their feet. More quickly than either person expected, the Majungasaur untangled itself and with a roar of fury, pivoted around to face them. Kavanaugh fought down a surge of panic. Although he had proved his courage hundreds of times in his life, the creatures of Big Tamtung did not seem like animals—they were like demonic forces unleashed from some unknown, nameless hell that pursued him for their own vicious reasons.

Honoré and Kavanaugh turned and ran. Ferns and thorns whipped at them, the needled tips of coniferous shrubs scored red lines across their arms and faces. Drooping lianas snagged at their necks and heads, but they fought free.

Behind them thundered the reptilian leviathan. Ripped up by the taloned feet, divots of the soggy earth pattered down all around like a rain. His lungs straining with the effort of breathing in the thick, humid air, Kavanaugh warred with the fear that ate away at his nerves like acid.

He and Honoré burst through a barrier of foliage, ignoring the sting of thorns on their bare arms and hands. The monster came crashing after them like an out-of-control locomotive.

Over the pounding of the creature's footfalls and their own hearts, they heard the snap-and-crack of gunfire. The Majungasaur's charge slowed and it turned to bite at the place on its thigh where a bullet struck. From somewhere in the forest, Crowe and Mouzi shouted wordlessly, trying to draw the animal's attention. It lurched to a halt and snarled, then licked at the bullet wound with a black, slimy tongue.

Kavanaugh and Honoré raced through a cluster of ferns, slapping the fronds aside—and nearly pitched into empty space. They dug in their heels, grabbing one another, rocking to clumsy stops. Directly in front of them the lip of a gully sloped downward for twenty feet. At the bottom of it spread a very smooth and invitingly open space of dark green.

Panting, sweat stinging his eyes, Kavanaugh said, "Maybe we can lose that goddamn thing down there."

Too winded to respond, her breasts rising and pressing against her perspiration-soaked shirt, Honoré shook her head. Bending over, she picked up a rock and tossed it down to the floor of the gully. It splashed against the green expanse and sank from view.

Swallowing hard, hands resting on her knees, she husked out, "Quagmire."

"Bad for us *and* old Stinky." Kavanaugh drew his Bren Ten from its clip-on holster at his waist.

Honoré stared at him uncomprehendingly through the tangled screen of her hair. She started to speak, coughed, turned her head, spat, and asked, "You mean to lure it down there?"

Kavanaugh nodded. "I don't think we'll be able to get away from it for very long. Listen—"

They heard the tramp of heavy feet, the crash of undergrowth and deep-throated, snuffling grunts.

"It's hunting us, sniffing us out," Kavanaugh continued, dropping his voice to barely a whisper. "Even if we sneak past it and hook back up with the others, it'll get wind of our scents and stalk us wherever we go."

"How can you be so sure of that? When did you become an expert on carnotaur behavior?"

Kavanaugh drew in a breath, common sense and pragmatism overwhelming the residue of panic. "I'm not, but I've been around this part of the world on enough hunting parties and expeditions to get a good idea of predator psychology. Do you know how Komodo dragons hunt?"

"No.".

"Like Stinky, they rely mainly on scent and what's known as a 'Jacobosen's organ', a vomeronasal sense. That means, with a favorable wind, they can sniff out prey up to six miles away. They're stalkers by nature, they take all the time they need. They're patient…they don't mind waiting. In fact, they've been known to get ahead of their prey and then charge out from ambush. Stinky apparently has an issue with one of us—and I'm betting it's me."

Honoré straightened up, raking her hair out of her eyes. "Majungasaurs and Komodo dragons aren't motivated by personal vendettas, Jack."

"Maybe not…but maybe whatever—or whoever—is nudging Stinky along has one."

Honoré blinked at him in confusion. "Are you proposing that this attack was *planned?*"

"And the kamikaze dive of the Quetzalcoatlus and maybe even the Sarcosuchus."

"I think you've been out here in the tropics so long, you've let your imagination run rancid. There was blood in the water, remember, and McQuay's wound had begun bleeding again, too. You said yourself that the Stinko—Majungasaur—hunted around the river banks."

"Yeah, but I never heard of one camouflaging itself before."

"That was probably due to foraging at the shoreline and it just picked up a covering of detritus by accident. I'm sure that wasn't a deliberate act."

"I wish I could be. What's that old saying: 'once is happenstance, twice is coincidence and three times is enemy action'?"

"That applies to mobsters in Chicago, not dinosaurs."

"It doesn't matter," Kavanaugh replied impatiently "What *does* matter is we're going to have to take action if we plan to stay alive on this island long enough to get off it—unless you just enjoy running around screaming like an extra in a Japanese monster movie."

"No," she stated stolidly. "I do not."

"All right. Let's go do something about it. How many bullets does that cannon you're packing have in it?"

Expertly, Honoré popped open the cylinder, spun it, slapped it back into place and announced, "Two."

"Let me handle the musketry, then."

As silently as they could, they retraced their steps, alert for any sounds, but they heard nothing but the inquisitive cheep of birds. They entered a small glade and looked all around.

Worriedly, Honoré said, "Perhaps it decided to give up on us and go after Captain Crowe, Mouzi and Bai Suzhen."

Kavanaugh nodded as if he considered the possibility, and turned slowly around, on the verge of calling out for Crowe. He had just opened his mouth when the Majungasaur crashed through the foliage, running at full speed with its head low, jaws wide in an unmistakable posture of attack.

Honoré cried out incredulously, "It was laying in wait for us—!"

The two people heeled around and began a frantic dash again. The monster bellowed behind them, a roar so loud and full of fury it hurt their ears. They plunged on through brush, trying to not waste time or risk a misstep by looking over their shoulders.

Kavanaugh and Honoré sprinted among fern trees, tearing their way through clumps of shrubbery. When they reached a copse of evergreens, the two people tried to disorient the snarling saurian by ducking around trees and leaping over fallen trunks. The carnotaur stumbled to a clumsy halt, its huge splayed feet trampling the spongy ground. It snapped viciously at Kavanaugh as he jumped over a log, its jaws closing around it and splintering the wood.

Kavanaugh bounded toward another tree and the Majungasaur followed him. Even though Honoré shouted and waved her arms, she failed to distract the animal from coming after him.

He slid around another tree and the thickly muscled, scale-sheathed tail of the creature battered deep into his midsection, slamming him off his feet. All the breath left his lungs in an agonized bleat between his teeth.

Kavanaugh was only dimly aware of collapsing to the ground, but he knew the monster's open jaws hovered above him. Although his vision was blurred, he saw the salvia-slick fangs champing only inches away. It was like glimpsing a slow-motion scene from a bourbon-fueled midnight nightmare.

Through the pain haze swimming across his eyes, he caught a foggy impression of Bai Suzhen bounding forward, her long sword upraised. She slashed at the creature's right flank, scoring a shallow, scarlet-leaking gash through the pebbled pattern of its scales. Voicing a sibilant snarl of anger, the Majungasaur spun toward her. She tried to run in the opposite direction of the monster's turn, but the long lashing tail clipped her at ankle level. Her legs swept out from beneath her, she hit the ground heavily on her back, with none of a dancer's grace.

Kavanaugh forced himself to his knees. He braced the Bren Ten with his left hand and squeezed the trigger. The reports of the pistol were far less loud than the scream of pain erupting from the throat of the carnotaur as the bullets punched dark little dots into its upper back.

Crowe appeared from behind a tree and fired his M15 General Officer's autopistol in a steady roll. Screeching, the Majungasaur lurched away from the hail of gunfire, wheeling around to face Mouzi, who triggered the carbine at its head. The two people arranged themselves to make the giant saurian the apex of a triangulated crossfire.

In a volcanic convulsion, the creature pivoted, bending almost double as its tail whiplashed against the trunk of a tree with sledge-hammer force. Flinders of bark flew from it and showered Mouzi with wood chips, driving her to cover.

Kavanaugh stepped forward, firing his pistol even though he knew shooting at the animal's body would have little effect. He could waste an entire clip trying to hit a vital organ. Only a head shot, through the eye into the brain, had any chance of killing the thing. The monster's sibilant snarling took on a high-pitched, keening note. Then the firing pin of the Bren Ten clicked dry on an empty chamber.

The Majungasaur turned toward him, and he leapt to the left, barely avoiding a pair of vicious, disemboweling swipes of the saurian's feet. Honoré jumped from behind a tree, the Casull in hand.

She worked the trigger of her pistol, holding it in a double-fisted grip, sending out booming shock waves of ear-shattering sound. The impact of the two steel-jacketed blockbusters against its left thigh sent the Majungasaur staggering sideways.

The creature continued to turn in the direction Honoré's bullets slammed it, spinning around and swinging its tail laterally. The tip struck Honoré a glancing blow on the right hip, knocking her headlong to the earth, the pistol bouncing end over end from her hand.

The carnotaur lifted a big, hook-clawed foot, preparing to stamp on the fallen woman. Yelling at the top of their voices, Crowe and Mouzi marched forward shoulder-to-shoulder, firing their weapons in tandem. To Kavanaugh's surprise, the creature recoiled from the barrage, stumbling backward.

Without hesitation, Kavanaugh heaved Honoré up from the ground and began running. He half-carried, half-dragged the dazed woman, the toes of her boots barely touching the earth as he bore her along. Within seconds he heard the snap of twigs and crash of shrubbery as the huge saurian rushed after them, like a ship pushed in front of a hurricane.

"Jack!" Crowe shouted. "What the hell are you doing?"

Kavanaugh didn't have the spare breath to explain. Honoré recovered sufficiently to do her own running. She put her feet down and sprinted flat-out. She panted, "This is *insane!* It should have retreated once it was wounded, run from all of us!"

"Told you," he husked out. "Personal."

They ran through the tangle, ducking and dodging, zigging and zagging, as if they were following a trail left by a broken-backed snake. They heard the Majungasaur's crashing progress through the undergrowth and its panting grunts of exertion.

Kavanaugh hazarded a quick, backward glance and glimpsed the animal still loping along behind them. The dull reverberations of the heavy footfalls slamming repeatedly against the ground sent little vibrations shivering up their spines.

The two people tore their way through a intertwining of vines and tottered on the lip of the gully, only a few meters from where they first emerged. Breathlessly, Honoré said, "How do we know it'll find us—"

Amid an explosion of leaves, twigs and jungle flowers, the Majungasaur burst through a wall of foliage, giving vent to prolonged, eardrum-compressing roar. Honoré and Kavanaugh sprang to one side just before the animal was upon them.

Roaring in maddened fury, the carnotaur dug in its hind claws, blundering to a halt at the edge of the gully, loose leaves and loam cresting up in front of it like a loose carpet. It teetered on its toes, tail held up straight behind it as it see-sawed back and forth, trying to regain its balance.

Kavanaugh lunged out from the brushline and delivered a fierce kick to its rear end. Snarling , the Majungasaur tipped forward, then it toppled headlong down the slope of the gully, rolling and thrashing, the weight of its body causing a dozen miniature avalanches. Its great hind limbs kicked spasmodically as if it were running in place.

At least five tons slapped into the quagmire. The impact sent mud cresting in a fountain, splattering Kavanaugh and Honoré. Very quickly the Majungasaur sank flank-deep into the mud, but it continued to flounder and flail.

Wiping the muck from her eyes, Honoré said hoarsely, "If it wasn't personal between you and Stinky before, it is now."

Chapter Twenty-Six

Honoré peered through the view-finder of the Nikon, brought the right forepaw of the Majungasaur into focus and pressed the shutter button. Unlike the first few times, it did not react to the high-pitched whine of the digital camera. It remained motionless, trapped in the bog, flies swarming over its blood and mud-coated body.

The creature panted noisily, eyes closed against the insects crawling over them. It assumed the attitude of dignified patience common to many injured animals. A big dragonfly, its carapace glistening like wet jade, landed atop the Majungasaur's head, its broad wingspan lending the saurian the impression of wearing a hair bow.

Honoré looked at her watch, suddenly realizing she had lost all sense of time since the chopper crashed on Big Tamtung. She he was shocked to see it was past six o' clock. At least a lifetime and a half felt like it had passed since first climbing into the helicopter.

The trees of the jungle were still, even birds and monkeys stayed silent as if they feared drawing the attention of the helpless Majungasaur. She wiped at the film of sweat on her forehead, desperate for an ice-cold ginger beer. Her shirt was plastered to her body, soaked through with perspiration. The humidity enclosed her without mercy. She tugged her shirt from the waistband of her jeans, unbuttoned it and knotted the tails beneath her breasts. The relief from the heat was negligible.

She wasn't sure if the temperature or post-adrenalin come-down made her entire body feel leaden. Anxiety about Belleau was at the forefront of her mind. Despite her anger at the little man, she couldn't help but worry about Aubrey. The pursuit and gun-battle with the Majungasaur should have drawn his and Oakshott's notice, regardless of how far they had walked from the riverside.

She looked toward the distant ramparts of the escarpment, rising from a shroud of haze above the treeline. She recalled Sir Arthur Conan Doyle's novel *The Lost World*, and the fabled plateau in Amazonia upon which prehistoric animals still frolicked. If what Belleau had told her held any truth, then she was standing in the actual Lost World, the real-life inspiration for Maple White Land.

Nor was the irony lost on her that she shared the surname with one of *The Lost World's* major characters, the big-game hunter Lord John Roxton. Although the Majungasaur was definitely big-game, she reminded herself with a wry smile, it had done the hunting of the Roxton this time around.

At the sound of rustling foliage, Honoré turned to see Kavanaugh and Crowe emerge from the brush. She smiled gratefully when she saw her Stetson in Crowe's hand.

"Thought you might want this," he said, passing it to her. "It's only a little stamped on."

"Thank you," she replied, brushing dirt from the crown and settling it on her head. "A ridiculous accoutrement I admit, but it helps me stand out in the crowd from the mob of celebrity paleontologists and naturalists."

Kavanaugh gestured toward the Majungasaur. "Stinky seems to have calmed down."

"I think he exhausted himself trying to escape. Did you bring anything to drink?"

From a back pocket, Kavanaugh removed a bottle of water and handed it to her. As she unscrewed the cap, she asked, "What about everybody else?"

"In pretty good shape," Crowe answered flatly. "Mouzi is backtracking, looking for the Darwin journal. Bai is limping, but nothing is broken."

Honoré eyed Kavanaugh. "What about you?"

"What about me?"

"You took quite the clout to the gut from Stinky's tail."

He shrugged. "Yeah, well...the fat absorbed the impact."

After taking a long swallow of the tepid water, Honoré said, "If you're hurting, best say so now. We can't have you collapsing on us."

"She's right," Crowe agreed

Kavanaugh pulled up his T-shirt. His belly was fairly flat, but a livid purple bruise stretched across it. Honoré winced and reached out with tentative fingers. Backstepping a pace, Kavanaugh tugged down his shirt. "It looks worse than it is."

"Hard to believe. Have you found any sign of Aubrey or Oakshott?"

Crowe shook his head. "No, but we haven't been looking very hard either. It's going to be dark in a couple of hours and we need to find a defensible place to spend the night."

"Do you think that Jimmy Cao fellow will try to sneak up on us?" she asked anxiously.

"I doubt it," Kavanaugh said. "The *Keying* has run aground on the opposite side of the river. Even though they have a couple of skiffs, most of those triad soldiers are too superstitious to paddle across so close to nightfall...especially with a fifty foot long prehistoric crocodile swimming around waiting for them to do that very thing."

"Speaking of prehistoric crocodiles," Crowe said, stepping to the edge of the gully, "why didn't it attack Stinky? The croc is actually bigger than he is."

"Stinky is under average size for a Majungasaur," replied Honoré. "Which makes a certain amount of sense... isolated populations of large animals tend to become smaller. The hippopotami in Madagascar became pygmies, for example. Elephant remains found in Sicily showed they had declined to the size of German Shepherds."

Crowe nodded. "Large animals trapped in small regions

downsize to maximize their population versus their food supply…but most of the dinosaurids here are damn big."

Honoré gestured toward the Majungasaur. "Stinky is still considerably different physically than most of the fossil reconstructions I've seen."

"What do you mean?" Kavanaugh asked.

"For one thing, his rib cage is more narrow and compressed than the standard specimen from the Cretaceous. That large flexible area between the thorax and the pelvic girdle allows him to have a long stride and be able to swivel from the hips to grab prey. We saw first-hand how maneuverable he can be. Even his neck is longer, and not quite as squat, which makes me think that Stinky might be a closer relation to a Tarbosaurus than a T. Rex."

"He looks like a T. Rex to me," muttered Crowe.

"There's a superficial resemblance. Most Tarbosaurus fossils have been found in Asia. The structure of their neck vertebrae was more elongated than the conventional T. Rex."

"Oh," Kavanaugh said, repressing a smile. "Conventional T. Rex, right."

Honoré pointed. "What I find the most intriguing is that even though the forelimbs are still small in comparison to the rest of its body, they're substantially longer than those of its Cretaceous ancestors, by nearly a quarter of a meter…not to mention that most Majungasaur fossils have only two fingers on their forepaws, and Stinky has three like the Giganotosaurus.

"Note the coloring of the scales, how they vary from yellow to medium brown to black. It's a sophisticated way of using shadows as natural camouflage…carnotaurs were thought to employ ambush tactics."

She tapped her nose. "That bony extension on its snout is part of the olfactory area and is probably full of air."

"Air?" echoed Crowe.

"The air spaces probably helped to lighten the load of the Majungasaur's skull, making it about 18 percent lighter than if the head were a solid structure. A fully fleshed-out T-Rex head likely weighed more than 500 kilograms…1,100 pounds, while the skull of a Majungasaurus might weigh 70 pounds. Neck muscles and can only support so much cranial heft.

"So if all the other features remained the same, the weight savings from having the air-filled pockets may have allowed T-Rex and Majungasaurus to have jaws that were the largest of any land animal, and capable of exerting incredible pressure… even a casual bite is around two tons per square inch.

"For that matter, perhaps the extension is used for long-range communication with others of its type, much in the way elephants communicate through infrasonic rumbles, too low for the human ear to hear."

Alarmed, Kavanaugh looked around. "Do you think it could call for help?"

Crowe shrugged. "Why not? There has to be more than one Stinkosaurus on the island."

"Exactly," said Honoré. "It would be a small breeding population, but apex predators tend have their own widely separated territories and only come together during mating season. There's nothing in the fossil record that—"

Honoré's voice trailed off. She uttered a jittery little laugh. "I can't believe I'm standing here, doing a comparative analysis between fossil reconstructions and an actual living specimen of a Majungasaurus. The only word for it is…humbling. Aubrey was right…here on Big Tamtung, the past has *not* stopped breathing. I feel like I'm in shock…or in a dream."

"Taking all that into account," ventured Crowe, "you think there's still been a form of evolution taking place here?"

"Not a form," Honoré said firmly. "Evolution is evolution. However, the changes aren't as dramatic as one would think, particularly after the passage of sixty-four million years. Aubrey suggested quantum evolution as a possible explanation, but I find that unconvincing."

"Quantum evolution?" Kavanaugh repeated.

"Yeah," said Crowe. "It's a theory that has gained some acceptance among biologists and geneticists. The main thesis is that the basic goal of any organism is to survive in its environment and reach an age where it can reproduce and pass on its genetic code, and any newly acquired mutations, for one more generation. In a closed ecosystem such as this one, any mutations would eventually achieve a state of equilibrium."

Honoré nodded thoughtfully. "That way, mutations are accumulated over time in the gene pool of any given species of any organism. Since not all mutations are created equal, only those that are beneficial to the organism, or only those that are *selected* for, are passed on to the next generation. Those are the mutations that do not negatively impact the organism's ability to survive in its environment."

"So," Kavanaugh said, "there wasn't an environmental reason for the dinosaurids to mutate in a dramatic way…they're already suited to survive in this environment."

Honoré absently brushed a strand of sweat damp hair away from her cheek. "True, but even that explanation doesn't take into account all of the—"

In the distance came a crack, like the breaking of tree branch. Honoré, Kavanaugh and Crowe reacted with surprise, heads turning in the direction of the sound. Another crack came and this time they recognized it as the report of the carbine. Crowe plunged toward the brushline.

"*Mouzi!*" he exclaimed.

*　*　*

Mouzi moved cautiously through the sunlight-splashed fringe of jungle and into the gloomier vaults at the edge of the rain forest. She was alert for venomous spiders, scorpions and even pythons hanging from low branches. She wasn't too worried about leopards, since any that might have been in vicinity high-tailed it to safer quarters once the Stinkosaurus came thundering ashore.

Although she had grown up in a ghetto, Mouzi possessed a natural affinity for the wilderness. She felt the most comfortable with herself when out-of-doors, relying only on her senses to get by. She carried the carbine over her right shoulder, finger resting on the trigger guard.

The sun shafting through the leaves of the trees cast a dappled pattern of shadow on her sweat-filmed bare arms and legs. Her tank top was so wet with perspiration it adhered to her body like a second layer of epidermis. Her small breasts thrust tautly against the damp fabric. However, she did not feel uncomfortable.

The dimensions of the ancient rain forest, where time had no meaning, reached out and embraced her. As far as she was concerned, the animals populating Big Tamtung were not freakish survivors of a bygone epoch. They belonged here on the island, whereas human beings did not—except for her, she told herself smugly.

Mouzi stumbled slightly in a depression on the ground. Looking down, she saw deep parallel tracks that had squashed and flattened the vegetation on the jungle floor. The outside edges of the prints showed the impression of huge splayed, three-toed feet.

Mashed down in the center of one print, lay the metal-case containing the so-called Darwin journal. Bending down, she dug the box out of the ground with her fingers. Although slightly warped and compressed, it looked intact.

She worked it loose of the damp earth and pried open the lid. The journal lay inside without so much a scuff mark on the leather cover.

"I'll take that, thank you."

Mouzi spun in the direction of the voice, raising the carbine at the same time her eyes registered the figure of Aubrey Belleau standing only a few yards away. An arm encircled her neck from behind, yanking her up and off her feet. Instantly, but with an accompanying surge of shame, she realized she had been outfoxed., distracted by the dwarf while Oakshott crept up behind her.

The giant grasped the carbine by the barrel, wrestling it

from her grip. She resisted, and squeezed the trigger twice. The echoes of the shots were swallowed up by the dense screen of the forest.

Mouzi back-kicked, fiercely clawed behind her with her fingers, and tried to sink her teeth into the forearm at her chin. She felt a thick thumb probe, then press into a nerve cluster below her right mastoid bone.

Oakshott released her and she fell to all fours, gasping in pain, every muscle tingling. A hundred needles felt like they pricked her neck and she wondered if the big man had dislocated vertebrae.

Then the pain and weakness ebbed. Raising her head, her heart trip hammering, she saw both Belleau and Oakshott standing nearby, paying little attention to her. Belleau examined the journal while Oakshott swiftly checked the rifle's box magazine, counting the rounds, then slamming it back in place.

"Only four bullets, doctor," he intoned.

Belleau nodded distractedly. "I doubt we will have to use more than one to get our point across."

Mouzi rose shakily to one knee, her neck aching fiercely. "What point?"

Belleau glanced at her as if slightly surprised she could speak. A chill finger stroked her spine when she saw how the man's bright blue eyes brimmed with anger and even hatred for everyone whom he could not bring under his direct control.

"The point," Belleau said softly, patronizingly, "is about who is in charge on this island."

Mouzi slowly got to her feet, not wanting to give Oakshott the satisfaction of seeing her massage her neck. "That's who again?"

Belleau smiled. "Perhaps we should demonstrate by ridding ourselves of redundant personnel…like you, for example."

Mouzi's lips twisted in a sneer. "And you said you were a decent fellow."

"Actually, I said I *used* to be a decent fellow," Belleau corrected. "I learned over the years that decency can only be measured on a sliding scale."

"Mouzi!" Crowe's voice floated to her, as well as the crackle and rustle of underbrush. "Where are you?"

Mouzi opened her mouth to reply, then glanced questioningly at Belleau. He nodded. "By all means, respond to the gentleman."

"Over here, Gus," she called. "Belleau is here, too!"

Belleau's smile widened. "Excellent. Now if you would be so accommodating as to kneel with her hands behind your back…?"

Anger blazed through her. "Not a fuckin' chance."

Belleau inclined his head toward Oakshott. "See that she cooperates."

Swiftly, Oakshott reversed his grip on the rifle and pounded the butt into the back of right knee. Agony flooded through her leg and it buckled beneath her. She cried out, thinking for a couple seconds the joint had been broken. Her senses swam, and her surroundings blackened at the edges.

When they brightened again, she became aware of movement, the thud of footfalls and the rasp of labored respiration. Lifting her head, she blinked back the pain haze and saw Oakshott aiming the carbine at Kavanaugh, Crowe and Honoré Roxton. The three people did not look happy, although Belleau's teeth gleamed in a vulpine grin of triumph.

"It's about time you got here," he said. "It's nigh onto evening and I'm wanting my supper."

Chapter Twenty-Seven

The pistols in the hands of Crowe and Kavanaugh trained on Oakshott. For a long moment, the tableau held, then Honoré asked, "Are you all right, Mouzi?"

The girl nodded, grimacing in Crowe's direction. "M'okay. Thanks for asking."

"Sorry," grunted Crowe, eyeing Oakshott warily. "But I kind of got distracted by the rifle pointed at my stomach."

"What's the deal, Aubrey?" inquired Kavanaugh. "A reprise of the finale of *The Good, the Bad and the Ugly?*"

The man's brow wrinkled in confusion. "I'm afraid I don't understand."

"It's a movie starring Clint Eastwood," Honoré said curtly. "Considered a classic of the so-called 'Spaghetti Western' genre…it ended with a three-way gunfight. None of the participants knew who was going to shoot first."

Belleau's eyebrows rose. "Ah. In this instance, I definitely know who is going to shoot first. Oakshott—"

Immediately, the giant swiveled the barrel of the carbine, aligning the bore with the back of Mouzi's head.

"Gentlemen, I suggest you drop your weapons," Belleau continued.

Crowe and Kavanaugh hesitated, exchanging brief glances, and dropped the pistols at their feet. They took steps back, raising their hands.

"Thank you," said Belleau. "Oh, there's no reason to raise your hands. This isn't one of your pasta-themed western movies. We're all going to have to rely on each other from hereon out."

"What does that mean?" Honoré asked suspiciously.

"Permit me to bring you up to date. Although Oakshott and I didn't witness your assault upon the *Keying*, we definitely saw the aftermath, safely hidden behind a tree. I was quite entertained to see you pursued so single-mindedly by the Majungasaur. It was a sight I shall never forget."

"That makes several of us," Crowe commented.

"I presume poor Mr. McQuay wasn't as fleet of foot as the rest of you?"

"You might say that," bit out Honoré.

"Where might the delectable Bai Suzhen be?" asked Belleau. "Not percolating in the beast's digestive tract, I hope, since we still have business to complete."

Kavanaugh shook his head. "She's all right…nursing a sore ankle. We were about to go back to where she's waiting for us and scout out a decent campsite for the night."

"Capital idea." He gestured grandly. "Lead on, please."

Honoré scowled at him defiantly. "Aubrey, I hope you have considered the consequences of your actions. What do you think you can accomplish with these tactics? Bai Suzhen will never agree to sell her shares of Cryptozoica Enterprises to you. Your partner, Jimmy Cao abducted her and murdered many of her crew, including poor Howard Flitcroft."

Belleau stared at her uncomprehendingly for a long moment. Then he asked faintly, "Murdered him?"

Honoré nodded. "That's what she told us."

Belleau snorted out a derisive chuckle. "And you believed her? My darlin', naïve Honoré…Bai Suzhen is of the same class as James Cao. She's a harlot turned professional criminal. Why would you take her word for anything?"

Kavanaugh said flatly, "Bai is not a liar, Aubrey…unlike some midgets I could name."

Belleau's eyes glinted with anger, quickly veiled by an insincere smile. "Lead on, Kavanaugh. Let's be off."

Oakshott tapped Mouzi with the barrel of the carbine. "That means you too, you little mongrel."

Mouzi slowly rose to her feet, wincing at the pain in her knee. Then she smiled sweetly at Oakshott. "This mongrel may not have big teeth, but she knows exactly where to bite."

Belleau collected Crowe and Kavanaugh's pistols, checked the loads and sighed in exasperation. "Empty, both of them. I'm surprised at you gentlemen, ex-military men, too. Don't you know enough not to run a bluff with unloaded guns?"

"We're a little out of practice...we'll know better next time," Crowe assured him.

The walk back to where Bai Suzhen waited for them wasn't a long or particularly difficult stroll. They followed the torn up ground left in the wake of the Majungasaur's pursuit.

Bai Suzhen sat with her back to a tree, wrapping her right ankle with an elastic bandage taken from the open first-aid kit. When she saw Oakshott and Belleau among the people, she reached out for her sword.

"Ah-*ah*," Belleau said. "There's no need for that, Madame. We're all in this together."

Bai's eyes were grim as they swung from left to right and fixed on the carbine in Oakshott's hands. "Then why do you hold my friends at gunpoint?"

Aubrey Belleau fluttered a dismissive hand through the air. "Some are more in this together than others. Are you able to travel?"

"If I can't?"

"Then you'll be left behind."

"Where are we going?" Honoré demanded.

"To the south...to find more salubrious ground than this to spend the night. We should do so while we still have light to see. Where might my satphone be?"

When no one answered the question, Belleau said mockingly, "Please don't tell me you lost it somewhere or that it was eaten by the carnotaur...because I won't believe you and Oakshott will punish Miss Mouzi Mongrel for your mendacity."

To emphasize his words, Oakshott laid a big hand atop Mouzi's head, the spread of his fingers entirely spanning her cranium. His grip tightened perceptibly and Mouzi drew in a sharp breath.

Her face expressionless, Bai Suzhen reached behind her and produced the satphone. Belleau took it from her with a gracious bow. Oakshott released Mouzi. Kavanaugh extended a hand to Bai, but she affected not to see it, rising to her feet by the use of her sword, as if it were a cane.

The people divided the equipment among one another, although Belleau burdened himself only with the metal box holding the Darwin journal. Bai limped, but she managed to maintain the pace without complaint.

"Madame," said Belleau, "I'm told you saw Mr. Cao murder Mr. Flitcroft."

"Among several others," she replied dispassionately.

"If true, I find that disquieting and not a little confusing as to his motives."

Kavanaugh made a scoffing sound. "Use your head, Aubrey. With Flitcroft dead, the Ghost Shadow triad is in a better position to leverage complete ownership of Cryptozoica Enterprises."

"Perhaps, but if he's convicted of murder—"

Honoré whirled on him, eyes bright with contempt. "Who is going to bear witness against him?"

Belleau's mouth pursed as he weighed her words, then he shook his head. "Academic, at this point."

"You hope," stated Crowe darkly.

The seven people wended their way among the endless columns of immense buttressed morabukea and greenheart trees. The trees grew to great heights and the crowns were so dense that they seemed to be one continuous canopy. Broken tree trunks lay on the ground covered with garland-like vines. Purple orchids hung from branches and now and then ill-tempered monkeys screamed at them from above, pelting them with fruit rinds and feces.

The abundance of plant life produced a musty perfume that tickled everyone's nostrils and even the backs of their throats.

Belleau consulted a small compass he took from a pocket and urged them all to keep walking south. Oakshott brought up the rear, not aiming the appropriated carbine at anyone in particular, but everyone felt the pressure of the bore at their backs.

After forty minutes of walking in the last of the light, Kavanaugh pointed out a pair of giant trees that had fallen crossways, forming a serviceable enclosure. Crowe and Mouzi built a fire with matches taken from the survival kit and collection of dry twigs. Mosquito repellent was passed around. Very quickly, the night surrounded the small fire with varying shades of purple and indigo. Huge moths swooped and fluttered around the firelight. Cicadas and tree frogs carried on lively conversations through inquisitive chirps and croaks.

As the people shared power bars, beef jerky and bottled water, they heard the coughing snarl of a leopard, the snort of a tapir and a mournful, trumpeting bellow that seemed to go on and on.

Honoré glanced anxiously in the direction the sound had come. "I believe that was the Majungasaurus—calling for help to get out of the bog."

"Perhaps summoning a mate for aid?" suggested Bai Suzhen, the firelight dancing on the golden swell of her breasts beneath her partly unbuttoned silk blouse. She was scratched and bruised and muddied like the rest of them.

"Are they intelligent enough to do that?" Mouzi asked.

Belleau said, "Perhaps if the theropods are warm-blooded, they're probably more intelligent than they've been given credit for."

"They couldn't have been all that smart," Kavanaugh said, "since most of them are extinct."

"Actually," Honoré replied, "the island itself might explain how why a group descended from Cretaceous dinosaurs survived…if there was a sudden cooling due to the K-T extinction event, these animals migrated to warmer climes and stayed put."

"Until a scientific study is conducted on the animals

here," Belleau said, "there is no way to gauge their degree of intelligence."

A thunderous crashing arose in the underbrush and briefly the ground trembled as with heavy footfalls. The cicadas and crickets instantly stopped calling to one another. Everyone fell silent, wide-eyed, until the sound of its crackling passage faded, all of them knowing that whatever the creature was, it had to be powerful and unafraid to make its way through the forest with so little attention paid to stealth. In a few moments, the oratory of the insects began again.

In surprisingly hushed voice, Honoré stated, "You still haven't said where you are taking us, Aubrey."

In response, he opened the metal case, removed the journal and passed it over to her. "Look at the next to last page, please."

Honoré did as he said, flipping through the Mylar sheaves. Reaching the page Belleau indicated, she glanced at it, then over at Belleau and handed the book to Kavanaugh. He held it near the firelight. The yellowed paper delineated a squiggly pattern drawn in faded ink with arrows and dotted lines specifying directions. A crude circle was labeled *Mystere Montagneux* in longhand.

"It's a map," he declared. "Of the area around the base of the escarpment."

"The southern side to be precise," Belleau stated.

"We surveyed that area," said Crowe. "There's nothing there."

"You overlooked it," Belleau retorted. "You stayed in the treeline, did you not? You didn't climb the bluffs?"

"No," said Kavanaugh bluntly. "You're very sure something is there?"

"Oh, yes."

"But you've never been there, either," Mouzi challenged.

"My great-great-grandfather, Jacque Belleau, was there, with Charles Darwin. But not even Darwin saw what he saw. Jacque made sketches and later they were fully rendered by the draftsman of the *Beagle*, Conrad Martens."

Kavanaugh lifted a sardonic eyebrow. "Really. And what did old Jacque see?"

Belleau smiled but it did not reach his eyes. "The secret of how life developed on Earth—and how humanity became the ascendant species."

No one spoke for a handful of awkward seconds. Then Bai Suzhen inquired coldly, "If these secrets were discovered over one hundred and seventy-five years ago, where have they been languishing for all this time?"

Belleau hesitated before saying, "In the proper protective hands."

With unmistakable sarcasm, Honoré said, "Those proper hands wouldn't happen to belong to this exclusive men's lodge of yours, would it? Your School of Night?"

"Oh, please," muttered Kavanaugh, rolling his eyes.

Belleau glared at Honoré through the flames of the fire. "Don't make sport of me, Honoré. The School of Night isn't a lodge, but a society of scholars founded in England, in 1592 by Sir Walter Raleigh. Throughout the centuries, the School has shaped the direction of scientific thought. We protected knowledge where it otherwise might have been destroyed or repressed.

"One piece of knowledge the School safeguarded was the so-called Enochian language. Through the translations by Dr. John Dee and later ones made by Jacque Belleau, the Tamtung islands were discovered."

"I don't understand," Honoré said, sounding intrigued despite the scowl on her face. "Decoding the Enochian language led Jacque Belleau here?"

Belleau nodded. "The key to breaking the Enochian code is binary. Dee found the first part in the fifteenth century but he died before he could decipher the other half. My great-great-grandfather accomplished that and thusly was inducted into the School. He joined the crew of the *Beagle* as ship's surgeon and botanist. He influenced Darwin to make landfall here, in May of 1836."

"It sounds to me like this School of yours suppressed the knowledge of the Tamtungs, rather than protected it," observed Bai Suzhen dourly.

Belleau hitched up a shoulder in a shrug. "Perhaps to an extent they did. They were wise enough to know that they did not know enough about the Tamtungs to reveal them to the world. Withal, they were able to glean something of a history of the island chain. When the original Enochian text was written, there were four Tamtung islands. Seismic activity must have caused the other two sink."

"How did they find out that out?" Kavanaugh asked skeptically.

"I'm getting to that, be patient. After Jacque Belleau's first and only visit here, several subsequent secret expeditions were mounted by the School of Night. Once photography came into fashion, we were able to maintain something of a pictorial record. That is how some people associated with the School learned about the Tamtungs...Arthur Conan Doyle, for one."

Crowe eyed him distrustfully. "You're joking."

"Not at all. Doyle read a few documents, saw a few photographs and wanted to expose the entire undertaking to the world. But we threatened him with ridicule if he revealed the truth of Big Tamtung. Inasmuch as his scientific credentials were already held in contempt due to his spiritualist beliefs, he agreed to write an altered account as fiction. And that is how *The Lost World* came to be written."

"That's a little hard to swallow," Crowe said.

"Not so much," Honoré said musingly. "It's common knowledge Doyle based Sherlock Holmes on a real person, a surgeon named Joseph Bell. Disguising an island in the South China Sea as an isolated plateau in the Amazon isn't that much of a stretch."

"Other people over the centuries came across clues to the existence of Big Tamtung," Belleau continued, "but the School of Night always managed to deflect those who came too close. Over time, true reports became so associated with legends, like those of the Isle of Demons, they were never taken seriously"

"Why?" demanded Kavanaugh. "If this society of yours is devoted to preserving knowledge, why fight so hard for so long to keep Big Tamtung a legend? Wouldn't the fields of biology and paleontology be advanced if the legend was actually revealed to be fact? Wouldn't this place be the ultimate living laboratory for naturalists?"

"Yes," Belleau drawled, voice heavy with sarcasm. "It also would be the ultimate living testament to anti-evolutionists, the creationists, the purveyors of the intelligent design 'theory'." He crooked his fingers to indicate quotation marks.

Bai narrowed her eyes. "I don't understand."

"If Big Tamtung was simply thrown out into the world," answered Belleau, "without strict controls on the release of information, then science as we know it would be awash in controversy. Nothing would ever be accepted from the scientific community, not new technologies, and not even new medicines. Religious pundits all over the world would vie with one another to claim Big Tamtung as the absolute proof of creationism.

"The danger of entering a new Dark Age, where the church once again wields more influence than scientific thought is a very real one. Reason would be subsumed by superstition. That part of our collective history should be never be repeated."

Everyone stared at the little man, surprised into silence. Then Kavanaugh cast a sideways glance at Honoré. "And you called *me* paranoid."

The corner of Honoré's mouth lifted in a smirk. "Aubrey isn't as paranoid about religion taking Big Tamtung away from him as he is the pharmaceutical companies."

Crowe frowned. "What?"

Honoré stared levelly at Belleau. "The reason why the School of Night in general and the Belleau family in particular was so obsessive about keeping Big Tamtung a secret under their influence is a little less grand than maintaining the purity of scientific thought. The profit motive figures into it very, very prominently."

"If that's the case," Kavanaugh said, "why didn't the School of Night interfere when we found the place and formed Cryptozoica Enterprises?"

Belleau chuckled contemptuously. "We didn't have to take any punitive action against you—your own inherent incompetence ensured the enterprise's failure. An eco-tourist destination resort—*really*. However, I will admit that several of the tabloid newspapers that we influence were eager to amplify the claims of fraud and hoax. Even if reputable scientists became curious as to the veracity of Cryptozoica, they shied away from the huckster stink of it all."

"Clever planning," Bai said bitterly. "Thank you."

"Don't thank me, Madame. Thank Tombstone Jack there. He couldn't have done a better job of discrediting Cryptozoica than if he were working under a full scholarship from the School of Night."

The flickering firelight made it difficult to read Kavanaugh's expression, but tendons stood out in relief on his neck. "You still haven't explained how your great-great-grandfather discovered the history of this place and what he really found here."

Belleau leaned back, half-reclining beside Oakshott. He gave the impression of enjoying all the attention immensely. "Jacque wasn't quite certain of what he found, but he had his suspicions...particularly after he copied several columns of Enochian glyphs. That's how he learned the history of the Tamtungs, by deciphering the alphabet. Turn to the last page there if you would, Honoré."

She did so, gazing at several columns of symbols canted at different angles away from a square central junction. She said, "These look like the same ones that were carved into the pillars."

"They aren't. My great-great-grandfather copied them from the sides of a stele, a monolith. Now, very carefully, bend the page in the middle in thirds. Don't fold it, just bend it."

Frowning in concentration, Honoré fumbled with the Mylar sheet, following his instructions.

"*Mad* magazine used to have a feature like that on the inside back covers," Crowe commented dryly. "It would give you a different picture than what you thought. What's this one show?"

Honoré didn't respond for a long moment. Then her eyes widened as she stared at the arrangement of glyphs. She breathed, "It can't be."

Belleau chuckled. "Oh, it be, darlin'. It very much be. The term DNA wasn't coined until long after Jacque's death and it wasn't until 1937 that an X-ray showed DNA had a regular structure."

"This isn't just a helix pattern," Honoré argued, "this is a Holliday junction… specific to genetic recombination."

Belleau sat up, eyes reflecting the firelight like two polished mirrors. "Exactly! The secret of the Darwin journal and of Big Tamtung is that a *non-human species raised humanity up from the ape.*"

He paused, as if he intended to say more, then asked, "May I have another piece of beef jerky, please?"

Chapter Twenty-Eight

May 13th

Kavanaugh turned to look at Bai. She was still asleep, her dark hair spread across the green pillow like an ebony fan. Her lips were quirked in a faint smile, as though her dreams were pleasant. She lay beside him in nude, damp exhaustion, the sheet tangled across her hips. He leaned down and kissed her on the corner of the mouth.

Bai's eyelashes flickered open and her dark eyes studied him gravely. She pressed up against him, the sweat-slick smoothness of her bare breasts sliding over his chest. She whispered, "I was dreaming about you."

"Poor way to spend your time," he replied.

"No," she said drowsily. "There was a message."

"What message?"

Bai's eyes opened inhumanly wide and they blazed forth with gold-green fury. She hissed, "If you return, you will die, Jack!"

Kavanaugh awakened instantly, his upper body snapping erect and dislodging Honoré's head from his shoulder. For a split second, he wasn't certain what had woken him, and then he realized it wasn't a sound but rather a sudden change in one. The steady chirping of the cicadas had risen in volume, clamoring wildly as they welcomed the rising sun. The change in the sound had penetrated even his dream.

Honoré groaned and pushed away from him, rubbing her eyes with the heels of her hands. Kavanaugh blinked and when his vision swam into focus, he saw Bai Suzhen sitting opposite at him, staring, her face as immobile and grave as if carved from ivory. He shifted further away from Honoré who rolled her neck, working out the kinks.

The first rays of sunlight penetrated the canopy of the tree tops, glistening on the fat drops of dew that dripped down from the leaves. In the tropics, the damp air of the jungle condensed among the towering trees and drizzled down until the air grew warmer.

The sky filled with a palette of blazing colors. As the sun climbed higher in the sky, then the cheerful notes of songbirds grew louder. Everyone slowly stirred in the campsite. A few wisps of smoke curled from the ashes of the fire. Oakshott stood leaning against a fallen tree, rifle in his arms. Kavanaugh didn't ask who had tended the fire all night—he really didn't care.

After Aubrey Belleau refused to answer any further questions, insisting they all rest up for the next day's journey, Kavanaugh, Crowe and Mouzi had tried to keep alert. They watched for any opportunity to jump Oakshott and disarm him. That opportunity never arrived. Kavanaugh did not remember falling asleep, certainly not with Honoré Roxton's head on his shoulder.

Belleau looked damnably clear-eyed and refreshed. He bustled about the camp, clapping his hands, admonishing everyone to make themselves ready, chanting "Hey-up, heigh-ho, let's go!"

"Oh, please, Aubrey," Honoré moaned, massaging her temples. "This isn't a health farm in Bath."

After washing down mouthfuls of power bars with swallows of bottled water, the seven people arose and stiffly moved southward through the jungle. Hanging from the trees, looped from the branches were rope-thick vines, acrawl with insects.

The heavy, humid air produced a greenhouse atmosphere. Honoré took off her Stetson and used it to fan her face.

The narrow trail they followed snaked through the forest. Insects and butterflies darted back and forth across the path and from their hiding places deeper in the jungle came shrill, warning cries. Once Honoré grabbed Kavanaugh's arm and pointed upward. He caught a glimpse of an archaeopteryx perched on branch high above them, staring down with beady, suspicious eyes.

Birds plumed in rich reds, deep greens and brilliant yellows cawed raucously. Tiny flying lizards glided short distances through the air above their heads. Frequently they heard snorts, which Kavanaugh attributed to the wild tapirs.

Within an hour of leaving the camp, a rain began to fall, a warm, wet drizzle that compounded their misery. Insects buzzed in clouds all around them, biting and flying, seemingly dedicated to achieving the single goal of crawling into mouths and eyes. Swatting and waving at the bugs, the group walked under arches made of massive trees leaning against one other. They scrambled over broken trunks lying on the ground, blocking their path.

"These trees look like they've been pushed over," muttered Belleau, glancing around anxiously. "By the same huge beast we heard last night, perhaps."

"No," said Crowe. "It's the rain. Some of the trees are over two hundred feet tall and after a couple of good monsoon-type rains, the ground gets spongy, the trees soak up thousands of gallons of water, and they can't support their own weight. They fall right over."

"That's comforting," said Honoré.

"This little rain isn't enough to do much," replied Mouzi, scratching at a bug-bite. "Except to make us feel like bags of waterlogged crap."

Favoring her bruised leg, Bai Suzhen stumbled on a root and nearly fell, but Kavanaugh managed to catch her and ease her down on a bed of soggy ferns. The warm rain, mixed with perspiration, streamed down her face, plastered her black hair to her head. She breathed heavily, her face flushed.

"Aubrey," Honoré called, "let's take a rest break."

"Not yet," the little man snapped over his shoulder.

"Bai Suzhen needs to take a breather," Crowe said.

Belleau came to a stop and glanced back at the woman with

annoyed eyes. Then he cut his gaze over to Oakshott. The big man transferred the rifle to his left hand and yanked Bai Suzhen to her feet with his right. The woman's eyes flashed, her hand tightening on the hilt of the jian sword.

"What the hell is your hurry?" demanded Kavanaugh angrily.

"I want to get to the escarpment before dark," Belleau replied. "While we still have light enough to explore."

Oakshott waved the carbine toward the south. "March."

Within half an hour, the rain slackened and ended but still the trickle of dripping, seeping water was everywhere. Wet heat arose from the ground, giving the jungle the stifling feel of a steam-bath with the outtake pipes at maximum.

The giant trees became less frequent, the overhead canopy less dense. Kavanaugh was surprised by the glimpses of open sunlight. The rain forest gradually changed over to a savanna of rich green grass carpeting a hilly terrain. The treeless slope ahead of them inclined to a hogback ridge.

To the south, the black bulk of the escarpment reached into the sky. The air around the summit appeared clear, but the permanent haze collected among the tumbled gray-green boulders at its base like an umbrella. It looked so far in the distance, it seemed they couldn't possibly reach it in a week, much less a day.

Belleau halted, wiping the perspiration from his neck with a white linen handkerchief. "We can afford to take a rest break."

Everyone dropped to the ground where they stood. Even Oakshott sank down. Although the breeze gusting over the tableland wasn't particularly cool, it felt fresher than the thick air trapped in the jungle. After passing around a bottle of water, Honoré asked, "Aubrey, what did you mean by non-human race raising humanity up from the apes?"

The little man shrugged. "I thought I was quite clear."

"You weren't, let me disabuse you of that right now. I presume you meant the entity you called the anthroposaur. Surely you're not postulating that an advanced reptilian race descended from dinosaurids actually *co-existed* with man."

"Why not? Consider the Troodon…paleobiologist Dale Russell speculated that a theropod species like the Troodon would have grown more intelligent and taken on a more humanoid appearance if not for the K-T event."

"Yes," Honoré conceded wryly. "But there *was* the K-T event. Besides, even if such a species existed, where is the historical record?"

Belleau gestured with both arms. "It's everywhere, in every culture, but like so much else, the knowledge was suppressed or dismissed as folklore. The mass of history definitely indicates the knowledge of an archaic science in the past."

Honoré nodded reluctantly. "True, but it's never been attributed to any single civilization."

"Of course it hasn't," he retorted bitterly. "But nor has any conventional historian ever identified the teachers of the ancient Egyptians, the Babylonians, the Sumerians. So why couldn't these culture-bearers have been a race of anthroposaurs descended from the Troodon? Almost every one of them, from the Mayan's Kulkulcan to Mesopotamia's Oannes was associated with serpents or reptiles."

Honoré gazed at him in dismay. "Linking legends with reality is not rational thought, Aubrey."

Belleau laughed. "Rational and irrational thought are divided by time frames. At the time Charles Darwin and my great-great-grandfather set foot here, the general belief in England was that Earth and man had been created simultaneously in 4004 BC. That was the prevailing wisdom less than two hundred years ago. Is it rational?"

"Of course not, but just because—"

A hooting cry rolled across the savanna. Hoarse and haunting, it held a deep bass note. Kavanaugh felt the ground tremble, ever so slightly, beneath him. He jumped to his feet. Within a second, everyone else did too.

They stared in silent awe at the huge creature lumbering slowly across the grassland from the fringes of the jungle. Its leathery hide was the color of pewter mixed with a yellow-green, the texture not unlike the skin of a rhinoceros. The four-legged animal moved in a relaxed saunter, dragging a short tail behind it. A great bony hood curved up at the rear of its skull.

Five horns sprouted from its head—two long ones above the eyes, a medium-sized horn on the snout and a pair of shorter, tusk-like protuberances curved out on either side of its jaw hinges, like truncated sabers. The tip of its left fore-horn was broken, leaving a jagged stump.

The animal looked to be at least eighteen feet long, from the beak-like mouth to the tip of the muscular tail. It stood six feet high at the shoulder.

"Triceratops," muttered Belleau.

"*Quin*terotops," Crowe corrected. "With all those degrees, didn't you ever learn how to count?"

Shading her eyes with her hands, Honoré intoned, "Five toes on both the front and back feet…the fan of the frill is broader and edged with longer, sharper points of epoccipitals, not unlike the earlier Styracosaurus. Two extra horns at the end of the frill. The frill itself is more round than the Triceratops. Although the Triceratops was one of the last dinosaur genera to appear before K-T, this is a cousin chasmosaurine ceratopsian—the Anchiceratops."

Mouzi regarded her with incredulous eyes. "I dare you to say that again."

The creature halted and turned its head slowly, looking behind it. Then, it broke wind explosively, lifted its tail and dropped a pile of dark green feces three feet high. It began walking again, tail swaying from side to side.

"It's heading in our general direction," Honoré said excitedly. "Let's follow it."

"Not too closely," Kavanaugh said. "We don't know what it had for breakfast and I'm not inclined to find out."

Without argument, the seven people fell into step a score of yards behind the Quinterotops as it ambled across the grassland and up the slope. It sniffed at the multi-colored wildflowers growing among the high grasses but didn't sample any.

Honoré ran ahead and took up a position several yards to its left, snapping a series of shots with her Nikon. Once the animal cast her a sour glance over its shoulder and opened its mouth to reveal a battery of blunt, powerful teeth, arranged much like those of a camel.

"Although it has changed from the Anchiceratops," Honoré said, peering through the view-finder "it's apparently still an herbivore, judging by the shape of its jaws and teeth. The Quinterotops probably uses the nasal horn to uproot tubers and the side spurs must be a defensive adaptation to protect their underjaws from small carnivores that attack from below."

Kavanaugh came up beside her during her monologue. "Interesting."

She lowered the camera, eyes rapt. "Interesting? The Quinterotops is completely fascinating."

"I didn't mean that," he said lowering his voice. "I meant that it's interesting that Aubrey has had his satphone since yesterday afternoon and has yet to place a call to Jimmy Cao."

Honoré blinked, trying to shift her concentration to a non-ceratopsian topic. "What do you think that means?"

"Maybe nothing at all. Or it could mean that Aubrey has had a change of heart about partnering up with the Ghost Shadows or he has business he wants to complete before he meets up with Cao again."

She nodded reflectively. "That pool…those ruins we saw the pictures of, perhaps."

They began walking, following the trail of stamped down grass made by the Quinterotops. Everyone else climbed up the slope ahead of them, although Oakshott let them know he closely monitored their progress.

In a voice barely above a whisper, Kavanaugh asked, "What did you mean that Aubrey was afraid of pharmaceutical companies?"

Honoré pushed back the brim of her hat. "Aubrey believes his ancestor discovered the equivalent of a universal panacea here on Big Tamtung. He calls it Prima Materia."

Kavanaugh frowned. "What the hell is that supposed to be?"

"Prime matter. It's part pseudoscience, part superstition, and half complete rubbish. There's a very old belief that all life on Earth sprang from a single source. Darwin referred to it as a warm little pond of ooze. Aubrey believes that was Darwin speaking in code, referring to the pool of prime matter Jacque Belleau found here."

"And you don't believe it exists?"

Honoré started to reply, then shook her head in good-natured frustration. "Three days ago I wouldn't have believed I'd be trailing a living, breathing, defecating Anchiceratops, so I'm not much of a judge on what exists and what doesn't. However, if there is such a thing as prime matter, there is probably no limit to the kind of medicines that can be processed from it."

"How so?"

"According to Darwin's journal, one of their party, a man named Hoxie, was mortally wounded by a Deinonychus. Hoxie's wounds were inadvertently exposed to a sample of the substance and he made a full recovery. It stands to reason one pint of Prima Materia would probably be worth ten times all the rain forest drugs in the world. No limit."

"No limit on the profits, either," Kavanaugh said.

"Exactly…as a world-renowned biochemist and botanist, Aubrey could probably put any research on the fast track. It doesn't hurt that he's a consultant to Maxiterm pharmaceuticals."

Kavanaugh smiled thinly "And another piece of the puzzle falls into place. No damn wonder Jimmy Cao is involved so deeply in this."

"Why so?"

"The triads connected to United Bamboo are always looking to invest in legitimate commercial ventures. It's one of their policies. That's why they put money into Cryptozoica Enterprises. But getting in on the ground floor of a whole new kind of drug development is a hell of a lot more profit-heavy than backing a tourist destination resort."

"That's a frightening idea," replied Honoré. She gestured toward Bai Suzhen who had almost reached the top of the hill. "What about her?"

"What about her?"

"Once Bai Suzhen learns about the possibility of reaping pharmaceutical profits, why wouldn't she throw in with Jimmy Cao? It would be easy to arrange tragic accidents to befall the rest of us."

Kavanaugh's thin smile widened. "You don't know Bai Suzhen very well."

"Do you?" Honoré challenged.

"I don't think anyone really does. She's definitely an enigma-wrapped-in-a-riddle kind of woman. But I know one thing about her—she doesn't betray people who have put their trust in her. She'd cut an enemy's throat and take a bath in his blood if she had the chance, but she'd never turn on her friends, regardless of how much money she might make."

Honoré nodded but said uncertainly, "That's the question, Jack—I don't know if she views me as a friend."

"I don't know that either," he said frankly.

"Then how—"

Standing on the ridgeline, Crowe turned and waved. "Jack! Move your ass! You've got to see this!"

Chapter Twenty-Nine

Honoré and Kavanaugh struggled up the face of the bluff. When they reached the top, she gazed in awestruck silence at the herd of dinosaurs milling around the cane-enclosed bank of a broad stream. They saw the massive horned heads and spurred frills of half-a-dozen Quinterotops and an equal number of squat-bodied, serpent-necked sauropods.

Mingling with the sauropods and ceratopsians were clusters of Parasaurolophus—bipedal orinthischia with bony, back-slanting crests on their skulls and splayed, duck-like snouts.

They were of an ochre hue, their hides striped with patterns of dark brown. They grazed on the tender shoots and hyacinths growing at the water's edge. The offspring of the different species moved fearlessly among the adults. Vocalizations not unlike those of lowing cattle and whale-song arose from the mixed herd.

Honoré lifted her camera and began snapping one picture after another. "I can only hope my memory card and battery holds out. This is the most amazing sight I have ever seen…the most amazing sight *any* human being has ever seen. But what you called an Apatosaurus looks more like the Saltasaur, a close but smaller relative…so-named because the first fossils were discovered in Argentina's Salta Province. They thrived during the late Cretaceous."

"They seem to play well with others," observed Bai Suzhen. "But there aren't many different kinds, either."

"The late Cretaceous showed a marked decline in the diversity of dinosaur species," Honoré replied.

"I wasn't talking about the goddamn dinosaurs," Crowe said impatiently. "Me and Jack have seen them before. Look over there."

Following Crowe's pointing finger toward the far side of the streambed, at a distance of an eighth of a mile, Kavanaugh saw a white concrete pylon rising twenty-five feet from the savanna. Atop it ran the narrow gauge monorail track. The bright, mid-morning sunlight glinted off a reflective surface and he squinted, trying to make it out. He picked out the details of the cylindrical, blunt-nosed shifter engine with the Cryptozoica logo emblazoned on the hull.

He said, "So *that's* where the monorail broke down."

"Exactly," Crowe said. "By my calculations, it's about ten to fifteen miles from the switch-back junction. Maybe me and Mouzi can get her running again."

"Why?" demanded Belleau

Crowe looked at him in disbelief. "So we can ride back to the Petting Zoo instead of being chased?"

"Duh," muttered Mouzi.

"How do you propose to reach the train itself?" Belleau asked. "Shinny up that post?"

"Something like that," Kavanaugh said. "We weren't quite as short-sighted as you try to make us out to be. There are ladder rungs on every pylon. We can climb up and walk along the track to the train."

"Ah." Belleau presented the image of pondering the proposal, then he blew out a regretful sigh. "Perhaps after we've reached out objective we can come back this way and find out if it's still useful."

Crowe gestured angrily. "If we can get her running, then we can also use her to cut at least ten miles off the walk to the escarpment you're so eager to visit."

Belleau's eyes narrowed. "How much of a delay are we talking about? How long will it take you to examine the train and ascertain if you can get it operational?"

"There's no way to tell until we crack her motor open," Mouzi said waspishly. "Thirty minutes, thirty hours, who knows?"

"We can't risk losing the time," Belleau stated, turning away from Crowe. "If we maintain our present pace, we should reach our destination by late afternoon."

Neither Crowe nor Mouzi moved. Oakshott stepped in front of them, regarding them with grave eyes, lifting the carbine suggestively. Just as suggestively, Mouzi drew a butterfly knife from the back pocket of her shorts.

"You can only shoot one of us before I cut your heart out," she said, her voice sibilant with spite.

Belleau looked over his shoulder, a smile of genuine amusement creasing his lips. "The question is which one of you will it be? Do you volunteer, little Miss Mongrel?"

"You can shoot me," she said, eyes seething with hatred. "Don't mean I'll die."

"Perhaps not, but I understand that bullet wounds to the stomach are exceedingly painful. You'll be out here in the wilderness with no medical help beyond the most rudimentary first aid. Of course, the volunteer doesn't have to be you. I can select someone else to serve as an example."

Sunlight flickered on the steel of Bai Suzhen's sword. She whipped the point of the blade sideways to rest against Belleau's throat. Oakshott instantly aimed the rifle at her.

"Having your throat cut is exceptionally painful, too," Bai said between gritted teeth.

"Steady on now, Madame," Belleau murmured. "Steady on. You don't want to take rash actions."

"Why not?" Bai exerted pressure on the sword, the point digging into Belleau's neck. He bit back cry of pain.

Raising a pair of conciliatory hands, Belleau said calmly, "If we do it my way, everybody lives. Nobody dies or so much as gets their toes stubbed. If we follow your course, all we will be doing is providing meals for the scavengers. You may kill me, but then Oakshott will be forced to kill you and as many of your friends as he can before he himself is killed. Seems rather a waste of resources and energy."

Bai's eyes narrowed to slits "If it had not been for you, Jimmy Cao would have never had the guts to move against me."

She snatched the blade away. "But we'll do it your way for the time being. However, I'm serving notice on you right now, you little *kom eu*—there *will* be a reckoning."

Belleau's eyes glinted with anger at being addressed as "shit dwarf", but he only touched the red mark at his throat and inspected his fingertips for blood. "I will make all of this up to you, Madame. To all of you…providing we reach our destination."

Head held high, metal box containing the Darwin journal tucked under one arm, Aubrey Belleau marched down the hillside and set out across the grassy plain in the direction of the stream. After looking at Oakshott, whose face remained an expressionless mask, everyone followed the little man.

The commingled herd of Saltasaurs, Quinterotops and Parasaurolophus paid their approach little attention. The six people walked at an oblique angle away from the animals, not wanting to go among them. Although the Saltasaurs weren't as gargantuan as the fossil reconstructions of Apatasaurus, their heads atop the very long necks still would have filled standard-size oil drums. One of the creatures stared at them steadily, a growl bubbling from lips curled back over long, peg-shaped teeth.

"I think that must be a bull," Honoré remarked. "Letting us know *he* knows we're here."

"Aren't sauropods supposed to be peaceful?" Mouzi asked. "Plant eaters?"

"Yeah," replied Crowe, "but you never know when one might decide to vary its diet."

"You'd think that even this small herd of Saltasaurs would strip the island of vegetation within a couple of years," said Honoré.

"You're forgetting the food chain," Belleau said. "There are predators about, make no mistake."

A Quinterotops swung its horned head toward them as they passed and uttered a warning rumble.

"I guess it takes one to know one, Aubrey," Kavanaugh commented.

"Very whimsical, Mr. Kavanaugh."

They walked through the brakes of cane, the tough stalks as big around as Oakshott's wrists. The ground was marshy and soft. The odor of sulfurous swamp gas became so strong that they all breathed through their mouths, although they ran the risk of inhaling handfuls of bugs.

The seven people paused at the edge of the stream, gauging its depth. Rainbow-tinted guppies and orange characins darted beneath the surface. The wavelets splintered the sun rays into little kaleidoscopic fragments.

They heard a sloshing and turned toward a Parasaurolophus slowly wading through the shallows toward them. It chewed thoughtfully on a stringy mass of vegetable matter. It looked toward them with eyes that were round and mild. Although it was built bipedally, the twelve foot tall animal walked hunched over, using its forepaws to support its weight. The creature took up a position in the stream directly in their path and uttered an interrogative snuffle. Everyone stopped and stared, then Mouzi stepped into the knee-deep water.

"What are you doing?" asked Honoré tensely.

"The snufflegalumps aren't aggressive," said Kavanaugh. "But they're curious."

"Actually, what you have there closely resembles a Bactrosaurus, one of the most common duck-billed Hadrosaurs."

Bai eyed her superciliously. "How can an animal that is thought to be extinct also be common?"

Honoré only shrugged.

Mouzi reached up with her right hand and the Hadrosaur lowered its head, still single-mindedly chewing. Caressing its skull crest, she said, "I might have met this one before, when she was a baby."

Belleau sighed in exasperation. "This isn't a Disney film, young lady. Send the beast on its way, so we can be on ours."

"Pay no attention to him, Mouzi," Honoré said, snapping photographs. "You and the snufflegalump will be the cover girls on the next issue of the *National Geographic.*"

The Hadrosaur suddenly jerked upright, venting a loud snuffle. Half-chewed plant bits fell from its jaws. It stared intently toward the savanna, the posture of its body suggesting fear.

Brushing masticated vegetable matter from her arms, Mouzi demanded irritably, "Now what?"

An icy hand stroked Kavanaugh's spine. The sweat on his face and under his clothes suddenly turned cold. The other animals stopped grazing, drinking and even moving. They appeared to cease breathing. The serpentine necks of the Saltasaurs arched as they stared in the same direction as the duck-bills.

The grasses swayed as if touched by the wind, but the movement was localized, restricted to small areas. Dark heads suddenly arose from the sea of grass, like the dorsal fins of sharks. They swiftly spread out, forming a circle around the animals clustered at the stream.

A faint sound reached Kavanaugh's ears, like the squeal of a nail being pried out of green wood, repeated over and over. He had heard the high-pitched noise before and the best he could describe it was as a "skreek", a blend of shriek and squeak.

"What is making that annoying sound?" Belleau demanded. "A flock of birds?"

"Not birds," Kavanaugh said flatly. "A flock of Deinonychus. I don't know if they're after the herd or after us, but they're on their way. We'd better find some high ground."

He pointed to the monorail pylon. "Some *very* high ground."

Chapter Thirty

They kicked up eruptions of water as they raced across the stream. Behind them they heard the wild bawlings and shrill outcries of animals in panic. The ground quaked at the pounding of the herd's feet as the creatures stampeded in terror.

Belleau stumbled and fell face-first into the stream, hugging the metal case to his chest. Without breaking stride, Oakshott snatched up Belleau and carried him the rest of the way over.

The seven people reached the opposite side and continued sprinting, tearing a path through the grass. The pain of a stitch stabbed along Kavanaugh's side and the muscles of his legs began to feel as if they were trapped between the jaws of a tightening vise. His vision was shot through with gray spots. Silently he cursed his last few years of drinking at the same time he prayed the nagging pull in his groin wouldn't get any worse. Nevertheless, he kept running although every footfall jarred his entire body, his bruised stomach muscles flaring with bursts of pain.

Mouzi, effortlessly maintaining a steady pace, took his arm to help him along. "Move it, old man!"

Kavanaugh shook her loose angrily. "I don't need your help!"

"Suit yourself." Her mocha-hued legs pumped and she pulled ahead.

The breath seared Kavanaugh's lungs and his heart pounded against his ribs. His laboring legs seemed filled with half-frozen mud. Outraged roars mixed in with high-pitched *skreeks* penetrated even the sound of the blood thundering in his head.

He risked a glance backward and what he saw chilled him clean through. A bellowing Quinterotops came blundering across the stream, sending waves of water cascading high into the air. The huge animal crashed through a stand of cane, snapping off the stalks like matchwood.

For a few seconds, Kavanaugh couldn't understand why the animal had chosen such a route—then he realized it ran blindly, desperate to rid itself of the six demonic figures hanging onto its hide by cruelly hooked claws.

Mouzi reached the pylon first. Gasping for breath, she hung onto the staple-shaped rungs imbedded in the concrete. Everyone gathered around the base of the column, swaying, panting, trying to regain their breath and slow the rapid hammering of their hearts.

The Quinterotops squalled in agony, shaking its great curved shield. Its armored skin showed fresh, bloody gouges, inflicted by sickle-shaped hind-claws. The Deinonychus were lean-limbed, slender creatures, predatory death stripped down to the very barest of killing essentials.

Their mottled, red-and-black striped hide was reminiscent of the deadly coral snake. The claw-tipped forelegs were the length of an adult human's arm and ropy muscles slid beneath the layer of scales. Their thickly muscled hind legs terminated in three toed feet, a scimitar-curved talon arching up and out from the second toe.

Their jaws gaped open, revealing rows of needle-pointed fangs thrusting up from purple gums. A crest of sharp quills, like those of a porcupine's spiked with red and yellow feathers ran vertically down the center of their skulls and along the lines of their spines. From the ends of their whiplike tails to their blunt snouts, they averaged six feet long.

If you return, you will die.

Kavanaugh pushed Honoré toward the rungs. "Everybody climb. Get going, Mouzi."

Crowe stepped aside to allow the Honoré to follow Mouzi. "They aren't paying us any attention, Jack."

"Yet...you go too, Gus—get aboard the engine and see what you can do to get her running."

Halfway up the pylon, Honoré looked down. "What about you?"

"I'll guard everybody's backsides. I need to have that rifle back, Oakshott...unless you're a world-class sharpshooter on top of all your other talents."

"Are *you?*"

Kavanaugh feigned a modest smile. "I qualified as a marksman-sharpshooter-expert. The Air Force even gave me a little bronze star on a ribbon. I don't have it on me, so you'll have to take my word for it."

The big man didn't respond until a soaking-wet Belleau blurted, "Give him the gun and give me a boost!"

Kavanaugh quickly checked the carbine over. He said to Bai Suzhen, "Go on up."

She hefted her sword, giving two short strokes to loosen her wrist. "I'll guard *your* backside, just in case you expose it."

"Yeah," he replied dryly, settling the stock of the carbine in the hollow his shoulder. "Just in case."

Roaring, the Quinterotops spun around in a circle, like a dog trying to catch its tail. With a gasping grunt of exertion, the animal rose up on its hind legs and tottered clumsily along the edge of the stream. It toppled backward in the attempt to crush its tormentors.

All six of the agile Deinonychus sprang away as the horned creature slammed into the ground with a sound like a boulder dropped from a great height. The slender raptors circled as the kicking Quinterotops struggled to get its legs underneath it.

"C'mon, Jack!" Crowe urged from the top of the pylon. "They still don't see us."

As if on cue, the head of a raptor whipped around, staring directly at Crowe atop the elevated monorail track. Its gaze lowered, taking in Kavanaugh and Bai Suzhen. Opening its mouth wide, it voiced a prolonged, nerve-stinging *skreek*.

The other three Deinonychus turned away from bedeviling

the Quinterotops, following the gaze of their comrade. Almost simultaneously, they performed a sideways hopping dance-step. To Kavanaugh, the movements looked like they were jumping with joy, anticipating a feast of human flesh.

Get up and run or you will die.

Softly, Kavanaugh said, "Get ready."

The six Deinonychus flung themselves across the grass as if launched from catapults. Kavanaugh achieved target acquisition and squeezed the trigger. A splotch of blood bloomed on a creature's breast and it tumbled head over heels, tail lashing the air.

The crack of the rifle startled the sprinting creatures. The raptors slowed, glancing in confusion at the death-throes of their companion.

"Perhaps they'll be scared off," Bai whispered.

"Not a chance," replied Kavanaugh grimly, aligning another Deinonychus before the sights of the carbine.

The five animals snarled and charged, moving in eye-blurring bounds. Instead of being frightened by the death of one of their number, they grew enraged.

Kavanaugh squeezed the trigger again and the top of a feather-crested skull floated away, surrounded by a misting of blood. The four survivors skreeked and from the far side of the stream, other members of the Deinonychus hunting troop answered the eerie call. They broke off harassing stragglers from the herd and came loping across the stream with relentless speed.

A pair of raptors ran in opposite directions, but swerved back toward the two humans standing at the base of the pylon. A fist clenched around Kavanaugh's heart. The Deinonychus displayed independent tactical thinking. They showed it by the way they came on in zigzag bounds to minimize the chances of falling victim to a weapon that, although new to them, knew was capable of killing from afar.

Kavanaugh's finger tightened on the trigger but he hesitated to squeeze it, knowing that he could not afford to miss with either of the two remaining bullets.

The feather-crested creatures surged over the ground, their maws gaping open in fanged grins of blood-lust.

Bai Suzhen and Kavanaugh stood back-to-back as the two Deinonychus made snarling, rushing feints toward them, eyes gleaming, teeth snapping.

A creature sprang upward and down, slamming into Bai with breath-robbing impact, the fanged jaws snapping for her throat. Claws ripped three vertical tears in her blouse. Staggering backward, she fell against the pylon. At the same time, she thrust with the jian sword into the raptor's belly.

The blade grated against the ribs. The animal twisted away with an agonized howl and went into death convulsions at her feet. Blood pumped out in spurts as it thrashed with its legs and tail in an effort to stand up.

Reversing his grip on the rifle, Kavanaugh swung it like a club. The stock crashed against the side of the remaining monster's skull, twisting its head around on its long neck with a crunch and crack of cartilage. It fell to the ground, rolling over and over in a spasm.

Bai Suzhen put a hand over the rips in her blouse. Not taking his eyes away from the advancing Deinonychus troop, Kavanaugh asked, "Are you all right?"

She nodded. "Superficial scratches."

From all around came a series of prolonged, paralyzing *skreeks!* as the Deinonychus hailed one another with their unnerving calls. They approached cautiously, hesitantly, moving in half-crouches, their attention divided between the growling, bleeding Quinterotops and the two humans standing over the bodies of their brethren.

"Up!" Kavanaugh said, spinning Bai Suzhen around to face the ladder. "Now, while we've got a few seconds to spare."

Hand over hand, she quickly scaled the pylon, not objecting even when Kavanaugh propelled her upward by a hand on her rump. "Go-go-*go!*"

Bai pulled herself to the top of the pylon and extended

a hand to Kavanaugh, gripping his forearm with surprising strength. She hauled him up over the edge. Glaring down at the raptors swarming around the base, she counted at least ten, with more arriving. They uttered little questioning barks to one another. The scene might have been cute, had they been otters and not bloodthirsty predators. One of them sniffed at the metal rungs, even nipping at them experimentally.

"Do you think they can figure out how to get up here?" Bai asked.

Before Kavanaugh had regained sufficient wind to answer, the curious Deinonychus hooked a rung with its foreclaws, then planted its hind feet on another.

"Yeah," Kavanaugh said grimly, putting the carbine to his shoulder. "I think they can figure it out."

"Jack!" shouted Honoré. "Come on!"

She stood about twenty yards away on a small platform at the rear of the bullet-shaped car. The monorail carriage was twenty feet long, ten in overall diameter. Most of the tube-shaped exterior was composed of curved, transparent panes of Plexiglass. The glass was streaked and dirty, but he saw everyone seated within.

Kavanaugh and Bai ran along the narrow track to the engine, climbing through the open hatch into the stuffy carriage. Belleau and Oakshott sat in padded leather chairs. Mouzi and Crowe kneeled down at the far end of the car, glowering into a square depression in the floor. The air in the coach was stifling. It stank of old mildew.

Kavanaugh remained by the open rear hatch, not just so he could keep watch for ladder-climbing Deinonychus, but also because of the drafts of fresh air. He called out, "What's the story, Gus?"

"Hell," Crowe retorted, pulling his Swiss Army knife from a pocket, "I don't even know the prologue yet. Keep in mind this thing has been sitting here dead for over two years."

From his seat near one of the transparent windows, Belleau said tremulously, "I thought monorails were powered by electric motors, fed by contact wires and the like. If there's no power at the Petting Zoo station, it can't be started, can it?"

"This monorail is a hybrid system," said Crowe shortly, extracting a screwdriver blade. "It uses a diesel motor to generate electricity for the rail motors. We designed a redundancy just in case the Petting Zoo station lost power. We've got an onboard high-efficiency Wankel."

Honoré cast him a perplexed glance. "You've got a *what?*"

"It's an engine," Kavanaugh explained. "State-of-the-art… or it was a few years back."

"Not that bleedin' efficient either," muttered Mouzi, reaching down into the engine module. "Give me the tool, Gus…my hands are smaller."

Kavanaugh watched the activity of the Deinonychus as they clustered around the pylon, but he was unable to see the creature that had showed interest in the ladder. He remarked casually, "They're smart little monsters, aren't they?"

Honoré swallowed hard. "And diabolically vicious. An adult has around sixty teeth, you know…think of them like great white sharks, only with legs and the brains of sociopathic six year-olds. Together with the Troodonids, the Deinonychosauria clade represents the group of non-avian dinosaurs the most closely related to birds."

"I wish they'd evolve wings and fly away," Kavanaugh replied. "If Gus can't get this thing rolling, I don't know how we're going to get out of this one."

Honoré gestured to the walls and roof. "I assume the train was designed for the maximum-range viewing, for the photographers who paid their fares."

"You assume correctly."

"How thick is the Plexiglass?"

Kavanaugh tapped a ceiling panel with the barrel of the carbine. "About a quarter of an inch, I guess. Tough enough, but we didn't test it against raptors."

Sitting in a seat beside the door, Bai Suzhen said drowsily, "We may have to, and sooner than we'd like."

Kavanaugh peered through the open hatch just as a Deinonychus raised its head above the top of the pylon, looking around alertly. Its eyes fixed on the coach and the people within it. Mouth opening wide, it gave vent to a long shriek that held a note of triumph.

Kavanaugh turned to speak to Bai Suzhen. Only then did he see that the front of her silk blouse was sodden with blood. She closed her eyes in pain, shock and exhaustion and leaned her head against the transparent pane.

Chapter Thirty-One

Honoré drew aside Bai's Suzhen's blouse, peeling the blood-wet fabric away from the three deep lacerations that extended down from her collarbone to the inner curve of her right breast.

"She needs doctoring and fast," she announced. "Where's the first aid kit?"

Mouzi arose, reaching for the case, but Kavanaugh said, "We need you on the engine. Aubrey, you can help Dr. Roxton."

To his surprise, Belleau didn't voice an objection. Instead he went swiftly to the front of the car and fetched the box. Honoré pulled out a padded thickness of gauze and wiped at the blood welling from the gashes.

"I don't think a major blood vessel has been severed," she said, "but the transverse thoraxic muscles are definitely hemorrhaging. Aubrey, give me a pressure bandage."

Belleau found the two-inch thick pad in the medical kit and waited for Honoré to pull away the bloody gauze. He laid the pressure bandage over the gash, affixing the adhesive to Bai Suzhen's flesh, giving it a little squeeze to bring the antiseptic gel to the surface. Bai showed no sign of regaining consciousness.

With effort, Kavanaugh kept his attention focused on the Deinonychus pulling itself atop the pylon. It crouched down on all fours, studying the rear of the car with bright, alert eyes. Its tail, held out behind it, switched like that of a cat about to pounce. He sensed the creature assessing him, gauging the threat level of the rifle in his hands, extrapolating on how it functioned. It turned its head toward the troop gathered below and uttered a series of yips and squeaks.

Under his breath, Kavanaugh murmured, "That's it, tell your

homies we're too dangerous, tell them we're too much of an unknown quantity. Go on, hell-spawn. Just back the fuck off."

Then between one eye blink and another, the Deinony-chus moved. It was so fast, to Kavanaugh's eyes, it looked like the creature had vanished from it where crouched and then reappeared several yards down the line. Its claws clicked in a maddened castanet rhythm against the rail. Behind it, another Deinonychus climbed atop the pylon, immediately followed by another.

Rather than risk missing the shot, Kavanaugh fell backward into the coach, dropping the rifle so he could use both hands to pull the door shut. The Deinonychus thrust an arm through before the door sealed completely. Kavanaugh avoided having his eyes clawed out by a fractional margin.

He launched a straight-leg kick at the door, trapping the creature's forearm just above the elbow joint between the edge and the frame. He maintained the pressure with his leg as Hon-oré snatched up Bai Suzhen's sword and slashed with the blade, the razor-keen steel opening up a horizontal gash in the scaled flesh of the raptor's arm. Very little blood spilled out, but the Deinonychus howled in pain.

Noting the denseness of the epidermal tissue, Honoré hacked again, using a swift, back and forth sawing motion until the blade grated against bone. The creature screamed, frantically struggling to free itself. Kavanaugh drew back his leg just far enough so the animal could pull its limb free. It went flailing across the track and over the edge, plummeting to the ground twenty-five feet below.

Kavanaugh dropped the aluminum locking bar across the door just as three other Deinonychus surged up. They slammed against it, their claws raking over the window. Terror rose in Kavanaugh as he saw how the talons scored the glass, gouging it deeply. Two of the Deinonychus leaped atop the car, affording everyone a view of the leathery soles of their feet. Their claws scrabbled loudly over the Plexiglass.

Honoré returned to attending to Bai Suzhen. Examining

the pressure bandage, she said, "I can't stop the bleeding. Even if I could, I'd only be prolonging her life for a few hours."

Belleau eyed her fearfully. "Why do you say that?"

She gestured with the blade of the sword. "We'll suffocate if we have to be locked up in here for more than two or three hours…less than that once the heat of the day hits. We'll be baked alive."

Kavanaugh knew she spoke the truth. The brutal mid-day sun would turn the interior of the car into an oven. They would all die of heat prostration before they ran out of oxygen. Several more Deinonychus came loping along the rail line and the hope of opening the door to allow an influx of fresh air disappeared.

Kavanaugh glanced toward Crowe who kneeled beside Mouzi, dabbing at her sweat-beaded forehead with a bandana, as if she were a surgeon performing an exceptionally delicate operation.

"Do you have any idea what the problem is?" he asked.

A mechanical throb arose from the floor plates. Little lights panels inset into the coachwork glowed, and then faded.

After the first jolt of jubilation, Kavanaugh demanded, "What the hell was that?"

"There's a loose coupling to the Wankel," Mouzi said between clenched teeth, her eyes squeezed shut in concentration. "I'm trying to reconnect it by feel, but this ain't the way to do it. I should pull the entire block and—"

A spark popped and a choked cry burst from the girl's lips. Her slight body spasmed as she rolled across the floor, hands knotted into fists. The engine drone filled the compartment and the coach lurched forward a few feet, a loud metal-on-metal squeal accompanying it.

"Thank God!" Belleau shouted happily, averting his face from the snarling visage of a Deinonychus only inches away on the other side of the transparent barrier. "Well done, young lady, very well done!"

Crowe pulled Mouzi into a sitting position, trying to prise open her clenched fingers. "'C'mon," he said gently. "Let me see."

"Just a shock," she said in trembling voice. "Not surprised it happened."

Crowe winced at the sight of the reddened flesh at the base of her fingers. "We need some analgesic cream over here."

Aubrey obligingly brought the tube to Mouzi, squeezing it onto her burns. Reacting to a touch of a cool breeze on his face, he saw a slotted air-conditioning vent on the floor. "We've got air! *Exceptionally* well-done, young lady!"

Mouzi only scowled at him.

Crowe helped Mouzi to her feet. They gazed at the landscape slowly sliding past the windows. The train picked up speed, the grinding of metal becoming less pronounced as rust deposits were scraped away. Then they felt a sudden surge of acceleration, which sent everyone staggering.

"Now we're cookin'!" Mouzi exclaimed.

"Yeah," Crowe said dolefully. "We've got air and we're moving, but we've got no control. The switch-back point has automatic brake settings, but I don't know if they'll still function."

"What will happen if they don't?" asked Honoré.

Before Crowe answered, his attention was commanded by a Deinonychus clinging to the side of the carriage, hanging spread-eagled but slowly slipping down the curve of the Plexiglass. Its claws gouged into the glass as it tried to tighten its grip. He feigned swinging a fist at its head. The creature flinched instinctively, lost its grip, fell off the side of the coach and toppled to the ground.

"Ain't that damn smart of a monster," Mouzi said with a snicker.

As the train picked up speed, the landscape changed. There were more clumps of trees dotting the expanse of savanna. Rock outcroppings rose from the grassy plain like unfinished sculptures.

Crowe faced Belleau. "If the brakes won't work, one of two things will happen—we'll crash to a dead stop at the switch-point and maybe even fly off the rail."

"There's a third option," pointed out Kavanaugh. "You

could disconnect the coupling again and just gradually slow us down."

Crowe looked out the forward port. "We've got about nine miles to make up our minds."

"It might not make a difference to Bai," Honoré declared, holding a finger to the base of the woman's neck. "Her vitals aren't good. Pulse is thready, heart-rate is erratic. Her temperature is very high. I think she's going into septic shock."

Kavanaugh gazed at her, feeling helpless and hating it. Bai Suzhen's eyes were closed, her face pale, sheened with perspiration. Her respiration was labored. Then he shifted his gaze to Belleau. "What about that tube of sludge?"

Honoré frowned, then her eyes widened. "Yes—Aubrey, you claimed exposure to the Prima Materia substance healed a mortally wounded man whom your great-great-grandfather was treating."

Belleau's face twisted in an expression of one who has been betrayed. "Honoré, surely you're not serious. The sample I have is the only one extant. It was collected by Jacque Belleau's own hands."

"Collect another sample," Honoré said, "this time with your own hands."

"The pool could be long gone by now, dried up or covered over. There may not be any more samples."

"That substance is the only thing we have left to try," stated Honoré matter-of-factly. "It's a matter of life or death."

"If the sample had any potency," argued Belleau, "it's probably long gone. It's been over one hundred and seventy-five years since it was found. There has to be an alternative."

Kavanaugh leveled the carbine at Belleau. "There is. If Bai dies, so do you."

Belleau glanced from the hollow bore of the rifle, to Bai Suzhen's face, and then he turned toward Oakshott. "The sample, please."

The big man thrust a hand into his pants pocket and produced the glass tube. Belleau took it from him, carefully picking away at the wax and solder seal. He said resentfully, "This was sealed by Jacque Belleau himself."

"Then who better that to break the seal than his direct descendant?" Honoré inquired.

A furious thumping and scratching came from above. On the roof, the pair of Deinonychus hammered at a pane of Plexiglass. At first, Kavanaugh assumed they vented their frustration, but he saw the corner of the panel pop loose from the lip of the frame. His throat constricted. By working with bloodthirsty diligence, the animals had found a weak spot.

Keeping his eyes on the raptors, he asked, "Gus, how fast do you figure we're going?"

Crowe looked out the window. "Thirty, maybe thirty-five miles an hour."

"No way to go faster?"

"I'm surprised we're maintaining this rate of speed. Why?"

Kavanaugh pointed to the creatures on the roof. "Remember what they used to tell us in training—that it was better to fight the enemy down the road than when they dropped into our laps?"

Crowe's brow furrowed. "Jesus Christ. How many rounds do you have left?"

"Two."

"If you shoot through the glass, you'll get a big degree of deflection."

"I know. And if we wait until they drop into our laps, we could find our laps in pretty clawed up conditions."

Crowe knuckled his chin contemplatively. "An outcome to be avoided."

Honoré swung her head up, her face registering a mixture of fear and confusion. "I'm not sure what you're talking about, but I don't like the sound of it."

"Join the club," Kavanaugh replied. "But if we don't do something, we're going to have a couple of very bad-mannered drop-ins."

He glanced toward Oakshott, who stared upward at the

Deinonychus. "Mr. Oakshott—do you happen to have a first name?"

The man nodded. "Hamish."

"Hamish, I'll need your help. I'm going to open the rear door, stand out on the platform and you're going to boost me up so I can shoot those goddamn raptors."

"What?" demanded Belleau in a ragged voice.

"Yes," said Oakshott, levering himself to his feet by the arms of the chair. "Yes, I can do that."

Belleau scowled. "I forbid it."

Oakshott said quietly, "Don't worry about it, Doctor. Everything is fine."

Belleau looked to be on the verge of arguing, then he finished scraping away the last of the seal on the tube and handed it to Honoré, who held it uncertainly. She sniffed the contents and asked, "What do I do with this?"

"How should I know? According to the journal, the material actually leaked into Bosun Hoxie's wounds."

Honoré eyed the substance within the vial dubiously. "Then I should just apply it topically to her injuries?"

"I've told you all I know," Belleau said with a resigned headshake.

Very carefully, Honoré lifted the pressure bandage away from Bai Suzhen's lacerations. Kavanaugh grimaced at the sight of the deep gashes, the flesh around them swollen and discolored.

"Here goes," Honoré whispered, tipping the vial over the wounds.

For a long moment, the sludge did not slide from the tube. Then, a fat drop oozed over the rim and plopped directly into the center cut. A second later, a sluggish stream flowed forth, spreading out and filling the raw gashes with bubbling slime.

Honoré drew back, murmuring, "Oh my God. It almost seems drawn to the areas of most trauma."

Feeling a little sick to his stomach, Kavanaugh gestured to Oakshott. "Let's do this."

The two men moved to rear door. Crowe and Mouzi stood directly beneath the Deinonychus, holding their attention by shouting and gesticulating.

Kavanaugh put his hand on the locking bar. "On three. One...two...*three.*"

He flung up the bar, and shouldered the door open, stepping onto the platform. At the same time, Oakshott bent, grasped him around the waist and lifted Kavanaugh straight up.

To Kavanaugh, an eternity elapsed between the time he opened the door and put the rifle stock to his shoulder. He half-expected to find himself staring directly into the snarling snout of a Deinonychus. He experienced a wave of relieved surprise when he saw that the two creatures were still engrossed in prying up the transparent panel from the roof. However, he had not expected the rush of the wind to be so strong and his eyes stung.

A raptor caught Kavanaugh's sudden appearance at the periphery of its vision. Its head whipped toward him, jaws opening either in astonishment or anger. Bracing his elbows on the edge of the train car roof, Kavanaugh sighted down the rifle and squeezed the trigger of the Kel-Tec.

The round punched through the roof of the creature's mouth and into its brain. Vomiting blood, it flailed backward, its tail slamming down hard against the roof of the coach. As it rolled off, the Plexiglass panel collapsed inward, carrying the second Deinonychus down with it.

Even over the sound of the rushing wind and the drone of the monorail's engine, Kavanaugh heard the blended screams and *skreeks.*

The Plexiglass panel narrowly avoided cracking Mouzi on the crown of her head, but the swinging tail of the raptor smacked into Crowe's right side, knocking him against a seat back. He struggled to stay on his feet. Shouting obscenities, Mouzi thrust at the Deinonychus with her butterfly knife.

The shrieking saurian struck at her hand, the jaws snapping shut so close to her wrist its snout brushed her skin. Crowe kicked at it, missed, and the Deinonychus responded by lashing out with its right foot. The sickle-shaped claw on its second toe ripped a long, deep rent in the seat cover.

Crowe swung a knotted fist in a ram's head backhand. The blow connected, the raptor's head jerked around on its neck and pain blazed through Crowe's knuckles, halfway up his arm. It was like back-fisting a statue. The Deinonychus staggered, then bent forward, pivoted around on its toes and clubbed him in the chest with its tail.

Crowe felt like his heart had been hit with an axe blade. His lungs seized and he doubled over. He collapsed into a seat, clutching at his ribs. Over his own agonized gasps, he heard Mouzi scream "Duck!"

A heavy weight thumped down near him. Drops of something warm and gelatinous splattered across his cheek. Gasping, he forced his vision back into focus and saw the head of the Deinonychus lying on the floor only inches from his face. Dark blood pooled at the stump of its sheared-through neck.

Crowe struggled up to a sitting position. To his amazement he saw Bai Suzhen standing directly behind him, her jian sword angled over her left shoulder. Although her face was nearly white, the haggard look was gone from her features and her eyes were clear. The breeze coming in through the open rear door stirred her sleek black locks.

"Bai," he managed to stammer. "Are you all right?"

Slowly, she lowered the sword, and then dropped into a seat. "I feel much better, thanks."

Chapter Thirty-Two

Belleau and Honoré stared at Bai Suzhen, surprised into silence. Less than a minute before, the woman had lain senseless. Then, mere seconds after the Prima Materia had entered her wounds, her eyes snapped open. She saw the threat presented by the Deinonychus, and without preliminaries, she arose, grabbed her sword and swiftly decapitated the creature.

"I don't believe it," faltered Honoré. "You were unconscious, feverish—"

Bai ran a trembling hand over her sweat-slick brow. "Still feel shaky."

She allowed Honoré to examine her wounds. Oakshott and Kavanaugh returned to the interior of the coach, standing nearby. "What happened?" asked Kavanaugh.

Honoré didn't answer immediately. The gashes on Bai Suzhen's torso were filled with a thick, semi-solid fluid. It bubbled and foamed along the edges of the lacerations.

Choosing her words carefully, Honoré said, "All I can think of is that this substance acts as both a natural coagulating agent as well as a stimulant...accelerating Bai's metabolic functions, boosting her immune system."

Belleau revolved the empty glass vial between thumb and forefinger, then brandished it over his head like an Olympic runner who has just passed the finish line with the torch. "My great-great-grandfather spoke the truth! Prima Materia, the one true thing!"

Kneading his rib-cage, Crowe glared at Belleau. "Do you even know what the hell you're talking about? Do you know what that sludge is made of?"

"Of course I do. It is the original soup of life. It is the autocatalyst from which all genetic materials on Earth sprang."

Crowe eyed him distrustfully, but he began to look intrigued. "You can prove that claim?"

"Of course I can, I wouldn't have made it otherwise." Belleau glanced over his shoulder at Oakshott. "Now, if you would be so kind—"

Without hesitation, the big man chopped with his right hand at the back of Kavanaugh's neck, just below his left ear. The blow numbed him. Dimly, he felt his knees folding and he tried to catch himself on a chair back, but his arms had no strength in them.

Oakshott easily wrested the rifle from his grip, aiming it at Crowe and Mouzi. Between clenched teeth, Crowe grated, "This is getting very old, Belleau."

"Oh, I entirely agree. That is why unless you force Mr. Oakshott to fire off the one remaining round in the rifle, you will cede authority of this expedition back to me."

"Expedition?" echoed Honoré in disgust. "That is what you call this series of abductions and hostage situations? This is intolerable!"

"You won't have to tolerate it for much longer, darlin'. No one will."

Rubbing the back of his neck, Kavanaugh slowly got up, turning around to face Oakshott. "You ever heard of the American concept of payback, Hamish?"

Oakshott shrugged. "I could've just as easily broken your neck, Jack. Consider yourself fortunate."

Belleau chuckled, but it sounded forced. "Don't take it out him. We're so close to the objective of the expedition, I don't want distractions."

"You're about to get a big one," Mouzi declared. "We're almost at the end of the line."

Everyone looked out the front window. The dark bulk of the escarpment loomed gigantic, almost filling the view. The rail ran straight and true, terminating in a T-shaped barrier cushioned by layers of rubber.

"We ought to be hitting the braking points any time now," Crowe said.

The coach lurched as if it rolled over a pothole and they heard a brief screech of metal.

"There's one of them," he went on.

Metal clanged loudly and a shower of sparks flew up from beneath the car. "And another."

"Can't you disconnect the power?" Belleau asked anxiously.

"Too late for that," replied Mouzi. "Best sit your ass down."

As everyone dropped into a seat, the train jolted and jarred. Sparks flew from beneath it like the fiery tails of crashing comets. The entire coach shook violently in a series of bone-jarring impacts as it continued to slide ahead. The smell of overheated metal and burning rubber drifted in.

Only when the nose of the coach slammed into the barrier did the train come to a full halt, tipping over slightly to the right. Hissings and clankings came from underneath. Kavanaugh found himself lying across the body of the decapitated Deinonychus.

He picked himself up quickly, turning around. To his disappointment he saw Oakshott had managed to retain his seat and his grip on the carbine. Bai Suzhen sat on the opposite side of the coach, her expression blank, hand held over her right shoulder. Honoré stirred beside her, face pale but composed.

Helping Mouzi to her feet, Crowe said, "We're without power now. The impact must've knocked the connection loose."

Kavanaugh fanned the air as the coach began fill up with smoke. "We also burned out some bearings. Time to get out. Let's get dump our headless hobo just in case we have to come back here."

The seven people filed out through the rear door. Crowe and Kavanaugh carried the corpse of the Deinonychus while Mouzi brought out the creature's head. They hurled both over the side and into the thick brush.

Belleau opened the Darwin journal, flipped to the map,

scanned the terrain and pointed toward the escarpment. The peak looked black against the blue-white of the sky. Cloud streamers whipped around the pinnacles of the extinct volcanic cone.

"That way," he announced. "We'll walk the same path to the Mountain of Mystery as my forebear."

Kavanaugh gestured toward the outer fringe of jungle, less than a mile distant. "Be our guest. We'll wait for you here."

Belleau shook his head. "No, that won't do. I have my reasons for not leaving anyone behind. But I assure you—there's no need for us to be antagonists, sir, not at this late date."

"If that's the case, you could tell Hamish to drop the rifle, right?"

"I could—but I won't. Not only are you an impetuous man, but Madame Suzhen has threatened my life. You can't blame me for preferring a bit of protection, even it's only a single bullet's worth."

To emphasize the little man's words, Oakshott leveled the carbine at Bai Suzhen. She affected not to notice the silent, implicit threat. Kavanaugh exchanged glances with Crowe and Mouzi, both of whom kept their expressions neutral, but their eyes said, *Now isn't the time.*

Kavanaugh shrugged. "All right, Aubrey. Lead on."

Honoré Roxton settled her Stetson on her head and quoted softly, "'Over the Mountains Of the Moon, Down the Valley of the Shadow, Ride, boldly ride.' "

Automatically she checked her watch and murmured wearily, "All of this before noon. Almighty God."

* * *

The jungle filling the ravines around the base of the escarpment was deceptive. It was not quite the tangled green hell as it looked from the verge. By following Belleau, they came upon a rutted pathway, laid with flat stones. It led through a rich maze of white orchids, clouds of whining insects and flowering plants of such brilliant colors they defied the imagination.

"Who made this path?" Crowe asked, the survival kit tucked under an arm.

Belleau grinned jauntily. "Would you believe that it was first laid by the second expedition to Big Tamtung, in 1840? And that it was kept up by various scholars of the School of Night?"

Crowe didn't respond.

Bai Suzhen brought up the rear. She remained silent, stoically enduring the flies crawling over her blood-caked blouse. Her detachment disturbed Kavanaugh because he could not afford to divide his concentration by worrying about her. He dropped back to walk beside her.

"How are you feeling, Bai?" he asked in a low voice.

She did not reply for so long he almost repeated the question. Then, softly, she answered, "I feel very strange, Jack. Like I'm not really here. I am dreaming this, aren't I? I'm lying in bed with you, dreaming about you."

Kavanaugh struggled to keep the sudden cold shock from registering on his face. He said, "Poor way to spend your time."

Bai whispered, "This is real, not a dream."

Kavanaugh forced a grin. "Maybe it is and you'll wake up in your dressing room in the White Snake club and wonder why the hell you were having a crazy dream with an ugly scarred-up American in it."

Bai's eyes cast him a penetrating stare. He met her gaze. Her smile was slow to come, but it grew like an unfolding blossom. Her long black hair half hid the smile and turned it into something mysterious and meaningful.

She whispered, "When you are ready to make your move, I will be, too."

She lifted her sword. He nodded in acknowledgement.

"Pick up the pace back there!" barked Belleau. "No need to conspire in whispers against me, either. You'll be thanking me soon enough."

Mouzi said angrily, "We're just humoring you, y'know. You

don't scare us. Because without that giant to back you up, you're just a damn dwarf with an attitude. "

"You're not the first to say so," Belleau shot back haughtily. "But you will most definitely be the last."

"Drop the threats, Aubrey," Honoré said.

He cast her a glance full of wounded innocence. "Threats? By no means...that was a promise."

The treeless summit towering over them was a monolith of dark, buttressed rock, slashed through with deep, shadowed crevices. The terrain gradually sloped upward toward it. The waterfall looked like a translucent veil over the face of a cliff. A thin mist lay over the high ridges.

The seven people walked under the permanent cloud that clung to the base of the escarpment. Under it spread the rain forest, damp and steamy. The sunlight became suffuse, as if they were at the bottom of a silt-clouded pond. The world seemed to turn a bilious green-gray around them.

The heat of the day increased and the air grew thicker, more difficult to breath. The path became less visible and they came across great mushrooms and huge spongy masses of fungus that grew six feet across.

The sour smell of mold and mildew clogged everyone's nostrils. Mouzi rubbed her nose with the back of a hand and muttered, "Place smells like my gran's basement."

The trail worsened, becoming very hard to see in the mist. A little stream ran near it, between high banks of dark soil. A bird twittered somewhere overhead and a heavy something made a crackling noise in the underbrush to their right.

After half an hour, it began to drizzle and within seconds everyone was soaked, but there was no relief from the heat. Their sweat mixed with the water and made for a slimy, slick coating on their skin, but they marched on until the rain ended a few minutes later.

Kavanaugh called for a halt when he saw Bai Suzhen stagger and nearly fall. Belleau gave him a hard, challenging stare but he didn't object. He moved on down the trail, to scout out what lay ahead, ordering Oakshott to stay behind.

Kavanaugh watched Bai stand uncertainly for a moment, then sit down on the path. Crowe and Mouzi seated themselves on either side of her. Honoré walked along the edge of the stream and sat down on the bank and unlaced her boots.

Kavanaugh sat down beside her with his back to broad-rooted tree, out of the sight of Oakshott. The air felt a little cooler beside the placidly flowing water. The top of the tree soared into invisibility, lost in the steamy fog. He asked her quietly, "How are you doing, Dr. Roxton?"

"I'm fine, except for my feet." Stripping off her socks, she plunged her toes into the purling water and sighed in relief. "What about Bai?"

"What about her?"

"She acts…strange. Out of it."

Kavanaugh glanced over at Bai Suzhen, peering through the fog. She sat between Crowe and Mouzi, hugging her knees and staring off into the mist, as if she were looking into another time or another reality.

"Yeah," he said. "Maybe it's a reaction to that stuff you treated her with. The Prima Materia."

Honoré nodded. "I wouldn't be surprised, particularly if its chemical composition is anything like Aubrey described."

"How so?"

"It's possible that the material increased Bai's own production of catalase and dismutase enzymes…jump-starting the healing process."

"Do you really think it could be a genuine miracle cure?"

"Isn't that what you and Flitcroft believed?"

"I just went along with the results of Howard's scientific tests. Still, I should have died when the Deinonychus gutted me. Anywhere else, the injuries would have been fatal."

Honoré opened her mouth to reply then shook her head. "I don't know anything anymore. I'm a scientist, I should have known better than to listen to Aubrey. But here I am, in the middle of nowhere, looking for the equivalent of the fountain of youth. I must be insane."

"I should've known better about a few things, too."

"Such as?"

"About letting Aubrey and Oakshott get the drop on us. At some point soon, we're going to jump them. They're going to get hurt, maybe very badly."

Honoré drew in a sharp breath. "I don't think that's necessary."

Kavanaugh said in a harsh whisper, "I don't want it to be, but that decision is totally up to them. I need to know which way *you're* going to jump."

She looked at him for a long, sober moment. "You know the answer to that, Jack. You can count on me."

"Thank you. That's all I needed to know."

Honoré smiled shyly at Kavanaugh. "You make me so curious about you. I don't really understand you. The self-indulgent drunk becomes the self-sacrificing warrior."

Feeling suddenly uncomfortable, hand reflexively going to the scar on his face, Kavanaugh said, "I'm nothing special, Honoré. I'm not much good to anyone. I've pretty much failed at everything worthwhile I ever tried. Nobody in the world—except for maybe Gus and Mouzi—would miss me too much if I died out here."

"I think you're wrong. You keep going in spite of all the things that could have destroyed you. I can relate to that."

"Why?"

"You do a lot of self-medication with alcohol, I noticed. But you haven't shown any signs of dependence out here."

"Maybe that's the difference between a drunkard and an alcoholic. I just like to get drunk, I don't *need* to."

With startling frankness she said, "I'm a recovering alcoholic, so I always feel the need."

His memory flew back to the meeting at the Phoenix of Beauty. "During the meeting with Flitcroft, you were the only one who wasn't drinking."

She smiled wanly. "Don't think I wasn't desperate for a drink. My life has been a struggle to control my impulses.

For example, I've had this mad impulse for the last couple of minutes to fuck you."

His eyebrows rose. "A *mad* impulse? Aren't those the worst kind?"

"They are, indeed. So this will have to suffice." Honoré leaned forward and kissed him hard on the lips.

Kavanaugh thought about Oakshott, about Bai watching them, and then he was only aware of the warmth and promise of Honoré's lips. Her hand cupped the side of his face, fingers tracing the scar. His own hand came up, pressing lightly against her left breast. She leaned into him and he felt her heartbeat, her nipple stiff against his palm.

Then she drew back, pulling her hand away, her breath on his cheek a rueful whisper. "I haven't wanted a man in a long time. I was married once, but I spoiled it due to my poor impulse control."

"So this is just another poorly controlled impulse?"

"Perhaps…so next time, my impulse will be a bit more premeditated…and in more conducive surroundings."

Kavanaugh chuckled. "That's the best reason I've heard to get out of here alive."

Belleau returned, seeming to materialize out of the fog. He gestured grandly. "To horse, to horse! We're almost there."

Reluctantly, groaning and biting back curses, everyone got to their feet. Honoré struggled back into her boots. Kavanaugh saw Bai Suzhen staring at him. Although her face held no particular expression, she quickly averted her eyes when their gazes met.

Feeling foolish and angry because he did, Kavanaugh fell into step behind the small Englishman.

They went on, following the trail. It crossed the stream on a rough log bridge, then crawled up a long slope, dipping down over the crest of the hill. The seven people stood on the brow of the ridge, looking down at a shallow valley backed by rocky outcroppings that melded into a vine-grown cliff-face.

The diluted sunlight made strange geometric shapes of ruined walls and crumbling structures. They saw how the rubble of collapsed roofs and statues whose features were eroded by centuries of rain formed a ghostly maze. An enormous stone column, nearly twenty feet tall and ten feet in diameter thrust up from the ground. The surface was almost completely overgrown with creepers.

Aubrey Belleau shivered, hugging himself in gleeful antici-pation. "Here we are," he chanted. "Here we are."

"Here we are where?" demanded Kavanaugh.

"Look closely at the pillar, Jack," Honoré said softly.

He squinted, peering through the mist. He was barely able to make out a series of carvings in the form of glyphs that Belleau had called Enochian.

Chapter Thirty-Three

As they walked down the hillside, they saw that the entire valley was one vast ruin, a tumbled labyrinth of overgrown walls, fallen roofs and sculpture that blended in with the encroaching jungle.

Enormous trees had grown up between cut blocks of stone and pushed them over to make room for their spreading trunks and root systems. Between them grass, weeds and saplings had forced their way toward the light. That alone was sufficient evidence for Kavanaugh that the structures had been built so long ago that even a whisper of their existence could only be measured in millennia.

"It's like a temple complex," Honoré said, squinting through the mist. "Similar in layout to Angkor Thom."

"Yes," agreed Bai Suzhen. "But on a smaller scale."

Time and the merciless hands of the elements had etched deep scars and grooves in low sandstone walls surrounding the grounds. The architecture of the few standing buildings was ornate, the facades swarming with sculptures and carvings depicting dancers, many-armed gods and multi-headed demons.

Some sections of the wall were so eroded they had fallen over altogether. They enclosed roofless arches and crumbling buildings containing nothing but empty shadows. Only silence and perpetual twilight filled the lanes and shattered structures.

Belleau paused, frowning. He ran a finger over a glyph inscribed in a free-standing stele, a square stone column covered on all four sides with carvings that formed swirling geometric abstractions. "My great-great-grandfather copied down these symbols."

Belleau looked all around, like a foxhound casting for a scent. "It should be close," he muttered. "It must be."

A broad avenue made of paving stones opened into a vast courtyard filled with the wreck and ruin of many buildings. Great blocks of basalt and granite lay sunken deep into the ground. But the inner arches still stood, and fragments of fretted galleries stretched to nowhere. Broken statues lay in the grass, their features mutilated by time and the jungle. Moss filled the carved eye sockets.

"I don't recognize this architectural style," Honoré said. "Or rather, the style is reminiscent of several cultures, but none predominate. That structure over there resembles the Gate of the Sun at Tiahuanaco in Bolivia."

Belleau chuckled briefly. "You might want to consider that the architecture here served as the inspiration for the styles adopted by other cultures. You've heard the theories that the many similarities between the cultures of Pre-Columbian Central American and the ancient East stemmed from a mysterious 'third-party' civilization."

Honoré didn't respond, but she looked closer at the few structures still standing.

Kavanaugh felt a sense of oppression and awe at the work that had been done here, yet sadness, as well, because of the way it had all fallen into ruin.

A sudden shifting of shadow, of a darker shade than the mist on the far side of he ruins made his shoulders stiffen. He wasn't sure if he'd glimpsed an actual movement or only a trick of the light. A chill finger seemed to stroke the base of his spine and he repressed a shudder. What kind of creatures watched their progress, he did not want to guess.

If you return, you will die

"Time to come clean with us, Aubrey," Honoré demanded. "What do you know about this place?"

"Like I told you before," Belleau said, consulting the journal again, "the School of Night has protected the secrets of Big Tamtung for nearly two centuries. In 1840, our society saw to the building of the first observation post here, a duck blind as it were, to study the flora and fauna. Once every twenty-five years, a volunteer was dispatched here with enough food and provisions to last him a year, while he observed and charted any changes in the island's ecosystem or biology.

"The School did this once every generation until the outbreak of World War II. Although the war in Pacific didn't quite reach this part of the world, it came uncomfortably close. The School feared discovery of the Tamtungs during all the post-war activity, and so the observation post wasn't occupied again until thirty-some years ago.

"After that particular volunteer's term was up, he never arrived at the rendezvous point to be retuned to England. He was a young doctor from an influential political family and the School kept an extraordinarily low profile during the investigation into his whereabouts. They feared exposure and scandal.

"The whole mission to maintain Big Tamtung under a protectorate was scrubbed, discontinued. Most of the other scholars placed very little priority on it, particularly with the rise of newer scientific disciplines."

"And then," Honoré said, "you became a scholar of the School."

She made a statement, she did not ask a question.

Belleau nodded. "Just so. I was inducted when I turned twenty-one. However, I wasn't able to revive the School's interest in Big Tamtung at that point. It required the publicity about Cryptozoica Enterprises to do that, many years later. In the interim, I was allowed to perform the first modern biochemical analysis on a sample of Prima Materia."

Bai Suzhen carefully probed her shoulder. "And what did you learn?"

Belleau smiled wistfully. "I only validated what my great-great-grandfather had long suspected. Prima Materia is the same legendary substance known throughout many cultures under a variety of different names—the Fifth Element, the Quintessence of Life, the Pool of Nectar, Soma Ras and Vasuki's Milk of Immortality. It is related to myths of Enoch, Thoth and even Ramses the Great and their supply of so-called *elixir vitae*. You'd be surprised by how so many legends of this miraculous life-giving substance are associated with serpents, but more on that later.

"According to Aristotle and alchemical lore, Prima Materia is the primitive formless base of all organic matter, from which every substance is created. It is considered to be *pure* matter, the same as primordial ooze, which contained all the biochemical ingredients considered essential for the development of life on the planet."

"I meant what is it actually *made* of?" Bai asked impatiently.

"The chemical composition is difficult to describe," replied Belleau. "But suffice it to say the Prima Materia exists as a multi-cellular organism unto itself, in a primal protoplasmic form. As you probably know, stem cells are found in all multi-cellular organisms. They have the ability to renew themselves through mitotic cell division and can differentiate into a very diverse range of specialized cell types, such as the abiotic synthesis of biomolecules. So what does that suggest to you?"

Crowe regarded the little man with an eyebrow angled at a steep, skeptical incline. "That it's a naturally-occurring, renewable source of stem cells?"

Belleau touched his nose. "On the money, Captain Crowe. Think about it—this substance can graft onto DNA and repair genetic defects, melding seamlessly with the pre-existing sequence, completely rewriting the code if necessary. No more birth defects, no more congenital autoimmune diseases, no more crippling spinal injuries."

Kavanaugh exchanged a sour look with Honoré and realized she was thinking the same thing as he—no more birth defects, spinal injuries and no more giant egos trapped in the bodies of dwarves.

"We can corner the market on an entirely new system of biochemistry," Belleau went on, his cheeks flushed, "that could conceivably grant a form of immortality through the synthesis of telomeres."

"What are they?" Kavanaugh asked.

"Sections of DNA that cap chromosomes," Belleau explained. "They keep them intact, except during cell division. There are some types of enzymes that work as a telomere repair system, even when a cell divides."

"So?" Bai demanded.

"So," replied Belleau, "cells that don't lose telomeres are virtually immortal, capable of dividing and self-replicating indefinitely and remaining intact."

"And a pool of that stuff is supposed to be around here?" Mouzi inquired dubiously.

"Yes, it is," answered Belleau. "It's my theory that the 'pool of that stuff' is why Big Tamtung became the most unique ecosystem in not just all of the world but in all of history."

They walked down a long, broad lane lined by monolithic columns carved with images of serpent-bodied warriors, princesses, devils and heroes. Every place the eye rested held serpent imagery. The stones of the floor bore colored tiles that formed the immense mosaic of a seven-headed cobra.

In a ghostly whisper, Bai Suzhen said, "The Naga queens and kings left their souls here.'

Belleau said quietly, "You are more correct than you know, Madame."

At the end of the hall, Belleau came to a halt to study the journal pages again. Honoré said, "I don't understand what you meant about Big Tamtung being a unique ecosystem. It most definitely is, but I thought you believed quantum evolution explained the Cretaceous survivors here."

A little distractedly, Belleau declared, "Small populations like this one, isolated from the gene flow, would maintain certain genetic combinations in stable adaptive peaks. I theorize that the Prima Materia has affected everything of an organic nature on this island, from plants to water to the animals."

"Explain."

"Over the centuries, over the aeons, the basic autocatalytic substance of the Prima Materia seeped into everything here, from the soil in which the plants grew to the ground water. The herbivores consumed the plants, the carnivores consumed the herbivores and they all drank the same water, a natural cycle by which they all ingested the same simple molecular replicator. That replicator maintained just about everything here in its most pristine state."

Belleau began walking again, touching walls as if trying to orient himself. "It's possible that the animals here are very old… perhaps the replicator slowed the aging process to a relative crawl, so even when offspring are born, it could take centuries before they reached mature breeding age. That would keep the population well within manageable limits, in balance with the ecosystem."

Honoré strode beside him, ignoring Oakshott. "Aubrey, is it your hypothesis that the Prima Materia *halted* evolution here on Big Tamtung? Gave it a time out?"

"Of course not. Evolution can no more be halted than gravity. You've pointed out the differences in several of the animals from the fossil record and the reconstructions. But I do believe that what evolution took place here was on a micro-level, changes within a species."

"I don't getcha," Mouzi said. "Example."

"Micro-evolution regarding whales would be their change from freshwater mammals to saltwater mammals," Crowe stated. "Macro-evolution would be like land animals going into the sea and evolving into whales."

"Oh," she said, still looking mystified.

"Darwin noted the biological variations among individuals of a species," explained Belleau. "He didn't know what caused the variations, but since his time we've learned they're caused by mutations. The general consensus of scientific thought is that useful mutations help a species survive. Darwin and his colleagues called this concept natural selection."

"Yes, yes," Honoré said impatiently. "Mutations are the result of changes in the DNA code from generation to generation of a particular species, usually a form of micro-evolution."

"That's because most mutations are neutral," declared Belleau. "Harmful or helpful mutations depend largely on the environment in which an organism lives. The organisms here on Big Tamtung were perfectly suited for their environment, so when they hit their adaptive peaks, they tended to stablize and stay there, except for a few, largely cosmetic changes, like the Majungasaurs developing a third finger or the Quetzacoatlus evolving the need for teeth. The basic, functional form remained the same.

"Of course, that's not to say a small number of Cretaceous survivors didn't become extinct here as they did in the outside world. An even smaller number actually underwent a form of evolution between micro and macro."

He paused and added quietly, "Like the Troodon."

Honoré's eyes widened. "You don't mean—the anthroposaur?"

Belleau nodded sagely. "The Nagas of Madame Suzhen's culture."

In an aggrieved tone full of exasperation, Honoré said, "Aubrey—"

Belleau brushed her off with a hand-wave. "Enough, Dr. Roxton. I've got to collect my bearings here."

He peered around as if he could see through the misty murk for a landmark.

"It's been a long time since that map was drawn," Kavanaugh said. "Things change, especially in a jungle."

"No," muttered Belleau. "It should be here. *It should be here.*"

"Hey," called Mouzi laconically, her figure looking like an apparition in the fog. "Is this what you're looking for?"

Belleau hustled toward her, elbowing his way between Bai Suzhen and Crowe. He rocked to a clumsy halt, a peculiar gurgling noise issuing from his mouth. His eyes bulged.

A path dipped down at a gradual incline, lined on both sides by square, squat columns. Inestimable centuries of weather had pitted and eroded the Enochian glyphs so they were barely visible. At the end of the double-facing row of monoliths, surrounded by a collar of interlocking stone slabs, lay a round pool ten feet in circumference. The inner rim was lined with an edging of silver ore that glinted with a dull iridescence. Every other stone slab was engraved with an Enochian symbol.

Mouzi stood at the rim holding a thick tree branch, six feet long. With the point, she prodded the surface of the pool. It looked more like a muck-filled, stagnant hog wallow. It smelled so foul and fetid that everyone recoiled from it.

Belleau circled the pool, as if his mind refused to accept what his eyes saw. "No, no. This isn't it, is it? No. *No.*"

A gaseous bubble on the surface of the sludge broke with a slow-motion flatulent *pop*, releasing a stench not unlike rotten eggs mixed with ammonia. Mouzi pinched her nostrils shut and shook her head in mock pity.

"*This* is what you dragged me to this part of the world to find?" Honoré shouted, whirling on Belleau, her eyes blazing with anger. "You put me through all of this, involved me in crime and murder to lay claim to this—cesspit?"

Belleau fell to his knees at the rim, reaching out a beseeching hand toward the bubbling muck. "This can't be," he whispered hoarsely. "This is unacceptable."

Oakshott stepped up beside him, intoning, "Don't worry about it, Doctor. Everything is fine."

Mouzi took a quick backstep, hefted the tree-branch in both hands and swung it like a baseball bat. The thick length of wood broke in half against the back of Oakshott's skull with a sound like a whipcrack.

The huge man stood stock still for a second, then he achieved a shambling half-turn before toppling over unconscious. As he fell, Mouzi expertly snatched the carbine from his hand.

"*Now* everything is fine," she stated matter-of-factly.

Chapter Thirty-Four

Belleau stood behind Oakshott, examining the back of his head. The big man sat near the edge of the pool, his face as expressionless as if graven in stone.

"Just a small contusion," Belleau said. "I don't think she hit you hard enough to inflict a concussion. You'll be as right as the mail in a little while."

Belleau swept his angry, reproachful gaze over Mouzi, Kavanaugh and Crowe. "Now that you have gained the upper hand again, what do you intend to do with it?"

"First thing," said Crowe, taking the carbine from Mouzi, "is to remove temptation."

Jacking the slide back and forth, he ejected the single bullet into his hand, which he then put into his pocket. He passed the rifle back to Mouzi.

Kavanaugh turned toward Honoré and Bai Suzhen, who stared at the surface of the pool. "Dr. Roxton, what time is it?"

She consulted her wristwatch. "Five minutes past three."

"Not much chance of walking back to the monorail before nightfall," Crowe observed.

"No," agreed Kavanaugh. "We're closer to the beach at this point. If we start out right now, we can probably make it by six." He extended a hand toward Belleau. "Your phone, please."

Belleau stared at him, feigning puzzlement. "Why?"

"Why do you think? I'll call Bert and arrange a pickup at the beach for this evening."

Reluctantly, Belleau reached under his shirt tail and removed the satphone from the holster at his hip. Kavanaugh pressed the power button, but no icons lit up. He tried it several times, then said flatly, "It's dead. The battery is drained."

Crowe took the phone, examined it quickly, then glared at Belleau. "You've had the triangulation tracer feature on all this time, haven't you? So Jimmy Cao would know where to find you?"

Belleau smiled but it held no humor. "Even if I had, the phone went dead some hours ago. I doubt Mr. Cao would be able to track us to this place."

"I don't," declared Bai Suzhen coldly. "He'll not give up if he thinks there's a fortune to be found here. He has no choice but to show something to United Bamboo, to justify why he went around the council and attacked me. He'll keep coming until he finds us."

Kavanaugh grinned. "And what he'll do to you, Aubrey, when you show him your fabled jacuzzi o' crap might be worth hanging around to see."

Crowe glanced around gloomily. "We're going to have to spend the night here, so we'd better find a defensible position. Belleau, do you know where the School of Night's observation post was set up?"

He shook his head. "No."

Crowe tapped Oakshott on the shoulder with the barrel of the carbine. "Up."

As the big man heaved himself to his feet, Kavanaugh gestured in the direction of the cliff-face. "Let's check over there for some high ground."

The seven people retraced their steps through the ruins. Belleau's gait was slow and trudging, his shoulders slumped. He muttered, "I don't understand…the pool should have continually renewed itself, self-replicated the micro-organisms. The sample in the vial retained all those properties. I don't understand."

"Anything could have happened to it over the years," Honoré said. "Perhaps the material finally just reached the end of its life-cycle. Pollutants might have contaminated it. There's no way to tell."

They wended their way among the fallen walls and free-standing arches until they reached a point where the ground met the cliff-face. Although nearly covered by a screen of vines, they saw a high, narrow fissure splitting the rock wall.

Honoré turned toward Belleau. "Did Darwin or your great-grandfather mention anything about a cave?"

Belleau opened the journal, thumbing through the pages until he found a small pencil sketch of a crack in the rock wall.

"This is it, but Jacque didn't explore it very deeply, although he suspected the tunnel passed completely through the escarpment and came out on the other side."

"If true," said Bai Suzhen, "it would save us some time."

Crowe removed a small flashlight from the survival kit. "We can take a look, but I doubt the battery in this will hold up for long."

Led by Crowe, Kavanaugh, Mouzi, Honoré, Bai, and Belleau went inside, with Oakshott several paces behind. High overhead, two hundred feet or more, the narrow crack of rock showed the clear afternoon sky, like a jagged spear point of brightness. The sunlight wasn't filtered through the mist. Rubble slid underfoot and each step was chosen with care.

The fissure gradually became a cave, widening at the bottom with the rock walls leaning toward each other at the top. Irregular stalactites hung from above. The narrow beam of the flashlight in Crowe's hand winked dully against a tin box resting atop a large boulder. The insignia of the School of the Night was barely legible on the lid.

Everyone gathered around it and stared, nonplussed. At a nod from Kavanaugh, Mouzi opened the box. Inside lay a small spiral-bound notebook and a long-handled silver flashlight.

Kavanaugh picked up the flashlight, pressed the switch and when nothing happened, he unscrewed a plate on the back and an L-shaped handle popped out on a spring. "It's an old dynamo-powered flashlight. You've got to turn the crank to build a charge. Makes sense, if you're going to be in a place where Radio Shack hasn't opened a franchise."

As he began turning the crank, Honoré flipped through the leaves of the notebook, holding it toward the little light cast by Crowe's flash. "Handwritten in English," she said, "by a doctor named David Abner Perry."

She glanced at Belleau. "Is that the name of the observer posted here who went missing all those years ago?"

"I believe that was his name, yes."

As Honoré read the notations, Kavanaugh's hand-cranking produced a weak, pallid halo around the lens of the flashlight. She leaned toward it, so she could scan the pages. "Perry left this record for anybody who might come looking for him. He hid weapons nearby...look for a marker."

Kavanaugh cast the light around and saw a little scrap of red cloth atop of cairn of stone. He and Mouzi went to it, while Honoré continued reading. Bai kept a watchful eye on Oakshott and Belleau.

"After only being here about three weeks, Perry did extensive explorations of this cave," she said. "Even excavation... he found something here that he had not expected. But he's not very precise about it. He claims he was very ill and couldn't be sure of much of anything, but he is certain that history, as humankind understood it, is basically a lie. He writes: 'Here on this island, in this cave, I have found the fingerprints of a vanished culture, one that molded human civilizations all over the globe, but one that our historians and churchmen conspired to keep from us.'"

"That's a little strong on the melodrama," commented Kavanaugh.

Lifting aside the stacked stones, he and Mouzi uncovered a long, canvas bag. He unzipped it and removed an M161A automatic assault rifle, and a box of cartridges, as well as a matched set of big-bored Colt Python revolvers with checkered walnut grips.

Kavanaugh said happily, "Heavy-duty stuff thirty some years ago, but it's still useful now. God bless Dr. Perry, melodrama and all."

"Not too wild about revolvers," Mouzi said sourly, hefting one of the Colt Pythons with both hands. She grimaced at the weight.

"If you're stuck for a year on a island populated by damn dinosaurs," said Crowe, "you'll want firepower that has the least amount of moving parts and the least chance of jamming on you. Revolvers fit the bill."

"Definitely," agreed Kavanaugh, popping open the cylinder and giving it a spin. "Got a full load here and about fifteen spares. Two full mags for the M16."

Crowe nodded approvingly. "Then we can give Hamish back his carbine. He looks naked without it."

With a grin, Mouzi handed the unloaded carbine to Oakshott, who folded his arms and looked away. She laid it down on the cairn and took the autorifle.

Seemingly oblivious to the conversation about the guns, Honoré continued to read from the notebook, "Young Dr. Perry opened a sealed tunnel or side gallery with an explosive. He was injured while doing so. Desperate, he ingested some of the Prima Materia."

Skeptically, Belleau demanded, "He *drank* it?"

"Evidently. Perry had come up with his own theories about the true nature of the Prima Materia, not too different from yours. He hoped the substance would produce self-replicating progenitor cells and speed up his healing process. Instead, he became very ill."

"Not surprising," Belleau said. "But unless his immune system was already compromised, he should have only suffered some flu-like symptoms and then made a recovery."

Honoré nodded. "He wrote this while he was ill... delirious. He thought he was dying. That's why he stated he couldn't be sure of anything. He claimed demons were watching him, waiting for him to let his guard down."

"What happened to him?" Bai Suzhen asked.

Honoré flipped through the pages at the rear of the notebook. They were blank. "That's it...his account just stops."

Mouzi swallowed hard. "Maybe the demons got him."

Handing a revolver to Crowe and the autorifle to Mouzi, Kavanaugh said, "Let's go see what he found…if anything."

They strode along the narrow passageway with the black rock walls pressing in on them. A brooding, unbroken silence bore down, like the pressure of a vast hand. Oakshott lowered his head between hunched shoulders and whispered, "Don't like this."

Kavanaugh chuckled tauntingly. "Are you claustrophobic on top of being a sucker-puncher, Hamish?"

Belleau said soothingly. "We'll only be in here for a minute, old fellow."

The flashlight beams showed the floor was scattered with loose shale. It was obvious the rubble had fallen within fairly recent times, shaken loose by either an earthquake or some other violent vibration.

They went on for a hundred yards, walking through darkness as absolute as eternity. The blackness seemed to suck the energy from their flashlights, giving them little more illumination than a struck match. Kavanaugh wondered if it was wise to go on. He tried to keep other worries and fears from intruding into his single-minded march.

The cavern abruptly ended against a blank wall, featureless except for a man-size cavity that been punched through it. A heap of broken rock and debris lay around it. Black scorch marks around the jagged edges indicated the hole had been made with high explosives.

Crowe inspected the area around the cavity and his flashlight touched a dust-covered shape humped up near a fissure. Stepping over to it, he lifted away a square sheet of canvas draped over a number of bulky objects. Kavanaugh joined him, looking at the assortment of pick axes, rock hammers and shovels arranged around a wooden crate.

Crowe prised open the lid and announced, "We've got some demolition charges here."

Honoré, Mouzi and Belleau murmured in wordless unease

and drew back, but Crowe said, "Don't worry. This is Titadyn."

He brandished three salmon-colored tubes, all of them one inch in diameter and six inches long. "It's a type of compressed dynamite, used mainly for mining in Europe. The stuff is pretty stable, not like standard dynamite that sweats out nitroglycerin over time."

Kavanaugh picked up a handful of small gleaming cylinders, each one tipped by long, thin cords. "Dr. Perry was using pyrotechnic fuse blasting caps. I'm not surprised he got hurt. Tricky stuff if you're not trained in explosives."

"Yeah," grunted Crowe. "Let's see if we can't be a little less careless with them."

He wrapped the sticks of Titadyn in his bandana and shoved them in his back pocket. Mouzi winced and said, "What happens if you piss me off and I kick you in the ass?"

He handed her small set of pliers taken from the crate. "Then that'll be you all over."

"What's this?"

"A crimping tool for the fuses."

"Are we planning some demolition work?" asked Honoré.

"You never know in this place." Kavanaugh put the blasting caps in his pants pocket and stepped through the cavity, shining the flashlight ahead of him, finger resting on the trigger of the Colt.

"Looks clear," he said. "Dark, like usual."

Belleau said, "I don't see the point in this spelunking escapade. I vote we return to the outside."

"*Vote?*" echoed Bai Suzhen with a mocking laugh. "Since when did this become a democracy?"

She laid the blade of the sword lightly against his neck. "You only have two options…to remain behind and be dead or go with us and stay alive. You will not be allowed to run free and join up with Jimmy Cao."

"Madame, I promise you—"

"—Oh, shut up, Aubrey," Honoré snapped. "Just shut the fuck up."

"Let's go, goddammit," Crowe said gruffly.

They found themselves in a short tunnel that led through a doorway and into a wider passage. Kavanaugh looked around, casting his light into the shadows, but seeing nothing but rock.

"These tunnels are quarried, man-made," he stated.

"You're about half-right," said Belleau with a macabre grin.

The gallery curved, turning almost at right angles. As they walked around the bend, the tunnel curved again, adding to the seven people's growing bewilderment and apprehension. As they made another turn, they were startled to see a patch of light far ahead. Vaguely rectangular in shape and of an unearthly greenish hue, it wavered and flickered. They heard a roaring, like a distant engine idling.

"What the hell is that?" Kavanaugh asked. "Where is that light coming from?"

"The outside, perhaps," whispered Honoré.

"Why are you whispering?"

"I have no idea."

The passage stretched toward a narrow archway. Upon either side of it loomed a pair of twelve-foot tall statues sculpted of dark stone, with their arms crossed over their chests like Egyptian pharaohs. Although the finer details had long eroded away, the shape of their heads and faces resembled those of serpents.

Belleau said faintly, "Those look like Sumerian statues of the Annunaki, uncovered in Ur a couple of hundred years ago."

"The Naga," Bai said quietly.

Mouzi said, "They look like bloody lizards to me."

"Same thing, young Miss Mongrel."

The chamber on the other side of the archway was vast and echoing. Every rustle of sound was answered from the high, vaulted ceiling. The walls were tiled in confusing patterns of blue, red and yellow, displaying Enochian glyphs.

The chamber opened onto a broad foyer, bracketed on either side by crumbling colonnades. They walked onto a narrow, smoothly paved causeway, rising several feet above the cave floor. On either side towered obelisks of obsidian, with Enochian glyphs still visible upon their faces.

"What the hell are we seeing here?" murmured Crowe, playing the beam of his flashlight over the monoliths. "The style almost looks Egyptian, but they have Mayan or Olmec characteristics, too."

"A little of all three, I should say," stated Honoré.

"Who built it?" Kavanaugh asked, feeling dread knot up inside of him. The wavering green patch of light had not grown any brighter, but the roaring grew in volume.

Belleau laughed suddenly, but it held a note of hysteria. "Off the top of my head, I would guess *they* built this place."

Everyone came to halt, shining their lights around, hearts pounding, moisture in their mouths drying. All around them dark shapes loomed. Blurred by the shadows, at first glance the figures looked like hideous travesties of humanity.

The beautifully polished stone of the ceilings and walls had been carved in elaborate reliefs, depicting events in the lives of creatures taller than Oakshott and leaner than Kavanaugh, lizard-things wearing high headpieces, holding scepters and dressed in the trappings of nobility.

Honoré, Crowe, Bai Suzhen and Kavanaugh stared wide-eyed, stunned, shocked and awed. The frieze stretched down the length of the great hall, displaying many different scenes, most of them surrounded by inscribed Enochian symbols.

"What are we looking at?" Crow demanded, the ghostly echoes of his voice chasing one another in the shadows. "A history of some sort?"

He played the beam of his flashlight over a sequence of reliefs that stretched out for several yards. The images depicted a naked human male and female surrounded by Enochian glyphs, twisting in on themselves to form a helix pattern. Even in the dim light, the features of the male and female looked brutish, with small craniums and pronounced brow ridges.

The next frieze showed the humans standing on either side

of a reptilian-featured entity, his arms around them. Their lower bodies were not visible. Instead, they appeared to rise from a stylized oval.

The final image depicted the male and female, holding the tiny hands of a baby, as if they were drawing it up from the oval. The baby's features looked very smooth, not possessing the outthrust supraorbital ridge.

"Watch your eyes," Honoré warned, lifting the Nikon to her face. She snapped flash pictures of the frieze, moving sideways so she could capture a continuous panoramic view.

Belleau quoted quietly, "'And it came to pass when the children of men had multiplied, and the Watchers lusted after them and Samyaza who was their leader, said unto them, 'Come, let us choose us wives from among the children of men, and beget us children ourselves.'"

Honoré lowered the camera. "What are you babbling about?"

"It's a verse from the Book of Enoch…quite possibly the most important clue to solving the mystery of homo sapiens sapiens."

"Are you claiming the Watchers are the same as the lizard people, what you've called the anthroposaur?" Kavanaugh snapped.

"Exactly. Anthroposaurus sapiens. Just consider—a small group of late Cretaceous-epoch dinosaurs survived the K-T extinction event here on Big Tamtung, the Troodon among them. Partly due to the effects of the Prima Materia on their genetic structure, they followed the original design Nature had for them, if not for the K-T.

"Over a period of several million years, their forelimbs became hands, their claws turned into opposable thumbs, their vision developed binocularly, and of course, the fact that they were already bipedal gave them a big advantage over the primitive mammals that might have been on the island."

Mouzi stared at him blankly, and then intoned, "So lizard-people built all of this, all of those buildings outside."

Belleau nodded. "I think so, yes."

"That's what you think, because you're *crazy!*"

Before Belleau or Oakshott could respond, Crowe asked, "If the Troodons evolved into humanoid forms, then why didn't the other dinosaurian species do the same over the last sixty million years?"

"A chimpanzee will not evolve into a human no matter how much time you give it," Belleau said. "The Troodon were already predisposed genetically to evolve in that direction...upright bipeds with hands, opposable thumbs and forward-facing eyes... not to mention the boost provided by the Prima Materia."

Kavanaugh pointed the flashlight toward the arch at the far end of the causeway. "Let's see what's on the other side there."

As they strode through the arch, their flashlight beams dissolved into a mass of green-white illumination. A wide fissure high in the rock ceiling allowed for fog-diluted sunlight to shaft in. It gleamed on the litter of bones and skulls spread out over the cavern floor. The chamber was a catacomb, a vast crypt. Hundreds of skeletons lay around them.

Bai Suzhen prodded a rib-cage with the point of her sword. "These aren't human bones."

"No," said Honoré kneeling beside a huge hollow-eyed skull topped by a bulging crest." They look mainly like the remains of Hadrosaurs, with some tapirs mixed in, too. Animal bones."

"Not all of them," Mouzi said, pointing with the barrel of the autorifle. "Look over there."

A yellowed human skull grinned up from the tumbled skeletons of animals. Crowe toed aside a rib-cage, dislodged a big femur and uncovered the scraps of a khaki shirt. A gold wristwatch and ring glittered among the fragments of bone. Picking up the ring, he revolved it between thumb and forefinger in a shaft of sunshine, highlighting the insignia of the School of Night.

"Dr. David Abner Perry, I presume," murmured Belleau.

"What is this place?" asked Bai Suzhen.

"A bone-yard," Kavanaugh stated grimly. "Like those in the backs of slaughterhouses or rendering plants. I worked in one when I was in high school in Evansville."

Honoré eyed him wonderingly, anxiously. "You're saying someone—or something—brought these animals in here for the sole purpose of slaughter...to butcher them?"

"That's what it looks like to me."

No one spoke for a long moment, but Honoré suddenly shivered as if with a chill.

Mouzi tensed, her shoulders stiffening. "I think I'll have to vote with Mini-me on this one...best we get out of here."

As they turned toward the archway, they glimpsed a hint of stealthy movement in the murk beyond. Pinpoints of red fire glowed, moving points of flame that seemed to dance and shift in weird rhythm. They heard the rustle of scales and the clatter of claws on rock, like the clicking of giant castanets, echoing in waves throughout the cave.

The sound was followed by a series of high-pitched, piping *skreeks*. A dozen Deinonychus advanced on them through the gloom, spreading out to surround them.

"Demons," muttered Mouzi, putting the M16 to her shoulder.

Chapter Thirty-Five

Several more of the Deinonychus emerged from the shadows, spreading out in a semi-circle. They thrust their heads forward, *skreeking* and hissing, eyes darting back and forth. Their angry cacophony filled the cave, pressing in on everyone's eardrums.

Crowe, Mouzi and Kavanaugh put Honoré and Belleau behind them, tracking the movements of the creatures with their guns. Oakshott picked up a big bone, a tibia, to use as a bludgeon while Bai Suzhen sidled to the rear, sword held high, to make sure they weren't attacked from that quarter.

A quick head count showed Kavanaugh at least twenty of the sinewy, red-and-black striped raptors, many of them with fresh blood glistening on their snouts and talons. Several others held chunks of raw, dripping meat in their forepaws. Their combined hissing hit painfully high notes, like a score of teakettles on full boil. Almost as one, their tails rose, the tips pointing toward the ceiling.

"I think they're getting ready to rush us," Crowe announced, finger curling lightly around the trigger of the Colt Python. "I sure hope this ammunition is still good after all these years."

Kavanaugh sighted down the barrel of the revolver, targeting the head of a Deinonychus who seemed particularly aggressive. "We'll find out the hard way. Dr. Roxton—"

"—Honoré," she corrected tersely.

"Honoré...when we start shooting, you and Aubrey run like hell for the next chamber."

"We don't know what's in there!" Belleau objected.

"We know what's out here, don't we?" snapped Honoré sarcastically. "Do as the man says."

Opening its jaws wide, a Deinonychus lunged forward—then halted, closing its maw with a loud clack. It tilted its head up, and cocked it to the side, as if listening to a sound that both puzzled and enthralled it. Slowly, its tail drooped. Kavanaugh stared in astonishment, then he heard the trilling of a bird, a rising and falling note. The sound touched off sweet, corresponding vibrations somewhere deep inside of him.

The Deinonychus slowly retreated, their sibilant hissing becoming a brief confused babble of little yips and chitters.

In a voice sounding as if it were forced through a constricted windpipe, Belleau husked out, "Darwin reported hearing a birdsong when Hoxie was attacked."

"Yeah," Kavanaugh said, not lowering the pistol, even though the Deinonychus no longer made a threatening display. "I heard it too."

The trilling whistle came again, a complicated series of notes. Several of the raptors stepped toward them, their heads jerking in upward nods, as if they were responding to the string-tugs of a puppeteer. Kavanaugh turned toward the aperture leading out of the bone-yard. "I think we're supposed to go that way."

Crowe eyed him worriedly. "You think? Why?"

"The monsters are being told to herd us over there."

"I don't necessarily believe that," Belleau said fearfully.

"It's either go that way, or try to walk through the raptors. They don't seem inclined to allow us to do that."

Bai Suzhen gazed at the greenish gloom on the other side of the opening, gingerly touched her injured shoulder and said quietly, "All things being equal, let's go that way."

She stepped through the arch, leading with her sword, held in a two-fisted grip. Kavanaugh followed her closely, and his sense of danger, of foreboding grew, so that he moved against it as a man breasted waves. He wasn't the only one who felt it—even Oakshott's normally placid expression showed apprehension.

The roaring increased in volume, becoming a steady

thunder. Shafts of late afternoon sunlight speared down from a dozen round holes cut in the rock ceiling. Each one appeared to be at least three feet in diameter.

The waterfall cascaded past the openings, spumes of mist collecting around the rims, glistening with a greenish glaze. A shifting umbrella of steam hung just below the cavern ceiling. Water dripped down from above—not quite a drizzle but every surface gleamed with moisture.

Kavanaugh came to a halt, and then moved aside to allow everyone else to come through. Belleau stopped dead, blinking owlishly at the contents of the chamber hewn out of solid rock.

It wasn't so much its contents that startled Kavanaugh as the sensation of stepping back in time several thousand years, into a clearing house for several ancient cultures.

A tall, round pillar bearing ornate carvings of Enochian glyphs, alternating with animal heads was bracketed by two large sculptures, one a hawk-headed man and the other a serpent with wings. Lacquered ivory screens depicting Asian ideographs hung from the walls. There were other screens, all bearing twisting geometric designs, a combination of cuneiform, Enochian and even hieroglyphics.

Ceramic effigy jars topped by animal-headed gods and goddesses from the Egyptian pantheon were stacked in neat pyramids. On the far wall hung tapestries worked in multi-colored threads that depicted scenes from ancient times—ziggurats from which sprouted terraced gardens, representations of animals long extinct, like the mammoth and the megatherium, of human and non-human faces. The images offered brief glimpses into a world lost many millennia ago.

A pedestal rose at the far end, a huge stone figure loomed atop it, sitting cross-legged in the lotus position. Six arms curved out like serpents from a body that was half-snake and half-woman, with provocative breasts and the coiled trunk of a constrictor for legs.

The huge room was an archeologist's paradise. Kavanaugh struggled to comprehend the enormity and age of the collection and why it was here. Finally, he realized it was a representative sampling from every human culture ever influenced by the long-dead race Belleau called the anthroposaur, and Bai Suzhen knew as the Naga. Empires had risen and fallen, their histories long forgotten. Nothing was left of their glory but their art.

"Amazing," Belleau said. "Beyond belief. Darwin was right again."

"About what?" Honoré asked.

"That humankind's earliest ancestors may have been reptiles. According to the Darwinian explanation of the origins of the human species, mammals evolved from reptiles and gained dominion over the Earth."

"What?" Crowe demanded incredulously.

Belleau gestured to the artifacts. "See for yourself…Egyptian, Sumerian, even Chinese. Don't you think it's rather remarkable that in so many ancient creation stories humans are said to be related to a superior reptilian race? In most cases, a great global cataclysm eradicated the earlier species and the survivors of the disaster started anew, eventually evolving into humans. Convergent evolution."

"Specious pseudoscience," said Honoré disdainfully, but she sounded doubtful.

Belleau shrugged. "An advanced reptilian species evolved from the Troodon would explain a great many mysteries about the origin of human civilization. Even Carl Sagan speculated that the leap in brain evolution among hominids in Africa and Asia was mysterious. He felt that it should have taken five to ten million years for humans to evolve, but the fossil record doesn't bear out that conclusion."

"And what's your conclusion?" Bai Suzhen challenged.

"I don't have one, per se, but I can propose an alternative." Belleau smiled slightly. "It is possible that advanced beings had a hand in accelerating the human evolutionary process. The anthroposaurs—let's call them the Naga for the sake of convenience—developed their own culture long before humankind graduated from stone tools and spread out over the world.

"They became culture-bearers, the source of all legends about wise serpents and dragons. Their interaction with humanity formed the basis of the belief that human royalty was descended from dragons...the kings and queens of Europe for example...the so-called Dragon Sovereignty, which allegedly can trace its origins back to the Annunaki in ancient Sumeria."

"I doubt there's any way you could conclusively prove that hypothesis," commented Honoré dryly.

Kavanaugh shifted his flashlight away from the tapestries and played the beam over a recess in the rear wall. Two figures sat there on seats of glassy volcanic stone roughly hewed into the likeness of thrones. The lean figures seemed at first to be strange works of sculpture, but as Kavanaugh stepped closer, he saw that the nearer figure was a cadaver. He felt the hairs lift on the nape of his neck.

The head tilted forward, with the mouth hanging open. A central ridge of bone curved down from the top of the domed skull to the bridge of a flattened nose. The dry flesh, stretched tight over the skeleton, had the texture and color of dusty leather. The eye sockets were empty black hollows. The body shone with a waxy sheen, as if it had been in dipped in lacquer.

In a voice hushed and thick with awe, Honoré whispered, "No myth, then. The serpent folk, the anthroposaurs."

"No myth, no mere legend," Belleau said. "The Oannes, the Anunnaki, the dragon kings actually existed, coexisted with humanity."

"The Naga," said Bai Suzhen faintly.

Impatiently, Mouzi asked, "Who the hell was doing that bloody whistling?"

The body seated in the second throne stirred, the lipless mouth opening slightly and from it issued a prolonged rhythmic whistle.

Everyone watched with wide eyes as a sudden spasm of movement shook the lean form. It turned its head and for the first time, Kavanaugh accepted it was a living creature, breathing and moving, aware of its surroundings. Its gold and black eyes swept over the people, then fixed on Kavanaugh. They stared straight into his soul.

"Jah-Kuh."

Chapter Thirty-Six

The gasping, liquid voice caused a fist of fear to knot in Kavanaugh's gut. The creature's pronunciation was slurred due to the structure of its mouth, but he understood it called him by name. In the depths of its eyes swirled the light of intelligence.

Honoré labored for breath as if she had just run a three minute mile. "She recognizes you, Jack! Oh my God--"

"Nobody move," Kavanaugh snapped in a fierce whisper.

With a faint, dry rustling, the figure pushed itself up from the chair. The dim light gleamed dully from an intricate pattern of tiny, glittering scales covering naked gray-black flesh.

The creature's posture was canted to one side, but she still stood taller than Oakshott. From down-sloping shoulders dangled long arms, the five fingers tipped with spurs of discolored bone. The neck was longer than a humans', the head blunt of feature with a wide, lipless mouth. The narrow, elongated skull held large, round eyes that were almost invisible under hard-edged brow ridges.

Honoré forced herself to look full upon the creature's seamed face. Pride was stamped there, as well as a dark wisdom. She was a queen without a kingdom, a ruler without subjects or a nation.

She heard herself whisper, "She's the last of her kind, just like you said, Jack. That must be her mate. God only knows how long he's been there, sitting beside her. His body looks like it was coated in some type of preservative."

Kavanaugh sensed that the female was old, so old that her soul wearied of trying to dredge up memories of youth. He couldn't recall the last time his heart had pounded so hard and violently within his chest.

She continued to shuffle forward, dragging a deformed, five-toed foot behind her. The leg was gnarled, twisted at the ankle and knee. She stopped and her head swiveled slowly from Kavanaugh to Belleau then back to Kavanaugh again.

"No nipples, no *mammalia*," Belleau murmured. "Oviparous."

"Or viviparous," said Honoré breathlessly. "There are some reptiles that give birth to live young. Just because we can't see external sex organs doesn't mean they're not there."

The creature pointed a trembling finger at Kavanaugh. "Jah-Kuh. Not kam bek you. Kam bek deed. Bad. Bad Jah-Kuh."

Crowe muttered, "What's she saying?"

Bai said, "She's telling Jack he shouldn't have come back. That he was bad to do so."

"I don't like the sound of that," Mouzi whispered, casting a glance over her shoulder at the Deinonychus standing by alertly.

Clearing his throat, Kavanaugh took a step forward, staring fearlessly up into the deeply lined, scaled face. "I didn't want to disobey you. We don't mean you any harm. What is your name?"

The creature gazed at Kavanaugh unblinkingly, impassively. Slowly, she reached out with her left hand and touched the outside corner of his right eye. He forced himself not to flinch. With a yellowed nail, she traced the curve of the scar down the line of his jaw. Faintly, as if sensing smoke rather than seeing it, a whisper impressed itself on his mind: *Get up and run, Jack.*

Kavanaugh laboriously formed words in his mind, visualizing how they sounded. *I did get up and run. I did not die. Thank you.*

"I don't think she understood you," Honoré said quietly. "Maybe her kind didn't have proper names except those given to them by humans. Or maybe she's so old, she forgot hers. I'll just go ahead and give her one—how about Wadjet?"

"Wadjet?" Crowe's brow furrowed as he stumbled slightly over the pronunciation. "What kind of name is that?"

Belleau chuckled briefly. "The cobra goddess of lower Egypt. As a patron and protectress, Wadjet was often shown coiled upon the head of Ra, the chief deity, in order to act as his protector. The asp on the headdresses of the ancient Pharaohs was the symbol of Wadjet."

In a voice made hoarse by amazement, Bai Suzhen said, "She actually could *be* Wadjet, couldn't she? The mother of the Nagas."

She kneeled, laying the sword on the cavern floor. Pressing the palms of her hands together, she steepled her fingers together at her chin and bowed deeply, respectfully. "She is the queen, the Deva-Naga of legend."

"You're babbling, Madame," commented Belleau.

As she rose, Bai cast him a venomous glare "Didn't you say the Prima Materia could make people and animals practically immortal?"

Belleau's eyes flickered and his expression registered a dawning excitement. He quickly stepped closer to Wadjet who drew back a pace. "Dear God, yes! Why not? It should have occurred to me!"

"You're frightening her," Honoré said, pulling him back.

"I don't think much of anything frightens her," Kavanaugh stated. "But there's no point in testing the theory, especially since I think she has a degree of control over the animals here."

A loose pouch of flesh at Wadjet's throat pulsed and a trilling issued not from her mouth but from her dilating nostrils.

"What's she doing?" Oakshott asked nervously.

With a click and clatter of claws, a Deinonychus pushed between them, uttering *skreeks* to warn everyone to get out of its way. It held a large chunk of blood-dripping meat in its foreclaws. Oakshott's big hands clenched around the length bone as the raptor went past.

"Don't do anything that's even remotely hostile," Honoré sidemouthed. "Don't move."

The Deinonychus handed the slab of flesh to Wadjet and backed away, glaring at the humans around it. As Wadjet tore off a little chunk of meat and put it in her mouth, Belleau said quietly, "This situation just becomes more and more amazing. Wadjet exerts influence on the fauna here, probably due to the absorption of the Prima Materia."

"That's what I just said," Kavanaugh whispered irritably. "She likely sent the Quetzacoatlus to keep us from getting too close to the escarpment and maybe she even directed the croc and Stinky, too."

"Perhaps," conceded Honoré. "She must rely on the Deinonychus to bring her food, like they're her attendants.. The Hadrosaurs and Parasaurolophus probably occupy the same niche as cattle...that's why she dispatched the Deinonychus to attack your hunting party, Jack. They threatened her primary food source."

To their surprise, Wadjet did not bring the meat to her mouth and rip into it with her teeth. Delicately, she tore off small bits of flesh with thumb and forefinger and put them in her mouth, chewing thoroughly with her mouth closed. The quality of the light peeping through the waterfall suddenly dimmed, as of the closing of a curtain.

"Getting on towards dark," Crowe observed. "Or a storm is coming. Either way, I think we're here for the night."

Mouzi eyed the Deinonychus assembled in the bone-yard as they squawked and squabbled over the raw meat they had carried in with them. "That's a comforting thought."

Belleau gazed in rapt fascination at Wadjet. "I don't think any of you quite grasp the enormity of this discovery."

"The last living member of a mythical non-human race?" Crowe asked dryly. "I think we've all made the connection between it and enormity."

Belleau shook his head. "You haven't, not really. Standing before us is not just the encapsulated lost history of humanity, but quite possibly its future as well."

Bai Suzhen eyed him suspiciously. "That sounds like a line of PR you fed poor Howard Flitcroft."

Belleau snorted. "Hardly. I could not have concocted such

a plan on my own. Consider—scientists have long puzzled over the similarities between the reptilian brain and the human brain. At the core of the human brain lies a vestige of our reptilian past, known as the R-complex."

He tapped his forehead. "It is what performs the dinosaur functions—aggression, territoriality, ritual, and establishment of social hierarchies, like families. The middle layer is called the limbic system, and that is thought to generate love, hate, compassion, and spirituality—characteristics believed to be strictly mammalian. The neocortex is believed to be the seat of reasoning and a sense of morality... where we differentiate between good and evil."

"And what's your excuse, then?" asked Kavanaugh. "Were you dropped on your neocortex as a baby?"

Belleau sighed. "I'll ignore that. Think about this...the knowledge of good and evil was given to humanity by a serpent...it caused the first woman and man to fall from grace with God."

Honoré mimed pulling the ends of a rubber-band. "Stretching, Aubrey. Very much so."

"I wish I were, darlin'. In an ancient Jewish document, known as the Haggadah, it is made quite clear that the serpent was not merely a snake. To quote from it: 'Among the animals, the serpent was notable. Of all of them, he had the most excellent qualities, in some of which he resembled man. Like man, he stood upright on two feet, and in height he was equal to the camel.' The document mentions his superior mental gifts despite having 'a visage like a viper.'

"Those superior mental gifts caused him to become an infidel. It likewise explains his envy of man, especially his conjugal visits...in punishment for tempting Eve, God said 'I created you to be king over all the animals...but you were not satisfied...I created you of upright posture...therefore you shall go upon your belly.'

"And of course the references to Watchers, good and bad angels, can be found in many ancient texts including the Old

Testament, which borrowed much from older documents, including the books of Enoch. It's not a coincidence that the Enochian alphabet is also known as angelic script."

"So?" Bai asked.

"So, I think it's safe to postulate that the Enochian alphabet was a phonetic rendering of the language the Nagas spoke. I think they also used it to express mathematical and scientific concepts. Over the centuries, the root of the language became confused, lost in legend and since Enoch was a patriarch, the assumption was the alphabet was the means he used to communicate with angels...instead of the Nagas, the Watchers of Biblical lore."

Crowe shrugged. "We can't deny that Wadjet's people interacted with humanity, but there's a big difference between having interaction and intercourse. I'm not a scientist, but I know mammals and reptiles can't conceive offspring. That's ridiculous."

"As you said," Belleau stated coldly, "you're not a scientist. If you were, you would know humans go through an accelerated process of evolution while in the womb. As repugnant as it may sound, I think Wadjet's people, using the Prima Materia as a propagation medium, engaged in transgenic experiments on primitive humans. There is a tradition in ancient Kabalist texts that the serpent of Eden didn't just tempt Eve, but actually seduced her and fathered Cain. That could be a report of early genetic engineering cloaked in myth and analogy."

"That's insane," bit out Bai Suzhen.

"And how would you know, Madame?" shot back Belleau. "Your only experience with DNA is mopping up after some of your less restrained customers. Have you ever heard of chromosomal crossover? No? It is when two DNA helices break, swap a section and then rejoin. Recombination allows chromosomes to exchange genetic information and produces new combinations of genes, which increases the efficiency of natural selection."

Honoré intoned dolefully, "The Holliday junction."

Belleau nodded toward her approvingly. "Just so, darlin', just so. The Holliday junction is a structure that can be moved along a pair of chromosomes, swapping one strand for another."

With both arms, he gestured to the cave, to the ruins outside, to Big Tamtung at large. "This island is quite possibly the largest genetics lab in history and Wadjet's people the first geneticists."

Belleau pointed to Wadjet. "And there we have the perfect living laboratory of everything we need to process the essence of the Prima Materia. Every cell is saturated with it, her blood flows with it and it's probably what has kept her alive for thousands of years or however long ago it was since her people retreated here...after some cataclysm, perhaps the Flood, devastated the world."

Wadjet regarded Belleau with mild interest, still single-mindedly chewing.

"Why wouldn't the animals here provide the same source?" asked Honoré.

Belleau glanced at her, frowning. "I think Wadjet directly partook of the pure Prima Materia on many occasions."

Kavanaugh inquired, "What makes you think she'd tolerate having her blood and spinal fluid be tapped and analyzed?"

"What makes you think she'd have any say-so in the matter?"

Honoré glared at Belleau first in surprise, then anger. "You don't intend to abduct her, take her away from here?"

"Why not?" he countered. "The longer she remains here, the more we run the risk of losing her to old age or any number of accidents. We can't allow her to die and her body to corrupt like the pool of Prima Materia, can we? Look at her...she's far gone in senility."

"Maybe so," Kavanaugh said. "But remember, she has some kind of telepathic or psychic ability. If you upset her, you might be upsetting her nasty domestic staff next door."

"I'll take that chance." Belleau stepped close to Wadjet, speaking in a low, soothing voice. "You wouldn't mind leaving here, would you, old girl? You'd be taken care of in your old age, and I'd make sure you'd want for nothing. Doesn't that sound nice?"

Wadjet stared down at him contemplatively, still chewing. She inserted a thumb and index finger into her mouth and removed a little chunk of raw, masticated meat. Leaning down, she thrust the blood and saliva-damp piece of flesh toward Belleau's mouth. Face twisting in revulsion, he recoiled so hastily he stumbled. Crowe and Mouzi laughed.

"She thinks you're the runt of the litter," Crowe said. "I guess she still has a maternal instinct…takes a reptile to love a reptile."

Aubrey Belleau's eyes flashed in sudden fury. "Don't make sport of me!"

Mouzi uttered a contemptuous laugh. "Lighten up. You've been calling me a mongrel for two days and here you are being force-fed Quinterotops steak tartare to bulk you up."

Teeth bared, Belleau whirled on her with a speed that deceived the eye. He lunged forward, grasped the barrel of the M-16, and using all of his considerable upper body strength, slammed the stock deeply into the pit of Mouzi's stomach.

Chapter Thirty-Seven

All of Mouzi's breath exploded past her lips in an agonized grunt. Belleau yanked the autorifle from her hands and she fell to her knees. He hammered the butt of the weapon against the back of her head, driving her face first to the cavern floor.

Almost in the same instant, Oakshott lashed out with the length of bone in his hands, smashing it down on a clump of ganglia on Crowe's right forearm. Crying out, his fingers lost all feeling and the revolver fell to the ground. A lightning fast follow-through with the tip of the cudgel slammed against his jaw and knocked him flat to the cavern floor.

Pivoting smoothly on the ball of his foot, Oakshott drove the blunt end of the bone into Kavanaugh's diaphragm. He folded over in the direction of the sickening blow and Oakshott jacked up a knee against his chin. It was like being kicked by a tree. Multicolored pinwheels spiraled behind his eyes.

Kavanaugh fell onto his side, agony spreading through his bruised torso. He tasted bile rising in a burning column up his throat, but he managed to keep it down and his eyes open, although he saw everything through a gray fog. He glimpsed Oakshott swing the bone at Bai Suzhen, who parried the blow with the sword, chopping out a fragment.

For a long moment, the two people exchanged a flurry of bludgeon-blows and sword strokes, but Oakshott used his greater strength and weight to batter the blade down and then smash his cudgel against the side of her head. She went staggering across the chamber and fell, the sword chiming briefly against the stone.

Oakshott spun and twirled the bone between the fingers of his right hand. His face creased in a superior smile as he played to a non-existent crowd.

Kavanaugh struggled to raise the Colt Python, but Oakshott whirled around and cracked the tibia against his wrist, knocking the pistol from his hand, and then swept his arms out from under him with a kick. A deep boring pressure at the base of his neck kept him prone, as Oakshott leaned his weight on the length of bone, grinding his face into the rock.

"Relax, Jack," Oakshott said in a low voice. "You really didn't think it would be that easy with me, did you? I'm a professional, ex-SAS…you're a barely talented amateur, a boozy flyboy."

Over the pounding in his ears and the thunder of the waterfall, Kavanaugh heard Honoré shout furiously, "Let him up, you bastard!"

Belleau said in a gloating croon, "Do as the doctor says, Oakshott."

Oakshott pulled the bone away, tossing it aside. Kavanaugh pushed himself up by shaking arms. The big Englishman stared down at him, a faint smile of disdain creasing his lips. Mouzi lay on the floor, unconscious, her hair clotted with blood seeping from a laceration on her scalp. Crowe stirred feebly. He could not even see Bai Suzhen.

A smirking Belleau held the rifle at waist level. He kicked both revolvers to one side. Wadjet stared in wide-eyed silent wonderment, apparently only perplexed by the sudden outburst of violence, not disturbed by it.

Honoré kneeled beside Kavanaugh. Her green eyes, blazing with loathing, fixed on Oakshott. "You're a coward."

"And you're a silly, obnoxious cunt, mum," Oakshott retorted quietly. "Pardon my French."

"Now what, Aubrey?" demanded Kavanaugh. "You think you can just waltz out of here, hand-in-hand with Wadjet, and somehow get her back to the world without drawing attention from customs or anyone else?"

"That's exactly what I think. Why else would I even consider going into business with a triad, if not to take to advantage of their smuggling lanes?"

"You're out of your mind," Honoré said raggedly. "Completely mad."

Belleau grinned wolfishly. "I'm thinking very clearly, darlin'. *You're* going to help me walk out of here with Wadjet."

"The Deinonychus will most likely eat out your heart," declared Honoré. "You don't understand the risk of this undertaking."

"What *you* don't understand is that I no longer care about risk. I'm not a big man, but even the smallest of men can move the world with a large enough fulcrum." He nodded meaningfully toward Wadjet.

"That's what she is to you?" spat Honoré. "The fulcrum by which you will stake out a monopoly on the new drugs processed from this poor creature's blood and bone marrow? You would damn her to a life full of torture, so you can achieve *that?*"

"I'd damn her, you and everyone else I know to the lowest pit of Hell, rather than continue to live in this body!" Belleau snarled out the words, drops of spittle flying from his lips. "A prince, a king, a modern Michelangelo, trapped in the twisted body of a monstrous child, a court jester, a *freak.*"

He kicked the motionless Mouzi on the hip. She did not react. "My last wife called me Quasimodo with a doctorate! The unfaithful cow…so that is what I am—a creature fit only to be made sport of by *harlots?*"

Looking into Belleau's rage-maddened face, Kavanaugh's stomach turned a slow flip-flop of nausea. Honoré stared at him with wild, wide eyes as if she couldn't believe what she had just heard.

She stammered, "All of this was done in the hopes of making yourself over…transforming yourself into your childish image of what a man is *supposed* to be?"

Belleau's face flushed red. "Not just my image—I see how you look at this Yank bounder. Tall, scarred, brave—even if most of his courage is poured from a fifth of bourbon. Irresponsible, arrogant and ignorant. All of you harlots murmur at the feet of these swaggering, faithless vessels who care nothing for anyone but themselves."

Belleau drew in a long breath through his nostrils. He stepped back. "The interesting thing is…how they squeal and soil themselves like pigs when they know they're about to die. Oakshott—show her what I mean."

Kavanaugh didn't hesitate. Tensing every muscle in his body, even those that throbbed, he performed the maneuver gymnasts call the kip-up. He thrust his legs straight out at a thirty-degree angle, bent his knees, planted his feet flat and used the momentum of the kick to spring upright.

For an instant he stood face-to-face with Oakshott, then he sprang forward, butting the big man squarely in the forehead, on the bridge of his nose. The impact sent shivers of pain all the way to the base of his spine, but Oakshott went staggering backward, arms windmilling as he tried to maintain his balance. The pallor of the man's face was brightened by the spattering of blood spraying from his nostrils.

Belleau shouted in wordless anger and whipped the rifle toward him. Kavanaugh glimpsed a blur of movement, then Crowe's arm throttled him from behind. Belleau struggled, twisting around with the M16, but Crowe back-fisted the barrel aside.

Belleau's finger closed over the trigger and he fired a stuttering burst into the ceiling. Thunderous echoes rolled. Ricochets screamed and rock chips and dust sifted down. Wadjet clapped her hands over the sides of her head, eyes wide in sudden fear, her mouth forming an O of wonder.

Growling deep in his throat, Belleau gripped the stock and barrel of the rifle, and threw his weight forward, muscling Crowe to the floor. He pressed the frame against Crowe's throat. Crowe wrenched and heaved, straining to keep the rifle from crushing his windpipe. Honoré dove forward, bowling into Belleau and all of them went down in a thrashing tangle of limbs.

Oakshott dabbed at the scarlet strings dripping from his nose and stared at Kavanaugh with a puzzled expression. Allowing a cold, taunting smile to play over his face, Kavanaugh assumed a combat posture, reservoirs of adrenalin pumping through his system. He beckoned to Oakshott with a forefinger and said, "C'mon, Hamish…show her what Belleau meant."

Face locked in a tight mask, Oakshott bounded toward him, fingers curled against his palms, swinging his hands in intricate, crisscrossing leopard's-paw strikes. Kavanaugh backed away from a slashing right hand, ducked the left and leapt forward, throwing his fists in a one-two jab at Oakshott's face with every ounce of his weight behind them.

Oakshott evaded both punches with lightning swift moves of his head. He swung his left hand viciously in return, fingers bent into hooks. The blow struck Kavanaugh across the ribs and the impact numbed his right side but he retained his footing. They stood toe to toe and traded blows and blocks. Kavanaugh landed a wicked shovel-hook uppercut, but then took a punishing upset punch to the belly.

He nearly doubled over as streaks of pain lanced through his solar plexus, but he managed to shift aside and stay upright. He estimated that Oakshott's strength was at least twice his own. His expression must have betrayed that realization to the big Englishman

Oakshott feinted toward his face and then thrust up his knee, seeking to pound Kavanaugh's testicles, but he twisted around so the impact landed against his upper thigh. Almost instantly, his leg went numb and buckled beneath him.

Snorting out a laugh, Oakshott closed in, his arms quickly curving up and under, hands linking at the back of Kavanaugh's neck. Kavanaugh's head went down under the relentless pressure of the giant's arms. He heard the creaking of cartilage and his breath blew out of his mouth in a hoarse cry. Skewers of pain lanced through his upper back.

Oakshott chuckled thickly. "You surprised me, Jack, you really did. But you're still just an amateur with some training and talent."

Oakshott cinched down harder. "And like all amateurs, I'll wager you'll squeal and soil yourself."

A red-hot knife stabbed through the back of Kavanaugh's neck. His throat constricted against the scream that tried to force its way past his lips. He felt a wispy brush against his mind, a question, a plea, and a command all at the same time.

Get up, Jack! Get up and run or you will die!

His mind formed desperate words: *I can't run, so I must die and you will be taken from here and be fed upon.*

He focused his thoughts on images of Wadjet being dragged away in a net, of her home looted, of the corpse of her mate cut into sections by big buzz-saws. He concentrated on visions of Wadjet strapped to an examination table, tubes and needles piercing her flesh, sucking out her blood. He imagined Oakshott standing over her, grinning in malicious triumph, thumbing a razor keen knife.

He powered all the images with a complete conviction, packing them with the ruthless unshakable certainty that the visions would come true and he was terribly grieved that he could not help her.

I should not have come back. I cannot run and I will die and so will you. I am sorry.

Suddenly, Oakshott's grip loosened, relaxed, and Kavanaugh fell limply to the floor. He rolled his head, gasping for breath, his heart trip-hammering and he saw Oakshott backing away, looking past Kavanaugh with an unreadable expression on his face.

As his vision cleared, he saw Wadjet approaching Oakshott, her eyes cold and savage, her yellow, red-filmed teeth bared in a silent snarl. Oakshott said something, lifting his hands, palm outward, but because of the roar of the waterfall, Kavanaugh couldn't hear what he said.

Wadjet seemed to lash out across almost twice as much distance as her arms should have been able to span and Oakshott staggered backward, his eye sockets raw, red jelly-smears.

There were blurred movements of flailing arms and claw-tipped fingers. Hands over his face, Oakshott fell to the floor, crashing against a stack of ceramic jars. Wadjet bent over his body, clawed open his shirt, and plunged her right hand into Oakshott's chest, punching through, flesh, bone and cartilage. He flung his head back and howled, blood flying from his lips. He convulsed, arms and legs spasming.

With a splintering of ribs, Wadjet yanked her hand out and up, holding Oakshott's quivering heart, squeezing it between her fingers. Blood pumped in crimson rivulets down her slender wrist and forearm. Kavanaugh tamped down a sudden surge of nausea.

Belleau fought his way out of the grapple with Crowe and Honoré, using the stock of the autorifle to beat them back. Shock froze him in place when he saw Wadjet holding Oakshott's blood-dripping heart. His eyes bulged and in a hoarse, horrified whisper he gasped, *"Hamish!"*

The man's name turned into a wild scream of fury. Belleau aimed the M16 at Wadjet who stared at him challengingly. Honoré lunged for the rifle. "Aubrey, no—!"

Belleau twisted away from her grasp, realigning the rifle. "It'll be just as easy to cart away samples carved from her body."

A shadow flitted between him and Wadjet. Metal flashed, like a mirror reflecting an errant sunbeam. Belleau uttered a thin cry of astonishment and went stumble-footing backward, the rifle clacking noisily at his feet. The plastic stock dropped in two pieces, sliced thorough cleanly.

Staggering on wide-braced legs, Belleau stared at the blood-jetting stump at the end of his right arm. His eyes lifted to Bai Suzhen, who advanced on him, sword angled up and over her head. The edge of the blade glistened carmine.

As if his mind did not comprehend what his eyes saw, Belleau lifted his wrist in front of his face. A stream of crimson squirted over his cheek.

By the time he reached down and plucked his amputated hand up from the floor, Belleau had dragged in enough air into his lungs to start screaming. He whirled and ran in raw panic, a gibbering explosion of mindless terror erupting from his mouth. He yelped with every footfall. Not even the raucous calls from the Deinonychus feeding in the bone-yard slowed him down.

The *skreeks* were repeated from Wadjet. Pushing himself to his feet, Kavanaugh watched the raptors moving aside, to allow the screaming Aubrey Belleau to run past.

Bai Suzhen turned to face Kavanaugh, slowly lowering her sword. "Are you all right, Jack?"

He nodded, despite the spasm of pain the movement caused in his neck muscles. "Think so. You?"

Gingerly she probed at the side of her head with careful fingers. "I was unconscious—I came to in time to watch Wadjet's open heart surgery technique on Oakshott." She smiled cruelly.

"I think you've been hanging around me too long," Kavanaugh commented, as Crowe and Honoré arose. Both of their faces showed abrasions and contusions sustained in the struggle with Belleau.

Crowe turned Mouzi over on her back, called her name and lightly slapped her face. Her eyelids fluttered, but did not open. He touched the back of her head and his fingertips came away wet with blood.

"We're going to have to get her out of here," he said darkly. "Where the hell is the first aid kit?"

Honoré went over to fetch it from where it had fallen on the floor. "We can't let Aubrey run free. He's hurt and very well may bleed to death."

"And that's an issue why?" inquired Bai icily.

Honoré started to reply, then shrugged. "I can't imagine."

She handed the kit to Crowe and eyed Wadjet, standing as motionless as the cadaver in the stone chair. Softly, she asked, "Why do you think she saved you, Jack?"

"I don't think she saved me so much as she saved herself, saved the memories of her people. As long as they still live in her, they haven't vanished completely."

He forced himself to look directly into Wadjet's eyes. *Thank you.*

Do not thank me. Her eyes poured a torrent of emotions into his mind—savage anger, outrage, and a deep abiding grief. A cold thought, like the slithering of a reptile, crawled across the surface of his mind: *If you return, you will die. All of you will die.*

Bai Suzhen stiffened, drawing in her breath sharply. She backed away from Wadjet. "She just told me to leave and not to come back under pain of death."

Kavanaugh said, "I think she told us all the same thing."

Crowe gathered Mouzi in his arms and heaved her up from the floor. "Let's do what she says, before she decides she's had enough visitors for this century."

Steepling her fingers beneath her chin again, Bai Suzhen bowed deeply to Wadjet and whispered reverently, *"Pai-yaa-na aak, ram laa."*

Chapter Thirty-Eight

They emerged from the mouth of the cave as the storm front slowly crept away, thunder rumbling off to the west. Flashes of lightning lit up the ruins. Trees creaked and bent beneath intermittent wind gusts. Although not in a torrent, rain fell in sporadic sheets of tepid water.

The Deinonychus had not interfered with their departure, although Kavanaugh suspected they followed them down the passageway, just out of revolver range. Honoré carried the autorifle and one of the Colt Pythons. Crowe carried Mouzi in his arms, as if she were a sleeping child.

Droplets of fresh blood glistened on the tunnel floor but they didn't catch a glimpse of Belleau. By the time they reached the point where David Abner Perry had conducted his demolition work, Mouzi regained consciousness.

Although her scalp wound still bled sluggishly and her vision blurred, she insisted she was fine and could walk. She took the M16 from Honoré, frowned at the sheared through plastic stock and Crowe muttered, "Don't ask."

They reached the mouth of the cave and waited for the rain to abate before leaving. Honoré ran trembling fingers over her forehead. Her face was paper-pale, her eyes dull with fatigue. In tone muted by horror, she whispered, "This has been like a nightmare."

"Worse," said Crowe tersely.

"How so?"

"Because there's no waking up from it."

Kavanaugh studied the ruins with slitted eyes. "I can't believe Aubrey made it this far, after he lost so much blood."

Honoré considered his words while gazing at the rainfall. "He's very resourceful, as you probably guessed. He could've made a tourniquet from his belt and boot-laces to stop the bleeding."

"Stop the bleeding and do what?" asked Bai, thumbing the edge of her sword.

"I think he's headed for the Prima Materia."

"What good would that pool of crud do him now?" Crowe demanded.

Honoré only shrugged. Kavanaugh frowned, first at her and then at the jungle on the other side of the ruins.

When the rain slackened to a drizzle, he announced, "Let's look for him there."

Bai Suzhen's eyebrows lifted toward her hairline. "Why should we?"

"If he's dead, that's one thing. If he's still alive, he can cause problems."

The walls and structures glistened with diamond-like drops of water in the dim light. The assembly of ruins looked depressing and forlorn in the suffused late afternoon sun, not awe-inspiring.

As they walked past a serpentine pillar, Kavanaugh heard a staccato pop-popping, like a string of firecrackers going off under a tin can. He threw himself down, pulling Honoré and Bai with him as the stone erupted and showered his shoulders and the back of his head with gravel.

"Jimmy!" Bai hissed between clenched teeth.

Everyone pressed themselves into the ground as if hoping to be absorbed by it. Bullets snapped above them like a steel flail. When the machine-gun fire stopped, they rolled and scrambled behind the green-stained head of a fallen statue. Faintly they heard the murmur of male voices speaking in Chinese.

Jimmy Cao's voice lifted in a shout: "All I want is Bai Suzhen and Aubrey Belleau!"

Kavanaugh exchanged startled glances with Crowe and Honoré. Bai whispered, "I assumed Jimmy had found Belleau.

Guess not."

Cupping his hands around his mouth, Kavanaugh shouted, "No deal! Not until we're all back on Little Tamtung. Even Aubrey thinks that's a good idea."

"Don't be a stubborn asshole!" came Cao's shrill, angry voice. The echoes in the ruins distorted it as to the direction from which it emanated. "After what me and my men went through getting here, there's no way we're going to let them out of our sight."

"Sorry about your men," Kavanaugh said. "How many of them made it here with you? How'd you find us?"

Jimmy Cao ignored the questions. He yelled, "Belleau! Talk to me! *Belleau!*"

"He can't talk right now, Jimmy," Bai called. "You'll have to deal with me."

Voice thickening with fury, Cao yelled, "You goddamn better bet I'll deal with you—I'll deal with all of you!"

The subguns hammered again, chewing notches out of the top of the statue. Kavanaugh ducked as a shower of rock ships pelted him. He hefted the revolver in both hands and said sarcastically, "Good strategy, Bai. Now they'll surround us."

"At least we'll find out how many of them there are," Crowe stated, handing his revolver to Honoré. "Hold this for me."

Hitching around, he pulled the bandana-wrapped sticks of Titadyne from his back pocket. "You still have those blasting caps, Jack?"

Digging around in his pocket, Kavanaugh pulled out the little silver cylinders. He had to raise his head a bit to do so and a subgun stuttered. Before he ducked back down, he glimpsed orange flame stab out of the encroaching twilight. Divots of dirt flew up all around as the bullets pounded a cross-stitch pattern in the ground.

Kavanaugh waited until the gunfire stopped, then he twisted around and came up on one knee, holding the big pistol in front of him. He squeezed off a shot, the echoing *boom* bouncing around the ruins.

A fist-sized chunk of scrollwork burst from a column and a screaming man lurched out into the open, clutching at the left side of his face. He dropped the Type 64 sub-machine gun.

Sitting back down behind the statue, Kavanaugh calmly unwound the fuses from the cylinders and laid them out in a neat row on the ground. Honoré eyed them skeptically. "Now what?"

Mouzi removed the pliers from her pocket and gave them to Crowe as he inserted the little silver cylinder in the end of the Titadyne stick. With the pliers, he squeezed the cap until he heard a faint crunch. "You crimp the fuse into place right here, so the ignition and the primary explosive mix. Give it a twist."

"Then what?"

From a pocket he pulled out the box of stick matches taken from the survival kit. "The fun and simple part. After you light the fuse, you have about five seconds to throw it before it detonates. Probably a good idea to know where you're going to be throwing it before you light up. Got it?"

Honoré swallowed. "Got it."

From another pocket he removed the black stub of a cheroot, barely two inches long. Putting it between his teeth, he struck a match into flame and lit the cheroot, sending up a plume of acrid smoke. Honoré coughed and fanned the air.

"Ghastly stench," she said.

"It'll keep the mosquitoes away," Crowe replied, puffing on the stub until the end glowed bright red. He took it from his mouth and held it out, his eyebrows raised questioningly. "Who wants to be responsible for it?"

Without hesitation, Bai Suzhen took it, sliding it between her index and third finger, she puffed on the end experimentally. "I'll keep it lit."

Crowe handed the Titadyne sticks to Honoré. "Start crimping."

Kavanaugh looked at Crowe. "Ready, Gus?"

"No, but let's do it anyway."

Carefully, they raised their heads up above the top of the statue. Almost immediately, a barrage of bullets spewed from three weapons, thudding into the sculpture, chopping out fragments, but not penetrating it. Crowe and Kavanaugh returned the fire, shooting blindly. The syncopation of the gunfire was deafening, but they fixed in their minds the two points from where the subguns blazed.

Crowe turned toward Bai. "Light me up."

She picked up a stick of the explosive, touched the fuse to the end of the cheroot in her mouth and when it sparked, slapped the cylinder into his waiting hand. He hurled the Titadyne in a looping overhand arc.

One of the Ghost Shadows saw the spark-spewing tube bouncing across the ground and he opened his mouth to scream a warning. A thunderclap blast slammed his words back into his throat.

For a microsecond, the area was haloed in a red flash. Flying tongues of flame billowed outward. The detonation of the Titadyne hurled two bodies into the air. A fine drizzle of dirt and pulverized pebbles rained down. Crowe and Kavanaugh looked up, over their stone shelter. Two men lay motionless, draped across the broken walls.

"Think that'll discourage them?" Crowe asked quietly.

"Depends on whether we got Jimmy."

As if on cue, Cao's strident voice lifted, screaming out commands in hard-edged Chinese. A wedge of men, at least half a dozen, ran around the far end of a wall in a milling rush. Wielding their Type 64 subguns, they began to fan out warily but swiftly around the perimeter, staying close the shadows of a long-stretch of wall.

Kavanaugh extended a hand toward Bai, who lit a fuse with the cheroot, and quickly placed the stick of Titadyne in his palm. He lobbed it around the curve in the wall. Eyes wide and fearful, the Ghost Shadow soldier in the lead dug in his heels and tried to stop, but the men behind him pushed him forward.

The explosive detonated in a tremendous cracking blast, a blinding burst of dirt and rock erupting from the ground.

The echo of the explosion instantly bled into a grinding

rumble as a long section of the wall toppled forward in a cascade of bouncing blocks and spurting dust. All the men were engulfed, buried by the down-rushing ton of basalt and limestone.

After the rolling echo of the crash faded, there came a stunned silence, stitched through with a clicking of pebbles and faint moans. Grit-laden dust hung in the air over the fallen mass of rock, blending with the perennial mist to make a nearly impenetrable haze.

Everyone cautiously stood up, coughing, waving the air in front of their faces. Mouzi whispered, "Think that did it?"

Kavanaugh opened his mouth to reply, and then held up a hand for silence. The steady reverberations of heavy weights slamming repeatedly against the ground sent corresponding shivers up his spine.

A dark shadow loomed against the cloud of smoke and mist. The revolting odor of rotten meat and the stench of excrement clogged everyone's nostrils.

Crowe groaned in heartfelt disbelief and disgust. "Oh, *no*-- don't tell me—"

Vegetation swished and crashed, saplings snapped and the Majungasaur bounded out of the undergrowth bordering the ruins, hopping like a kangaroo afflicted with St. Vitus Dance. The creature lowered its head and bellowed, overwhelming everyone with its carrion and septic-tank breath. Its armored hide crawled with flies, caked with dried mud and blood.

"How the hell did it escape the quagmire?" demanded Honoré in a high, wild voice. "And why did it track us down?"

Kavanaugh pulled her back by her left hand. "Like I said before—it's personal."

"That's *mad*." She looked ill, her eyes darting wildly like a trapped animal's. "Insane."

He tightened his grip on her hand. "Don't go simple on me, Dr. Roxton." He pitched his voice at calm, unemotional level. "I don't want to have to slap you."

Honoré's eyes flicked toward him and she forced a chuckle.

"That's a good thing...for you."

From behind fallen pillars and heaps of stone, two men bolted in terror, running in blind, screaming panic. One of them brandished a dao sword. Bai leaned forward intently, the smoldering cheroot dropping from her fingers. "That's Jimmy!"

"I think he's gone raw prawn," Mouzi observed dryly.

The Majungasaur's head whipped back and forth as if trying to decide which sprinting human would be the easier prey. It sneezed explosively, and then dug at its nostrils with three-fingered foreclaws.

"All this smoke acts as an irritant," Honoré observed, bending down to pick up the stub of the cheroot. "Probably bothers its eyes, too."

"Let's take advantage of that," Crowe said grimly, "We'll spread out, and confuse this damn thing. Grab the dynamite and start running."

The Majungasaur pivoted and pounced, its talon-tipped toes tearing out great clots of damp earth.

Chapter Thirty-Nine

The Majungasaur, with its upper body parallel to the ground and head outthrust like a missile, raced after the screaming Ghost Shadow soldier. The man ran among a row free-standing megalithic stones, squeezing through the narrow space between them, hoping to delay the animal even by a few seconds.

Without slowing, the carnotaur slammed into the slabs of stone, uprooting and knocking them over, causing a domino effect. Pillars and walls toppled.

The man sprinted only a few yards before the giant jaws of the creature closed over his head and shoulders. The crack of bone sounded sickeningly loud, as the man's skull and rib-cage broke like rotten latticework.

The saurian let the slack-limbed body drop from its blood-flecked maw as it stood upright, tiny eyes surveying the landscape, looking for more victims. Kavanaugh realized the creature wasn't for hunting food but for revenge.

Slowly, it turned its head, nostrils dilating and flaring. Its vision fixed on Mouzi crouched in the shadowed lee of two pillars and part of a fallen roof. Bellowing, the Majungasaur charged her. With a cry of fright, she flung herself in a backward somersault beneath the roof overhang. The animal stooped over, trying to jam its huge head under the rubble

Raising her M16, Mouzi squeezed off a short burst, the reports barely audible over the beast's snarls. The snarls were replaced by a roar and it scuttled backward, blood spurting from the wounds on its snout. Lifting one hind leg, the carnotaur stomped down hard on the section of roof under which Mouzi crouched. It collapsed with a crash.

She dove out headlong, then dodged between the legs of the infuriated Majungasaur, evading by a hands-breath a snap of the six-inch long fangs. She spun and ran in the opposite direction.

She heard loud gunshots as Crowe drew the animal's attention with his revolvers. The heavy caliber bullets pounded into its flank, knocking it off balance long enough for Crowe to take Mouzi by the hand and run toward the far end of the ruins.

The carnotaur roared angrily as its prey sprinted away, crashing through the broken columns, knocking aside giant stone blocks and trampling heaps of masonry in a single-minded juggernaut pursuit. The two people separated, running in opposite directions.

The animal paused, confused about which human to pursue, then it spied Honoré and Kavanaugh standing before a wall. The saurian launched its huge body directly at them, head down, mouth open as it bellowed in vicious triumph.

Although the Majungasaur changed direction far faster than Kavanaugh and Honoré thought, they didn't move until it was only a couple of yards away. Both people kicked themselves backward, shoulder-rolling through an intact archway and over the stone littered ground.

Saliva-and-blood wet fangs clashed shut within inches of Honoré Roxton's toes. She and Kavanaugh scrambled away from the snout of the raging Majungasaur. It wedged its entire head and upper body through the arch.

Snapping its jaws at the two humans just out of reach, the enraged predator strained to reach them with twitching, talon-tipped fingers. A network of cracks spread through the archway and wall, flakes of stone and ancient mortar popping loose.

Honoré applied the fuse of the Titadyne stick to the stub of the cheroot jammed into the corner of her mouth. When it sparked, she tossed the sizzling cylinder into the maw of the giant saurian. The jaws closed on it with a loud clack.

She and Kavanaugh whirled away just as the head of the

Majungasaur dissolved in a hellfire bloom of flame, smoke and red, wet flesh. The concussion struck them like a wave. Hunks of bone, shreds of muscle and fragments of teeth pattered down all around, accompanied by a crimson drizzle.

The body of the Majungasaur collapsed into a strange, half-crouching position, only a misshapen travesty of its massive skull barely recognizable.

Honoré and Kavanaugh slowly climbed to their feet. They stared at the settling corpse of the dinosaur without speaking, as if they feared that if it heard their voices, the creature would be restored to full, vengeful life.

Kavanaugh coughed, cleared his throat and said quietly, "Well, I guess his head *was* full of air."

Honoré smiled abashedly. She took the cheroot out of her mouth, blew a stream of smoke, then turned around and vomited.

• • •

Needles of pain jabbed through Bai Suzhen's shoulder as she clambered over the wall. Breathing hard, she looked behind her at the yawning entrance to the cavern then back to the ruins that spread out before her.

Upon hearing the explosion, she had gone to ground and waited to hear anything further, but when no sound was forthcoming, she climbed atop the low wall. Even with a slightly elevated vantage point, she could not see far. Visibility was limited due to the smoke-and-cloud veiled sun. In a short time, night would fall and she doubted even the light of the full Moon would penetrate the clinging umbrella of mist.

She jumped off the wall and the chipped masonry clattered beneath her shoes—so loudly she didn't hear the crunch of running feet until Jimmy Cao was almost behind her.

He slashed wildly with the dao sword, shaving a lock of hair from Bai's head. He wheeled around and Bai backpedaled carefully, parrying Cao's thrusts and swings, steel clashing loudly against steel.

"You must be the last one left of your crew," Bai said softly, tauntingly. "You can't go back to Zhou Zhi or the council now. United Bamboo will expunge you and your triad from the scrolls."

Jimmy Cao didn't reply and Bai realized he understood all of that. His clothes hung in tatters, his hair was plastered with sweat and he breathed deeply through expanded nostrils. Purple veins throbbed on his temples. He stank with a strong, vile odor more animal than human. All he cared about was killing her before he died.

He lashed out with his blade, a decapitating stroke. Bai twisted aside and slashed swiftly in return, a half-cut, half-thrust at Jimmy Cao's groin, seeking to sever the femoral artery.

He skipped backward, and then lunged back in, whipping his sword in whistling left-to-right arcs, trying to overpower her. Bai parried desperately, metal clanging and rasping, little starbursts of sparks flaring from the points of impact.

Although he wasn't an accomplished swordsman, what training he had combined with psychopathic rage made him very dangerous. One of the cuts got through her guard and shallowly sliced into her left forearm. Fiery pain streaked down into her hand.

Wrenching her body backward, she blocked an overhead strike with the jian. The force of the blow staggered her. As she tried to recover her balance, a piece of masonry broke beneath her weight and she stumbled. Jimmy Cao launched a straight-leg kick that connected solidly with her midriff. She went with the force of the kick and threw herself to one side as a follow-up swing of the dao missed her throat by a finger's width.

Bai Suzhen hit the ground hard and she heard the man husk out a low chuckle, a savage gloating sound. He stood above her, sword angled up and over his shoulder, preparing to deliver a stroke that would sever her head from her shoulders.

Then she heard the high-pitched *skreek*.

Jimmy Cao heard it, too and looked up just as a Deinonychus slammed into him, flying from the gloom in a spring-legged

bound. A swipe of the scimitar toe-claws flayed his shirt and almost all the flesh from Cao's torso. He went down screaming, amid liquid ribbons of crimson.

As Bai Suzhen watched with horrid fascination, the Deinonychus gutted Jimmy Cao with two more slashes of its hind claws. Loops of blue-pink intestines spilled out onto the ground.

The jaws of the raptor closed around the man's head with a crunch and the Deinonychus jerked him fiercely back and forth. The cracking of vertebrae sounded like a series of distant finger-snaps.

The Deinonychus gathered itself and bounded toward the cave entrance, the eviscerated body of Jimmy Cao hanging head first from its blood-streaked jaws.

Bai slowly rose to her feet, weak and trembling in every limb, stunned by the blinding-fast ferocity of the animal's attack. Her eyes followed the trail of the Deinonychus. She watched it disappear into the darkness of the cavern opening and caught a fleeting hint of a tall figure in the shadows. Words impressed themselves into her mind, like whispers borne on the breeze of a forgotten childhood.

Paì-yaa-na aak tiì-daa, ram laa.

Farewell, Naga daughter.

Bai Suzhen nodded, tears stinging her eyes. She pressed her hands together beneath her chin and for the second time in an hour, she murmured, *"Paì-yaa-na aak tiì-daa, ram laa…*farewell, Naga mother."

Chapter Forty

May 14th

The dawn air felt cool for about twenty minutes, and then as the sun topped the treeline, the heat trapped beneath the cloud cover turned the rain forest and the ruins into a vast open-air steam bath.

Honoré Roxton flipped through the leather-bound journal and winced when her fingers touched a sticky spatter of half-dried blood on the inside back cover.

Kavanaugh squatted on the collar of interlocking stone slabs that surrounded the pool of Prima Materia. He poked at the thick surface with a stick, trying not to make too obvious a show of breathing through his mouth.

He said conversationally, "If Aubrey jumped in here, he sank straight to the bottom. There's no telling how deep it is."

Honoré sighed. "I'm afraid you're right. He's the type of man to take desperate measures, particularly if he was out of his head with shock and pain."

Rather than attempt to track Aubrey Belleau the evening before, the five people voted to find a defensible place to camp in the ruins. After the events of the day, Kavanaugh was astonished he had fallen asleep so quickly. He was keyed-up, his mind racing like an out of control engine. He had stretched out on the ground, thinking only to rest. He slept until daybreak, jerking awake to find his head in Bai Suzhen's lap and a loudly snoring Mouzi using his ankles as a pillow.

They had eaten the last of the power bars and beef jerky and then engaged in a search for Belleau. Kavanaugh's guess that he would head for the pool of Prima Materia had been borne out by the blood trail that led directly to it. They found Darwin's journal lying on the ground at the base of a glyph-covered pillar.

Crowe and Mouzi returned from circling the perimeter. "Nothing," the man said flatly. "If Belleau wasn't three-quarters dead when he jumped in the wallow, then he drowned pretty damn quick. There's no sign he climbed out."

Honoré tucked the book under an arm, then lifted her camera to her eyes and snapped a photo of the glyphs. "We can at least try to decipher the Enochian alphabet and learn if these characters actually do deal with genetic engineering. I would imagine any conclusive answers are years away."

Crowe said, "If we wanted to get ourselves torn to pieces by the Deinonychus, we could always try to get a DNA sample from Wadjet. Maybe you could ask her real nice, Jack. She seems to have a little something for you."

Kavanaugh stared at him stonily but did not reply.

Honoré said, "Actually, I have a theory about that. I think Wadjet is so old, her higher brain functions are subsumed by the old R-complex instincts. Her maternal impulses are very, very powerful. She thought Aubrey was an undernourished child and she probably thought you were the wayward bad-boy son, Jack. All you needed was some tender loving understanding."

Mouzi snorted. "Please."

Honoré smiled. "There's a lot of figuring out yet to do."

Kavanaugh sighed and stood up, tossing aside the stick. "We'd better figure out a way to get out of here."

"Done," announced Bai Suzhen as she approached through the mist shrouding the columns. "Transportation is on its way."

She extended the satphone in her left hand. "This is Jimmy's. I found it over by the cave. He used it to track Belleau here and I'm guessing he came most of the distance downriver, in the *Keying*'s launch. There was just enough juice in the battery to make one call."

"To who?" asked Crowe.

"Bertram...Bert."

"Bert?" Kavanaugh echoed, raising an eyebrow.

She smiled slightly, seductively. "We're on a first name basis now. I apologized for the loss of his fingers and he apologized for trying to feel me up. He claimed too much liquor and I claimed too much heat and not enough sleep. It was a bad combination for a first meeting. Now he thinks this may be the beginning of a profitable friendship."

Bai shrugged, eyeing Honoré and Kavanaugh standing shoulder-to-shoulder. "There are stranger partnerships, I suppose. Bert said to meet him on the beach in about two hours."

"How's your shoulder, Bai?" asked Mouzi.

She pulled aside the collar of her stained, torn blouse and touched the discolored, scabbed-over flesh. "It looks like it's been healing for a month, so the Prima Materia in the vial was still potent. It doesn't even itch this morning."

"We can analyze what's in the pool," commented Honoré. "Compare it to the traces in the vial, see if there's been a change on the molecular level."

Bai Suzhen stretched her arms over her head, arching her back, her breasts thrusting tautly against the silk. "The white serpent of good fortune is prospering at last."

Gazing levelly at Kavanaugh, she asked softly, "Won't it be wonderful to lie naked in a tub of ice cubes again?"

Honoré's eyes narrowed to slits and she cast Kavanaugh a sidewise glance. Rather than respond to Bai's question or Honoré's stare, he busied himself checking the cylinder of his revolver.

"I'll go for just some cool sheets and a soft bed under me," Mouzi said cheerfully. She rubbed the back of her head and turned a grimace of pain into a grin. "We ought to choreograph this whole thing, put it to music and stage it as a joint tour package production of Cryptozoica Enterprises and Horizons Unlimited."

"Yeah," said Crowe dourly. "I can just see the Triple A travel reviews: 'Great family fun, until my wife was disemboweled by a Deinonychus.'"

Nobody laughed. All of them were too tired, dirty, scratched, bruised and battered to find much humor in anything.

As Crowe, Mouzi, Bai Suzhen and Kavanaugh wended their way among the stone columns, Honoré said quietly, "This story is bound to get out, Jack. A man of Aubrey's standing can't just go missing without somebody asking questions and I'm the person they'll be asking them of, since he was last seen in my company."

"And?"

"And, although I hate to sound like Aubrey, we need to control the release of information and secure this site."

"Why?"

"The concept of turning Big Tamtung into a living laboratory where the flora and fauna can be studied by qualified people is still a sound one. We can make it the most unique and famous nature preserve in human history."

He smiled ruefully. "No tourist destination?"

Honoré chuckled. "I'm afraid not, no. Admittance would be restricted. It would have to be…creationists and Darwinists and every fringe belief in between would try to turn Cryptozoica into their own private Mecca to further their agendas. Like Aubrey said, everything is different now. What we think we know about the origin of humanity, of all life on Earth, will have to be re-evaluated."

"Didn't you say Aubrey worked for a pharmaceutical company?"

"Maxiterm. I think they're based in Switzerland."

"They could come calling with their hands out, too."

"Aubrey denied being involved with them in this undertaking, but I probably shouldn't take his word for that."

"It won't be easy pulling it all together, you know," Kavanaugh said reflectively. "This is a wild and unstable part of the world. It's pretty damn lawless, what with pirates and the triads jockeying for position. And if Belleau's group, that School of Night he talked about, wants to get involved with Big Tamtung again, this could turn into a hell of a mess. Credibility won't be easy to establish."

Honoré tugged at the brim of her Stetson. "That's why I'm willing to be the front-person, Jack, the spokeswoman. I may not have much else going for me, but I *do* have credibility—and one more thing besides."

Kavanaugh glanced at her quizzically. "What's that?"

"A catch-phrase." She used her hand to place blocks of invisible copy on a transparent billboard. "Cryptozoica—Where the Past Has Not Stopped Breathing."

Kavanaugh laughed—then he heard a monstrous roar beyond the treeline, a prolonged, eardrum-compressing bellow that seemed to have no fixed point of origin, but embodied everything savage, fearsome and ancient about the island.

Everyone came to a halt, bodies tensing, hands gripping weapons. Honoré Roxton glanced around with wide eyes. "What in the name of God was *that?*"

Quietly, Jack Kavanaugh said, "That was Cryptozoica...where the past hasn't stopped breathing and can still eat you *alive.*"

Epilogue

May 15th

The storm swept through as a wild, howling fury, bringing a hot wind that whirled over the ruins and filled every hole, crevice and crack with rainwater.

Wadjet squatted on her heels beside the Womb of the Earth, hugging her knees. She chewed slowly, noting how a layer of wind-torn foliage covered the surface of the pool.

She sat and waited as she had since dawn, impervious to the lash of the wind against her skin, her eyes never leaving the womb. She was used to waiting. Wadjet's thoughts were not channeled into the measurements of time, since her people had long known the perception of its passage was a subjective phenomenon. Another few hours, days or even years squatting beside the pool made no difference to her.

The leaves on the surface suddenly stirred, bulging upward as if pushed from below. Wadjet did not move, she only chewed and watched. Thunder rumbled, rolling across the island.

A hand thrust up through the scraps of foliage, fingers clawing wildly as if to grasp a fistful of life and light. Skin gleamed whitely beneath the coating of dark sludge.

Reaching out, Wadjet grabbed the wrist and pulled upward. A small body came loose from the embrace of the mire with a protracted sucking sound.

Gently, she laid out the small man on the collar stones and straightened his limbs, even the under-developed legs. She laid his hands atop his chest, only glancing at the little web-fingered paw sprouting from his right wrist.

The rain sluiced away the muck from his hairless skull. His eyelids fluttered, his chest rose, fell and rose again.

Wadjet turned his head to one side and he coughed, spewing out a jet of thick, green-black fluid. His blue eyes opened, staring about in uncomprehending wonder. He inhaled a raspy breath, lips writhing back over toothless gums.

Wadjet removed the piece of raw meat from her mouth and pressed it to the small man's lips, cradling the back of his head in her hand.

Aubrey Belleau sucked at it greedily.

The Science *of* Cryptozoica

The Possibility of Dinosaurid Survival

A growing school of scientific thought postulates that a form of living dinosaur is not a zoological impossibility, particularly in areas that have been geologically stable for the past sixty million years.

Some scientists have put forward arguments that legends and ancient works of traditional art depict dinosaurs interacting with humans, such as the Peruvian Ica stones, not to mention the fossilized footprints of hominid and dinosaurid that were found imbedded in rock strata from the same era. A carving resembling a Stegosaurus was recently discovered on a temple wall in Cambodia's Angor Wat.

There are frequent reports of sauropods in Africa, notably the Mokele-mbembe and the Iguanodon-like creatures allegedly sighted in New Guinea.

There is of course, the coelacanth, a fish believed to have died out even before the dinosaurs, that is still swimming off the coast of Africa, not to mention a wasp believed extinct for twenty-five million years, that was discovered to have survived in California.

Quantum Evolution

Scientist George Gaylord Simpson conceived a multi-tempoed theory of evolutionary change in the 1940s. According to Simpson, some lineages in the fossil record evolved with extraordinary slowness, others more rapidly. He observed that in most phyletic lines, evolution occurred in a moderate and steady manner, while others showed fluctuating patterns of evolutionary descent. The most rapid of these tempos was dubbed "quantum evolution."

Simpson believed that major evolutionary transitions would arise when small populations—isolated and limited from gene flow—would fixate upon unusual gene combinations and maintain them in stable "adaptive peaks."

Feathered dinosaurids

A theory that has gained popularity among paleontolo-

gists and dinosaurologists is that feathers first evolved as in-
sulating structures on warm-blooded dinosaurs. In the 1970s,
Dr. John Ostrum published his work on the Deinonychus,
arguing that it possessed many of the features evident in the
Archaeopteryx and therefore the theropods—bipedal predatory dinosaurs—were the ancestors of birds.

Anthroposaurs

Paleontologists have long speculated that the bipedal
Troodon, a species of theropod, were separated from other
dinosaurs by a gulf comparable to the division between men
and apes. If not for the ecological catastrophe at the end of
the Cretaceous period, they would have evolved into humanoid dinosaurs. By historical times, their brain size would have
been within the human range.

In an experiment conducted in 1982, paleontologist Dale
Russell conjectured that the species would have evolved into a
humanoid intelligent form not unlike our own. The Troodon
had manipulative fingers, opposable thumbs and binocular
vision. Russel speculated that like most dinosaurs of the
Troodon family, this creature, the anthroposaur, would pos-
sess large eyes and a minimum of three fingers on each hand.

As with most modern reptiles and birds, its genitalia
would have been internal. Russell theorized that the anthroposaur would have required a navel, as a placenta aids the
development of a large brain case, however it would not have
possessed mammary glands, and would have fed its young,
as birds do, on regurgitated food. Its language would have
sounded somewhat like bird song.

Prima Materia

According to Aristotle and alchemical lore, Prima Materia
is the primitive formless base of all matter, from which all
substances are created. It is considered to be "pure" matter,
and it is conjectured to be the same as primordial ooze, which
contained ingredients considered essential for the development of life on the planet.

Exobiologists at the University of California, San Diego's Specialized Center of Research and Training, are studying the abiotic synthesis of biomolecules to determine which ones could have been present on Earth before life arose and, thus, may have been instrumental to the first living organisms.

The research provides evidence for the presence of an important ingredient in the original soup of life. It has been demonstrated that amino acids can form abiotically in a number of ways and are used by modern organisms for the manufacture of proteins. Sugars, however, which are components of modern genetic materials such as DNA or RNA are thought to be too unstable to have been widespread on Earth before life arose. The remaining "Big Question" is how and when did non-living molecules turn into life forms and begin to make copies of themselves, although the study of autocatalysts is providing a new road map.

Autocatalysts are substances which catalyze the reproduction of themselves, and therefore have the property of being a simple molecular replicator.

Enochian Alphabet

The Enochian language is the name applied to an occult alphabet recorded in the journals of Dr. John Dee in the late 16th century. Dee and his seer, Edward Kelly, claimed that the alphabet was revealed to them by angels.

Although most scholars believe Enochian to be a coded language constructed for the purposes of spying and smuggling secret messages, Dee referred to the alphabet as "Adamical", claiming it was the language Adam and Eve spoke in the Garden of Eden. He also claimed that Enoch was the last human who could speak, write and read the language, which prompted historians to refer to the language as Enochian.

Some researchers have proposed that the builders of Solomon's Temple expressed their architectural secrets in Enochian and that the Masonic lodge holds the key to understanding the language.

Mark Ellis is a novelist and comics creator whose many credentials include *Doc Savage: The Man of Bronze, The Wild, Wild West, The New Justice Machine, Death Hawk, The Miskatonic Project* and *Star Rangers*. In 1996 he created the best-selling *Outlanders* series for Harlequin Enterprise's Gold Eagle imprint. He is the author of 50 books and co-wrote with his wife Melissa Martin-Ellis, *The Everything Guide to Writing Graphic Novels*. He has been featured in *Starlog, Comics Scene* and *Fangoria* magazines. He has also been interviewed by Robert Siegel for NPR's *All Things Considered.*
www.markellisink.com

Jeff Slemons is a Colorado illustrator who has been involved in a variety of projects over the last two decades. He contributed work to *CARtoons* magazine and illustrated the popular *Hollow Earth Expedition Sourcebook* and *Hollow Earth Expediton: Secrets of the Surface World Sourcebook*. His other credentials include the *Luna Moon-Hunter* graphic novel, the online comic *SCAPS Agent* and the covers for the *Armor Quest* novel series. He shows his fine art in Houston, Vail and Denver. His work has been featured in *Heavy Metal* magazine and *Spectrum 17: The Best in Contemporary Fantastic Art*.
www.slemonsillustration.com

Melissa Martin-Ellis is a professional artist, writer, graphic designer and photographer. She co-wrote *The Everything Guide to Writing Graphic Novels* and is the author of *The Everything Guide to Photography (2nd Ed.)* and *The Everything Ghost-Hunting Book*. Her work as a writer and photographer has appeared in *Newport Life Magazine, The Boston Globe, The Providence Journal, Newport This Week, Newport Daily News* and *The Horseman Yankee Peddlar.*
www.mellissart.com

Acknowledgements

Usually it's difficult to thank everybody involved in a project like this, but fortunately this time it's not a strain. To the Museum of Natural History in New York City for planting the seed of *Cryptozoica* in my mind; to mega-talented Jeff Slemons for his enthusiasm; to our daughter Deirdre DeLay Pierpoint; to Wayne Quackenbush, Elizabeth Bell Carroll and all of the members of the Newport Roundtable; to Jim Mooney and Darryl Banks; to influences like Doc Savage, Milton Caniff, *I Spy*, Sir Arthur Conan Doyle, John D. MacDonald, Stephen Marlowe, Donald Hamilton, Richard Prather, Edward S. Aarons and Robert E. Howard; to the fans of my *Outlanders* series, particularly Christopher Van Deelen.

And last but definitely not least, Melissa, my wife, editor and art director, whose painstaking work, support and love brought *Cryptozoica* to its present form.

50517485R00260